P. W. Grant

The Revelation of John

an exposition

P. W. Grant

The Revelation of John
an exposition

ISBN/EAN: 9783337398620

Printed in Europe, USA, Canada, Australia, Japan

Cover: Foto ©Andreas Hilbeck / pixelio.de

More available books at **www.hansebooks.com**

HE REVELATION

OF

ST. JOHN

By WILLIAM MILLIGAN, D.D.

PROFESSOR OF DIVINITY AND BIBLICAL CRITICISM IN THE UNIVERSITY
OF ABERDEEN

London

MACMILLAN AND CO.

1886

TO

MY CHILDREN

PREFACE

In giving to the Public the following Lectures on *The Revelation of St. John*, the author can do little more than refer to the opening sentences of the first Lecture for a statement of his deep sense of that responsibility which he has felt to be involved in undertaking such a task. It is an old conviction with him that, so long as that book is retained in the Canon of the New Testament, the Church lies under an imperative obligation to endeavour to understand it, and that no difficulties met with in its interpretation can justify neglect of what she receives as a portion of the will of God revealed to her in Scripture. The present work is, therefore, simply an effort on the part of the writer to contribute what he can to the discharge of this responsibility; and, in the circumstances, he can only hope that, whatever criticism his views may have to meet, he will not be charged with arrogance or self-sufficiency in expressing them.

In publishing the Lectures the author labours under

one great disadvantage, which he has found it impossible to overcome. They ought to have been accompanied by a series of Discussions on important texts of the Apocalypse, and on the principles adopted in their interpretation. Without these too much may seem at times to have been taken for granted, and many may be of opinion that assumptions have been made without their correctness having first been proved. To have attempted this would, however, have swelled the volume to an unreasonable extent. Whether such a series of Discussions may be published at some future day will depend on the amount of interest taken in the inquiries here pursued. Meanwhile the author would venture to refer to his " Commentary on the Apocalypse," in the *Commentary on the New Testament*, edited by Professor Schaff, and published by the Messrs. Clark, Edinburgh. The views expressed in that Commentary have not indeed in every case been now adhered to. In particular, the exposition there offered of Rev. xix. 11 to xxii. 5 has been modified in several particulars, of which the meaning assigned to the words "a little time" in chap. xx. 3, and to the "loosing" of Satan in connection with them, may perhaps be said to be the most important. In other respects there is no material change ; and if, in alluding to this perplexing passage, the author reminds his readers that his interpretation of the "thousand years" was published long before[1] Kliefoth adopted a somewhat similar interpretation of the figure of time there used, he does this from no desire to claim originality, but that he may not be charged with not acknowledging obligations that have no existence.

The list of books referred to at p. xv. is not to be regarded as a summary of the literature of the subject. It is no more than a list of those actually quoted in this work, and it is given where it is for a twofold purpose—that the references to these books may be afterwards shortened, and that the reader may see more clearly what particular editions it was in the writer's power to consult.

In conclusion, the author has only to express his earnest hope, not that the view of the Apocalypse taken in this volume may be accepted as a whole,— that were too much to hope for,—but that his labours may help forward the study of one of the most instructive, elevating, and consolatory portions of the sacred volume.

THE UNIVERSITY, ABERDEEN,
    March 1886.

[1] In *Contemporary Review*, September 1871.

CONTENTS

LECTURE I.

Introductory.

LECTURE II.

Influences moulding the Conception of the Apocalypse.

LECTURE III.

PART I.

Structure and Plan of the Apocalypse.

PART II.

Minor Points of Structure.

LECTURE IV.

The Interpretation of the Apocalypse.

LECTURE V.

Design and Scope of the Apocalypse.

LECTURE VI.

Exposition of Chaps. xix. 11 *to xxii.* 5.

APPENDICES

*It may be well to give here the full titles of the principal
\ks referred to in the following work, and to say that the texts
the New Testament quoted in English are, with little exception,
m the Revised Version.*

FORD, H. ....*The Greek Testament* .   .   .   . Lond., 1854.
DREAS ....*In Apocalypsin Commentaria,*
             Bibl. Vet. Patrum.
te-Nicene Christian Library .   .   .   . Edin.
ETHAS ....*Explanationes in Apocalypsin* .   Paris, 1631.
BÉ, B. ....*Histoire des Persécutions de l'Eglise* Paris, 1875.
BERLEN, C. A...*The Prophecies of Daniel, and*
             the Revelation of St. John .   . Edin., 1856.
GUSTINUS ....*De Civitate Dei* .   .   .   . Tauchnitz, 1825.

UR, F. C. ....*Kritische Untersuchungen über*
             die Kanonischen Evangelien Tübingen, 1847.
CK, G. T. ....*Erklärung der Offenbarung*
             Johannis, Cap. i.–xii. .   Güterslohe, 1884.
YSCHLAG.........*Die Offenbarung.*
lical Review, and Congregational Magazine .   .   .   . 1846.
EEK, F. ....*Lectures on the Apocalypse,*
             edited by Davidson .   .   . Lond., 1875.
itish and Foreign Evangelical Review.
USTON, C. ....*Le Chiffre* 666 .   .   .   .   . Paris, 1880.

NDLISH, R. S....*The Fatherhood of God,* 5th edit. Edin., 1869.
ARTERIS, A. H...*Canonicity* .   .   .   .   . Edin., 1880.

Commentary on the New Testament, edited by
Schaff. Vol. ii., *The Gospel of St. John*, by
Drs. Milligan and Moulton, referred to as *Comm.*   Edin., 1880.
Vol. iv., *The Revelation of St. John*, by Dr.
Milligan, referred to as *Comm.* . . . . . .   Edin., 1883.

DAUBUZ, C. . . . . *A Perpetual Commentary on
the Revelation of St. John*   Lond., 1720.
DAVIDSON, S. . . . .*Introduction to the New
Testament* . . . . . .   Lond., 1868.
DE WETTE, W. M. L. *Einleitung in das N. T.*, 4te
Ausg. . . . .   Berlin, 1842.
Dictionary of the Bible : Smith . . . .   Lond.
Dictionary of Christian Biography : Smith and
Wace . . . .   Lond.
DÖLLINGER. . . . .*The first age of Christianity,*
translated by Oxenham,
2d edition . . . . . .   Lond., 1867.
DÜSTERDIECK, F. . . . . . .*Krit.-Exeget. Handbuch über
die Offenbarung Johannis,*
2te Ausg. . . . . .   Göttingen, 1865.

ELLIOTT, E. H. . . . .*Horæ Apocalypticæ*, 3d edit. .   Lond., 1847.
EUSEBIUS. . . . .*Eccles. History*, translated by
Crusé, 4th edit. . . . .   Lond., 1847.
EWALD, H. . . . .*Die Johanneischen Schrif-
ten* . . . .   Göttingen, 1861.
Expositor, The.

FAIRBAIRN, P. . . . .*On Prophecy* . . . . . .   Edin., 1856
FARRAR, F. W. . . . .*The Life of Christ*, 5th edit. . .   Lond
FROMMANN. . . . .*Der Johann. Lehrbegriff* . .   Leipzig, 1839
FÜLLER, T. L. . . . .*Die Offenbarung Johannis* Nördlingen, 1874

GEBHARDT, H. . . . .*The Doctrine of the Apocalypse*   Edin., 1878
GIESELER. . . . .*Eccles. History* . . . .   Edin.

ìODET, F...............*Studies on the New Testament* Lond., 1876.

ÍERDER, J. G. VON... *Werke* .   .   .   .   . Carlsruhe, 1820.
ÍERZOG...............*Real-Encyklopädie*   .   . Hamburg, 1854.
ÍILGENFELD, A.......*Historisch-Kritische Einlei-
               tung in das N. T.*   .   . Leipzig, 1875.

ournal of Philology .   .   .   . Lond.

ÌEIM, THEOD.........*The History of Jesus of
               Nazara, translated by
               Ransom* .   .   .   .   . Lond., 1876.
        ,,   *Rom und das Christenthum* . Berlin, 1881.
ÌITTO, J..............*Journal of Sacred Literature* . . Lond.
ÌLIEFOTH, TH. ......*Die Offenbarung des Johannes* Leipzig, 1874.

ÌARDNER, N..........*Works* .   .   .   .   .   . Lond., 1838.
ÌEE, W...............*Commentary on Revelation of
               St. John in Speaker's Com-
               mentary* .   .   .   .   . Lond., 1881.
ÌIGHTFOOT, J. B......*On the Galatians* .   .   .   . Camb., 1865.
        ,,   *On the Colossians, 2d edit.* . Lond., 1876.
        ,,   *The Apostolic Fathers, part 2,
               S. Ignatius, S. Polycarp* . Lond., 1885.
ÜCKE, FR.............*Versuch einer vollständigen
               Einleitung in die Offen-
               barung des Johannis, 2te
               Aufl.* .   .   .   .   .   . Bonn, 1852.

ÌACDONALD, J. M.... *The Life and Writings of St.
               John* .   .   .   .   .   . Lond., 1877.
Ì'LELLAN, J. B.......*The New Testament, vol. i.
               The Four Gospels* .   .   . Lond., 1875.
ÌEDD, P. G...........*The One Mediator.* .   .   . Lond., 1884.

ÌEANDER, A..........*General Church History, trans-
               lated by Torry* .   .   .   . Edin.

OVERBECK, F....... { *Studien zur Geschichte der alten Kirche, Heft i.* }   Schloss-Chemnitz, 1875.

Parousia, The . . . . Lond., 1878.

RENAN, E.............*L'Antechrist*, 3me ed. . . Paris, 1873.
REUSS, ED............*History of Christian Theology in the Apostolic Age* . . Lond., 1874.
  ,,   *L'Apokalypse* . . . . . Paris, 1878.
  ,,   *History of the Sacred Scriptures of the New Testament* Edin., 1884.
RIGGENBACH, C. J....*Die Zeugnisse fur das Evang. Johannis* . . . . . Basel, 1866.

SCHAFF, P.............*Hist. of the Christian Church: Apostolic Age* . . . Edin., 1883.
SCHENKEL, D..........*Bibel-Lexikon* . . . . Leipzig.
  ,,   *Das Charakter-Bild Jesu* . Wiesbaden, 1873.
SCHWEGLER, A........*Das Nachapostolische Zeitalter* . . . . . . Tübingen, 1846.
STIEREN, A............*Sancti Irenæi quæ supersunt omnia* . . . . . . Leipzig, 1853.
STUART, MOSES.......*A Commentary on the Apocalypse*, 3d edit. . . . Lond., 1854.
Studien und Kritiken . . . . Hamburg.

Theologische Jahrbücher . . . . Leipzig.
TODD, J. H............*Six Discourses on the Apocalypse* . . . . . Dublin, 1846.
TREGELLES, S. P.......*Canon Muratorianus* . . . Oxford, 1867.
TRENCH, R. C.........*Commentary on the Epistles to the Seven Churches*, 2d ed. Lond., 1861.

VOLKMAR, G..........*Commentar zur Offenbarung Johannis* . . . . . Zurich, 1862.
VÖLTER, D. ....*Die Enstehung der Apokalypse* . . . . Tübingen, 1882.

WESTCOTT, B. F......*The Canon of the New Testament* . . . . . . Lond., 1855.

,,　　　　*The Epistles of St. John* . . Lond., 1883.

WILLIAMS, ISAAC......*The Apocalypse with Notes and Reflections* . . . Lond., 1873.

WINER, G. B.........*Grammar of New Testament Greek*, edited by Moulton　Edin., 1877.

WITTICHEN, C.........*Der Geschichtliche Charakter des Evang. Johannis* . Elberfeld, 1868.

WORDSWORTH, C......*Lectures on the Apocalypse* . Lond., 1852.

ZÜLLIG, F. J.........*Die Offenbarung Johannis* Stuttgart, 1834-46.

LECTURE I.

No one who has paid careful attention to the Revelation of St. John will doubt the sincerity of the author of the following lectures when he says that he approaches the subject before him under a profound sense of its difficulties. These do not arise merely from the strange and mysterious nature of the book with which he has to deal. They spring even more from the thought of that amount of feeling which discussion of the topics connected with it seems always to provoke. The Christian community may be said to be divided upon this point into two great classes,—one seeing no meaning in the Apocalypse, the other attaching to it so definite a meaning that it regards as impiety every interpretation but its own. Nowhere is the tendency to dogmatize upon matters that least admit of dogmatism more observable than here. Nowhere do inquirers show less toleration for conclusions differing from those to which they have themselves been led. On no questions of Biblical interpretation are opponents more frequently referred to in terms approaching to contempt. The fact is discouraging, but it is at the same time a striking testimony to the remarkable interest of the book, and to the power which it exerts over the student. Our effort must be to avoid the spirit thus frequently exhibited by others. In studying the Revelation of St. John, humility, calmness, openness to conviction, singleness of desire to ascertain the truth, and charity are even more than usually required.

There are two important questions connected with the Apocalypse which it is necessary, in the meanwhile, to set aside as unsuitable for discussion in this place and way. They relate to the authorship of the book and to the date of its composition. Consideration of these questions must, therefore, be reserved for an Appendix. For the present it is assumed that the Apocalypse is an authentic and genuine production of its reputed author, and that it was written towards the close of his life, during the reign of the Roman Emperor Domitian. Such has been the general belief of the Church from the beginning of her history down to very recent times ; and, although it cannot be denied that not a few distinguished scholars of all shades of opinion have been led of late to a different conclusion, an effort will be made to show in the Appendix that the belief so long and so universally entertained upon both points is right. No one, therefore, will complain that, as an hypothesis, it is now taken for granted, and its effect upon interpretation tried.

Taking then the book of Revelation as it lies before us in the Bible, the object of the following lectures is to endeavour, in some degree at least, to dispel the perplexity which surrounds it; to ascertain its meaning; and to claim for it that place in the estimation of Christian men to which it is entitled. It is not enough that every one who sees, or imagines that he sees, a meaning in it should at once acknowledge the singular fascination of the book; that, notwithstanding its difficulties, he should constantly return to it; and that he should, without hesitation, pronounce it to be one of the most sublime, instructive, and consolatory portions of the sacred volume. What it is to such persons it ought to be to all who acknowledge that it is divine.

Notwithstanding this, there is no exaggeration in saying that, to the great majority of Christians, the Revelation of St. John has long been, and still is, an object of suspicion and distrust. In the earlier ages of the Church it was far less read than the other books of Scripture. St. Chrysostom and other eminent Greek Fathers abstain from making use of it;[1] for many centuries we possess no commentary upon it from any writer of the first rank; while its very strangeness led not unfrequently to its being denied canonical authority. In later times Luther undervalued it. Calvin did not venture to comment upon it. Herder refers to those who in his day considered it the mark of a sound understanding to abstain from the study of it. The old Lectionary of the Church of England, replaced by a new one but a few years

---

[1] Comp. Smith's *Bible Dict.*, iii. 1035.

ago, contained only three lessons from it, while all the rest of the New Testament was read in order three times a year. Even in the new Lectionary portions of it are omitted. Nor is it otherwise with the general body of the Christian community. Multitudes think it wise to neglect it, and to occupy themselves with those other books of the Bible which, whether really more intelligible or not, appear at least at first sight to be so. To numbers it is not only absolutely sealed ; they imagine, and are content with imagining, that no loosing of the seals is possible. Sometimes deliberately, almost always practically, the book is laid aside. The effect is more than negative ; the result worse than loss. The symmetry and completeness of Scripture are marred. The idea of revelation is disturbed. If one portion of the Divine Word may be dispensed with, why not all? Conclusions of this kind are so disastrous that it seems an imperative duty to attempt to counteract them. The attempt may be reproached or ridiculed ; or it may only lead to deepened confusion of thought upon the point. There is no help for it. The book is there, and it must either be excluded from the New Testament, or the Church must continue her struggle to comprehend it until she succeeds in doing so. Consider—

1. In the first place, that we start with the supposition—a supposition denied by none of those to whom these lectures are addressed—that the Revelation of St. John is part of the Word of God. That consideration settles the whole question. The simple fact that a book has been given by the Almighty to man con-

stitutes man's obligation to make every effort to understand it. It may be hard to do so. We may be long defeated. Not less is the effort one that we are bound to make; using all the appliances in our power, and watching, if we still feel that we are in darkness, for the first symptoms of light. Nothing is more certain than that, had it not been intended that we should use this book, the exalted Redeemer would not have given it by revelation to His servant John.

2. In the second place, the language of the book itself confirms what, from the very nature of the case, is a matter of unquestionable inference. Its title is—"The *Revelation* of Jesus Christ, which God gave Him to *show unto His servants*, even the things which must shortly come to pass."[1] Some of the earliest words uttered to the Seer by the glorious Person who appeared to him are—"What thou seest, *write in a book, and send it to the seven churches.*"[2] Almost the last instruction of the angel when he had brought to an end the visions of this prophecy are—"*Seal not up* the words of the prophecy of this book, for the time is at hand;"[3] while, with still more explicit reference to the application to be made of it, the Saviour Himself declares—"I Jesus have sent mine angel *to testify unto you these things for the churches.*"[4] The words of this revelation then, unlike the words of Daniel's prophecy of which it was said, "Shut thou up the vision, for it belongeth to many days to come,"[5] were not to be shut up. They

[1] Chap. i. 1.   [2] Chap. i. 11.   [3] Chap. xxii. 10.
[4] Chap. xxii. 16.   [5] Dan. viii. 26.

were to be spoken, to be testified, to man; and, if so, can it be for a moment doubted that they were to be listened to, to be apprehended, to be taken home, by man? The exhortation, so solemnly repeated in each of the seven epistles to the churches of Asia, may be applied, if indeed it was not expressly intended to be applied, to the whole of that book with which these epistles are so intimately connected—"He that hath an ear, let him hear what the Spirit saith unto the churches."[1]

3. In the third place, there is even a special blessing promised to the student of the Apocalypse, and a special woe denounced upon him who tampers with it—"Blessed is he that readeth, and they that hear the words of the prophecy, and keep the things which are written therein; for the time is at hand."[2] Such is the preface, and not less striking is the conclusion—"I testify unto every man that heareth the words of the prophecy of this book, If any man shall add unto them, God shall add unto him the plagues which are written in this book: and if any man shall take away from the words of the book of this prophecy, God shall take away his part from the tree of life, and out of the holy city, which are written in this book."[3] Words like these are attached to no other book of the Bible; and they constitute an impressive warning not to neglect the visions of the Seer, and a not less impressive call to study them.

The prepossessions hitherto referred to are easily

[1] Chaps. ii. iii.　　　[2] Chap. i. 3.　　　[3] Chap. xxii. 18, 19.

dispelled. There are, however, other and more serious difficulties not unfrequently leading to the same conclusion. On the one hand, many are offended with the extravagance, the fanaticism, the sensuous and unspiritual ideas of divine things so often associated with the gorgeous pictures of the Apocalypse, and the tendency of which is to destroy every intelligent conception of Christianity in the minds that entertain them. On the other hand, not a few appeal to the endless diversity of interpretations that have been given of the book, to the obviously mistaken conclusions arrived at in connection with it by even the most distinguished expositors of other parts of the New Testament, or to the falsification by the event of every attempt made to fix from it the date of the Second Coming of the Lord; and then they ask, not unnaturally, Is it possible to understand it? Is not rather the impossibility of doing so proved by the whole history of the Church? Is not the book so unregulated not only in its style, but in its thoughts, as to be out of keeping with all ordinary writings, and to be subject to no rules of interpretation, however otherwise well established? May not every inquirer make of it what he pleases? The objections are important and must be answered.

Of the first of them indeed little need be said. If fanaticism has been fostered by false interpretation, it is only the more necessary to reach an interpretation that is true. If calm and rational believers hand the book over to ignorance and folly, what ground have we to expect a satisfactory result? Besides which it is well to remember that the liability of the Apocalypse to be abused, and made an instrument of nourishing carnal expectations of Christ's kingdom, is neither peculiar to it, nor without analogy in the history of God's dealings with His Church. The prophecies of the Old Testament were not less abused before the First Coming of our Lord. But, because they were so, would it have been better for Israel to have wanted, or to have made no serious efforts to comprehend, them? Surely not. There were always some who used their advantages aright, "searching what *time*, or what manner of time, the Spirit of Christ which was in them did point unto, when it testified beforehand the sufferings of Christ, and the glories that should follow them;"[1] and, although many took a false view of prophecy, by that very view, when the Redeemer came, they were tried. The dreams, therefore, of enthusiasts who, whether carnally or spiritually minded, have found their strength in a one-sided and imperfect interpretation of the Apocalypse, cannot make us underestimate the real value of that book, or persuade us that it does not attain its end. It is to us what Daniel and Isaiah and Ezekiel and others of the prophets were to the Jewish Church. Many may misapprehend its meaning. Many may gather from its pages those outward notions of Christ's kingdom which are so natural, and so difficult to eradicate. Yet without its prophets Israel could not have prepared itself for the coming of the Son of God in the flesh; and without the revelation of the Apocalypse our know-

---

[1] 1 Peter i. 11.

ledge of His coming in glory would be equally imperfect.

The second objection is more important than the first. It is equivalent to a denial of the inspiration of the book. To suppose that the Almighty has given us a sacred writing of which it is as easy to make one thing as another, is to put it out of analogy with what He has done in every other department both of His works and of His Word. That it should be obscure or mysterious would in no way startle us. Obscurity and mystery meet us everywhere. We have no reason to complain of such arrangements. It is an altogether different thing when we are told, not that a part of revelation is difficult, but that it is from its very nature unintelligible, and that it is constructed with so little reference to common processes of thought and rules of language as to place a distinct conception of its meaning beyond our reach. This is simply to deny the operation of the Divine Spirit in the construction of the book. Everything that has proceeded from the Almighty has a meaning distinct, definite, and one. Man may not immediately comprehend it, just as thousands of years passed before he comprehended the structure of the earth, or the movements of the heavenly bodies. But the voice both of the earth and of the heavens was never in itself less fixed or certain than it is now. They were capable of being interpreted; and at last they received their interpretation. It is the same with the book before us. He who regards it as divine must believe that its meaning is as definite as that of sun or moon or stars or rocks, and as likely to yield itself to carefully conducted and patient investigation. Many mistakes may be made; much disappointment may be experienced; there may be long delay; but the meaning is there. That is the point with which we are concerned, and it brings with it the pledge that we shall one day attain our end.[1]

The whole theory indeed as to the impossibility of understanding the Apocalypse proceeds upon a false notion of the nature of figurative language. It is supposed that figures are amenable to no rule, whereas

[1] Herder, referring to this subject, exclaims, "They (the prophets) have all one spirit, one design. One builds upon another; one explains another; and as gold have all been preserved. No imagery-language has remained purer or been better preserved. None is in any measure so deeply embedded in the genius of the people, its writings and its idiom. Hebrew poetry is as it were all symbol, imagery, holy and lofty diction. Even the prose-writers and historians must needs speak in a tropical way because their language demands it; still more must this be done by teachers and prophets. No language loves and furnishes imagery like this. Here a fiery glance, there a breathing full of the spirit of the Lord. In this way speak the Old and New Testament; and so speaks the Apocalypse which contains the sum of both. It is an anile fable that a peculiar key belongs to it, or that the key is lost. Who ever writes a book without an adequate key? Specially, who writes such an one for seven churches? Did John attach a peculiar key to it when he sent it to them? How did it look? Who has seen it? How came it to be lost? Is it in the sea near Patmos, or in the Mæander? John writes a book for others, for many; a book about whose contents he was so seriously anxious that he arrays curse upon curse against any one who detracts from it, and blessing upon blessing for him who reads, hears, and obeys it; and yet this book is said to be an unintelligible enigma, a kind of raving wholly sealed up, which no one except its author can understand, and which even he himself perhaps did not understand. Can anything be more absurd?"—*Works*, vol. xxxix. p. 371.

they are not less the expression of thought than the most ordinary terms of speech or writing ; and they are used with a not less definite intention by every one who deals honestly with his audience. We may not always have a right conception of their force, because our modes of thought may differ widely from those of the nation or the age in which the figures were employed. But, considered in themselves, they are not more ambiguous than many terms of the baldest philosophic or didactic treatise. Our commonest words are ambiguous, or even meaningless, to the man who is unable to put their meaning into them. Nothing more is necessary to make figurative language as clear as the plainest, simplest, and most unadorned statements than first, that a writer always use his figures in the same sense ; and secondly, that the reader know the ideas for which they stand. They then take their place along with all those other artificial signs of thought on which we depend for maintaining the daily intercourse of life.

These considerations ought to go some way towards settling an important question which has been raised in connection with the Apocalypse. St. John, it has been said, uses symbolical language in that book on purpose to conceal his meaning from the heathen, especially the Roman, authorities; and to his dread of drawing down fresh persecutions either upon himself or his fellow-believers we owe in no small degree the obscurity of the book.[1]   There is not the smallest

[1] Beyschlag, *Die Offenbarung*, p. 23. Dr. Farrar does not appear to be perfectly satisfied how far the motive alluded to in the text

foundation for the statement. So far is it from being
correct that we not only find the Apostle often telling
us what his figures mean, as in the case of the stars and
of the candlestick in chap. i. 20, of the white-robed
company in chap. vii., of the great dragon in chap.
xii., and of the New Jerusalem in chap. xxi., but that
the very vision in which, according to these interpreters,
he ought to have been most reserved, that relating to
the beast and the harlot in chap. xvii., is precisely the
vision of which he gives the fullest explanation. Besides which, such words as those of chap. xiii. 18, "*He
that hath understanding* let him count the number of
the beast," are obviously used not to favour concealment of the mystery, but to provoke to the investigation
of it, as one to be known, either then or in due season,
by the spiritual mind. The figures of the Apocalypse
flow from no effort at concealment, and from no dread
of danger. They are the natural result of the Seer's
own temperament, training, circumstances, and mood
of mind at the time he writes; and they are designed
to lend a force and vigour to his style which would
not have been gained by simpler speech.

We must not, therefore, allow ourselves to be startled

prevailed in the age of the New
Testament. In his *Life of Christ*
(vol. ii. p. 173) he accounts for the
omission in the Synoptists of the
raising of Lazarus by their un-
willingness to bring the family of
Bethany into "dangerous prominence." But he prefers another
explanation of the fact that the
name of Peter (as the assailant
of Malchus) is not given in the
Synoptists than this, that "it
was purposely kept in the background in the earliest cycle of
Christian records." Yet this last
he thinks neither "absurd nor
improbable."—(Vol. ii. p. 323,
note.).

by the fact that in the case of no other book of Scripture has interpretation been marked by so much unsettledness and diversity of view as in the case of the Apocalypse, that the wildest theories have been connected with it, and that its predictions have been assigned with the utmost confidence to times and places separated from each other by many centuries or by half the circumference of the globe. These things prove no more than the weakness and blindness of men. We dare not allow them to lessen our estimate of the definiteness of the Word of God.

With these preliminary remarks we may now turn directly to the book before us. Our object is to understand it, and so to determine its place and meaning in the scheme of revelation that we may derive from it the instruction or encouragement, the warning or comfort, which its Divine author intended it to convey. We have to lay aside, as far as possible, all preconceived notions of its meaning. The principles of historical criticism must be applied by us with the strictest faithfulness. We must judge of the book mainly by considering its own contents, by taking into account what we otherwise know of the writer, and by keeping in view the special circumstances amidst which he wrote.[1]

---

[1] "In order to a right interpretation of the Apocalypse, the best help is to be found in the Apocalypse itself. St. Augustine has well observed that this book is composed in such a manner as to exercise the diligence of the interpreter (*De Civ. Dei.*, xx. 17), and that by comparison of one passage with another the obscure parts may be illustrated and made clear. Indeed there is scarcely a

There can thus be no hesitation as to the course to be pursued in the present lectures. The internal characteristics of the Apocalypse first claim our notice. In proceeding to them it ought to be distinctly borne in mind that our aim is not the gratification of literary curiosity or interest. We desire simply to interpret, or to ascertain the meaning of the book. To this aim everything else must be subordinated. On this everything else must be brought to bear.

1. The first characteristic of the Apocalypse claiming our attention is that the revelation contained in it is given by means of visions. There are indeed one or two parts of the book which seem to be historical,—the first eleven verses of chap. i., in which the writer speaks of himself and relates the occasion of his writing; chaps. ii. and iii., describing the condition of the churches he was commissioned to address ; and the two closing verses of chap. xxii. With these exceptions the rest of the book is communicated in visions. St. John was "in spirit on the Lord's day,"[1] in the small rocky island of Patmos in the Ægean Sea. Then the unseen world was opened to him ; and, as in a great drama, successive visions—though not, as we shall see, always representing the events with which they deal in chronological order—passed before his view. Whether all the visions of the book were presented to the Seer without inter-

phrase or sentence in the Apocalypse, however difficult it may seem to be at first, which may not be elucidated by means of some other phrase or sentence in the same book."—(Bp. Wordsworth, *Introd. to Apoc.*).

[1] Chap. i. 10.

ruption from the beginning to the end, or whether there were intervals of time between the different groups, is not easily determined; and, for the purpose of interpretation, the inquiry is unnecessary. That all were connected with Patmos is unquestionable; and, were we to understand "the Lord's day" spoken of in chap. i. 10 of the first day of the week, the words of the preceding verse, which warrant the conclusion that the visions belong to Patmos, would lead us also to infer that they were granted on the same day.[1] But the expression, "the Lord's day," has in all probability another reference; and, besides this, one statement of the writer distinctly shows us that changes did take place in his condition. At chap. iv. 2 we read, "Straightway I was in *the* spirit," or rather, "I passed into *the* spirit,"[2] although we know that he had been in that state before. There may also have been other points of transition, such as the moment of chap. xvii. 3, "And he carried me away in spirit into a wilderness," and of chap. xxi. 10, "And he carried me in spirit into a mountain great and high." It is unnecessary, however, to determine the

---

[1] It does not seem necessary to enter upon any lengthened discussion as to the meaning of the expression "the Lord's day." The writer can only say that, in the absence of all proof that the first day of the week was so designated in early Christian times, and taking into account the general tone of the Apocalypse, it seems more natural to understand the Seer as meaning by that term not any particular day, but the whole of that Christian dispensation which, notwithstanding the sufferings of Christians, was to him, in its deepest characteristics, the day of the Lord—the time when the Lord was ruling in the earth and preparing to make His glory manifest.

[2] ἐγενόμην.

question.   On either supposition the meaning of the visions will be the same.

For a like reason it is unnecessary to ask whether the visions passed before the Seer in the forms in which he relates them, or whether, having had only certain truths divinely impressed upon his mind, his poetic fancy led him to clothe these in the shapes before us. Even were the latter supposition correct, it would in no degree modify either the extent of his inspiration or the value of his teaching.   The Spirit of God adapts Himself to every method of expression suggested by the peculiarities either of a writer or his age.   The human element can no more be excluded from the plainest than the most ornate sentence, from the simplest than the most complex figure.   It is not the words but the man who is inspired.   It is not with the words as such, but with the truth contained in them, that we have to do. That truth may be conveyed in figures of many kinds determined by the era, the country, or the immediate purpose of the author.   If we can learn what the truth itself is, and if at the same time we have reason to believe that it comes from God, we need inquire no further.

Yet there is every reason to think that these visions were granted to the Seer exactly as he records them. They do not stand alone in Scripture, and they probably come under the same law as others which it relates. The state of Abraham must have been similar when, before being warned of the fate that was to overtake his seed, "an horror of great darkness fell upon him."[1]   So

----

[1] Gen. xv. 12.

also must have been the state of Balaam when he "saw the vision of the Almighty, falling into a trance, but having his eyes open,"[1] while the prophecies of Ezekiel and Zechariah are mainly presented to us in visions of the same character. Nor are visions confined to the Old Testament. St. Paul was favoured with "visions and revelations of the Lord." "I knew a man in Christ," he says, "(whether in the body I know not, or whether out of the body I know not, God knoweth), such a one caught up even to the third heaven. And I know such a man (whether in the body, or apart from the body, I know not, God knoweth), how that he was caught up into Paradise, and heard unspeakable words, which it is not lawful for a man to utter;"[2] and St. Peter is described as having fallen into a trance at the time when the vision which led to the extension of the Gospel to the Gentiles passed before him.[3] In these and in every similar instance it would seem as if the Spirit of God had come upon the subject of His influence with such

---

[1] Numb. xxiv. 4.

[2] 2 Cor. xii. 2-4. Reuss has endeavoured, but without success, to draw a broad line of distinction between the visions of the Apocalypse and those of St. Paul; looking upon the latter as more momentary in duration, more limited in object, and marked rather by a suspension than by a greater than ordinary action of the writer's freedom and spontaneity of spirit (*L'Apocalypse*, p. 23). The first two character-istics are of too external a nature to justify the distinction drawn; and it may be fairly pled that the spirit of both St. Paul and St. Peter was as active during the visions vouchsafed to them as was the spirit of St. John. St. Paul knew what he had seen and heard, though he felt that it was "unlawful" for him to utter it. St. Peter understood perfectly the bearing of his vision at Joppa after it was over.

[3] Acts x. 10.

an overwhelming power that he was, as it were, lifted out of the body, and swept away into a higher world, where he beheld in sensible expression the realities which had previously only filled his thoughts. Then what are called visions presented themselves to the eye or reached the ear, sights and sounds of an exalted and transcendental nature, the imagination being quickened into a far greater than ordinary activity, though the powers of reflection and of reason remained unshaken. The "Tongues" of the early Church may have been the utterances of a similar state; and hence the words used by St. Paul to denote that gift, when he speaks of it as "spiritual things," or simply as "the spirit."[1]

Visions of this kind were eminently adapted to the position in which St. John was placed, and to the peculiar nature of the task assigned to him. He was an Apocalyptist rather than a Prophet; and the function of the one differed from that of the other, although both had so much in common that the former may not unfrequently be spoken of as prophetical, the latter as apocalyptic, in his work. There seems, however, to have been a real and essential difference between them. Yet that difference did not consist in this, that the Seer "stood upon a loftier altitude than the prophet, and had visions of things to come more explicit, more detailed and consecutive than were afforded to any of the other prophets."[2] Such a distinction touches only the more external characteristics of the work of each. Nor is it

<hr>

[1] 1 Cor. xiv. 1; 1 Thess. v. 19.   [2] Fairbairn *On Prophecy*, p. 120.

to be found in this, that "the prophets of the Old Testament, like the epistolary writers of the New, write primarily and specially for their own times, for the present emergencies of the kingdom of God," while an "apocalypse is not given primarily or specially for present but for future times, is not the immediate product of any particular present emergency, and has as its primary object to serve as a guiding lamp for the people of God during those dark periods when there is no revelation." [1] The last words of this extract may be accepted, but not the rest. No prophet wrote more directly for his own time than the Apocalyptist did. The latter was called forth by "present emergencies" not less than the former. His utterances were emphatically "present truth." [2] The difference between the

---

[1] An anonymous writer in the *Ecclesiastic and Theologian* for April 1857. Comp. Dr. Westcott in Smith's *Bible Dictionary*, vol. i. p. 391.

[2] Daniel (*the* Apocalyptist of the Old Testament) was, not less than Isaiah, a prophet in the first place *for his own age*. Take, for example, his visions of the Four World-Empires which were to usher in the establishment of the kingdom of God. These giant powers began in Daniel's time. They were not only something new in the world's history; their rise involved of necessity a great change in the outward form of the Theocracy. With them in the field such a monarchy as David's was impossible. Moreover, they had attractions of their own which might seduce men's hearts from their true allegiance. They awed the imagination by their magnificence and pride ; they gave to the nations peace, though at the expense of liberty. Under them even faithful souls might be tempted, on the one hand, to despair of the Theocracy ; on the other hand to "wander after" them, and to worship their rulers as earthly deities. Daniel's position as a high minister of state under the two first of those World-Empires—the Babylonian and the Persian—gave him an intimate personal knowledge of them. He was just the man, therefore, for

two would appear to have been of a deeper kind than
is expressed in either of the above suppositions. It
depended upon the fact that, in the times when the
Apocalyptist spoke, prophecy had delivered its message
and had little that was new to say. The Apocalyptist
then came in as an interpreter rather than as a Prophet.
He did not take his stand in the future rather than the
present; to him the future was the present, and the
present embraced the future. He did not enjoy fuller
communications of the Divine purpose than those previously given; he rather only beheld more clearly the
contents of what had already been revealed. He belonged to an era in which one Divine Dispensation had
either closed or was closing around him, and another
was taking possession of the field. With this last as a
present era he had to do; and his charge was to set it

his twofold function, (1) to reveal the really brutal and earth-
born character of these imposing
powers (even the fairest of them—
Alexander's—he showed had the
insatiableness, if it had also the
beauty, of the panther); and (2)
to promise that under them all
Jerusalem should be preserved till
the erection of an everlasting kingdom in the hands of a Son of man.
It is indeed much more as unveiling the essential *character* of the
world's kingdoms and of Christ's
respectively than merely as seeming to fix beforehand the date of
Christ's appearing, that Daniel
holds his high rank in the prophetic college. Commentators
have estimated aright, or undervalued, his importance precisely
as they have connected him with,
or disconnected him from, the
position and the needs of Israel at
the time when God raised him up.

In three respects the position of
Daniel resembled that of St. John.
Both stood at the beginning of
long periods of anti-theocratic
empire. Both had personal experience of persecution under these
imperial foes of God's kingdom.
Both had revealed to them the
inmost character (and out of that
the fortunes) of the powers whose
conflict they beheld.

forth in its true character, so that the Church of God might face her inevitable trials in a strong and hopeful spirit. The "prophet" of the Old Testament was succeeded not by the Apocalyptist but by the "teacher" of the New. The apocalyptic function passed from the one Dispensation to the other unchanged in its essential features.[1]

St. John, therefore, had not, like the prophets of the Old Testament, to unfold "by the word of the Lord" successive steps in the evolution of a Divine plan which was to culminate in the appearance of the Hope of Israel. That plan had already culminated in the coming of Christ, although a part of His manifestation of Himself was still awanting. The Church was already in "the last days," and no further prophetic revelation was needed. Men of God were now to interpret the revelation given in the Son. They were to penetrate more deeply than had yet been done into the mystery of His person and work in its relation to the world, in order that thus unveiling its contents they might apply them, with growing insight, for the warning of the sinner and the encouragement of the saint. Their commission was therefore less to predict the future than to see the present, and to trace in what was happening around themselves the working of those eternal principles which were about to be manifested in their full sweep of power. With events yet to take place, except in so far as these were the natural consequence and outcome of what Christ was known to be, of the contest He was to

---

[1] 2 Peter ii. 1.   Comp. Fairbairn *On Prophecy*, p. 131.

carry on, and of the victory He was to win, they had nothing to do. In Christ Himself and in His teaching was included everything of which they needed to be informed; and hence visions of what was took the place of prophecy of what was to be. In these considerations we seem to have an explanation of that extraordinary burst of apocalyptic literature which marked the close of the first and the first half of the second century.[1]

While thus adapted to the position of the Seer, visions were not less appropriate to that of those for whom he wrote. They were more concrete and life-like than mere general description would have been. There was a vividness and a graphic power about them far surpassing that of ordinary teaching. They presented pictures to the eye; they appealed to the imagination; they gave scope for boundless range of thought amidst the things which they expressed. Let us place ourselves in the circumstances of the early Christians, with burdens or trials like theirs to meet, and we shall be more alive to the value of the visions of a Seer as compared with the utterances of a prophet.[2]

2. A second characteristic of the Apocalypse is its use of symbols. Its visions are presented to the Apostle

---

[1] In connection with what has been said in the text it is of great importance to notice the true meaning of John xvi. 13. "The things that are coming" there spoken of are not so much revelations wholly new as new applications of what had already been revealed, the things that happen when He who is to come begins in the power of His Spirit the conflict of the Church with the world. (Comp. *Comm. in loc.*).

[1] Comp. interesting remarks of Reuss, *L'Apocalypse*, p. 11.

in symbolic forms,—that is, in images drawn from material and earthly objects, or from combinations of impressions produced by them, for the purpose of teaching spiritual and heavenly truth. This method of instruction, more or less resorted to by all nations, is peculiarly appropriate to the religious spirit and the lively imagination of the East. There everything is full of a present Deity, and becomes the utterance of His will. It is equally prominent in the Old Testament, where the Jews, and therefore also the early Christians, had long been familiar with it. The prophecies of Daniel, Ezekiel, Hosea, Zechariah and others abound in symbols. Numerous objects in nature — fire, winds, floods, lightning and thunder, earthquakes, eclipses of sun and moon and stars, cities, buildings, trees, gold, silver, jewels, garments and colours—are constantly laid hold of in order to convey in a more visible and telling manner than belongs to abstract statement, the lessons to be proclaimed. Distinct traces of the same style of thought appear in other books of the New Testament as well as in the Apocalypse. To say nothing of symbolical action, which hardly belongs to our present subject,[1] we find our Lord using symbolical language when he speaks of sitting down with Abraham and Isaac and Jacob in the kingdom of heaven, when He warns the sons of the kingdom that they shall be cast forth into the outer darkness, or when he exclaims, "I beheld Satan

[1] Comp. on this remarks by the writer in the *British and Foreign Evangelical Review* for October 1871.

fallen as lightning from heaven."[1]   In the fourth Gospel symbols meet us at every step.   All the figures applied in that Gospel to the Saviour—the bridegroom, the vine, the living water, the bread of life, the door of the sheep, the shepherd, the temple—are symbolical. They do not simply compare Him to these persons or things, so that we have to search for the features of resemblance between Him and them: that is a similitude.   They do not simply relate incidents of everyday experience in order to illustrate by what passes upon earth the Divine administration of heavenly things: that is a parable.   Nor do they employ real or imaginary, though probable, events of this life in order to set forth the manner in which eternal issues are produced: that is an allegory.   The symbol differs from these figures of speech in this, that when we hear it its deeper meaning alone starts to view.   We concern ourselves about its essence in itself.   The object which supplies it has in its own world a purpose, a meaning, a force, a mission, belonging to itself and to no other object.   In the higher world, which rests upon the same principles and is ruled by the same laws, the object symbolized has a precisely similar purpose and meaning and force and mission.   The symbol guides us straight to these.   It is not introduced in a manner leading us to think of the pleasure always experienced when two things in which we did not at first suspect resemblance are shown to resemble one another.   It at once suggests the thought which it embodies; and its

---

[1] Matthew viii. 11, 12 ; Luke x. 18,

value consists in its power to flash, by a single stroke, ideas into the mind which might lose much of their force through the number or the weakness of the words that would be otherwise needed to describe them. The basis of the representation is so familiar to us, is so intimately connected with our ordinary lives, that it cannot be mentioned without instantly awakening numerous associations. In spiritual things symbols are not less powerful if the world of spirit is as real to us as the world of nature.

What has been said will be confirmed, and light will be at the same time thrown on the general character of the Apocalypse, if we note one or two particulars connected with its symbols.

(1.) They are for the most part suggested by the religious position, training, and habits both of the writer and his readers. The Apostle had been a Jew, in all the noblest elements of Judaism a Jew to the very core. We know it from what is told us of his history in the Gospels. We know it not less from numerous little marks which stamp the fourth Gospel, penned by him, as one of the most genuine productions of a Jewish mind. It is true that we do not meet in that Gospel figures exactly similar to those of the Apocalypse. The difference is easily explained. In the former St. John was writing narrative and describing facts. In the latter he dwells upon the spiritual impression which the facts produce ; and it was natural that, in doing so, he should adopt the method and the style of those old prophets whose work had been the glory of his nation, and whose words had fed the loftiest and brightest hopes of his own heart. We may expect that what is written from such a point of view will breathe the very essence of Old Testament prophecy · more especially in its apocalyptic parts, will be moulded by its spirit, be at home amidst its pictures, and be familiar with its words. Why consider this inexplicable? Why deny to a Christian Apostle the right of clothing his ideas in forms of speech sanctified to him by all that was best in the bygone history of his people and (may we not hope) also sanctified to us? We do not make it an objection to Isaiah or Ezekiel or Daniel or Zechariah that they adopted in their communications with men the style which they actually employed. Why should we complain that St. John adopts a similar style? How indeed could he have done otherwise? Having fired his soul amidst these pictures of his earlier days until he was "weary with forbearing and could not stay;" knowing that God was the same, and man the same, in every age; seeing in the future, by the light of the Incarnation, not a time entirely different from what had been, but only the fulness of a long preparatory course of ages, how could he avoid speaking in the tones most familiar to him, when he spoke upon the same subject? Or how could he fail to behold the fortunes of the Church through the medium of figures that till then had completely possessed his thoughts? These very figures of the Apocalypse, the symbols that it employs, the language that it speaks, are a testimony to the thorough reality of the writer, to the depth of his convictions, and to the profoundness of the emotions which stirred his soul.

Then, again, we have to remember that he was addressing persons familiar with this style of thought. The Old Testament was the Bible of the Church. The books of the New Testament had not yet been gathered into a volume. If the earlier date of the Apocalypse be correct some of them had not been written. The Christian Church, even among the Gentiles, had been grafted upon the stem of David. She had an interest in Zion and Jerusalem; she saw in Babylon the type of her enemies; she felt herself to be the true Israel of God. She was well acquainted with the tabernacle and the temple, with their pillars and incense, with their different altars, with the high priest's robes, with the seven-branched golden candlestick, with the ark of the testimony, with the hidden manna, and with the parchment rolls written both within and on the back. These symbols were therefore closely adapted to her condition, and must have gone home to her with peculiar power.

(2.) When the symbols of the Apocalypse are not closely connected with the Old Testament, they are drawn from the most familiar objects in nature. The phenomena to which the writer has recourse are, in the forms of their manifestation employed by him, almost peculiar to the East. Lightnings, great thunderings, hail of the most destructive severity, earthquakes, burnings of trees and grass, seas appearing to be mingled with flame, and meteoric stones play their part. We read of the wilderness into which the woman with the man child was driven; of the dens and rocks of the mountains in which the terrified inhabitants of earth shall hide themselves from the wrath of the Lamb; of the frightful locusts of the fifth trumpet-plague; of fowls that fill themselves with the flesh of men. In like manner we read of eagles, of the sound of the millstone, of olive trees and palm branches, of the vintage, and of the products of an Eastern clime—odours, ointments, frankincense, wine and oil. All these are directly associated with the locality to which the first readers of the book belonged. Even objects well known in other lands are viewed in the light in which the East, herein differing from the West, regards them, as when horses are presented to us not so much in the magnificence as in the terror of their aspect, or as when the sea, instead of being the symbol of beneficence or eternal youth, is spoken of as the symbol of all that is dark or terrible to man. In this respect the symbols of the Apocalypse correspond to those of the Prophets and of our Lord. They are always taken from well-known things. Had it been otherwise the imagery would not have answered its purpose. Drawn from unfamiliar objects it might have been understood, but a much slighter impression would have been produced by it.

Similar remarks may be made with regard to the historical events referred to in the Apocalypse. Such events often lie at the bottom of its symbols, but it may be doubted if there be a single instance in which the incident taken advantage of by the Seer was not both well known and of the deepest interest to his readers. Nothing, in short, is more marked in the whole character of this book than the desire of the writer to give to the truths with which he deals the utmost possible degree alike of clearness and of fulness of effect.

In connection with this point, and even as in itself a matter of importance for the interpretation of the book, it is interesting to observe that there seems to be no symbol in the Apocalypse taken from heathenism. Such is not the case with the other writers of the New Testament, who do not hesitate to enforce their arguments by considerations drawn from the customs of the heathen lands around them. But the symbolism of the Revelation is wholly and exclusively Jewish. Even "the crown of life" in chap. ii. 10 is not the wreath of the victor in the Grecian games, but the Hebrew crown of royalty and joy—the crown of " King Solomon, wherewith his mother crowned him in the day of his espousals, and in the day of the gladness of his heart." [1] The "white stone," with the new name written in it, of chapter ii. 17, is not suggested by the white pebble which, cast in heathen courts of justice into the ballot box, expressed the judge's acquittal of the prisoner at the bar, but in all probability by the glistering plate borne by the high priest upon his forehead. And all good commentators are agreed that the palms of chap.

[1] Song of Songs, iii. 11.

vii. 9 are not the palms of heathen victors either in the battle or the games, but the palms of the Feast of Tabernacles when, in the most joyful of all her national festivals, Israel celebrated that life of independence on which she entered when she marched from Rameses to Succoth, and exchanged her dwellings in the hot brick-fields of Egypt for the free air of the wilderness, and the " booths " which she erected in the open country.[1]

(3.) The symbols of the Apocalypse are to be judged of with the feelings of a Jew, and not with those of our own country or age. No one will deny that in the symbols, both of the Old Testament prophets and of this book, there are many traits which, looked at in themselves, cannot fail to strike the reader as in a high degree exaggerated, extravagant, and out of all keeping with nature or probability. They are not conceived of according to the laws, as we should consider them, of good taste ; and they cannot, without seriously offending us, be transferred from the pages of the book to the canvas of the painter.[2] Take even the sublime description of One like unto a Son of man in the first chapter —" Clothed with a garment down to the foot, and girt

---

[1] Comp. Trench on the *Epistles to the Seven Churches*, p. 103.

[2] To say nothing of others, Albert Dürer attempted this in a series of etchings "illustrative" of the Apocalypse. But not even his genius could achieve the impossible. His drawings are only grotesque, and rather need to be explained by the sacred text than in any way interpret it. On the other hand the Italian masters who, in the frescoes of the Cathedral of Orvieto—the preaching of Antichrist, etc. — have endeavoured not so much to represent the visions as to interpret them, have at least succeeded in telling very plainly what they understood to be St. John's meaning.

about at the breasts with a golden girdle. And his head and his hair were white as white wool, *white* as snow; and his eyes were as a flame of fire; and his feet like unto burnished brass, as if it had been refined in a furnace. . . . And he had in his right hand seven stars; and out of his mouth proceeded a sharp two-edged sword; and his countenance was as the sun shineth in his strength;"[1] or the description of the Lamb in the fifth chapter—"And I saw in the midst of the throne and of the four living creatures, and in the midst of the elders, a Lamb standing as though it had been slaughtered, having seven horns, and seven eyes, which are the seven Spirits of God, sent forth into all the earth. And He came and He taketh the book out of the right hand of Him that sat on the throne;"[2] or of the vintage of the earth in the fourteenth chapter— "And the angel cast his sickle into the earth, and gathered the vintage of the earth, and cast it into the winepress, the great *winepress*, of the wrath of God. And the winepress was trodden without the city, and there came blood from the winepress, even unto the bridles of the horses, as far as a thousand and six hundred furlongs;"[3] or of the New Jerusalem in the twenty-first chapter—"And the city lieth foursquare, and the length thereof is as great as the breadth; and he measured the city with the reed, twelve thousand furlongs; the length and the breadth and the height thereof are equal;"[4] and we feel at once in all these

[1] Chap. i. 13-16.
[2] Chap. v. 6, 7.
[3] Chap. xiv. 19, 20.
[4] Chap. xxi. 16.

instances, as in many others of a similar kind, that nothing can be less in harmony with the realities of things. This incongruity of imagery with nature strikes us even more in the descriptions given of the composite animals in many of the symbols of the book, as in the case of the four living creatures of the fourth chapter, which were " full of eyes before and behind," and which had " each of them six wings ;" [1] or of the locusts of the ninth chapter, the shapes of which were "like unto horses prepared for war ; and upon their heads as it were crowns like unto gold ; and their faces were as men's faces. And they had hair as the hair of women, and their teeth were as the teeth of lions. And they had breastplates, as it were breastplates of iron ; and the sound of their wings was as the sound of chariots of many horses rushing to war. And they have tails like unto scorpions and stings ;" [2] or of the beast that rose up out of the sea in the thirteenth chapter, "having ten horns and seven heads, and on his horns ten diadems, and upon his heads names of blasphemy. And the beast was like unto a leopard, and his feet were as the feet of a bear, and his mouth as the mouth of a lion." [3] But the truth is, that in all such cases the congruity of the figure with nature, or with notions of propriety suggested by her, was altogether unthought of. It is possible that the style of some of these representations may have been brought by the Jews from Assyria, the wonderful sculptures of which exhibit the very same features—

[1] Chap. iv. 6, 8. [2] Chap. ix. 7-10. [3] Chap. xiii. 1, 2.

almost entire ignorance of beauty of form, but massiveness, power, strength, greatness of conception in what was designed either to attract or overawe or terrify. The sculptor in Assyria, the prophet in the Old Testament, and precisely in the same manner St. John in the Apocalypse, had an idea in his mind which he was desirous to express ; and, if the symbolism effected that end, he did not pause to inquire whether any such figure either existed in nature or could be represented by art. As he felt so did spectators and readers feel. In their eyes it was no objection to the symbol that the combination of details was altogether monstrous. Their sole consideration was whether these details lent a force to the idea which would not or could not have been given to it by other means. When, accordingly, we consider the symbols of the Apocalypse from this point of view, our sense of propriety is no longer shocked. We rather recognise in them a vivacity, a spirit, and a power in the highest degree interesting and instructive.

(4.) There is a natural fitness and correspondence between them and the truths which they are intended to express. In his choice of symbols the Seer was not left to the wildness of unregulated fancy, or to the influence of mere caprice. Consciously or unconsciously he worked within certain limits of adaptation on the part of the sign to the thing signified.[1] Just as in the

---

[1] Nothing can thus be more unfortunate or confusing to the reader than the rendering of the Authorised Version, which in so many passages of the Apocalpyse translates the word ζῶον by our English word "beast," making the object denoted the repre-

parables of our Lord all the representations used by Him rest on the deeper nature of things,—on the everlasting relations existing between the seen and the unseen, on that hidden unity between the different departments of truth which makes one object in nature a more suitable type or shadow of an eternal verity than another,—so is it here. "In the symbol," says Auberlen, "as well as in the parable the lower is used as a picture and sign of the higher, the natural as a means of representing the spiritual. All nature becomes living: it is a revelation of God and of the divine mysteries and laws of life in a lower sphere, as much as the kingdom of heaven is in a higher. There is a deep fundamental harmony and parallelism between the two grand spheres of cosmic being, that of nature and that of spirit ; or, as the latter is twofold, both psychical and spiritual, between the three kingdoms of nature, history, and revelation. It is on this correspondence that symbolism and parabolism are grounded. The selection of symbols and parables in Scripture therefore is not arbitrary, but is based on an insight into the essence of things. The woman could never represent the kingdom of the world, nor the beast the Church. . . . To obtain an insight into the symbols and parables of Holy Scripture, nature, that second or rather first book of God, must be opened as

sentative of brute force and unregulated passion instead of redeemed creation. The term "beast," or "wild beast," ought to be strictly confined to the $\theta\eta\rho\iota\alpha$ so often mentioned, and the word $\zeta\tilde{\omega}o\nu$ to be translated "living creature" (comp. Ezek. i. 20, 21 ; x. 17).

well as the Bible."[1] The principle thus expressed is one of great importance, and the correct interpretation of some of the symbols of St. John depends in no small degree upon its being kept steadily in view.

(5.) In the symbols of the Apocalypse it is not necessary to suppose that each minute particular has a definite meaning; or, if it has, that that meaning must be understood by us before we can appreciate the force of the symbol as a whole. Many of its symbols indeed at once explain themselves. There can be no doubt that the judgments of the Almighty are expressed by thunder, and His mercy by the rainbow; that mountains denote worldly kingdoms, and the roaring of the sea the tumult of the nations; that white is the emblem of purity, red of the thirst for blood, and black of mourning and desolation ; other symbols of a much more elaborate character can also be easily and un-hesitatingly explained. But there are not a few every detail of which we do not understand, and when, therefore, the objection may be made that we do not under-stand the symbol.

Is it really so ? Let us look at the parables of our Lord. It is probable that even the smallest particulars mentioned in them had a meaning to Himself. We cannot measure the infinite extent of His wisdom or the amount of instruction which, at least to His own mind, lay in His simplest utterance. When He explains some of His parables He includes much in the explanation of which without His guidance we

---

[1] Auberlen, *Dan. and the Rev.*, p. 87.

should hardly have thought. In the parable of the Sower He shows us that the field, the birds of the air, the heat of the sun, the thorns and brambles, the thirty, sixty, and an hundred fold have all a meaning. Nor is it otherwise in the parable of the Tares and the Wheat. How readily might we suppose that the reapers were only subordinate to the harvest, and that it was unnecessary to connect with them any particular idea. There cannot be a harvest without reapers. Yet "the reapers are the angels."

On the other hand, where no explanations of this kind are given, it is often impossible for us to interpret particulars that meet us in a parable without the risk of our interpretation being either fanciful or erroneous; as when, in the parable of the Prodigal Son, we infer that the robe, the ring, and the shoes given to the returned wanderer denote distinct blessings of the Covenant; or when we imagine that the equal division of the ten virgins into five wise and five foolish, points to an equality of numbers between the saved and the lost. Incidents or notices like these may be introduced simply for the sake of preserving the verisimilitude and heightening the effect of the story. The abuses indeed, which have sprung from the supposed necessity of interpreting every minute particular in a Scripture narrative, will not unfrequently make calm interpreters cling to the belief that their main duty is to gather the general impression. Still it by no means follows that because, by their own confession, they cannot interpret everything, therefore they can interpret nothing.

It is the same with the symbols of the Apocalypse. We may not be able to explain every particular which they contain. But it may not have been intended that we should ; and it is quite possible that, without doing so, we may in each case reach the lesson of the symbol as a whole.

(6.) One remark more has to be made, but one so obvious that, forgotten as it too frequently is, it will not be necessary to dwell on it,—the symbols of the Apocalypse must always be interpreted in the same way. They are a form of speech, and therefore subject to the rules that regulate the interpretation of all speech. The most common words indeed may vary in their signification, and the context may have often to determine their special shade of meaning at a particular time. But where there is nothing to demand the contrary, the same word must invariably be understood in the same sense, and that the sense fixed by usage. This general principle is applicable in all its strictness to symbolical language. There is no reason in the nature of the case why a symbol should be more uncertain in meaning than any other word. The power of that convention which links a certain sense to a certain sound in ordinary terms is not less binding in the presence than in the absence of metaphor of any kind whatever. Thus, where we read in the Apocalypse of the "sea" as an emblem of the troubled and sinful nations of the earth, we are bound, unless forbidden by the context, to carry that interpretation through, and to understand the "sea" spoken of in chap. xx. 13—"And the sea gave up the dead which are in it"—not of the ocean in which so many have found a "wandering" grave, but of the troubled and sinful world. In the same way, when we find the expression, "they that dwell on the earth," unquestionably used on many occasions not of all the inhabitants of the world but of the wicked as distinguished from the good, we are bound to apply it always in this sense unless it can be shown that the writer would himself lead us by his other statements at the time to a different conclusion.[1]

Still more important is the application of this rule to the numbers of the Apocalypse. That many of these numbers are without a doubt symbolical is admitted by every interpreter of the book. Instances might easily be produced in which no one would think of maintaining that the number 7 meant seven, or the number 3 three, or the number 10 ten. Notwithstanding this there has been a tendency on the part of even eminent interpreters to play fast and loose with the apocalyptic numbers. More particularly has this been the case, for example, with the number 7. It is admitted by all interpreters worthy of regard that, when applied to the seven churches of Asia, that number represents not seven in the numerical scale, but the idea of totality; and

---

[1] The difficulty of applying this rule is undoubtedly great. Probably every commentary will supply illustrations of it. No one has seen the rule more clearly than Dr. Fairbairn, of whose valuable work on prophecy the portion devoted to the Apocalypse is by no means the least important. Yet even he supposes the "great city" of chap. xvii. 18 to be a city situated on seven literal mountains, because in verse 9 we read that "there are seven mountains on which the woman sitteth," p 372.

the same thing may be said of it in many other passages of the book. When, accordingly, we read in chap. xvii. 9 that "the seven heads are seven mountains upon which the woman sitteth," it is impossible at once to draw the conclusion that the city spoken of was built literally upon seven hills; and, in like manner, when we read in the same chapter of "seven kings," it is not less at variance with strict rules of interpretation to maintain that these must be seven emperors of Rome, because a king is an emperor and seven is seven. The first and most legitimate inference in both cases is rather that we are dealing with a seven which must again in one way or another express a totality. Similar remarks may be made with regard to the two witnesses of chap. xi., the three and a half years of chap. xii.,[1] and the thousand years of chap. xx., figures which have been claimed as an exception to the ordinary practice of the Seer, and have been supposed to refer literally to witnesses in number two, or to years in number three and a half or a thousand. No wonder that a book is dark where the best understood rules of interpretation are systematically neglected. The darkness is largely due, not to it, but to ourselves. We have only to adhere faithfully to the common and well-understood laws of language in order to see much at least of its obscurity disappear.

[1] By what right can Renan be allowed to interpret the three and a half years literally, and yet the "one hour" of chap. xvii. 12 as *un temps limité? (L'Antechrist,* p. 433), or how can Volkmar be justified in making three and a half years equal thirty-five years, while a thousand years are literal years? (*Comm.,* p. 9, 301).

In conclusion, it may be remarked that the principle now spoken of, applicable to all books, is peculiarly applicable to the Apocalypse, for no one who has paid attention to that book can fail to have been struck with the singular care bestowed on its composition. Everything connected with it bears witness to the fact that in general structure, in selection of figures, and in the choice of particular constructions and words, there has been exercised an amount of deliberate thought and plan certainly never surpassed, perhaps hardly ever equalled, in either secular or sacred literature. So far from being wild and unregulated, never was a book written displaying on the part of the writer a clearer consciousness of the aim which he had in view, or showing even in minute particulars more pains to reach it. The result may be something to which we are wholly unaccustomed ; but it is needless to say that in proportion to the perfection of that result must have been the deliberate and fixed nature of the steps by which it was attained. In the nature of things, therefore, a book so written ought to admit of a definite sense being assigned to it. It is not the careful but the careless, not the perfect but the imperfect, structure that at once baffles our efforts and excuses our failure to comprehend it. The more real the meaning of any work of art, the more ought that meaning to disclose itself to the diligent and persevering student.

LECTURE II.

INFLUENCES MOULDING THE CONCEPTION OF THE APOCALYPSE.

WE have considered the form—that of visions and symbols—in which the revelation contained in the Apocalypse is presented, and we may turn now to the influences moulding the conception of the book. Novel and strange as its contents appear at first sight to be, we shall find that they exhibit a singular amount of dependence upon what is otherwise well known to us, and must have been equally well known to the Seer and his immediate readers.

In entering upon this inquiry no one surely will imagine for a moment that any doubt is thrown by it on the belief, always and reasonably entertained in the Church, that the visions of the Apocalypse are substantially due to that glorified Lord who alone knows the end from the beginning. But we are dealing with historical phenomena which must be investigated on the same principles as all other phenomena of a similar kind. Our sacred books claim to be received as historically authoritative, and we can only respond to their appeal when we have examined them as we examine every historical document submitted to our judgment. No inquiry is more legitimate than that relating to the origin of any one of the four Gospels. Whence did the writer gather his materials? Was it from general tradition, from the information of immediate eye-witnesses, or from personal recollection? What motives prompted him to write? What influences shaped his work? Answers to these questions need not of themselves disturb our conclusions as to the reality or extent of the Divine inspiration under which he wrote; for no one will deny that the Spirit of God, in fitting His instruments for their task, avails Himself of the preparation afforded them by the ordinary course of Providence. Similar questions therefore cannot unfavourably affect our estimate of the Divine origin of the Apocalypse, but they may exert an important influence on its interpretation. Let us look at the facts.

I. In the first place, the Apocalypse is moulded by that great discourse of our Lord upon "the last things" which has been preserved for us in the first three Gospels.[1] The parallelism between the two is to a

---

[1] Matt. xxiv. 4 – xxv.; Mark xiii. 5-37; Luke xxi. 8-36; comp. xvii. 20-37. It is remarkable that we find no account of this discourse in the Gospel of St. John; nor does it seem a sufficient explanation of the omission that the later Evangelist was satisfied with the records of the discourse already given by his predecessors. The author of *Parousia* has adverted to this fact, and has suggested that "the difficulty is explained if it should be found that *the Apocalypse is nothing else than a transfigured form of the prophecy on the Mount of Olives*," p. 374. The explanation seems by no means improbable.

certain extent acknowledged by all inquirers, and is indeed in many respects so obvious that it can hardly escape the notice of even the ordinary reader. Let any one compare, for example, the account of the opening of the sixth seal in Rev. vi. 12-17 with the description of the end in Matt. xxiv. 29, 30, and he will see that the one is almost a transcript of the other. Or let the three series of apocalyptic visions,—the Seals, the Trumpets, and the Bowls, be compared with the other parts of the discourse, and it will be found that, speaking generally, they are filled with the same thoughts,—with wars, pestilences, famines, earthquakes, signs in sun and moon and stars, false teachers doing wonders and trying to deceive the very elect, the elect preserved, angels sent forth to gather them with the great sound of a trumpet, the victorious progress of the Gospel, the Son of man coming in the clouds of heaven, the final deliverance of the good, and the just judgment of the wicked. These things reveal in a way not to be mistaken a very intimate relation between the last prophecy of Christ and the Revelation of St. John. When we look still further into the matter, the correspondence is much more marked. The main particulars only can be here adverted to.

In the first place, we have to determine the manner in which we are to divide our Lord's discourse into its different parts. This question has exercised the thoughts and taxed the powers of every student of the Gospels; but it is impossible to speak now of what has been done by others. The matter must be approached directly. As given in its greatest fulness in the twenty-fourth chapter of the Gospel of St. Matthew, the discourse before us is an answer to a question of the disciples contained in the third verse of the chapter,— "Tell us, when shall these things be? and what shall be the sign of Thy coming and of the consummation of the age?" The chief part of the answer to the question occupies the verses extending from the fourth to the thirty-first. The verses preceding these relate the circumstances under which the question was asked; the verses following give the practical application of what had been said. We may confine ourselves at present to the central and most important part of the discourse —verse 4 to verse 31.

This portion of the chapter ought to be divided into three, and not, as sometimes, into two; or, as at other times, into many parts.

The first of the three extends from verse 4 to verse 14, and contains in its most general form our Lord's reply to the question of the disciples in verse 3. That question had been apparently a double one—(1) "When shall these things be?" When shall that overthrow of the temple take place of which Jesus had spoken in verse 2, and the thought of which had produced so profound an impression on His hearers? (2) "What shall be the sign of Thy coming and of the consummation of the age?" But, though apparently double, the question had been in reality a single one. The disciples had mixed up two things with one another. Our Lord distinctly separates the two, and in verses 4 to 6 He confines Himself to the first, warning the disciples that the signs by which the destruction of Jerusalem should be preceded were not intimations of " the end."   " The end," He said at the close of verse 6, " *is not yet.*"   At this point, at verse 7, He turns to the second element in the disciples' question,—" the consummation of the age."   He regards the present dispensation as a whole, and follows it to its " end."   No longer occupied with the interests of the disciples as Jews, or with the events, however important, that were to happen in Judea, He looks at " all the nations," [1] and occupies Himself with the fortunes of His Church on her widest scale.   A multitude of particulars are grouped together in brief and rapid outline upon the canvas—wars; famines; and, as St. Luke adds,[2] pestilences; earthquakes in divers places; and, as St. Luke again adds, terrors and great signs from Heaven.[3]   For the followers of Christ there shall be hatred and tribulation and death; or, in the still more graphic language of St. Luke, they shall be delivered up to synagogues and prisons, and shall be brought before kings and governors for Christ's name's sake.[4]   The effect of all this shall be, that many shall stumble and many be led astray by the false prophets who shall arise; and that, because iniquity shall be multiplied, the love of the many shall wax cold.   Yet, in the midst of calamity and defection, the true children of God, as we read especially in the second and third Gospels, shall be preserved; the very malice of their

---

[1] Verses 9-14.

[2] Luke xxi. 11.

[3] Luke xxi. 11.

[4] Luke xxi. 12.

enemies shall turn unto them for a testimony; not a hair of their head shall perish; and he that endureth to the end the same shall be saved.[1] Meanwhile the preaching of the Gospel of the kingdom shall be extended to "the whole inhabited earth for a testimony to all the nations," and "then shall the end come" (verse 14).

Such is the first picture of the discourse. It is particularly to be observed that it relates *both* to the Church and to the world; and it is obvious that it carries us down to the final judgment. Many traits of it are wholly inconsistent with the idea that it is limited to the time preceding the destruction of Jerusalem. The mention of "all the nations," the preaching of the Gospel "in the whole inhabited earth," and more especially the contrast between the words of verse 6, "but the end is not yet," and those of verse 14, "and then shall the end come," are conclusive upon the point. It is only, however, in great and general outlines that the picture is drawn. The history of the Church, and of the world in its relation to her, are both set before us in their broadest features.

The second great picture follows at verse 15 and extends to verse 28. There is no chronological continuation of the first, and there could not be, for the first had already brought us to "the end." We return rather to the beginning, and we have again before us the whole history of the Christian Church from the moment when she was planted in the world to the moment when her

---

[1] Comp. Mark xiii. 11, 13; Luke xxi. 14, 15, 18.

Lord shall come again to introduce her to everlasting blessedness. We are not dealing with Jewish Christians alone.   It is true that the fall of Jerusalem is especially mentioned in these verses, that we read of them that are "in Judea" fleeing to the mountains, and that the disciples are instructed to pray that their flight may not be on "a Sabbath." [1] But the words of verses 17-19 were words used by our Lord, as we learn from the third Gospel, with a universal application. [2] We cannot confine the words "no flesh" of verse 22 to Jews; and the remarkable omission by St. Mark, in his report of the discourse, of the words "on a Sabbath" [3] is a clear proof that the exhortation of Jesus was understood by him to apply also to the Gentiles. St. Luke, as might be expected from the object of his Gospel, is still more specific. He not only omits the words " on a Sabbath," but speaks of "the times of the Gentiles,"—those times which were to prevail everywhere and to the end—of distress of nations "upon the *earth*," and of the things that were coming upon "the world" or "*the inhabited earth*." [4] Throughout this second part of the discourse the whole world is before us; and, as is distinctly shown by the word "immediately" of verse 29, is before us to the end. [5]

[1] Verses 15, 16, 20.

[2] Comp. Luke xvii. 30-37.

[3] Mark xiii. 18.

[4] Luke xxi. 24-26.

[5] It is one of the subordinate testimonies to the correctness of the arrangement here proposed that we are able to understand the εὐθέως of the original (verse 29) in its natural and necessary sense. The torture to which that word has been exposed forms a curious chapter in the history of New Testament Exegesis (comp. Morison *in loc.*).

Still more important, however, is it to observe, in connection with these verses (15-28), that they really divide themselves into two parts dominated by entirely different thoughts, the first part extending from verse 15 to verse 22, the second from verse 23 to verse 28. In the former we have the *external* history of the Church in the world, and her preservation in the midst of all the trials that surround her there. The "great tribulation" spoken of bears less immediately upon her than upon those who are opposing and afflicting her. The woes that here come upon the earth are woes occasioned by its own sinfulness; and they would be much greater than they are, were it not that for the elect's sake the days shall be shortened. These shortened days must thus, from the very circumstance that their "shortening" is referred to as it is, be the days that immediately precede "the end." The latter half of the passage (verses 23-28) gives us the *internal* history of the Church. It begins with a direct address to "the elect," who had been spoken of at the close of the preceding paragraph, and its object is to warn them to resist apostasy and to flee from the judgments by which apostasy shall be overtaken. It exhorts to watchfulness against declension; and the dangers to which it alludes are not so much those of the world as of the Church. Finally, therefore, its threatenings are not directed against unbelievers, but against professing Christians who deny their faith; and the "carcase" spoken of in verse 28 is not that of the world but of all who in any age or in any land—"*wheresoever* the carcase is"—act over again the part of degenerate Jerusalem and of the false theocracy. A "carcase" is something that has fallen from life, not something that was always dead.[1] Once more, it may be observed, we are at "the end."

The third great picture is easily understood. It is given in the verses extending from verse 29 to verse 31, and it presents us with a view of what is to happen when the present Dispensation has run its course. It takes up "the end" mentioned in verse 4, and to the beginning of which we had been brought in verses 23 and 28, as come, and it describes the different fate in store for the foes and for the friends of Jesus,—the one wailing at His presence, the other (still styled His "elect") "gathered together from the four winds, from the one end of heaven to the other."

Such are the leading particulars of this great prophecy of Christ, and such is the manner in which it seems proper to arrange it.

When we turn to the Apocalypse and compare it, from the point at which the action opens, that is from chap. vi., with the discourse now spoken of, more especially when we compare with that discourse the three great series of visions, the Seals, the Trumpets, and the Bowls, the parallelism between the two is of the closest and most remarkable kind.

---

[1] It is in this sense that the word $\pi\tau\hat{\omega}\mu\alpha$ is to be here understood, not as referring to a world sunk in corruption (Morison, Meyer, *in loc.*). It might thus be applied to Jerusalem, did not everything else in the prophecy compel us to think of something wider. The main point is that the saying, whether proverbial or not, is here applied by our Lord not to the world but to a degenerate Church.

Let the following particulars be noted :—

1. As compared with the Trumpets and the Bowls the Seals are general.[1] There is less minute specification of details ; and the subject with which they deal corresponds exactly to that dealt with in the first section of our Lord's discourse (Matt. xxiv. 7-14). There are the same wars and famines and pestilences; there is the same wide preaching of the Gospel, and the same preservation of the elect. But the whole series is of a general and preparatory kind, although in the space of time which it embraces it reaches to "the end."

2. The two series of the Trumpets and the Bowls are in a certain sense to be taken together, in this respect exactly corresponding to the second section of our Lord's discourse—that section which, as we have already seen, presents a second picture of the whole history of the Church from two different points of view (verses 15-28). It has indeed been maintained by many inquirers that the three series of the Seals, the Trumpets, and the Bowls are entirely independent of one another; by many that they are developed out of one another,—the Trumpets out of the Seals and the Bowls out of the Trumpets. A closer examination of the text will satisfy us that both alternatives are wrong. The opening verses of chap. viii. clearly show that there is an intimate connection between the Trumpets and the Seals—"And when he opened the seventh seal, there followed a silence in heaven about the space of half an hour. And I

---

[1] Comp. Lecture iii. p. 93.

saw the seven angels which stand before God; and there were given unto them seven trumpets,"[1] after which comes the incident of the prayers of all saints; and only at the sixth verse of the chapter do the angels prepare themselves to sound. We cannot, therefore, separate the Trumpets from the seventh Seal. The former are not independent of the latter, but are evidently developed out of it, although the succession is one of thought rather than time. When we turn to the seventh Trumpet at the close of chap. xi. there is no similar connection with the immediately following series of the Bowls. There is no introduction, there is no mention, of the Bowls. An entirely new start, taking us back to the beginning, is made in chap. xii., and not until we reach chap. xv. 7 do we read of the seven angels to whom were given the seven Bowls full of the wrath of God. The contrast with the transition from the Seals to the Trumpets is striking, and it warrants the conclusion that the Bowls do not stand to the Trumpets in the same relation as the Trumpets to the Seals. There is no development now of the one out of the other. The legitimate inference is that there is a sense in which the Trumpets and the Bowls taken together form one great section of the Apocalypse, that, however distinct from one another, there is some thought common to them both, that there is a point of view from which (like the verses in Matt. xxiv. 15-28) they constitute one series, and that both are developed out of the Seals. They are a fuller, a more detailed, a more definite ex-

[1] Chap. viii. 1, 2.

plication of what the Seals contain. In other words, the two later series taken together stand to the earlier series in precisely the same relation as that in which the second section of our Lord's discourse, with its two divisions, stands to the first.

3. This inference will be confirmed, and the parallelism insisted on will be brought still more fully out, if we further attend to the contents of the Trumpets as distinguished from the contents of the Bowls. That both these series embrace the whole history of the Church will be afterwards more fully seen; but they embrace it with a difference.

The Trumpets refer peculiarly to judgments on the world and to the preservation of the elect in the midst of them. That the elect are affected by the judgments is true.[1] They live in the same world as the wicked, engage in the same occupations, discharge the same duties, are exposed to the same trials, are mingled with them in the same bonds of the family, the neighbourhood, and the state. The time has not yet come for the separation which shall finally take place. Were the tares to be rooted up the wheat would be rooted up with them. But although the righteous suffer,

---

[1] This had been the experience also of the Old Testament Church. No distinction was made between Israel and the Egyptians till the close of the third plague. The waters were turned into blood for both alike; the frogs and the lice were upon both alike. It will be noted that the judgments under the Trumpets in the Apocalypse are called plagues (chap. ix. 20), and that several of them just reproduce in an intenser form the plagues of Egypt—the water turned into blood (*ibid.* viii. 8), the darkness (*ibid.* viii. 12), and the locusts (*ibid.* ix. 3).

the judgments of the Trumpets fall directly on the world alone. Numerous indications prove this.

Thus it is of importance to notice the manner in which the Trumpet judgments are introduced. They are an answer to the prayers of "all saints," which were offered up by the angel of chap. viii., along with the incense which he presented upon the golden altar that is before the throne. But these prayers are directed against the world that has persecuted the Church, against those who are spoken of under the fifth seal as "they that dwell on the earth."[1] It is true that the apostate Church is a persecutor, in this book even the great persecutor, of the people of God. But against her the saints cannot pray. To them she is still the Church. God alone can separate the true from the false within her pale. That against which the prayers of all saints are offered is the world. Again, in chap. viii. 13, the three woes of the three last Trumpets are denounced upon "them that dwell on the earth," an expression invariably applied in the Apocalypse to those who are partakers of the sinful spirit of the world. Now it is a principle of interpretation, to be applied to all the three series of the Seals the Trumpets and the Bowls, that what is mentioned under any one member of each series belongs equally to its other members, and that the judgments, while in a certain sense seven, are in another one. The three woes therefore express the character of the whole group to which they belong. Again, in the account given of

---

[1] Chap. vi. 10.

the fifth Trumpet at chap. x. 4, the children of God are clearly separated from the ungodly, so that judgment shall not touch them. The locusts of that Trumpet are not to "hurt the grass of the earth, neither any green thing, neither any tree, but *only such men as have not the seal of God in their foreheads.*" Finally, let us notice that the seventh Trumpet, in which the Trumpets culminate, and in which therefore the special character of the whole series is expressed, deals peculiarly with judgment on the world : " *The nations* were angry, and Thy wrath came, and the time of *the dead to be judged . . .* and to destroy them that destroy the earth." [1] When we put all these circumstances together, we shall be satisfied that the series of the Trumpet-plagues presents us with the same thought as the first half of the second section of our Lord's discourse. It deals not with the Church but with the world, or with the world in its relation to the Church.

If from the Trumpets we turn to the Bowls the following particulars claim our notice :—(1) The very mention of Bowls at once connects us not with the world but with the Church. The vessels so designated were not vials but bowls or basins, broad and shallow rather than narrow and deep. They were gifts presented by the princes of the twelve tribes of Israel for the service of the Tabernacle,[2] and they were used for offering on the golden altar of the sanctuary the incense which had been kindled by coals from the altar in the court. They were thus instruments of religious

---

[1] Chap. xi. 18.   [2] Numb. vii.

service, and were peculiarly fitted, according to the *lex talionis*, the law of recompense in kind pervading the whole Apocalypse, to contain those judgments of the Almighty which were designed not for the world but for the faithless Church.   It was thus that in Malachi the corrupt Jewish Church was threatened, " I will curse your blessings " (chap. ii. 2 ; comp. Psalm lxix. 22, 23). (2) A similar remark applies to the fact that, as mentioned in chap. xv. 6, the angels which bear the seven last plagues come forth from the " temple " or innermost shrine of the tabernacle of the testimony in heaven, dressed as priests in pure white linen and with golden girdles.   Nothing of this kind is said of the angels of the Trumpets in chap. viii.   The thought of the *lex talionis* again leads us to the degenerate Church as the object of the judgments to be inflicted by these angels.   (3) By the time we reach the judgments of the Bowls in chap. xvii. the peculiar struggle of the children of God with their great adversaries has begun. The three enemies of them that " keep the commandments of God and hold the testimony of Jesus " [1] have been described in chaps. xii. and xiii.   The preservation of the sealed has been set before us in chap. xiv.; and in chap. xv. they that come victorious from the beast, and from his image, and from the number of his name, have been beheld upon the glassy sea, having harps of God and singing the song of Moses the servant of God and of the Lamb.   Like the great leader of Israel of old, like the Lamb of God Himself in the days

[1] Chap. xii. 17.

of His flesh, they have conquered not merely the world in its coarser forms, but a degenerate theocracy, the world in the Church. (4) The contents of the third Bowl are discharged upon those who had "poured out the blood of saints and prophets,"[1] and it has already been remarked that the object of judgment mentioned under any one member of a group throws light upon the object of judgment under its other members, although under them it may not be so distinctly noted. But this description of those who are judged under the third Bowl is elsewhere applied in almost the same terms to Babylon the apostate Church.[2] (5) The seventh Bowl, like the seventh Trumpet, treats of the final judgment, yet with the obvious difference that, while the latter, as we have seen, deals with the "world" and the "nations," the former deals with "the great city" and "Babylon" —"and the great city was divided into three parts, and the cities of the nations fell: and Babylon the great was remembered in the sight of God, to give unto her the cup of the wine of the fierceness of His wrath."[3] This "great city," this Babylon, is the apostate Church.[4] (6.) On the supposition now before us it becomes possible to give an easy and natural explanation of the words of chap. x. 11, "And they say unto me, Thou must prophesy, a second time, over many peoples and nations and tongues and kings." Why do these words come in at the point at which we meet them? Because we are about to pass from the world considered in itself

---

[1] Chap. xvi. 6.
[2] Chap. xviii. 24.
[3] Chap. xvi. 19.
[4] Comp. p. 181.

to the world as the theatre of the Church, as the stage upon which the Church's fortunes are the chief object of interest to angels and awakened men.   There is a fitness, therefore, in calling our attention to that second proclamation of the Gospel by which the Church was constituted among the Gentiles.[1]

Let us again put these circumstances together, and we shall be led to the conclusion that the series of the Bowls has a special relation not to the Church in the world but to the Church considered in herself, and to her internal rather than her external history.   In other words, the series of the Bowls gives expression throughout to the same thought as the second half of the second section of that discourse of Jesus with which we are now comparing the Apocalypse.

On the correspondence between the third section of our Lord's discourse and the closing scenes of the Apocalypse it is unnecessary to dwell.

Thus strikingly then do the leading visions of St. John correspond to that discourse of Jesus in which He pointed out in great lines to His disciples the nature of the events that were to happen between His own day and "the consummation of the age."   The correspondence is not merely general, it is minute and special;

---

[1] It is not without interest to compare the words of chap. x. 11 with those in the Gospel of St. John iv. 54.   The importance which St. John attached to this latter statement, as shown in the very peculiar structure of the verse, has been pointed out in the Comm. (*in loc.*).   In Rev. x. 11 we have again his πάλιν, and that in connection with the very same thought—the extension of the Gospel tidings to the Gentile world.

and it exists to such a degree as to admit of only one conclusion, that the Apocalypse is the enlargement of the discourse. This conclusion is more than interesting and curious : it is in the highest degree important. Two consequences in particular may be noticed. (1) The Revelation of St. John is at once separated from all the other apocalyptic writings with which it is so often compared. The direct authority of the Saviour is lent to it, and we see at least how naturally it may have been the production of that disciple who knew so much of the mind of his Master. (2) The book being the enlargement of the discourse, it is not unreasonable to think that what the discourse contains is contained also in the book, and that what the discourse does not contain is not to be looked for in the book.

It may be well, before passing on, to present the above analysis of Matt. xxiv. and of the Apocalypse in a tabular form, taking in only for the sake of completeness the whole discourse :—

I. The situation, Matt. xxiv. 1-3.

II. The discourse, part i., Matt. xxiv. 4-31.

    1. Reply of Jesus to the first part of the question after He had separated it into its component elements, When shall these things be ? (verses 4-6).

    2. Reply of Jesus to the second part of the question, What shall be the sign of Thy coming and of the consummation of the age ? (verses 7-31, in three parts).

a. General outline of the history of the Church and of the world to the Second Coming (verses 7-14); corresponding to the seven Seals of the Apocalypse.

b. Same subject resumed under two special aspects (verses 15-28).

First Aspect.

The Church in her relation to the evil world (verses 15-22); corresponding to the seven Trumpets of the Apocalypse.

Second Aspect.

The Church in her relation to the evil in herself (verses 23-28); corresponding to the seven Bowls of the Apocalypse.

c. The Second Coming (verses 29-31).

III. The discourse, part ii., Matt. xxiv. 32—xxv. 46. Application to the truths stated in part i.

1. To question regarding the destruction of the temple (verses 32-35).

2. To question regarding the consummation of the age (chap. xxiv. 36—xxv. 46).

II. In the second place, the conception of the Apocalypse is powerfully moulded by St. John's recollections of the life of Jesus. What these recollections were we know from that Gospel which is also the production of his pen; and the strong individuality of which, stamped upon its every line, reveals not the influence of a general tradition as it appears in the three earlier Gospels, but the manner in which St. John himself recalled the life of his Divine Master upon earth. The remarkable fact, then, with which we have now to do is this, that the parallelism just spoken of between the Apocalypse and our Lord's discourse to His disciples upon "the last things" is not more close or striking than is that between the same book and the delineation of the life of Christ contained in the fourth Gospel. When we compare the two we shall find that, alike in general scope and in particular details, the Gospel is the model of the Apocalypse; that all the lines of the one are followed in the other; and that, separated as the two books are in many of their outward features by what is often thought an impassable gulf, the later is yet, in the deeper conceptions which pervade it, a repetition of the earlier.

One point of distinction must indeed be kept steadily in view. The two books are written from a different standpoint. The Gospel is the record of the Word made flesh, of the Life come down from heaven to give life unto the world, of the creation of the union between Christ and His people. In the Apocalypse this union has been formed and is seen subsisting. The Son of God in the glory of His Ascension-state is still the Son of man, and the latter aspect of His Person becomes prominent. In the very first vision He is spoken of as "like unto a Son of man."[1] He is the great High Priest and King of His people, not so much the eternal Logos (although He is that also) as He who became dead, and behold, He is alive for evermore. He holds the seven stars in His right hand, walks in the midst of the seven golden candlesticks, and is the constant and

____
[1] Chap. i. 13.

faithful Guardian of His flock. It is Christ in His Church, therefore, rather than in Himself; or, in other words, it is the Church as she is in Christ, and is one with Him, whose fortunes we are here to follow.

With this thought, however, another immediately connects itself,—that union with Christ not only in inward spirit but in outward fortune is the abiding mark of the Church, one of the deepest and most essential characteristics of her life; that the Church must tread the same path as that which her Redeemer trod; that she must drink the same cup and be baptized with the same baptism. Hence the life of Christ, remembered as St. John remembered it, supplies the type to which the history of His people shall be conformed : or, in other words, the Gospel of St. John moulds the conception of the Apocalypse.

We see it in the general arrangement of the seven successive parts of the book, in every one of which a thought may be observed precisely parallel to that which appears in the corresponding stage of the life of Jesus.

The prologue in chap. i. corresponds to the prologue of the Gospel, with the difference in the aspect of Jesus already noticed (comp. John i. 1-18). Then the presentation of the Church as she occupies her position in the world, in chaps. ii. and iii., corresponds to the presentation of Jesus on the field of human history (comp. John i. 19—ii. 11). Chaps. iv. and v., which follow, contain pictures of coming victory in every respect analogous to those found in the third section of the Gospel, so that before the conflict with the world begins the mind is filled with confident and joyful hope as to the issue (comp. John ii. 12—iv. 54). The conflict itself, extending from chap. vi. to chap. xviii. 24, is next presented to our view, reminding us of the conflict of Jesus with His enemies, containing similar opposition, similar triumph over it, similar advance in judgment, and similar pictures, marked by ever-increasing brightness, of the security of the righteous. Yet, strange to say, it closes with the same sad tones; for the Church of Christian, no less than of Jewish, times has become degenerate, and God's faithful ones can only be saved by listening to the cry, "Come forth, my people, out of her, that ye have no fellowship with her sins, and that ye receive not of her plagues" (comp. John v. 1—xii. 50). The conflict is next followed by the pause of rest and accomplished victory, from chap. xix. 1 to chap. xix. 10; and it is impossible to mistake the resemblance to that blessed pause in the life of Jesus when, His conflict over, and every element of darkness driven away, He celebrated the Last Supper with His disciples, addressed to them His last words of peace, and poured forth His heart in that high-priestly prayer in which we breathe the very atmosphere of heaven (comp. John xiii.-xvii.). The resemblance is so close that, just as in chap. xiii. of the Gospel the Last Supper is celebrated, so even in the Apocalypse *there is a supper*. For the first time in the book we read of "the supper of the marriage of the Lamb,"[1] for that "marriage is come

---

[1] Chap. xix. 9.

and the Lamb's wife hath made herself ready." [1]   But the pause is not to last (chap. xix. 11 to chap. xxii. 5). The eternal rest is not yet come.   There is a fresh outbreak of war at chap. xix. 11.   First, the Lord Himself appears in all the glory of His victorious might; and the description is peculiarly interesting because it takes up again several of the most striking particulars contained in the description given of Him on His first appearance, and not since that time alluded to.   He rides upon His white horse; He is called Faithful and True; in righteousness He judges and makes war; His eyes are as a flame of fire; out of His mouth proceedeth a sharp sword ; He ruleth the nations with a rod of iron; He is King of kings and Lord of lords.[2] Next "the beast" is seen with "the kings of the earth and their armies gathered together to make war against Him that sat upon the horse and against His army," and he is accompanied to the field by "the false prophet that wrought the signs in his sight."   Lastly the devil himself comes forth "to deceive the nations which are in the four corners of the earth, Gog and Magog, to gather them together to the war." [3]   The war thus spoken of corresponds to that renewed outburst of evil, occurring at chap. xviii. of the Gospel after the rest of Jesus, which here as well as there is unsuccessful, and which, followed in the history of our Lord by the "lifting on high" of the cross and the resurrection, is followed in the visions of the Seer by the casting of the

[1] Chap. xix. 7.

[2] Comp. with the particulars of the description in the text, chaps. vi. 2; i. 5; iii. 14; i. 14; i. 16; ii. 27; i. 5.

[3] Chap. xx. 8.

Church's last enemies into the lake of fire, and the perfecting of the happiness of the saints amidst the glories of the New Jerusalem (comp. John xviii.-xx.). Of the epilogue (chap. xxii. 6-21) in the Apocalypse it is unnecessary to speak. It ends, as the Gospel does, with the Second Coming of the Lord (comp. John xxi.)[1]

In reviewing these particulars there is a risk that they may appear to many too artificial to be true. But the more they are reflected on the more will this impression disappear. Let us once satisfy ourselves, and no student of St. John can long be insensible to the fact, that union, that identification, of Christ's people with their Lord was one of the deepest convictions of the beloved disciple; let us learn from all his writings how strongly he felt that every member of Christ's Body must share the fortunes of its Head, and we shall not be surprised that his conception of the history of the suffering Church should shape itself in his mind according to the history of the suffering Lord.

Not only, however, does the idea now spoken of appear in the general conception of the book, it appears also in individual passages.

Let us turn, for example, to the history of the two witnesses in chap. xi., and we can hardly fail to see

---

[1] The writer may be permitted to refer to his paper in the *Expositor* (second series, v. p. 102) in which the above point is more fully dwelt on. Any difference of view now expressed relates only to the point at which section vi. of the Apocalypse should begin, there at chap. xx. 7, here at chap. xix. 11.

that the description of their death in the seventh and eighth verses of that chapter is suggested by the closing hours of the Redeemer's life.   The opening words, " And when they shall have finished their testimony," take us at once to the scene on Calvary as it is described in the fourth Gospel—" When Jesus therefore had received the vinegar, He said, It is finished : and He bowed His head, and gave up the ghost." [1]   Other particulars of the correspondence are not so minute; but few will doubt whence the general idea of them is drawn,—" And the beast that cometh up out of the abyss shall make war with them, and overcome them, and kill them.   And their dead bodies lie in the street of the great city, which spiritually is called Sodom and Egypt, where also their Lord was crucified."   A similar remark is applicable to the vindication which the witnesses receive at the hands of God.   Probably no commentator hesitates to recognise in it particulars furnished by the Resurrection and Ascension of our Lord,—" And after the three days and a half the breath of life from God entered into them, and they stood upon their feet ; and great fear fell upon them which beheld them.   And they heard a great voice from heaven saying unto them, Come up hither.   And they went up to heaven in the cloud ; and their enemies beheld them."

Again, in chap. xii. 4, the attitude of the great red dragon towards the woman delivered of the man child is thus described: " And the dragon stood before the woman which was about to be delivered, that when she

<hr>

[1] John xix. 30.

F

was delivered, he might devour her child." Whatever else may be implied in this, it surely reflects that fact in the history of Jesus with which St. John, though he does not mention it in his Gospel, must have been perfectly familiar,—that Herod sought the young child's life to destroy him,—a fact again repeated in the history of the Church. And when, at verse 5 of the same chapter, the child is caught up to God and to His throne, what is this but the catching up of the faithful (for they are included in the child) to the heavenly places, after the manner of Him who ascended to "His Father and our Father, to His God and our God"?

Again, the relation now spoken of between the fourth Gospel and the Apocalypse explains the representation given in the latter of the great enemies of the Church. In the Gospel the enemies of our Lord are three in number, the devil, the Roman Government, and that degenerate Judaism which persuaded the Roman Government to become the tool of its guilty purposes. But three great enemies appear also in the Apocalypse, the dragon, the first beast, and the second beast. That the dragon of the Apocalypse is the same as the devil of the Gospel admits of no dispute. In chap. xii. 9 he is expressly said to be "the old serpent, he that is called the Devil and Satan." The second enemy, or the first beast of chap. xiii., is almost universally allowed to be the power of the world represented at the time by that of Rome; and the more carefully the particulars mentioned of the second beast of the same chapter are examined, the more will it appear that the description rests upon that fanatical spirit of "the Jews" which led them to incite Pilate to the condemnation of the Christ at the moment when he himself, saying "I find no fault in Him," sought to release Him.[1]   There may be nothing surprising in the fact that a writer who delights as much as St. John in the use of the number 3 should see especially three enemies bringing about the death of Jesus ; but that, when he comes to the history of the Church, the same three should again appear cannot fail to show us how closely the fortunes of the Church are moulded upon those of Christ.

One other passage may be referred to in illustration of this point.   At chap. xvii. 16 we read, " And the ten horns which thou sawest, and the beast, these shall hate the harlot, and shall make her desolate and naked, and shall eat her flesh, and shall burn her utterly with fire. For God did put it in their hearts to do His mind, and to come to one mind, and to give their kingdom unto the beast, until the words of God should be accomplished." The passage is one of the most startling in the book of Revelation, and its statement comes upon us as a result totally unexpected and unaccounted for.   The harlot had been sitting on the beast, and guiding the beast in perfect harmony with its designs.   The two are friends and fellow-workers.   All at once the scene is changed. Defeat has taken place, and what is its effect ?   The bond which in prosperity had bound together the partners in wickedness is dissolved; they who had co-operated in sin fall out; the one turns round upon the

---

[1] John xix. 6, 12.

other; and she who had found ready instruments in the beast and its heads for accomplishing the work to which she had spurred them on, now sees them, in the hour of their common despair, fall upon herself and mercilessly destroy her. We need not ask whether events then future, or future still, are symbolized by this language. A great principle, one often exemplified in the world, is proceeded on,—that combinations of the wicked speedily break up, leaving the guilty associates to turn upon and destroy one another. The question that at present mainly concerns us is, What are the historical circumstances lying at the bottom of the vision? And, when we ask that question, it is difficult not to think that there was one great drama present to the mind of the Seer and suggestive of the picture of the harlot's ruin, that of the life and death of Jesus. The degenerate Jewish Church had then called in the assistance of the world-power of Rome, had stirred it up, and had persuaded it to do its bidding against its true Bridegroom and King. An alliance had been formed between them; and, as the result of it, they crucified the Lord of glory. But the alliance was soon broken; and, in the fall of Jerusalem by the hands of her guilty paramour, the harlot was left desolate and naked, her flesh was eaten, and she was burned utterly with fire.[1]

It is possible that other illustrations of the point now

---

[1] The quarrel of the fallen Jewish Church and the Roman power was *consummated* in the fall of Jerusalem. But the beginning of the quarrel took place *as soon* as our Lord was delivered up. St. John notes it in the words of Pilate in chap. xix. 22 — "What I have written, I have written."

before us may be found ; or, if the principle of contrasts, which we have yet to see plays a large part in the structure of the Apocalypse,[1] be resorted to, the conclusion arrived at may find support in it, for the binding of Satan and the sealing of the abyss in chap. xx. seem to be a mocking counterpart to the binding of Jesus and the sealing of the stone rolled against the mouth of His tomb. Enough, however, has been said to show that the Apocalypse is penetrated in a remarkable manner by the tendency to present the history of the Church as corresponding in every respect to the history of the Church's Lord.

To such an extent is what has now been said the case, that the Apocalypse may without impropriety be spoken of as the complement of the fourth Gospel. It stands to it in a relation similar to that of the Acts of the Apostles to the Gospel of St. Luke, or of the Epistle to the Ephesians to that to the Colossians. We may divide into two parts the words of our Lord's high-priestly prayer, "As Thou didst send Me into the world, even so sent I them into the world;" and, if we do so, they will severally describe the books before us, "As Thou didst send Me into the world,"—that is the Gospel; —"Even so sent I them into the world,"—that is the Apocalypse. But the one is history, the other is apocalyptic vision ; and in giving the latter through the Seer the Spirit of God simply availed Himself, as He always does, of the preparation found in the Almighty's providential arrangements, and of the mould made ready to His hand in the prophet's mind.

[1] P. 110.

These considerations will afterwards help us to understand the mysterious book with which we are dealing. In the meantime it is enough to say that the mistakes committed in its interpretation have flowed mainly from this, that men have not apprehended with sufficient clearness the singleness, the simplicity, and the purity of the ideas which it is its purpose to unfold.

The fact now adduced draws again a wide line of demarcation between the Apocalypse and the general apocalyptic literature of the time. It connects it with the rest of the New Testament in a manner and to an extent totally wanting in the other books of a similar character which have come down to us. It makes it the unfolding of a thoroughly Christian idea, and it even helps to give us a standard by which our interpretation of particular passages may be tried. Here, if anywhere indeed, it would seem that we are to find the key of apocalyptic interpretation; for the whole Apocalypse is but a presenting over again, in the mould supplied by our Lord's own history, of the difficulties, the sorrows, the conflicts, and the triumphs of the members of His Body.

III. In the third place, the Apocalypse is largely moulded by the historical and prophetical books of the Old Testament. No characteristic of it is more remarkable than the extent to which this is the case. That a great resemblance should exist between the two might have been expected. As He who is the God of Abraham and Isaac and Jacob is the God of His people now; as He who guided Joseph like a flock is the ever-living

Shepherd of Israel, it is natural that His dealings with the saints of old should be viewed by the Christian mind as typical of His dealings with their children and their children's children to the end of time. The prophets too extended their glance not merely to the coming of Christ into the world, but to the final issues of the Christian dispensation. They testified not only the sufferings of Christ, but the glories that should follow them (1 Pet. i. 11). They were enabled to behold afar off the coming of an age when all evil should be overthrown, and all good be for ever triumphant. Again, therefore, it was natural that the great apocalyptic book of the New Testament should adopt their forms of thought and their very words. The Church of Christ is essentially one with that of the earlier covenant. Though in another and higher stage of progress, she has the same God for her guide, the same Redeemer for her life, the same Spirit to give her light and strength and comfort. She has the same pilgrimage to pursue, the same enemies to contend with, the same promises for her support, the same inheritance for her ultimate reward. With all, therefore, that is Divine in her the same, and all that is human the same in its fundamental principles, we need not wonder that language addressed to the Church at one period of her development should also, though with a wider meaning, be found suitable to her at another.

Yet, even admitting this, such considerations alone would very imperfectly prepare us for the singular dependence of the Apocalypse upon Old Testament history and prophecy. The book is absolutely steeped in the memories, the incidents, the thoughts, and the language of the Church's past. To such an extent is this the case that it may be doubted whether it contains a single figure not drawn from the Old Testament, or a single complete sentence not more or less built up of materials brought from the same source. Nothing can convey a full and adequate impression upon the point except the careful study of the book itself in this particular aspect of its contents. But it may be well to give one or two illustrations of what has been said.

Let us look at its references to persons. Is a particular heresy predominant in Pergamum? It is not merely that of the Nicolaitans but of Balaam;[1] or is Thyatira tolerant of evil? the angel of the Church is charged with "suffering" his wife Jezebel instead of putting her down with a strong hand.[2] Have the two witnesses, amidst all their trials, a might greater than that of their enemies? the description takes us back to Moses and Elijah, and is rendered all the more graphic because we read of deeds similar to theirs without any mention of their names.[3] When a leader of the angels of heaven against the dragon is introduced to us, it is that Michael whose prowess more than one passage of Daniel records;[4] and, when the king of the frightful locusts of the abyss is spoken of, it is by a name familiar to the reader in the original of the books of Job and Psalms and Proverbs.[5] If from persons we turn to

[1] Chap. ii. 14.   [3] Chap. xi. 6.
[2] Chap. ii. 20.   [4] Chap. xii. 7.
          [5] Chap. ix. 11.

places the same rule is observable. Jerusalem and Mount Zion and Babylon and the Euphrates and Sodom and Egypt, all familiar to us in the history of Israel, play their part in order to denote the holiness and happiness of the saints, or the coming in of judgment, or the transgressors from whom the righteous must separate themselves.[1] The battle of Har-Magedon has undoubted reference to one or other, if not to both, of the two great slaughters connected in the Old Testament with the plain of Megiddo, the one celebrated in the song of Deborah and Barak in the book of Judges (chap. v. 19), and again alluded to in the Psalms (Psalm lxxxiii. 9); the other that in which, as related in the second book of Kings (chap. xxiii. 29), King Josiah fell.[2] While nothing can explain the last attack upon the saints as a gathering of Gog and Magog from the four corners of the earth but the fact that these names had already been consecrated to a similar purpose in the prophecies of Ezekiel (chaps. xxxviii., xxxix.)[3]

Again, how many are the objects of Old Testament history mentioned in this book in order to bring out the New Testament ideas which it breathes. The promises to the seven churches, instead of being clothed in purely Christian language, are given under the form of " the tree of life which is in the paradise of God," of " the hidden manna," of " the white (or glistering) stone, and upon the stone a new name written which no man knoweth but he that receiveth it," of

---

[1] Chaps. xxi. 2; xiv. 1; xvi. 19; ix. 14; xi. 8.

[2] Chap. xvi. 16.

[3] Chap. xx. 8.

"the sceptre of iron" breaking the nations to pieces like "the vessels of the potter," of "the morning star," of "names that shall not be blotted out of the book of life," of "the pillar in the temple of my God," of the feast to which Jesus will come in, "supping" with the believer, and the believer with Him.[1] Heaven itself is described under the image of the Tabernacle in the wilderness, with its outer court and its inner sanctuary, its altar of burnt offering, its golden altar of incense, its ark, and its cherubim in the midst of the throne and round about the throne;[2] while the great Being who sits upon the throne shines like the precious stones mentioned by Ezekiel, is encompassed by the rainbow of the Covenant, and has perpetually sung to Him the holy *Trisagion* of Isaiah.[3] The preservation of the people of God from the attacks of their enemies is represented under the figure of the crossing of the Red Sea and of the river Jordan, mixed up with the fate of Korah and his companions in rebellion.[4] The song of the redeemed, who have gotten the victory over the beast, and his image, and his name, and the number of his name, is the song of Moses the servant of God as well as of the Lamb;[5] while the redeemed themselves are marked out as high priests consecrated to God by having their Father's name written on their foreheads.[6] The plagues of Egypt are continually appealed to— water changed into blood, hail and fire and thunder and

---

[1] Chaps. ii. 7, 17, 27, 28 ; iii. 5, 12, 20.

[2] Chaps. xi. 1, 19 ; vi. 9 ; viii. 3 ; xi. 19 ; iv. 6.

[3] Chap. iv. 3, 4, 8.

[4] Chap. xii. 15, 16.

[5] Chap. xv. 3.

[6] Chap. xiv. 1.

lightning and darkness and locusts.[1]   The terrible horses of the sixth trumpet-plague have their features gathered from different passages of the Old Testament ; [2] and the fall of Babylon is moulded upon the fall of Jericho and of Tyre.[3]   The great earthquake of chap. vi. is taken from Haggai; the sun becoming black as sackcloth of hair and the moon becoming blood, of the same chapter, from Joel; the stars of heaven falling, the fig tree casting her untimely figs, the heavens departing as a scroll, in the same chapter, from Isaiah; the scorpions of chap. ix. from Ezekiel; the gathering of the vine of the earth in chap. xiv. from Joel; and the treading of the winepress in the same chapter from Isaiah.   The wings of the eagle upon which the woman is borne for protection to the wilderness are those of Deuteronomy and Isaiah, and the whole description of the New Jerusalem in chap. xxi. is moulded upon Ezekiel.

If we look at several of the larger visions we shall have the same lesson brought home to us—that of the throne in heaven in chap. iv. having its prototype in Isaiah and Ezekiel; that of the roll in chap. v. in Ezekiel; that of the opening of the seals in chap. vi. in Zechariah; that of the beast from the sea in chap. xiii. in Daniel; that of the olive trees in chap. xi. in Zechariah, that of the measuring of the temple in chap. xi. in Ezekiel and Zechariah; that of the little book in chap. x. in Ezekiel.

Or, once more, if we take any single vision and

---

[1] Chap. viii.

[2] Chap. ix. 17 etc.

[3] Chap. xviii.

examine its details, we shall find that its various portions are often gathered out of different prophets, or different parts of the same prophet. Thus, in the very first vision of the book, that of the glorified Redeemer, in chap. i. 12-20, the golden candlesticks are taken from Exodus and Zechariah; the garment down to the foot from Exodus and Daniel; the golden girdle from Isaiah and Daniel; the hairs like white wool from the same two prophets; the feet like unto burnished brass from Ezekiel; the voice as the sound of many waters from Ezekiel; the two-edged sword from Isaiah and the Psalms; the countenance as the sun shineth in his strength from Exodus; the falling of the Seer as dead at the feet of the Person who appears to him from Exodus, Isaiah, Ezekiel, and Daniel; the laying of the right hand of Jesus upon the Seer from Daniel.

It is impossible to enlarge without going over every chapter, verse, and clause of the book, which is a perfect mosaic of passages from the Old Testament, at one time quoted verbally, at another referred to by distinct allusion, now taken from one scene in Jewish history, and now again from two or three together.

Not indeed that the writer binds himself to the Old Testament in a slavish spirit. He rather uses it with great freedom and independence, extending, intensifying, or transfiguring its descriptions at his pleasure. Yet the main source of his emblems cannot be mistaken. The sacred books of his people had been more than familiar to him. They had penetrated his whole being. They had lived within him as a germinating seed capable of shooting up not only in the old forms but in new forms of life and beauty.   In the whole extent of sacred or religious literature there is to be found nowhere else such a perfect fusion of the revelation given to Israel with the mind of one who would either express Israel's ideas, or give utterance, by means of the symbols supplied by Israel's history, to the purest and most elevated thoughts of the Christian faith.

All this has to be studied as more than a remarkable phenomenon.   It draws once more a wide line of distinction between the Apocalypse and the other apocalyptic literature of the early Christian age; and it has the closest bearing on the interpretation of the book.

IV. In the fourth place, there is still another influence to be adverted to which is often supposed to have powerfully affected the conception of the Apocalypse, but which must be mentioned only to be, at least in some measure, set aside.   It is urged by many recent interpreters that the book owes its contents to the religious opinions, especially as to the future, prevalent among the Jews of the first century.   A comparison is made between it and the apocryphal book of Enoch, the fourth book of Esdras, the Ascension of Isaiah, the Sibylline books, and others of a similar kind ; and the result is declared to be that it in every respect resembles them, exhibiting the same wild speculation, the same narrow, intolerant, and Judaizing spirit.   The question raised is a fair one, and the expounder of the Apocalypse is bound to determine the relation in which he stands to it.   In doing so it may be at once admitted that, as it is impossible to separate the author from the other circumstances of his time, so it is equally impossible to separate him from its apocalyptic literature. That literature had begun in the book of Daniel, and it found expression, although it is difficult to determine the precise dates, from the Maccabean period to the second century of the Christian era, in the works that have been mentioned, and in others resembling them. But it does not follow that the Apocalypse of St. John is to be placed upon the same footing, and to be regarded in the same light as these. There were many apocryphal gospels in the first century of the Christian era; but our canonical gospels, though belonging to the same general class, were able to vindicate for themselves an entirely different position; and, under the Divine guidance which she enjoyed, the Church, with the approval of all subsequent generations, separated them from the mass of which they might have seemed to form a part. There were spurious epistles also in circulation at the same date, but again their existence did not prevent the Church from pronouncing a firm and consistent verdict both against them and in favour of our canonical epistles. Nor is it of any moment to determine whether the true or the apocryphal came first. We know that before St. Luke wrote his Gospel there were "many" others in circulation, and some of these at least the Church put unhesitatingly aside. Mere priority of date did not persuade her to accept them. The same may have been the case with the Epistles, for epistolary writing was in these days both understood and practised.

Apocalyptic literature, it is true, is more strange to *us* than that which is historical or epistolary ; and we are, therefore, under a greater temptation to throw all writings of that kind into a common heap, and to suppose that they must have had the same origin.   But if apocalyptic writing was *then* as common as either historical or epistolary, such a conclusion is obviously illegitimate.   The fact that so many then wrote apocalypses forbids our placing them in a separate group in which no distinction may be drawn between one Apocalyptist and another.   They come under the operation of the same general principles of judgment as the writers of histories and epistles.   We must apply the same tests and judge by the same rules in order to distinguish between the spurious and the true.

When, accordingly, we do so, it will be found that the Apocalypse of St. John differs so widely from these other works, and exhibits a spirit so entirely different from theirs, that we can only ratify that judgment of the Church by which it was at the very first, and more even at the first than afterwards, treated as standing by itself.   That it possesses much in common with them is undoubted, but what is common ground is ground common to humanity at large.[1]   The perplexing problem of

[1] "From the beginning of its history," says Godet (*B. S.*, p. 297), "humanity has lived in a state of expectation, of disquieting fears, and of glorious hopes.   This expectation concentrated and purified itself in the heart of the people of Israel. . . . Through Jesus this Divine aspiration became that of the Church ; and the book of the Apocalypse is the precious vessel in which this treasure of Christian hope has been deposited for all ages of the Church, but especially for the Church *under the Cross.*"

the existence of sin in the world, the weariness of the struggle with it, the longing to be free from it, the belief in a righteous Governor of the earth who will ultimately vindicate His ways, the expectation that good and evil will yet be recompensed according to their deserts, —these and such like truths have always had a strong hold of the human heart, and their existence in the Apocalypse is no more a proof that that book is merely human, than the longing for redemption before Jesus came is a proof that He was nothing more than the creation of natural desires and hopes. We may allow without hesitation, therefore, that in a general sense the Apocalypse was moulded by the spirit of its age; but that is only to allow that it proceeded from a genuine teacher, true alike to the Divine fountain of his inspiration, to himself, and to those whom he would instruct.[1]

It is not necessary to say more. We have considered the main influences by which, under the guiding hand of God, the Apocalypse was moulded into the shape which it assumed. The considerations that have been adduced rest upon the facts of the case as they are presented by the book itself, and ought always to be present to our minds when we endeavour to interpret it.

---

[1] On this point it may be well to remember the words of Lücke, who says of the author of the Apocalypse, that "the later apocryphal, even the apocalyptic, literature *steht ihm, wie es scheint, fern*" (*Versuch*, p. 378).

LECTURE III.

PART I

STRUCTURE AND PLAN OF THE APOCALYPSE.

HAVING considered the influences moulding the conception of the Apocalypse, the next point claiming our attention is its structure and plan; and, as before, the object to be kept steadily in view is not mere literary inquiry or the gratification of curiosity, but the interpretation of the book. Upon this interpretation the subject now before us will be found to have an immediate and important bearing.

There is indeed a fear on the part of many that the idea of plan is inconsistent with simplicity of purpose. Principles of arrangement, the existence of which earnest inquirers in examining the structure of our canonical books have been unable to deny, have not unfrequently seemed to these inquirers themselves too artificial to be correct. Even while accepting their own conclusions they have shrunk from them. They have been afraid of yielding to their convictions lest, by doing so, they should destroy the naturalness of the Word of God; should introduce into the utterances of the sacred penmen too much of what in a modern writer would be conscious design; or should even disparage the work of the Spirit by ascribing to Him those contrivances through which merely human authors endeavour to lend force and attractiveness to their works. The fear is groundless. In the first place the question, like every other, must be determined by the facts, and not by prepossessions of our own. In the second place, admitting the facts, it is impossible to deny that the Spirit of God, in bestowing His inspiration upon men, has in innumerable instances made use of the very instrumentality thus thought to be too human for His purpose. Metaphor, parable, allegory, the tropical sense of words, even the use of paronomasia or pun, strophe and antistrophe in the Psalms, the poetic clothing of the most solemn prophecies, the arrangement even of didactic passages in Epistles upon what are incontestably the principles of Hebrew parallelism—such and similar phenomena are sufficient to show that in these, as we might call them, human devices, there is nothing inconsistent with simplicity, or with the desire to produce a moral and religious result. If, in proportion to the degree in which we were constrained to acknowledge their presence in Scripture, we felt at the same time compelled to admit that the Divine element in it was giving way to the human, the effect would be that we should lose the former in exact proportion to the amount of sublimity or pathos, of power or tenderness, by which it was really indicating its presence. Lastly, it ought to be remembered that such artistic arrangements are improperly designated when spoken of as device or artifice. However strange to us, they were the very mould and fashion of Jewish thought. Precisely in proportion to the degree in which the prophet or poet of Israel was impassioned, did his language shape itself into their most perfect forms. The form had a meaning to him. It was part of his inspiration to adopt it. Not because he hoped to gain an adventitious influence over men did he so speak, but because he had no alternative. He was making his nearest approach to what he recognised as the Divine ideal. He was using the only mould adequate to the expressions of the Divine conceptions with which his breast was filled. Consciousness, or rather self-consciousness, there was none. The artificial form was so natural to him, was so much a part of his whole habit of mind, that, when most true to his message and himself, he fell most naturally into it. So far, therefore, is artificial arrangement in a book of Scripture from being an argument against the truth of the contents, that it may be the reverse. It may be a valuable token of the inspiration of the writer. It may be a pledge to us of the exalted state of mind in which he wrote. It may be strictly a part of the Divine method. If we sink ourselves into the style of Hebrew thought, and no one will deny that in studying a Hebrew book we ought to do so, it may be full of valuable instruction, and may commend the lessons of the book to us with double force. All that we have to beware of is the substitution of our own fancies for the objective phenomena. When we allow ourselves to be guided simply by the latter; when our effort is only to penetrate into all parts of the Divine idea ; when we resign ourselves to Him who teaches, not only in Scripture but in nature, by form as well as substance ; when we see that the form is substance, inseparably connected with it, and adapted to it as its appropriate vehicle, we have no need to be afraid of form. Not only is the effort to discover it full of interest, but the form when discovered may be full of power.

Numerous illustrations of these remarks might easily be given both from the Old and the New Testament,[1] but it is unnecessary. Everywhere in both we encounter structures that may at first sight be deemed simply artificial. But they are so in nothing but appearance. In reality all is natural, and the mind of the writer is only unfolding itself in artistic arrangements as plants shape themselves into their forms of symmetry and beauty. If, therefore, we meet artificial form in all parts of Scripture, even in prosaic passages, much more may we expect it in a book written like the Apocalypse in the noblest spirit of prophetic and poetic enthusiasm. Several particulars demand attention.

I. The first particular to be noticed is the singular extent to which the structure of the Apocalypse is moulded by the use of numbers. Many numbers play a part in it, but we may confine ourselves to one or two which even the superficial observer cannot fail to notice. These are seven, four, and three.

[1] Reference may be made in the Old Testament to such passages as the following :—Psalm cxix. ; the Lamentations of Jeremiah ; Proverbs xxxi. 10-31 : in the New Testament—John x. 14, 15 ; Romans, iii. 7-10.

Let us take in the first place the number seven, and that not merely as it is used to denote so many individual objects, but as, without being expressly named, it influences the structure of the book. With its use as a number every one is familiar. There are "seven spirits which are before the throne of God," "seven churches," "seven golden candlesticks," "seven stars" in the right hand of Him who is like unto a Son of man, "seven lamps of fire burning before the throne," "seven horns and seven eyes" of the Lamb, "seven seals" of the book in the right hand of Him who sat upon the throne, "seven angels" standing before God, "seven thunders" uttering their voices, "seven thousand" slain in the great earthquake which attends the ascent of the two witnesses into heaven, "seven heads" of the great dragon and "seven diadems" upon his heads, "seven heads" of the beast that came up out of the sea, "seven angels" with seven trumpets, and again with the seven last plagues, "seven mountains" upon which the mystic Babylon is seated, and "seven kings," of whom five are fallen, and one is, and the other is not yet come.

All this is in itself sufficiently remarkable, but the use of the number is still more worthy of notice when we find it moulding the structure of the narrative in many a passage where no direct mention of it is made.[1] Thus in chap. v. 12 seven attributes of praise,

---

[1] The principle of structure here noticed is to be found also in the Old Testament. One interesting illustration may be given. The blessing on Jacob in Gen. xxviii. 13-15 divides itself naturally into seven parts, of which the fourth and central is the great covenant promise, "And in thee and in thy seed shall all the families of the

" power, and riches, and wisdom, and might, and honour, and glory, and blessing," are ascribed by the multitude about the throne to the Lamb that was slain. In chap. vii. 12 the white robed company worship God with a similar number, saying, " Blessing, and glory, and wisdom, and thanksgiving, and honour, and power, and might, be unto our God for ever and ever." And in chap. ix. 7-10 the terrible locusts of the fifth trumpet are described in seven particulars. They have on their heads as it were crowns like unto gold; their faces are as faces of men; they have hair as hair of women; they have teeth as teeth of lions; they have breastplates as it were breast-plates of iron; the sound of their wings is as the sound of chariots of many horses rushing to war; they have tails like unto scorpions and stings. Even longer and more varied passages are dominated by the number seven. The preparatory vision of chap. xiv. 6-20 con-sists of seven parts, each part except the fourth, which in a series of seven is always the central and most im-portant, being introduced by an angel,[1] while in the fourth part we have the leading figure of the movement, *one* like unto a Son of man sitting on a white cloud, on His head a golden crown, and in His hand a sharp sickle.[2] Similar observations apply to a still more lengthened passage extending from chap. xvii. 1 to chap. xxii. 5, where it will be found that three angels introduced at

earth be blessed." The three parts preceding this are promises of a general character, the three follow-ing are special to Jacob. The punctuation adopted by the Re-visers shows that they had failed to notice the correct division of these parts.

[1] See verses 6, 8, 9, 15, 17, 18.

[2] Verse 14.

chaps. xvii. 1, xviii. 1, and xviii. 21 precede the fourth part, the appearance of the conquering King of kings at chap. xix. 11, and are followed by other three angels at chaps. xix. 17, xx. 1, and xxi. 9, no angel appearing at any intermediate point, and these seven appearances embracing the whole closing drama of the book from the time of the judgment on Babylon to the establishment upon earth of the New Jerusalem.

Nay, not only does the remark apply to both the shorter and the longer passages of the book, it applies also to the Apocalypse as a whole. There is no small reason for adopting the idea that it contains seven visions or sets of visions;[1] and, whether we agree with this or not, it naturally divides itself into the seven sections that have been already spoken of.

The number four plays if not so important yet a similar part throughout the book. "Four living creatures full of eyes before and behind" are seen in the midst of and round about the throne;[2] "four angels" stand at the "four corners of the earth," holding the "four winds of the earth;"[3] "four angels" are bound at the great river Euphrates, prepared for a moment fixed in the counsels of the Almighty, and noted by the mention of four periods of time—an hour and day and month and year.[4] The blood of the winepress extends to 1600 furlongs, that is to the square of 4 multiplied by 100;[5] and the New Jerusalem lieth foursquare.[6]

[1] Comp. Züllig, vol. i.; *Parousia,* p. 377, and many others.
[2] Chap. iv. 6.
[3] Chap. vii. 1.
[4] Chap. ix. 14, 15.
[5] Chap. xiv. 20.
[6] Chap. xxi. 16.

Again also, as in the case of the number seven, the thought of four often regulates the structure without our attention being expressly called to it. In the visions of the Seals, the Trumpets, and the Bowls, the first four numbers of each series refer to objects different in character from those of the last three, and constitute separate groups of four. The inhabitants of the earth are summed up in "tribes and tongues and peoples and nations;"[1] prophecy is to be uttered over "peoples and nations and tongues and kings;"[2] when authority is given to Death upon his pale horse to kill over the fourth part of the earth, he is to do so "with sword, and with famine, and with pestilence, and by the wild beasts of the earth;".[3] when the judgments of God are about to be revealed, there are "thunders and voices and lightnings and an earthquake;"[4] guilty Babylon solaces herself with four classes of musicians, "harpers and minstrels and flute-players and trumpeters;"[5] and when the kings of the earth turn round upon the harlot to destroy her, they "hate her, and make her desolate and naked, and eat her flesh, and burn her with fire;"[6] the sins of which men repented not, even after the desolation caused by the horses of the sixth trumpet, are classified as "murders and sorceries and fornications and thefts;"[7] and they that have their part in the burning lake are divided into two successive groups of four, or four successive groups of two.[8]

[1] Chap. v. 9.
[2] Chap. x. 11.
[3] Chap. vi. 8.
[4] Chaps. viii. 5 ; xvi. 18.
[5] Chap. xviii. 22.
[6] Chap. xvii. 16.
[7] Chap. ix. 21.
[8] Chap. xxi. 8.

More remarkable still is the use of the number three, so remarkable and continuous indeed that it would require an analysis of the whole book for its perfect illustration.[1] And again it is not simply the mention of the number that arrests us, as when we read of the "three" woes, of the "three" unclean spirits like frogs, of the "three" parts into which Babylon is divided, or of the "three" gates on each side of the foursquare Jerusalem. It is the mode in which this number is mixed up with the entire structure of the book that is especially worthy of notice. A few illustrations only can be given. The first three epistles to the seven churches are evidently distinguished from the remaining four by the place assigned in them to the call, "He that hath ears to hear, let him hear what the Spirit saith unto the churches." The last three Seals are not less clearly separated from the first four, and the same remark applies to the Trumpets and the Bowls. In chap. iv. 5 three things, "lightnings and thunders and voices," proceed out of the throne. In the same chapter the four and twenty elders have three characteristics— they sit, they are arrayed in white garments, they have on their heads crowns of gold.[2] When they pay homage to Him that sits upon the throne three acts of homage are ascribed to them,—falling down, worshipping, and

---

[1] A very long and apparently exhaustive inquiry into the use of the number three in the Apocalypse will be found in Stuart's *Introduction to his Commentary upon the Book*, section 7 a. The same author inquires with a large amount of care into what he calls the "numerosity" of the Apocalypse generally.

[2] Chap. iv. 4.

casting their crowns before the throne ; and when they lift their song to their Lord and their God, they celebrate Him as worthy to receive three things, the glory, the honour, and the power.[1] In the same chapter we meet with the *Trisagion* "Holy, Holy, Holy," and that *Trisagion* is sung to Him who, as "the Lord," has three attributes of glory,—God, the Almighty, He which "was" and which "is" and which "is to come," the last of the three again consisting of three parts.[2] In chap. vii. 1 three things are mentioned on which the wind is not to blow. In chap. xi. 1 three things are to be measured, and in chap. xii. 16 the earth does three things for the woman's help. In chap. xviii. 8 three plagues come upon Babylon in one day ; and in the same chapter, verses 9-19, three classes of persons are introduced, one after another, lamenting over her fall. One other illustration of the point before us must suffice. Let us look at the first chapter of the book. That chapter consists of three parts :—

1. Description of the book, and its importance, verses 1-3.

2. Salutation of the writer to the persons addressed by him, verses 4-8.

---

[1] Chap. iv. 10, 11.

[2] Chap. iv. 8. This is one of those passages, and there are not a few of the same kind throughout the book, in which attention to the structure of the Apocalypse supplies an important rule of interpretation. In the Authorised Version we read, "Holy, holy, holy, Lord God Almighty," etc. ; in the Revised Version "Holy, holy, holy, *is* the Lord God, the Almighty," etc. But Westcott and Hort, in their Greek text, punctuate otherwise and rightly. They place a comma after κύριος "Lord," thus yielding the translation given above.

3. Vision of the great Priest and King presiding over His Church, verses 9-20.

Let us take now the first of these parts—verses 1-3, and it again divides itself naturally into three.

1. The source of the revelation, verse 1 to the words "shortly come to pass."

2. The medium of the revelation, verse 1 at the words "and he sent" to the end of verse 3.

3. The importance of the revelation, verse 8.

Once more let us take each of these three subordinate divisions, and it will be found that it also is distinguished by triplicity of parts ; for in the first division we have mention of three persons,—Jesus Christ, God, and the servants of Jesus ; in the second division we find a threefold description of that to which witness is borne by the Seer,—the Word of God, the testimony of Jesus Christ, and all things that he saw ; while in the third division the persons for whom a blessing in connection with it is reserved are portioned off into three groups,—"he that readeth," "they that hear the words of the prophecy," and "they that keep the things that are written therein." [1]

Enough has been said to show to how great an extent the structure of the Apocalypse is dominated by numbers. But they who would form an impression upon the point as strong as is warranted by the facts must examine for themselves. The more they do so, the more will they be struck with the singular extent to which numbers rule the plan of the apocalyptic writer ;

[1] Comp. *Biblical Review*, vol. i. p. 423.

and the more powerfully this conviction is brought home to them, the better will they be prepared for the interpretation of his book.

II. The second particular to be noticed in connection with the structure of the Apocalypse is the symmetrical arrangement of its parts. Even in smaller sections this symmetry forces itself upon our notice. The seven epistles contained in the second and third chapters are composed upon precisely the same plan. They consist of seven parts, following each other in the same order in each epistle—the superscription to the church addressed; a special aspect of the Saviour who addresses it ; an account of the spiritual condition of the particular church ; words of commendation or censure adapted to its state; exhortations founded upon that state ; promises to him that overcometh ; and a call to every one to hear. One part of the arrangement may indeed seem to disturb the symmetry ; for in the first three epistles the general exhortation, "He that hath an ear, let him hear what the Spirit saith unto the churches," occurs in the middle of the epistle, immediately before the promises ; whereas in the last four it is transferred to the close. This, however, is universally admitted to be part of that higher symmetry, meeting us in other portions of the book, by which the number seven is divided into its two parts three and four or four and three.[1]

When we turn to the body of the Apocalypse sym-

[1] The writer would refer for an attempt to explain the division of seven into three and four, rather than four and three in these epistles, to his paper in the *Expositor*, second series, vol. iv. p. 57.

metrical arrangement presents itself in a still more striking light. Comparing the first four numbers of each of the three groups of the Seals, the Trumpets, and the Bowls, we see at once that they all relate to the same objects taken in the same order [1]—

SEALS.		TRUMPETS.		BOWLS.	
Chap. vi.		Chap. viii.		Chap. xvi.	
1.		1.	(Land.	1.	(Land.
2.	} Earth. [1]	2.	} Earth. { Sea.	2.	} Earth. { Sea.
3.		3.	{ Rivers, etc.	3.	{ Rivers, etc.
4.		4.	(Sun, etc.	4.	(Sun.

At the introduction of the fifth number of each group the scene is changed, and in a similar direction, from the world of sense to that of spirit—

SEALS.	TRUMPETS.	BOWLS.
Chap. vi. 9.	Chap. ix. 1.	Chap. xvi. 10.
Altar in heaven.	Pit of the abyss.	Throne of the beast.

For reasons springing out of considerations adduced in the last lecture, the symmetry of the sixth and seventh numbers of the groups is to be expected only in the case of the Trumpets and the Bowls, and then it comes before us in a marked degree—

Sixth Number.

TRUMPETS.	BOWLS.
Chap. ix. 13.	Chap. xvi. 12.
The river Euphrates.	The river Euphrates.

Seventh Number.

TRUMPETS.	BOWLS.
Chap. xi. 15.	Chap. xvi. 17.
The close of all.	The close of all.

---

[1] It is important, in confirmation and illustration of what is said in Lecture ii. p. 50, to notice here the *general* character of the Seals as compared with the more *detailed* statement of the Trumpets and the Bowls.

Still further, it is to be observed that, except in the case of the Bowls, the several numbers of these groups do not run on in uninterrupted succession to the end of the group. Between the sixth and seventh Seals the two visions of the sealing of the 144,000 and of the great multitude standing before the Lamb are interposed;[1] and, exactly in the same way, between the sixth and seventh Trumpets we meet the visions of the measuring of the temple, and of the two witnesses who were faithful unto death and triumphant over it.[2] These are visions of comfort, episodes of consolation, intended to sustain our hope in the last great outburst of the wrath of the Most High; and if, in the case of the Bowls, the similar visions of chap. xiv., instead of coming before the seventh Bowl, precede the series, the reason seems obvious, that the Lord is now rapidly winding up the present dispensation, and, with the suddenness of a thief in the night, making a short work upon the earth.[3] When the struggle is over, and the end come, that is our consolation, and we need no more. The element of climax, in short, here modifies that of perfect regularity; but only in conformity with a higher principle, for visions of consolation are still afforded, though at an earlier point.

Another illustration of the symmetrical structure of the Apocalypse lies upon its surface. Of the seven parts into which it naturally divides itself, the first, the prologue, corresponds to the seventh, the epilogue; the second, the Church in her mixed earthly condition, to

---

[1] Chap. vii.   [2] Chap. xi. 1-14.   [3] Chap. xvi. 15.

the sixth, the true members of the Church in their ideal repose ; the third, pictures of the Church's victory anticipated, to the fifth, her victory realised; while the fourth or main section of the whole occupies, as according to the structural efficacy of the number seven it ought, the central place.   This symmetry of the Apocalypse, alike appearing in its smaller parts and marking it as a whole, more particularly this correspondence of each pair of its leading sections, when they are counted either from the centre to the circumference or from the circumference to the centre, deserves the most careful observation.

III. A third particular to be noticed in the structure of the Apocalypse is the synchronism, rather than the chronological succession, of its visions.   These visions are for the most part comprised in the groups of the Seals, the Trumpets, and the Bowls.   Now it is no doubt true that the three groups follow one another. It was absolutely necessary that they should do so, both in the visions of St. John and for the apprehension of his readers.   The one could not see, the other could not apprehend, them all at the same moment.   But they do not on that account contain a definite succession of events extending from the opening of the first to the close of the third group.   The first group, on the contrary, brings us to the end ; and the next two groups, so far at least begin at the beginning, that they present to us the evil world and the degenerate Church as exposed throughout all their history to the just judgments of God, although the heaviest judgments are reserved for the close.

Let us look at the Seals. The first Seal introduces the horseman upon a white horse, who "comes forth conquering and to conquer."[1] It is undeniably the opening of the gospel age. The sixth Seal (the peculiarity of the seventh will be noticed by and by), after a striking description of convulsions of nature and terrors of men, speaks of "the face of Him that sitteth on the throne, and of the wrath of the Lamb ; for the great day of their wrath is come, and who is able to stand?"[2] These words can hardly refer to anything but the final judgment. They describe no partial manifestation of Christ made at some intermediate point of the Church's history, but the great day of the Lord itself. And this interpretation is confirmed, were more needed to convince us, by comparing the words of the Seer with those of Christ in Matt. xxiv. 29, 30, in which the phenomena are the same, are spoken of in almost the same language, and are followed by expressions that can be understood of nothing but the winding up of the world's history.

Let us look at the second or Trumpet group of visions. When the seventh angel sounded, we read that "there followed great voices in heaven, and they said, The kingdom of the world is become the kingdom of our Lord, and of his Christ :" and again the four and twenty elders said, "Thy wrath came, and the time of the dead to be judged, and the time to give their reward to Thy servants the prophets, and to the saints, and to them that fear Thy name, the small and the great ; and to destroy them that destroy the earth."[3] Whether we

---

[1] Chap. vi. 2.　　[2] Chap. vi. 12-17.　　[3] Chap. xi. 15, 18.

interpret these words in themselves, or in their relation
to other and similar expressions in the same book, they
lead directly to the final issues of the present dispensation, so that we are thus anew conducted to a point
previously reached, and are compelled to regard the two
groups of the Seals and of the Trumpets as synchronous
rather than as historically successive.

This conclusion is greatly strengthened when we turn
to the third group of visions (that of the Bowls) which,
like those of the two groups going before, are also seven
in number, giving evidence by this very fact of their
completeness in themselves in that line of things of
which they treat. At the pouring out of the seventh
Bowl we are told that "there came forth a great voice
out of the temple, from the throne, saying, It is done;"
while a little farther on it is said that "every island
fled away, and the mountains were not found." In
neither case can these words lead us to anything but
the end, while in the latter they have the closest possible resemblance to those words of chap. xx. 11, which
are referred with the unanimous consent of interpreters
to the final judgment, " and I saw a great white throne,
and Him that sat upon it, from whose face the earth
and the heaven fled away; and there was found no
place for them." The succession of these three groups
of visions cannot therefore be chronological. It must
be one of ideas and not of time.

The view thus taken is confirmed by the singular parallelism running through the judgments of the Trumpets
and the Bowls, and exhibited in the following table :—

	TRUMPETS Relating to	BOWLS Relating to
First.	The earth, chap. viii. 7.	The earth, chap. xvi. 2.
Second.	The sea, chap. viii. 8.	The sea, chap. xvi. 3.
Third.	Rivers and fountains of the waters, chap. viii. 10.	Rivers and fountains of the waters, chap. xvi. 4.
Fourth.	The sun and moon and stars, chap. viii. 12.	The sun, chap. xvi. 8.
Fifth.	The pit of the abyss, chap. ix. 2.	The throne of the beast, chap. xvi. 10.
Sixth.	The great river Euphrates, chap. ix. 14.	The great river Euphrates, chap. xvi. 12.
Seventh.	Great voices in heaven, followed by lightnings, and voices, and thunders, and an earthquake, and great hail, chap. xi. 15, 19.	A great voice from the throne, followed by lightnings, and voices, and thunders, a great earthquake, and great hail, chap. xvi. 17, 18, 21.

A simple inspection of this table is of itself almost
sufficient to convince us of the great improbability of
the supposition that the two series in question embody
a succession of time rather than of thought. "It is
surely," says the late Principal Fairbairn in adverting
to it, "against all reasonable probability to suppose that
these two lines of symbolic representation, touching at
so many points, alike in their commencement, their
progress, and their termination, can relate to dispensa-
tions of providence wholly unconnected, and to periods
of time separated from one another by the lapse of
ages. It is immeasurably more probable that they are
but different aspects of substantially the same course
of procedure, different merely from the parties subjected
to it being contemplated in somewhat different relations.
Nor would it be possible, if two entire series of symbolical delineations following so nearly in the same
track were yet to point to events quite remote and

diverse, to vindicate such delineations from the charge of arbitrariness and indetermination." [1]

The conclusion thus come to, and certainly supported by a comparison of the three leading series of visions in this book, may be confirmed by other illustrations. Thus at the beginning of chap. xii. we have the vision of the woman clothed with the sun, and the bearer of a man child who is to rule all nations with a rod of iron. This vision, in so far as it refers to a historical event, can refer only to the birth of Christ, and yet it comes in *after* the visions of the Seals and of the Trumpets have both been closed, a clear proof that the Seer is not guided by the thought of historical succession. We have another striking instance of the same kind in the same chapter, where the flight of the woman into the wilderness at verse 6 is not a different flight from that spoken of at verse 14, the two being only different aspects of the same event. In both we have a flight into the same wilderness, for the same purpose, and for the same space of time,—the one only bringing out the particulars in a way different from the other. [2] So also the assault of the beast upon the two witnesses in chap. xi. 7 is the same assault as that described in chap. xiii. 7. The war to which the kings of the whole world are gathered in the great day of God, the Almighty, at chap. xvi. 14, is the same war afterwards more fully described in chap. xix., with all its disastrous consequences to the enemies of the Lamb. Finally, though more will need to be hereafter said upon the point, the description given

<hr>

[1] On *Prophecy*, p. 402. [2] Comp. p. 120.

of the binding of Satan in chap. xx. 1-3 is not essentially different from his being cast out of heaven into the earth in chap. xii. 9, while the reign of the saints in the same chapter (verses 4-6) is but a fuller expression of what we are told at chap. xii. 5 of the catching up of the man child unto God and unto His throne.

These considerations establish the conclusion that one of the structural principles of the Apocalypse is to set before us different series of pictures relating not so much to successive events as to the same events under different aspects, each series complete in itself, and inviting us to think less of its temporal relation to those which precede and follow it, than of the new and different light in which it presents an idea common to itself and them. The principle was not a new one when St. John wrote. It had been familiar to the sacred writers, and especially when they wrote in a prophetic or poetic strain. The Song of Songs and the book of Daniel display a similar plan; and the same principle is followed by our Lord, not only, as we have seen, in Matt. xxiv., but when, in the parable of the Wicked Husbandmen, He points to the doom of those who reject His messengers.[1] The dominating thought in the three messages of the owner of the vineyard, and in the threefold reception given to them, is not that of succession of time, as if each later rejection involved certain historical events subsequent to those of the rejections preceding it. Our attention is called to the same picture of criminality throughout, although the guilt of the

______

[1] Luke xx. 9-16.

husbandmen is marked by special characteristics in each case. A certain succession of time there no doubt is, for the rejection of a second message must follow that of a first, and the rejection of a third that of a second; but the main consideration is, that this succession of time is subordinate to that of the stages of an ever-deepening obstinacy and sinfulness, yet an obstinacy and a sinfulness which may belong, in different individuals, to any part of the whole period embraced within the scope of the parable.

Thus also with the visions of the Apocalypse. There may be in them succession, even in a certain sense succession of time. But it is succession of another kind upon which we are asked to dwell; and the point to be now mainly noticed is, that the different visions of the book do not follow one another in such a manner that each takes up the thread of a continuous history where the one before it ends. Each of the three groups, in particular, of the Seals, the Trumpets, and the Bowls, starts from the beginning of the Church's fortunes upon earth, and takes us by its own path to their close.[1]

[1] This idea of synchronism, rather than of succession, in the visions of St. John, was entertained at an early period in the history of the Church. Thus we find Victorinus, Bishop of Pettau, who flourished towards the end of the third century, in his comment on Rev. vii. saying, "We must not regard the order of what is said, because frequently the Holy Spirit, when he has traversed even to the end of the last times, returns again to the same times, and fills up what He had (before) failed to say. Nor must we look for order in the Apocalypse; but we must follow the meaning of those things which are prophesied" (Clark's *Anten. Libr. Tertullian*, vol. iii. p. 414). The same view was taken by Augustine in the fourth, and by Berengaudus in the eighth century. The thought of chrono-

IV. A fourth particular marking the structure of the Apocalypse is the element of climax. This meets us everywhere throughout the book, and not unfrequently in the most unexpected ways. Let us look at the Epistles to the churches, and the theme so frequently referred to in them, the Second Coming of the Lord. In each of the Epistles, except that to Smyrna, the Second Coming has a place; but, taking first the first group of three, it will be observed that to Ephesus it is said, "I come to thee;" and to Pergamum, "I come to thee quickly."[1] Proceeding to the second group of four, a difference in the same direction is perceptible. To the first of the four, Thyatira, is said only "Till I come;" to the second, Sardis, "I will come as a thief;" to the third, Philadelphia, "I come quickly;" to the fourth, Laodicea, "Behold I stand at the door and knock."[2] As

logical succession appears to have come in only in the fourteenth century, when it began to be supposed that the Apocalypse contained a prediction of the main events in the history of the Christian Church, from the days of the apostles to the end of time (Todd, *Lect.*, p. 50). The correctness of this method of interpreting was, however, by no means universally conceded, and it was again departed from by many. Daubuz (on *Rev.*, p. 22) says that Mede was the first to return clearly to the idea of synchronism, and the principle may be said to be now accepted by a great number of the most distinguished modern in-terpreters. It is indeed characteristic of the Hebrew prophetic literature to set forth in each prophetic vision some new phase of what had been already treated of. Either the whole delineation is resumed and lifted up to a higher platform, or details noticed only generally in an earlier part of the prophecy are separated from their former setting, and dwelt upon more at length. Comp. Renan, *L'Antechr.*, p. 391; Isaac Williams on *Rev.*, p. 392; Wordsworth, *Lect.*, p. 96; Fairbairn *On Prophecy*, p. 396.

[1] Chap. ii. 5, 16.

[2] Chaps. ii. 25; iii. 3, 11, 20.

we pass from church to church the Coming draws continually nearer, till at last He who comes is heard knocking at the door.

A similar climax is observable in the promises to "him that overcometh" contained in these Epistles. From those of the first group to those of the second there is distinct advance. In the first all is quiet, appealing to the gentler susceptibilities of the soul. Believers are rewarded with the privileges and enjoyments of a child that has not yet left its father's garden, or known the struggle of the world. In the second we enter upon bolder and more manly figures, which presuppose fiercer trials and a hotter conflict, and are therefore full of a more glorious reward.

Again the element of climax meets us, when we compare the consolatory visions between the sixth and seventh Seals and those occupying a corresponding position between the sixth and seventh Trumpets. Chap. vii. gives the one, but it is simply a vision of Christians "sealed;" and even if, in the second vision of that chapter, we are told of saints that "have come out of great tribulation," we have not seen them suffering. Chap. xi. gives us the other, and when we read it we feel at once that there is progress in the thought. It is no longer the waiting, but the working, witnessing Church with which we have to do; and, instead of the simple mention of sufferings past, and probably forgotten, we behold them inflicted by the beast with all that rage and power with which he ascends out of the very centre of his dark and cruel kingdom.[1]

---

[1] Chap. xi. 7.

The same element of climax is also to be traced in the fact that, in interpreting the several members of the Seals, the Trumpets, and the Bowls, we are not to imagine that the plague of each successive member is completely over before that of the next is inflicted. Each successive plague would seem rather to be added to those that go before, so that under the operation of each its predecessors are still active, until all the terrors of the Divine judgments are concentrated in the last.[1]

Again the same principle applies to the three great groups of visions, the Seals, the Trumpets, and the Bowls, considered in the totality of their effect. Parallel and synchronous as they largely are, they are not repetitions of one another. They are exhibitions of the same principle under different aspects and in different circumstances; and the judgments of which they warn us go on in an ascending line. Comparing, *e.g.*, the Trumpets with the Seals, the very fact that the former are trumpets indicates a higher, a more exciting, a more terrible, unfolding of the wrath of God than in the latter. The trumpet is peculiarly the warlike instrument, summoning the hosts to battle: "Thou hast heard, O my soul, the sound of the trumpet, the alarm of war;"[2] "That

[1] The point noticed in the text is one of great importance for the general interpretation of the plagues. It seems to come very clearly out in the case of the Bowls. Thus, on the pouring out of the fourth Bowl, we read that men "blasphemed the name of God which hath the power over *these plagues*," not "that plague" (chap. xvi. 9). Thus also in verse 10 of the same chapter the mention of the gnawing of the tongue for pain is remarkable, for the pain could not proceed from the darkness of the fifth Bowl. It could only come from the effects of the previous plagues.

[2] Jer. iv. 19.

day is a day of wrath, a day of trouble and distress, a
day of wasteness and desolation, a day of darkness and
gloominess, a day of clouds and thick darkness, a day of
the trumpet and alarm against the fenced cities." [1]   It
is thus peculiarly associated with the judgments of God,
"Blow ye the trumpet in Zion, and sound an alarm in
my holy mountain; let all the inhabitants of the earth
tremble: for the day of the Lord cometh, and it is nigh
at hand." [2]   The trumpet has also, no doubt, other associations in the Old Testament; but, used by St. John
in connection with judgment, there can be little doubt
that it intimates more terrible judgments than under
the Seals.   That the Bowls again are still more potent
than the Trumpets appears both from their position in
the book and from the manner in which they are introduced.   As to the former, they naturally succeed the
Trumpets, for the plague is first called for by the Trumpet, and is then poured out of the inverted Bowl.   As
to the latter, we read in chap. xv. 1, "And I saw another
sign in heaven great and marvellous, seven angels having
the seven last plagues; for in them is filled up the wrath
of God."   They are the "*last*" plagues; the wrath of
God is "*filled up*" in them; they are the consummation
of all judgment, the most complete manifestation of Him
who not only prepares His reward for the righteous, but
who, throughout the whole of this book, is a God judging
in the earth.

The fact now before us becomes more obvious when
we bring into comparison the individual members of the

---

[1] Zeph. i. 15, 16.   [2] Joel ii. 1.

groups. In the first four Trumpets judgment is more definite and precise than in the first four Seals. The objects upon which it falls are detailed at greater length, and the "fourth" part spoken of in the earlier passes into a "third" part in the later plagues. The climax is still more marked when we turn to the first four Bowls and compare them with the first four Trumpets. The first Trumpet affects only the third part of the earth and the trees, and all green grass :[1] the first Bowl affects men.[2] Under the second Trumpet the third part of the sea becomes blood, and the third part of the creatures which are in the sea die, and the third part of the ships are destroyed.[3] Under the second Bowl the third part of the sea is changed for the whole ; the blood assumes its most offensive form, "as the blood of a dead man ; " and not the third part only but " every " living thing dies in the sea.[4] The same change takes place under the third and fourth Bowls compared with the third and fourth Trumpets, for under the latter the great star falls only upon the third part of the rivers and upon the fountains of the waters, and only the third part of sun and moon and stars and day and night is smitten (chap. viii. 10-12); whereas under the former all the rivers and the fountains of the waters become blood, and the whole of the sun has power given him to scorch men with fire (chap. xvi. 4, 8). This higher potency of judgment, seen in the first four members of each of our three groups, continues to make itself felt in

---

[1] Chap. viii. 7.
[2] Chap. xvi. 2.
[3] Chap. viii. 8, 9.
[4] Chap. xvi. 3.

the remaining members. At the fifth Seal heaven is opened, and the heavenly altar is disclosed to view, having under it "the souls of them that had been slain for the Word of God, and for the testimony which they held" (chap. vi. 9); under the fifth Trumpet the bottomless pit is opened, and terrible locusts come forth so tormenting men that they shall "seek death, and shall not find it; and shall desire to die, and death shall flee from them" (chap. ix. 6); while the fifth Bowl is poured out upon the throne of the beast, "and his kingdom is full of darkness, and they gnaw their tongues for pain, and blaspheme the God of heaven because of their pains and their sores" (chap. xvi. 10, 11). At the sixth Seal there is a great earthquake and the day of God's wrath is come, but all the men "of the earth" have time to flee to the dens and rocks of the mountains (chap. vi. 12, 15); under the sixth Trumpet the four angels bound by the great river Euphrates are loosed, and an innumerable army of horsemen ride forth actually destroying the third part of men (chap. ix. 14-19); while under the sixth Bowl, poured out upon the great river Euphrates itself, unclean spirits go forth out of the mouth of the three great enemies of the saints, and gathering together all the powers of earth at the place called Har-Magedon, prepare them for their immediate and final overthrow (chap. xvi. 12-16). At the seventh Seal we are told only of "silence in heaven about the space of half an hour (chap. viii. 1); under the seventh Trumpet this silence gives place to "great voices in heaven, intimating that the world is subdued and the time of judgment come" (chap. xi. 15, 18); while under the seventh Bowl "a great voice comes out of the temple of heaven from the throne, saying, It is done." Judgment actually falls. Every island flies away, and the mountains are not found (chap. xvi. 17-20). The climax in these individual members of the three groups cannot be mistaken.

If, instead of looking at the members individually, we look at the three groups as a whole, the same thing will appear. In the series of the Seals we have the effects of the proclamation of the Gospel presented to us in their most general point of view. They describe indeed the judgments of God, and thus imply the sinfulness of man, for otherwise there would be no judgment; there would be simply peace, not a sword. But this sinfulness of man is not brought to light, and the specific reference of judgment to it is not unfolded. Even the souls under the altar are only told that their brethren shall be killed. The killing itself is reserved for a later stage; and the different riders who come forth upon their horses are described as "having power given them" to inflict judgment, rather than as exercising their power. The series of the Trumpets marks an advance on this. It is not merely hinted now that the saints shall suffer upon earth. They *have* suffered. The Christian brethren who, like the Old Testament saints of the fifth Seal, are to be killed, have not only been presented to us in the second consolatory vision of chap. vii. as persons who have " come out of the great tribulation;" they have been sending up their prayers, before the series of the Trumpets opens, to Him who will avenge His elect. The judgments now inflicted are accordingly a direct answer to these prayers, and they are spoken of with specific and minute detail through all the members of the Trumpet group. The same progress is continued in the Bowls, not so much in time, in historical succession, as in the wickedness of those who suffer, and in their deliberate and determined rejection of the truth. We pass from a sinful world to a faithless Church, from those who have never known that the Lord is gracious to those who were once enlightened, and have tasted of the heavenly gift, and been made partakers of the Holy Ghost, and have tasted the good word of God and the powers of the world to come, and yet have fallen away. Which class is the most guilty? Surely there has been advance in sin. Prophecy has again been uttered before many peoples, and nations, and tongues, and kings (chap. x. 11). The faithful witnesses have witnessed and been slain, and have ascended up to heaven in the cloud; but they that dwelt upon the earth have only rejoiced over them, and made merry, and sent gifts one to another (chap. xi. 10). The dragon, the beast, and the false prophet have successfully played their part (chaps. xii. xiii.) Therefore judgment falls, and falls naturally, with intensely increased severity.

Thus it is that we mark a more important succession in the visions of this book than any mere succession of time. As sin deepens, judgment deepens. Every abuse of mercy brings with it increased punishment. This shall be the case not in future ages only but now. A Divine vindication of righteousness is always pressing on the skirts of sin, and the one shall always be in strict proportion to the other. There is a climax in that succession upon which our thoughts are fixed.

PART II.

The particulars spoken of in the first part of this lecture are of themselves sufficient to establish the artistic nature of the plan upon which the Apocalyse is constructed. To such an extent, however, does the interpretation of the book depend upon this fact that it seems desirable to illustrate it with still greater fulness. Two or three minor points connected with the structure adopted by the Seer therefore claim our notice.

I. The principle of contrast. In their broader features the contrasts of the Apocalypse at once strike the eye. No reader can fail for a moment to perceive that, like Aaron when he stood between the dead and the living,[1] St. John stands in this book between two antithetical and contrasted worlds. On the one hand he sees Christ, life, light, love, the Church of the living God, heaven, and the inhabitants of heaven; on the other he sees Satan, death, darkness, hatred, the syna-

---

[1] Numb. xvi. 48.

gogue of Satan, earth, and the dwellers upon earth.   In
all history, whether during the time of the old covenant
or the new, he beholds a record of the struggle between
these opposing forces,—the former often apparently
crushed, but destined to ultimate triumph; the latter
not unfrequently to the eye of sense victorious, but
doomed in reality to ignominious and everlasting defeat.
It is not enough, however, to observe this.   The contrasts of the book are carried out in almost every particular that meets us, whether great or small, whether in
connection with the persons, the objects, or the actions
of which it speaks.

If, at one time, we have an ever-blessed and holy
Trinity, the Father, the Son, and the Holy Spirit,[1] at
another we have that "great antitrinity of hell," the
Devil, the Beast, and the False Prophet.[2] If we have
God Himself, even the Father, commissioning the Son
and clothing Him with His authority and power,[3] we
have the dragon commissioning the first beast and giving
him his "power, and his throne, and great authority."[4]
If the Son, when He manifests the Father and conveys
His message to mankind, appears as a Lamb with seven
horns,[5] the dragon, when he speaks in the second beast
or false prophet (for the first beast has no message; he
opens his mouth only to blaspheme), has two horns like
a lamb, though he speaks as a dragon.[6] If the name of
the one is Jesus or Saviour,[7] the name of the other is

---

[1] Chap. i. 4, 5.   [3] Chap. i. 1; vi. 2.   [5] Chap. v. 6.
[2] Chaps. xii. xiii.   [4] Chap. xiii. 2.   [6] Chap. xiii. 11.
                          [7] Chap. xxii. 16.

Apollyon or Destroyer.[1]   If the one is the bright, the morning, star shining in the heavens,[2] the other is a star fallen out of heaven into the earth.[3]   If the one has the keys of death and of Hades, opening and none shall shut, shutting and none openeth,[4] the other has the key of the pit of the abyss.[5]   If the one has His throne,[6] the other has also a "throne," not (as the Authorised Version unhappily renders it) a "seat."[7]   If the one is celebrated in the Old Testament as having none like unto Him,[8] the followers of the other magnify him with the words, " Who is like unto the beast ?"[9]   If the one in carrying out his great work on earth is the Lamb " as though it had been slaughtered,[10] the other, as we are told by the use of the very same word (a point unfortunately missed both in the Authorised and Revised Versions), has one of his heads " as though it had been slaughtered unto death."[11]   If the one rises from the grave and lives,[12] there cannot be a doubt, when we read in precisely the same language of the beast that he hath the stroke of the sword and lived,[13] that here also is a resurrection from the dead. If the description given of the Divine Being is " He which is, and which was, and which is to come,"[14] that given of diabolic agency is that it " was, and is not, and is about to come up out of the abyss ;"[15] and if in the one case, when the Lord is thought of as come, the last term of the description is dropped,[16] in

[1] Chap. ix. 11.
[2] Chap. xxii. 16.
[3] Chap. ix. 1.
[4] Chaps. i. 18; iii. 7.
[5] Chap. ix. 1.
[6] Chap. iii. 21.
[7] Chaps. ii. 13; xvi. 10.
[8] Psalm cxiii. 5; Isaiah xl. 18.
[9] Chap. xiii. 4.
[10] Chap. v. 6.
[11] Chap. xiii. 3.
[12] Chap. ii. 8.
[13] Chap. xiii. 14.
[14] Chap. i. 4.
[15] Chap. xvii. 8.
[16] Chap. xi. 17, R. V.

the other case, when the beast comes in his final manifestation, a similar omission is made.[1]   In the hour of His judgment we read of the "wrath of the Lamb,"[2] and when the devil, cast out of heaven, goes down unto the earth and the sea, we are told that he has "great wrath," knowing that his time is short.[3]

Many other particulars meet us in which the same principle of contrast rules.   Believers are sealed with the seal of the living God;[4] unbelievers are marked with the mark of the beast.[5]   The seal is imprinted upon the forehead;[6] the mark upon the forehead or the hand.[7]   The contents of the seal are the name of the Lamb and of the Father.[8]   The contents of the mark are the name of the beast or the number of his name.[9] The "tribes of the earth" are in contrast with the tribes of Israel;[10] the false apostles of Ephesus with the true apostles of the Lord;[11] and the harlot Babylon[12] with the Bride, the Lamb's wife, the holy city Jerusalem.[13] Nay, the contrasts even go at times beyond the facts specifically mentioned in the book to facts only known to us through the Gospel history; for, as already in part noticed, it is hardly possible not to feel that, in the binding of Satan at the beginning of the thousand years, in the casting him into the abyss, in shutting it, and sealing it over him,[14] we have a counterpart of the bind-

---

[1] Chap. xvii. 11.
[2] Chap. vi. 16.
[3] Chap. xii. 12.
[4] Chap. vii. 2.
[5] Chap xiii. 17.
[6] Chap. vii. 3.
[7] Chaps. xiii. 16 ; xx. 4.
[8] Chap. xiv. 1.
[9] Chap. xiii. 17.
[10] Chap. i. 7.
[11] Chap. ii. 2.
[12] Chap. xvii. 18.
[13] Chap. xxi. 10.
[14] Chap. xx. 2, 3.

ing and burial of our Lord, and of the sealing of His tomb.[1]

II. The principle of *Prolepsis* or Anticipation; that is, the tendency of the writer to anticipate in earlier sections, by mere allusion, what he is only to explain at a later point of his revelation. This principle is exemplified in the promises made to " him that overcometh " in each of the Epistles to the seven churches of Asia, for all of these find their fuller explanation and application in subsequent chapters of the book. The tree of life of the first Epistle meets us again in the description of the New Jerusalem.[2] The second death, spoken of in the second Epistle, is not explained till the final judgment is complete.[3] The writing upon believers of the new name promised in the third Epistle is almost unintelligible until we behold the 144,000 upon Mount Zion.[4] The dominion over the nations, and more especially the gift of the morning star, referred to in the fourth Epistle, cannot be comprehended until we are introduced to the vision of the thousand years and the last utterances of the glorified Redeemer.[5] The white garments of the fifth Epistle can hardly be rightly understood until we see the white-robed company standing before the throne and before the Lamb.[6] The mention in the sixth Epistle of " the city of my God, the new Jerusalem, which cometh down out of heaven from my God," remains a mystery until we actually witness her

---

[1] Comp. Matt. xxvii. 60, 66; John xviii. 12, 24.

[2] Chaps. ii. 7; xxii. 2, 14.

[3] Chaps. ii. 11; xx. 14.

[4] Chaps. ii. 17; xiv. 1.

[5] Chaps. ii. 26, 28; xx. 4, 5; xxii. 16.

[6] Chaps. iii. 5; vii. 9, 14.

descent.[1]   And, finally, the sitting in Christ's throne of the seventh Epistle is only elucidated by the reign of the thousand years *with Him*.[2]

Not a few other illustrations of the same principle are to be met with.   Thus it is that we are told of the two witnesses that " they went up to heaven in the cloud, and their enemies beheld them," [3] but we only know what "the cloud" means when later in the book we read of " a white cloud, and on the cloud one sitting like unto a Son of man," [4] for " the cloud" is not a cloud to veil the witnesses from view : it is that on which the Lord Himself, accompanied by His people, comes to judgment.[5]   Thus it is that, in the account given us of the fate of the same two witnesses upon earth, we find mention of " the beast that cometh up out of the abyss, who shall make war with them, and overcome them, and kill them," [6] while it is only after a considerable interval that we are made fully acquainted with this terrible enemy of the children of God." [7]   Thus it is that an angel at one point of the visions of the Seer proclaims "Fallen, fallen is Babylon the great,"[8] although a lengthened period has to pass before the guilty city is actually overthrown.[9]   Thus it is that " the beloved city" in chap. xx. 9 is an anticipatory notice of the New Jerusalem to be fully described in chap. xxi. ; and finally, it is thus that the Elders in their triumphant song under

[1] Chaps. iii. 12 ; xxi. 2, 10.
[2] Chaps. iii. 21 ; xx. 4.   Comp. Trench, *The Seven Epistles*, p. 87.
[3] Chap. xi. 12.
[4] Chap. xiv. 14.
[5] Comp. chap. xiv. 14-16.
[6] Chap. xi. 7.
[7] Chaps. xiii. xvii.
[8] Chap. xiv. 8.
[9] Chap. xviii.

the seventh Trumpet speak of a judgment of the dead as come,[1] while the judgment itself does not take place till we are near the close of the book, after the thousand years are finished.[2]

Other illustrations of the same principle abound, but those given are sufficient to show that we have often to pass from one part of this book to another, and to bring its later parts to supplement its earlier, sometimes its earlier its later, if we would understand the Seer.

III. The principle of double representations or pictures of the same thing. It is impossible to discuss this point at any length. But the principle, strange to us, was natural to a Jew. It seems to have been characteristic of the Hebrew mind that, in uttering its thoughts, it loved to express the same or nearly the same thing twice, the second expression rising higher than the first. The speaker or writer was not satisfied with one utterance. After he had spoken for the first time he brought the same point a second time before him, worked upon it, enlarged it, deepened it, and set it forth in stronger and more vivid colours. The whole system of Hebrew parallelism is an illustration of the principle, although there the element of climax may not be always present. Simple repetition gave the sentiment force, and brought it home to the mind with greater power than it would have possessed had it been stated only once. In a narrative belonging to the earliest times of the Old Testament we may find the explanation. When Joseph interpreted Pharaoh's

---

[1] Chap. xi. 18.   [2] Chap. xx. 12.

dreams of the fat and lean oxen and of the full and blasted ears of corn, he added, "And for that the dream was doubled unto Pharaoh twice, it is that the thing is established by God, and God will shortly bring it to pass."[1] The doubling of the dream lent it impressiveness and certainty. A similar remark may without hesitation be applied to Joseph's own two dreams of the sheaves in the field and of the sun and moon and eleven stars doing him obeisance.[2] The prospect of more sure and speedy execution was associated with the repetition of a thought ; and hence the words of the Psalmist, "God hath spoken once ; yea, *twice* have I heard this, that power belongeth unto God."[3]

The principle finds its application in not a few passages of the Apocalypse. When we read in chap. xi. 18 of "the saints and of them that fear Thy name," we shall be mistaken if we suppose two different classes to be alluded to. The two are in reality one, though they are beheld by the Seer in two aspects, the first taken from the sphere of Jewish, the second from that of Gentile, thought. They who are to be rewarded in the great day spoken of are at once the true Israel of God and those whom God has redeemed out of every tribe and tongue and people and nation. Similar observations apply to what may at first sight seem to be descriptions of two different classes of heretics in the Church at Pergamum, "some that hold the teaching of Balaam," and "some that hold the teaching of the

---

[1] Gen. xli. 32. 　　　　　　[2] Gen. xxxvii. 7, 9.
[3] Psalm lxii. 11.

Nicolaitans." [1] Between these two there is in reality no difference, for the best (to say nothing of its seeming to be also the most generally accepted) explanation of the word Nicolaitan regards it as not derived from Nicolas, mentioned in Acts vi. 5, but as compounded of two Greek words equivalent in meaning to the two component parts of the Hebrew name Balaam. Thus the Balaamites and the Nicolaitans are the same, considered in the one case from a Jewish, in the other from a more general, point of view. In like manner the "song" of chap. xv. 3 is not a double but a single song, its first appellative " of Moses, the servant of God," awakening the remembrance of all that God did for Israel through Moses, the great deliverer of the Old Testament dispensation; its second pointing not less clearly to the sun and centre of the universal dispensation of the New Testament,—" the Lamb of God which taketh away the sin of *the world*." [2] Even the two figures of the seven candlesticks and the seven stars in chap. i. seem to be best explained when we consider them as a double figure of the Church, which is a "golden candlestick" while she burns in the secret place of the Most High unnoticed by human eyes, but a "star" when, set in the firmament of heaven, she diffuses her light far and wide, and shines not for God only but for man. Finally, the same principle explains the essential sameness of the two consolatory visions of chap. vii.—those of the sealing of the 144,000 and of the white-robed multitude—the persons in both cases

[1] Chap. ii. 14, 15.   [2] John i. 29.

being the same, though they are first contemplated as a Church gathered out of the tribes of Israel, and next as gathered out of the tribes of the earth.[1]

In all these cases we see a principle of structure not dependent upon facts, but deliberately adopted, and faithfully carried out by the writer because it expressed certain ideas of his own.

A fourth point is closely connected with the last.

IV. In double descriptions of the same thing the first seems to be not unfrequently occupied with the ideal, the second with the actual aspect of the object spoken of. The Apocalypse itself supplies us with the explanation of this characteristic of the writer's style. Part of the song of the four and twenty elders, when they celebrate in chap. iv. the glory of Him that sat upon the throne, is in the following words,—"Thou didst create all things, and because of Thy will they were (not, as in the Authorised Version, 'are',) and were created."[2] They "were," and they "were created." How could they be before they were created? One explanation alone is possible. God knew what He would make before He made it.[3] There exists in the Divine mind an eternal type of everything that is called into existence. There is a pattern in the mount

---

[1] This interpretation of chap. vii. is no doubt much disputed. For a full defence of it see *Comm. in loc.*

[2] Chap. iv. 11.

[3] "For He was not ignorant of what He was about to create when He did create. No accession to His knowledge comes from His creatures to Him, nor did He know them after He had created them in any other way than before; but they existing when, and as, was meet, His knowledge remained as it was."—S. Augustine.

after which each pin of the tabernacle is fashioned. There is an ideal before there is an actual.

Let us apply this principle to the difficult task of grouping the paragraphs of chap. xii., and it will afford us help of which we shall be otherwise in want. The relation of the first paragraph of this chapter (verses 1-6) to the third (verses 13-17) has long been a matter of dispute. In the one we read of the woman's flight into the wilderness and of her nourishment there for a thousand two hundred and threescore days (verse 6). In the other we read of what appears to be the same flight and the same nourishment (verse 14). The second passage is, in consequence, often regarded as a mere repetition of the first, or as a more specific detail of what had been mentioned in verse 6, after the natural course of events had been interrupted by verses 7-12. But, rightly regarded, the first and third scenes of the chapter are not the same, nor is the narrative interrupted at verse 7 in order that the war in heaven may be described, and again resumed at verse 13. There is a marked difference between the two scenes contained in verses 1-6 and verses 13-17, and the difference consists in this, that the first is ideal, the second actual. Strictly speaking, the woman in verses 1-6 is neither the Jewish nor the Christian Church. She is light from Him "who is light, and with whom is no darkness at all," light which had been always shining before it was partially embodied either in the Church of the old or the new covenant. Her actual conflict with the darkness has not begun. We behold her in her own glorious existence, and it is enough to dwell upon the potencies that are in her as " a light of men." In like manner the dragon is not yet to be identified with the devil or Satan. That identification does not take place till we reach verse 9. The former differs from the latter as the abstract and ideal power of evil differs from evil in the concrete. As the woman is at first ideal light, light before it appears in the Church upon earth, so the dragon is ideal darkness, the power of sin before it begins its deadly warfare against the children of God. Thus also we learn what is intended by the Son who is born to the woman. He is not the Son actually incarnate, but the ideally incarnate Son, "the true light, which lighteth every man coming into the world" (John i. 9). More difficulty may be felt in answering the question whether, along with the Son Himself, we are to see in this "Son, of man's sex," the true members of Christ's body. Ideally, it would seem that we are to do so. All commentators allow that in the Son's being "caught up unto God and unto His throne" there is a reference to the Ascension and Glorification of our Lord. But, if so, it is hardly possible to separate between the risen, ascended, and glorified Lord and those who are in Him risen, ascended, and glorified. We cannot part Him from them or them from Him. Everything therefore in these verses is ideal. We see light and darkness, their natural an-tagonism to each other, the fierce enmity of the dark-ness against the light, the apparent success but real defeat of the darkness, the apparent quenching but real triumph of the light. All this, however, we see ideally. The actual forces are not yet upon the field.

In the third paragraph we have the actual Church before us in her conflict, her flight into the wilderness, her nourishment there, and her victory. We have a translation into the concrete of what we had previously witnessed in the abstract.

The second paragraph of the chapter (verses 7-12) is thus no interruption to the narrative. It is a distinct advance upon the first, and an equally distinct preparation for the third. We pass from the dragon, the ideal representative of evil, to the devil or Satan, known to us as the source of all the sin and misery from which earth suffers. Further, we learn why the Church on earth has to contend with this great adversary. He has been cast with his angels out of Heaven. It is God's decree that the main and last struggle between good and evil shall be fought out on earth. Among men, not angels, the issues of the plan of redemption shall be achieved. To impress these thoughts upon us—thoughts necessary to the comprehension of the conflict—is the reason why the second paragraph of this chapter has its place assigned to it in the grouping of the several parts.

The whole chapter presents a most striking parallel to the opening paragraphs of chap. i. of the Gospel of St. John.

If the principle now advocated be just, we venture to ask whether it may not be applicable to a still more important passage—the description of the first beast in chap. xiii., with the mention of which are associated the mysterious numbers six hundred, sixty, and six. The identity of this beast with that of chap. xvii. has been eagerly disputed ;[1] and it must be allowed that on ordinary methods of interpretation there is some difficulty in maintaining it. Yet if there be a difference between them the whole narrative is thrown into confusion. May the principle now advocated afford us light? May the description in chap. xiii. be ideal rather than actual, the first beast of that chapter being thought of in its existence in itself, while only in chap. xvii. do we see it in its real manifestation? Some points of the description favour this conjecture. Thus in chap. xiii. the beast is spoken of as if it were *come*, but in chap. xvii. its coming is rather a thing of the *future* than the present. In chap. xiii. 1 it comes up out of the " sea," thus leading us to the thought of its *original* source ; but in chap. xvii. 8 it comes up out of the " abyss," into which it is only plunged when, *in the course of history*, conquered by the Redeemer (chap. xx. 1). In chap. xiii. 2 we are told what it was like, but no mention is made of its "scarlet" colour, that fact being reserved for chap. xvii. 3, when its bloody conflict with the saints is before the Seer's mind. In chap. xiii. 3 we read of its head slaughtered and cured ; but in chap. xvii. this is not mentioned, apparently because it is now *acting* in its capacity as a beast risen from the dead, come up out of the abyss. In chap. xiii. 2 also the gift to it by the dragon of the dragon's power and

---

[1] As, *e.g.*, by Züllig.

throne and great authority has the appearance of an original investiture. The same remark applies to the *gift* in verse 5 of the mouth speaking blasphemies, and of *authority to continue* for a certain time ; as well as of the *gift* to make war in verse 7, the word "given" in the language of St. John leading us back to the primal rather than the historical grant. In like manner, if the description of the second beast of chap. xiii. be, not less than that of the first, ideal, we may better understand why we are not led to know it as " the false prophet" until we reach a later period of the book.[1] This character may properly be attributed to it only when it speaks to men. If there be any ground for these remarks they will help to confirm, what indeed may be otherwise proved, that in the mysterious eighteenth verse of the chapter the *abstract thought* of the name corresponding to the number, rather than the concrete name itself, is the point upon which we are to dwell. " His number is six hundred and sixty and six." These ominous numbers describe primarily the *character*, and only subordinately the *name*, of the beast referred to. The words of the same verse, " for it is the number of a man," will then mean that, just as the name of a man is, or originally was, an expression of his character, and may be given in numbers which, when properly interpreted, afford the same expression of it, so the number of the beast will be found in due time to correspond to a name equally pregnant with the thought of wickedness and of woe to the saints of God.

[1] Chaps. xvi. 13 ; xix. 20 ; xx. 10.

One more particular of structure must be briefly noticed.

V. The use of Episode.   Every student of the Apocalypse is familiar with this point, and it is not necessary to enlarge on it.   The visions of consolation in chap. vii. are strictly episodical.   They interrupt the narrative of the opening of the Seals.   The words of chaps. viii. 13; ix. 12; and xi. 14, have a similar character. So have the consolatory visions of chap. xi. and chap. xiv.   Episodical remarks also frequently occur, as in chaps. xiii. 18; xiv. 13; xix. 9.   Finally, along with this may be noticed the tendency to go back upon a thought the moment it is uttered with the view of presenting it in that contrasted aspect by which it may be made fuller and more impressive, as in chap. ii. 9, "which say they are Jews, *and they are not*, but are a synagogue of Satan;" and chap. iii. 9, "which say they are Jews, *and they are not*, but do lie."

The use to be made of all these particulars will appear in the next lecture.

LECTURE IV.

FROM the structure and plan of the Apocalypse we have now to proceed to the principles to be applied in its interpretation. Upon this point, as upon every other connected with the book, the widest diversity of opinion has prevailed, or still prevails ; and some notice of these divergent views it is impossible to omit. They rather claim our first attention, because it would seem that, for the most part at least, they must be set aside ; and because, after setting them aside, the field will be cleared for the further prosecution of our task.

I. The first system of interpretation to be noticed is that known as the historical, or the continuously historical. According to it the Apocalypse contains a brief sketch of the Church's progress from her first propagation to her consummation in glory.[1] The most important crises in the history both of the Church and of the world find a place in it; and the book establishes alike its Divine origin and its value by the minuteness of its manifold predictions, and by the

---

[1] Daubuz, *Prel. Disc.*, p. 16.

wonderful accuracy with which they have been fulfilled. No system of interpretation has exercised so
powerful an influence over those who have concerned
themselves with the study of this book. From the
thirteenth century until recently it may be said to have
had undisputed possession of the minds of men.[1] It
rallied to it, especially in the different branches of the
Reformed Church, the most distinguished expositors.
It pervaded largely the writings even of many who did
not accept it as a whole.[2] It not only awakened the
interest but secured the enthusiastic submission of
thousands upon thousands of pious minds. To this
day no belief is more commonly entertained than that
in the visions of St. John we may read of the establishment of Christianity under Constantine, of Mohammed, of the Papacy, of the Reformation in the sixteenth
century, of the French Revolution, of not a few in short
of the greatest movements by which, since the beginning
of the Christian era, the Church and the world have
been stirred.

The objections to this system are fatal to it.

One alone might suffice. It is impossible to reconcile with it those particulars regarding the conception, the structure, and the plan of the book that

---

[1] The Abbot Joachim, at Floris
in Calabria, is generally recognised as the earliest authoritative
interpreter of this school, although he extended the history
of the Kingdom of God given in
the book as far back as the creation (Lücke, *Versuch*, p. 1008.
Comp. also the history of the
school as given in Elliott, *H. A.*,
vol. iv. p. 415, etc.).

[2] Such as Alford, Auberlen,
Isaac Williams.

have been noticed in previous lectures. Either these are fanciful, or the Apocalypse is in no sense a continuous history. History does not accommodate itself to such rules as those under the guidance of which it was composed. The dependence of the book upon our Lord's discourse on the last things ; its singular parallelism to the fourth Gospel ; the selection of its figures to so great an extent from the Old Testament, or their creation out of materials derived from that source ; the degree to which its structure is regulated by the numbers of the arithmetical scale; its symmetry ; its synchronism ; the climactic character of its successive parts ; its contrasts ; its use of *Prolepsis* or Anticipation ; its double pictures ; its presentation of subjects in their ideal before it introduces them in their actual form, and its episodes—all these things forbid our regarding it as a history of actual events. The course of human progress from age to age is too free to admit of its steps being scheduled according to the peculiarities of any individual mind. For the sake of illustrating a particular conception of a person or age an historian may select and group events that have already taken place. Predicted events, if the truth of the prediction is to be recognised, must be submitted to us in the order in which they are to occur, and not in that which an ideal view of them may suggest. Here accordingly the external characteristics of the Apocalypse mentioned in the last two lectures find their most important application. If we are satisfied that they are to any considerable extent, even if not wholly, correct, the continuously historical interpretation of the book must be abandoned, whatever form it may assume.

Another conclusive objection to this system of interpretation is that, were it well founded, the Apocalypse would have been useless, alike to those for whom it was originally written and to the mass of humble Christians in after times. It would have had no connection with its own age; and nothing has been more conclusively established by recent Biblical inquiry than that even a prophetic, to say nothing of an apocalyptic, book must spring out of the circumstances, and must directly address itself to the necessities, of its original readers. Those into whose hands it is first put must feel that they are spoken to. It may be designed for others, but for them it must be designed, or the very idea of revelation is destroyed. Revelation implies not merely an unfolding of the Almighty's will, but such an unfolding of it that those to whom the revelation is given shall be able, if willing, to apprehend it. God always deals with His people in the condition in which they are found at any particular stage of their progress. There is, accordingly, a marked growth of revelation throughout the Bible. The light afforded corresponded with the capacity of the eye to see, and the eye was thus gradually opened to receive the fuller revelations that were to follow. Had another method been adopted, men would have been blinded by the strength of the illuminating force; and, instead of accepting the communication and storing it up for future use, would have been unable even to admit it into their minds. The whole history of prophecy establishes this truth. To the men of his own day the prophet spoke, and their responsibility to listen would have been removed had he spoken in terms which only future ages could understand. A principle thus applicable to all the other books of the Bible is not less applicable to the Apocalypse, for no book bears upon it stronger marks of having aimed at the immediate instruction and comfort of the then existing Church.

We may indeed admit that the events found in it by the historical interpreter would have been instructive or consolatory to the early Christian, if he could have thoroughly apprehended them. But the real difficulty lies in this, that such apprehension was then impossible. The first generation of Christians could have attached no proper meaning to the establishment of Christianity under Constantine, to the rise of Mahomedanism, to the accoutrements of Turkish Pashas, to the varying fortunes of the Lutheran Reformation, to the seven Dutch united provinces, or to the French Revolution. These things were all to happen in an age so different from their own that details of them, revealed in prophecy, would have been unintelligible. It needed a stage of the world's progress which had not yet come to give them meaning. No good effect therefore could have followed communications of this kind. They would have possessed no present power. They would have failed to make the men of the day either wiser or better. They would have substituted a vain prying into the future for the study of those Divine principles which, belonging to all time, bring the weight of universal history to enforce the lessons of our own.

While thus useless to the men first addressed by them, the visions of the Apocalypse would, upon this system, have been equally useless to the great body of the Christian Church, even after they had been fulfilled, and their fulfilment recognised by a few competent inquirers. The poor and the unlearned have always known, and will probably always know, little of the historical events supposed to be alluded to. Could it be a part of the Divine plan to make the understanding of a revelation so earnestly commended to us dependent on an acquaintance with the ecclesiastical and political history of the world for many hundred years? The very supposition is absurd. It is inconsistent with the first promise of the book, " Blessed is he that readeth, and they that hear the words of the prophecy." [1]

The two objections now taken to the historical method of interpreting the Apocalypse do not stand alone. Various others may be urged ; and as no true progress can be made in the interpretation of the book until this system is finally abandoned, it may be proper to allude to them with as much brevity as possible.

1. The selection of historical events made by the system is in a high degree arbitrary, and cannot be said to correspond to the degree of importance which these events have vindicated for themselves in the course of history. All historical interpreters, for ex-

---

[1] Chap. i. 3. Comp. Todd's *Lectures*, p. 44.

ample, cling with a curious pertinacity to the fortunes of Western Christendom. They make little mention of the Eastern Church, although the latter has in all probability numbered, through successive centuries, as many adherents as the former. Turning even to the West itself, we find no mention of the discovery of the Continent of America, or of the progress of that Christian Church there which has grown up to be so bright a jewel in the Redeemer's crown, and so powerful an instrument for the world's good. Nothing is said of the Reformation in Bohemia, or France, or Spain, or of its disastrous retrogression in these lands after having made in them a start so full of promise. The invention of the printing-press has no place in this scheme of interpretation, although it would be difficult to think of anything more intimately associated with the progress of Christ's Kingdom. The rise of the missionary spirit in the Protestant Church, one of the most remarkable phenomena of her history, is equally unknown to it. Nor are we told of that breaking up of the Church into many different and hostile sections, which has done so much to defeat the purpose of her existence in the world.

It may be replied that these things are not found in the Apocalypse by the historical interpreter simply because they are not there, and that it is his duty to elicit what is in the text, not to impose upon it incidents left unnoticed. Yet, allowing it to be so, the fact that such things as those now spoken of are left unnoticed cannot but throw some measure of suspicion upon a system inviting us to look for them. A Divine book purposing to deal with the whole history of the Church both in herself and in her relation to the world ought not to pass some of the grandest events in that history without at least recognising them.[1]

2. The events in which the historical system of interpretation finds predictions of the Apocalypse fulfilled are not unfrequently of the most puerile and trifling kind. One is pained to speak in this connection of the red stockings of Romish Cardinals, of the horse tails worn by Turkish Pashas, or of Sir Robert Peel's motion, in 1841, of want of confidence in the Whig ministers.[2] It may be asserted with perfect confidence that the thought of such things would have been at once dismissed by the excellent men who have suggested them, had not attachment to a theory destroyed the soundness of their judgment, and blinded them to the correct proportions of historical fact.

3. Akin to this difficulty is that afforded by the manner in which the historical interpretation so often degrades the sublime language of the book, and brings down its figures to a level upon which they lose their power.

4. Even were these objections less weighty than they are, the continuously historical interpretation

---

[1] Finding the French Revolution in the earthquake of chap. xi. 19, even Elliott says, " It was a political convulsion and revolution of magnitude such that the apocalyptic prophecy would have been altogether inconsistent with itself had it not noticed it " (*H. A.*, iii. p. 289).

[2] See mention of this last in Todd's *Lectures*, p. 217, *note*.

would be discredited by the hopeless disagreements of its advocates. In almost nothing are they at one; and there is hardly a single vision of the book in regard to which the greatest diversity of interpretation does not prevail among them. But prophecy thus interpreted long after its fulfilment must have taken place ceases to deserve the name of prophecy, and becomes no better than an uninstructive and disappointing riddle.

5. Even these results of the historical system of interpretation are in many instances only gained by mistranslations of the original,[1] by forcing upon words meanings which they will not bear,[2] by strained and unnatural inferences,[3] and by an arbitrary mixing up of literal and figurative renderings in the case of ob-jects that are clearly dependent upon one another.[4]

Finally, it may be added upon this point that it is difficult to estimate the amount of loss which has been sustained by the Church of Christ through the attempts of historical interpreters to limit the passages explained by them to particular events. Even the most plausible interpretation thus offered—that which finds in Baby-lon Papal Rome—has not only deprived Protestants of some of the most solemn warnings addressed to them

---

[1] Thus Elliott renders chap. ix. 15, where we read of the angels prepared "for the hour and day and month and year," "at the ex-piration of these periods of time aggregated together" (*H. A.*, i. p. 489).

[2] The same author applies "thousands" to provinces after the manner of the English term "hundreds" (*U. S.*, ii. p. 420).

[3] Thus the "hail" of chap. xi. 19 is applied by Elliott first to nations, and then in particular to the nations of the North (*U. S.*, iii. p. 288).

[4] Comp. Fairbairn *On Prophecy*, p. 141.

in the Bible, but has taught them to use a book not less fitted to humble than to elevate the heart, as a store-house of weapons for every species of partizanship, recrimination, and strife. The system has, indeed, been supported by men whom in every other respect it is alike a duty and a delight to honour; but, however numerous or illustrious its defenders, it may be said without exaggeration that nothing has tended more to diminish the value and to discredit the general accept-ance of the Revelation of St. John. The taste, however, for such interpretation is rapidly passing away, probably never to return.

II. A second system of interpretation is proposed. According to this view almost the whole, if not the whole, book belongs to a future which may be even yet distant. It relates exclusively to the Second Coming of the Lord, with its attendant signs and circumstances; "and we are therefore to look for the fulfilment of its predictions neither in the early persecutions and heresies of the Church nor in the long series of centuries from the first preaching of the Gospel until now, but in the events which are immediately to precede, to accompany, and to follow the Second Advent of our Lord and Saviour."[1]

This system of interpretation is no more defensible than the last. That it possesses an element of truth it is indeed impossible to deny. The Apocalypse does deal in a most distinct and emphatic manner with the Second Coming of the Lord; and every description

---

[1] Todd's *Lectures*, p. 68.

which it gives, whether of the destruction of the ungodly or of the protection and blessedness of the Saints, has reference to that event. From the beginning to the end of the whole book the Seer is continually in the presence of the great day, with all in it that is at once so majestic and terrible. The Lord comes : He comes quickly : He is knocking at the door. Such is the attitude in which He is always presenting Himself to the believing and the watchful heart. But it by no means follows from this, that St. John has passed over the events alike of his own time and of all succeeding centuries till the last moment comes, and that he mentions nothing but what is to occur in a few closing years of the Christian Dispensation. Were it really so his prophecy would have been deprived of a large measure of its value for those to whom it was originally addressed. Nor could even the Church of any later age have seen it in the power of present and immediate reality, because it could never have been possible to recognise in their true character the events of which it speaks until Christ were come. Even the Church living on the very eve of the Lord's return would not know that it was the eve, until she looked back upon it from the full light of the following day. The meaning of the prophetic intimations of the book would be uncertain, and the issue could alone interpret them. The Church, therefore, could never, upon this system, apply the lessons of the Apocalypse directly to herself, because she could never know whether her lot had been cast in the days alluded to until the days were over.

The main considerations, however, against this system spring, as in the case of the system already spoken of, from a just interpretation of the book. Let us look at one or two clauses particularly depended on,—"The revelation of Jesus Christ, which God gave Him to show unto His servants, even the things which must shortly come to pass;"[1] "Blessed is he that readeth, and they that hear the words of the prophecy, for the time is at hand;"[2] "He which testifieth these things saith, Yea: I come quickly."[3] Upon what principle of interpretation, we may well ask, is it possible to find in expressions such as these no more than an intimation that the events which are to precede and accompany the Second Advent of the Lord shall take place in a short and rapid space of time?[4] On what principle can we imagine that, in thus speaking, the Seer intended to throw himself forward hundreds of years; and to say only that, when the winding up of the drama came, it would be brief? We must start from the circumstances amidst which he was placed when he wrote, and from that point measure the time that was to elapse to the end. When he said "Blessed is he that readeth, and they that hear the words of the prophecy," he certainly had in view the readers and the hearers of his own age; and when, therefore, he immediately added, "for the time is at hand," he not less certainly intended that the course of "the time" thus spoken of was to take its beginning from their day. Throughout the whole book the Church

---

[1] Chap. i. 1.
[2] Chap. i. 3.
[3] Chap. xxii. 20.
[4] Todd's *Lectures*, p. 65.

is addressed as she was when the Apostle wrote, and is told what was to be done to her and for her at the instant when she first read the prophecy.

Another exegetical difficulty in the way of this system of interpretation, and one hardly less fatal than that now spoken of, arises from the necessity involved in it of applying an extreme literalism to what is said both of the duration and of the events of the closing scenes. The three and a half years, for example, or forty-two months, or twelve hundred and sixty days, frequently mentioned in the latter half of the book, must be understood simply of the space of time which the words express in ordinary language. For otherwise they can only be interpreted according to the usual symbolism of numbers prevailing elsewhere in the Apocalypse; and this, in the light of history, would imply a length of time incompatible with that literal interpretation of the phrases "the time is short" and "I come quickly" upon which the system rests. The same consideration makes it necessary to refer each vision of the book, from the opening of the first seal onward, to events which are either immediately to precede or to accompany the Second Advent. The coming forth of Christ under the first Seal, "conquering and to conquer;" the wars and famines and pestilences of the next three Seals; even the slaughter of Christian martyrs pointed at, upon the supposition with which we are now dealing, under the fifth Seal; the whole subsequent development of the Trumpets and the Bowls, and the fall of Babylon,—every one of these must

belong to Christ's appearance the second time without
sin unto salvation. Nay, it ought rather to be said
that they *follow* that appearance, for the first Seal must
be interpreted of the Second Advent,[1] and no one will
deny that, in point of time, it takes precedence of the
remaining visions of the Seer. Such an idea, however,
cannot be entertained for an instant.

But this literalism is not confined to such things.
It connects itself also with views as to the rebuilding of
the temple, the restoration of the Jewish polity, the
settlement of the Jews in the ancient inheritance of
their fathers, and their predominance, alike in dignity
and Christian work, among the other nations of the
earth, of which it is not too much to say that they are
out of keeping both with the general revelation of the
New Testament, and with that method of interpreting
the prophecies of the Old Testament which is suggested
in the New. This second system can no more be
accepted than the first.

III. The two systems of interpretation now considered have no longer the weight that they once had
in the mind of the Church. Within recent years they
may be said to have been in great measure superseded
by another which asserts for itself an exclusive
possession of the improved methods of modern re-
search.[2] It demands, therefore, and is entitled to, our

[1] Todd's *Lectures*, p. 99.

[2] There is something extraordinary in the confidence with
which this third system of interpretation is urged upon us. "If,"
says Renan, "the Gospel is the
book of Jesus, the Apocalypse is
the book of Nero" (*L'Ant.*, p. 477).
Archdeacon Farrar describes the
Nero-story as the key of the

attention. Upon this third system it is supposed that the Apocalypse is confined to events either surrounding the Seer or immediately to follow—in particular to the overthrow of Judaism and heathenism, of degenerate Jerusalem, and of pagan Rome. These two great enemies of the Christian faith were face to face with the Apostle. His heart was torn by the sufferings which they inflicted upon the flock of Christ; but he knew that the risen and glorified Redeemer was against them; and, in the glowing pictures of a righteous indignation, he prophesied of their fall. The system possesses, like the last, an element of truth. It may be at once allowed. that from what he beheld around him, either fully developed or in germ, the Seer did draw those lessons as to the dealings of God with the Church and with the world which he applies to all time. He starts from contemporary history, and it is quite possible that at the bottom of each judgment which he depicts, when he does not rely simply upon the Old Testament, there may be something which his own eyes have seen or his own ears heard. Nor can it be urged that to speak of events of his own day alone would have been unworthy of his inspiration, for the same reasoning would deprive of permanent value much of the teaching of the New Testament. Nay, it is not even a just argument against this method of interpretation that, if it be true, the contents of the book have been falsified in important particulars by

.book (*Expositor*, May 1881, p. 335).   others attach equal importance to
Gebhardt, Hausrath, Bleek, and   it.

the issue. Another conclusion might be unavoidable, for the book might be apocryphal, and unworthy of its place in the Canon.

The true objection to the proposal to limit the meaning of the Apocalypse by the events of the writer's own day rests upon exegetical grounds, partly of a general and partly of a more special kind.

As to the former, the book bears distinctly on its face that it is not confined to what the Seer beheld immediately around him. It treats of much that was to happen down to the very end of time, down to the full accomplishment of the Church's struggle, the full winning of her victory, and the full attainment of her rest. The Coming of the Lord so frequently referred to was certainly not exhausted in that destruction of the Jewish polity which we now know was to precede by many centuries the close of the present dispensation; and the enemies of God described continue their opposition to the truth not merely to a point near at hand, when they are checked, but to the last, when they are overthrown finally and for ever. There is a progress in the book which is only stopped by the final advent of the Judge of the whole earth; and no just system of interpretation will permit us to regard the different plagues of the Seals, the Trumpets, and the Bowls as symbolic only of wars which the Seer had beheld in their beginnings, and which he knew would end in the destruction of Jerusalem and Rome. Against the idea that St. John was limited to the events of his own day the tone and spirit of the book are a continuous protest. Nor can it be pleaded that he combines these with those that were to happen at the last, leaving, for reasons unexplained by him, a long interval of time unnoticed. There is no trace of an interval. The lightnings flash and the thunders roll in close succession from the beginning to the end of the book. Judged even by its general character, the Apocalypse cannot be interpreted upon this modern system.

The special interpretation of particular passages is not less fatal to the theory, for it is invariably, if not inseparably, bound up with two assumptions,—that the beast of chaps. xiii. and xvii. is the Emperor Nero, and that the Babylon which plays so large a part in the later chapters of the book is Rome. The second of these assumptions will meet us in the next lecture for another purpose. We may, therefore, at present confine ourselves to the first, that the beast of chaps. xiii. and xvii. is Nero.

The identification of the two is regarded by not a few leading scholars of the day as the great discovery of modern times in connection with the Apocalypse,[1] and there is a disposition to accept it which may almost be spoken of as general. The main strength of the argument rests upon the words of chap. xiii. 18—"He that hath understanding, let him count the number of the beast; for it is the number of a man; and his number is six hundred sixty and six." St. John, it is said, is dealing with that ancient and mystic system of

---

[1] Comp. Reuss, *Hist. of N. T.*,   October 1863 and December 1873;
p. 156 ; Réville, *Rev. d. d. Mondes*,   Renan, *L'Ant.*, chap. xvii.

numbers by which the letters of a man's name had their numerical value assigned to them, so that, when added together, they supplied a number instead of a name as his designation. The letters of the two words "Neron Cæsar" make up the number 666; and St. John, by thus telling us that the beast is Nero, gives us the key to the principle upon which he wrote his book.

One consideration alone ought to be enough to demonstrate the mistaken character of this interpretation. It puts St. John *in direct conflict* with those particulars of his own day to which he is supposed to be giving expression in his vision. Observe the words of chap. xiii. 3, "and I saw one of his heads as though it had been slaughtered unto death; and his death stroke was healed." This head, according to the theory, is Nero; and the symbolism rests, it is said, upon the fact that when that Emperor was reported to have put an end to his life, he had not really died, but had escaped to the distant land of Parthia, whence he would yet return to take vengeance upon Rome. The passage before us however speaks of something entirely different from flight and return from flight; it speaks distinctly *of death and of resurrection from the dead.* The words of the original are unfortunately translated in our English version, "and I saw one of his heads as it were wounded to death."[1] They are better, but not adequately, translated in the Revised Version, in which for "wounded to death" we read "smitten unto death,"

____

[1] Chap. xiii. 3.

with the margin "slain" for "smitten." The true translation is "slaughtered unto death," for the Greek word used occurs, in addition to the present instance, seven times in the Apocalypse, in every one of which it must be translated "slain," or "slaughtered," or "killed." How can it be otherwise translated here? Not only so; the statement in the verse before us is the counterpart of that in chap. v. 6, where we read of the "Lamb as though it had been slaughtered." In both cases there is death, not flight. The head of the beast had died as really as the Lamb of God had died on Calvary, and the Seer saw that it had done so. Nay, more, it had experienced a resurrection from the dead. As we read in chap. xiii. 3, its "death-stroke was healed;" still more fully in chap. xvii. 8 it is spoken of as the beast that "was, and is not, and is about to come up out of the abyss;" and again, in the same verse, as the beast that "was, and is not, and shall be present." But these words are the counterpart of those used by Jesus of Himself in chap. i. 18—"I am the first and the last, and the Living one; and I became dead, and behold, I am alive for evermore." Hence, accordingly, we read in chap. xi. 7 of "the beast that cometh up out of the abyss" as that by which the two witnesses are killed. The whole representation, in short, of the beast implies that it had not merely died as Christ had died, but that it had also risen as He had done; and it is not simply as the beast "slaughtered unto death," but as the beast with "its death-stroke healed," that in chap. xiii. 3 it receives the homage of the world.

But all this was wholly different from what either took place in the history of Nero or was ascribed to him by popular rumour.   Rumour did not say that he had died, but that he had fled.   It did not say that he would rise from the grave, but that he would return from Parthia.   We know that he did not rise, that he did not return, that he was not received with the acclamations of his adherents.   If St. John means that Nero is the beast, he has founded his representation not upon contemporary occurrences, but upon a wild imagination of his own.   By the application of this single test the elaborate structure of the Nero-hypothesis crumbles into dust.

Much more might be urged upon the point.   In particular it might be shown that the theory is discredited by the mistake of confounding the heads of the beast with the beast itself ; by its misunderstanding the force of the word "name ;" by its putting that emphasis upon the word Nero which really belongs to the number 666 ; by its misapprehending the relation between numbers and names which the Seer has in his mind ; by its unnatural spelling of Hebrew words in order to accomplish its end ; by its inability to secure that secrecy at which it is supposed to aim ; and by its suggesting a mere puzzle or play with numbers for a Divine mystery, the thought of which, when he alludes to it, fills the Seer's mind with awe.[1]   Enough, however, has been said to show that the beast cannot be Nero. If so, the whole system of interpretation so much relied on in recent times falls to the ground.

[1] These points will be noticed more fully in Appendix III.

No doubt the Seer did start from the events of his own day, and likewise spoke to it. But it is impossible to limit his meaning to what was then happening around him. He beheld in that only one manifestation of the deeper principles which, always true, would never fail to exhibit themselves in action until the end came.

The different systems of interpretation now considered must thus be set aside; and it remains for us to mark one or two general principles that may help us both to understand aright the purpose of the Seer, and to appreciate the manner in which that purpose is accomplished.

I. The Apocalypse embraces the whole period from the First to the Second Coming of the Lord, but without positively determining whether it shall be long or short. That the beginning and the end of the Christian Dispensation are before us in the visions of St. John cannot be doubted. It can only be a question whether the intermediate space of time is not omitted. That it is not is clear from this, that there is no pause in the action of the book. From first to last there is continual development and uninterrupted progress. The explanation is, that the Seer has separated the ideas to which he gives expression from all thought of the time needed to embody them in fact. It is true that in not a few passages he speaks as one who felt that the close was at hand ; but such language, we shall immediately see, admits of an easy explanation. In the meanwhile it is of more importance to remark that the renouncing on the part of the apostle of any attempt to indicate the number of days or years or centuries which were to pass before the end is in strict accordance with the teaching of our Lord.

When the disciples of Jesus asked their Master on one occasion regarding the "consummation of the age," He replied, "Of that day and hour knoweth no one, not even the angels of heaven, neither the Son, but the Father only."[1] Again He said to the twelve, immediately before his Ascension into Heaven, "It is not for you to know times or seasons, which the Father hath set within His own authority."[2] In words like these our Lord distinctly eliminated from what He reveals to us of the end every trace of allusion to either its nearness or its distance. From the Divine point of view, "one day is as a thousand years and a thousand years are as one day;" and it was from the Divine point of view that Jesus spoke. His words, therefore, contain a principle of the utmost importance to the interpretation of what is said by His apostles either in the Apocalypse or in other books of the New Testament. If we introduce into their writings the thought of any definite length of time whatever, we are directly at variance with the principle laid down by Christ. It may indeed be urged that they speak in the language of men, and that by the ordinary laws of such language they must be understood. The remark is just ; but these ordinary laws of language require that a Prophet or a Seer shall be understood according to the laws of prophetic or apocalyptic language. As he was filled with the prophetic or apocalyptic spirit, we can only comprehend him when we

---

[1] Matt. xxiv. 36.   [2] Acts i. 7.

share that spirit, when we move in the same Divine region of thought as that out of which he speaks.

Two errors, therefore, on the point now spoken of, have to be avoided in the interpretation of the Apocalypse.

In the first place, it may be said that, had we not possessed the visions of that book, we could hardly have imagined that the interval between the beginning and the consummation of the Christian age would have been so great ; or that the waves of sin and judgment, of trial and victory, would have been so manifold.[1] But it is precisely of the extent of this interval that the Apocalypse says not one single word. These successive waves of judgment are obviously successive in thought rather than in time. They may come at distant intervals, or they may be crowded wave upon wave. Nothing in the book entitles us to say which of these will be the case. Even such a word as "hereafter," in the statement "The first woe is past : behold, there come yet two woes hereafter,"[2] does not prove that lapse of time is the main consideration present to the Seer's mind. For anything told us, the drama, with all its varied scenes, may be quickly closed.

In the second place, it may be, as it often has been, said that the expressions, " the things which must shortly come to pass," "the time is at hand," and " I come quickly," necessarily imply only the briefest possible period between the time when they were uttered and the consummation of the age. But, again, we have no right to say so. The style of speech thus adopted

---

[1] Fairbairn *On Prophecy*, p. 174.   [2] Chap. ix. 12.

arises out of a method of conception peculiar to early Christianity, and nearly if not altogether strange to the later history of the Church. Owing in all probability simply to the fact that Christian history has already embraced so many centuries of the world's progress, we look at the period between the First and Second Coming of the Lord as simply a part of a regular and continuous course which the world has been running since the creation of man. It is distinguished from the pre-christian age by having brought with it clearer light, higher privileges, and greater responsibilities. Yet it is to us only a stage in a process that has been always going on, and that, like the morning light, has been shining more and more unto the perfect day. To the early Church, however, the time which began to run with the coming of Christ presented itself in an entirely different aspect. It was separated from the past by a more distinct line of demarcation, by a broader and deeper gulf. It was not merely a more signal period of preparation for the end than any previously given; in one sense *it was the end itself.* Not indeed that there might not be still much to happen before the Lord of glory actually appeared; but, even though it were so, the age was His in an altogether peculiar sense. He was ruling in it in a way in which He could not be said to have ruled before. He had not only died, but risen again, and ascended to the right hand of the Majesty ·in the heavens. There at that very moment He was carrying out, not the *preparatory,* but the *final* purposes of His wisdom and love. The earth was even now the stage upon which the *last* act of the world-drama was accomplishing.

Hence, accordingly, that separation between two distinct ages which, appearing · first in the Jewish, afterwards appears also in the Christian, Church,—the two ages being known as " this age (or world)" and " the age (or the world) to come." The former, before Christ came, was the age of preparation, when all things went on in their ordinary course, although in the midst of them God, by His special dealings with men, was bringing about an ever-increasing " fulness of the times." The latter, after Christ had come, was the age of consummation, when everything which God intended to do for the execution of His covenant had been done, when the scheme of revelation had been completed, when it was no longer needful to add dispensation to dispensation, or age to age, in order to fill up the times, but when their " fulness " had been at length attained.[1] Everything, it is true, of which prophecy had spoken, and which was included in the promises of the covenant, had not yet been realised. So far from this, it seemed as if the state of matters for the Church of God were worse instead of better. She was more oppressed and persecuted than she had ever been, while the world was more godless and wicked. Still it was the Gospel age, the new dispensation, " the world to come." The

---

[1] Nothing can show this more clearly than the fact that in Hebrews vi. 5 " the powers of the age to come" are classed with " the heavenly gift," " the Holy Spirit," and " the good Word of God," as things of which those Hebrew Christians who were in danger of falling away had *already* tasted.

Church could not abandon that conviction without abandoning her faith that Jesus was the Messiah, and, along with this, the very basis of her existence. She consoled herself therefore with the thought that the age had not yet been revealed in all its glory, that she had as yet seen only one side of it, that there was another and a brighter behind, and that what she had to wait for was not a new stage of time, but only a manifestation, a revelation, an *Apocalypsis*, of what was really in existence.[1] It will thus be observed that to the early Church glory darted its rays into the midst of shame, heavenly triumph into the midst of earthly defeat. It was not so much that the shame and the defeat were the only things known in this world, but were to be followed in a better world by the glory and the triumph. That is our way of looking at it. The early Church saw the latter already reached in the person of the Redeemer who made over to her all that He Himself possessed. They were not then *to be* won—they *were* won. Nothing more was needed than that Christ, now hidden, should "appear," and should make the glory, already potentially His people's, shine out, so that they too might "appear" with Him in glory, and enjoy their Epiphany as He had enjoyed His. The thought of the early Church was thus not, like ours, a double thought

---

[1] The second chapter of the Epistle to the Hebrews is in this point of view especially instructive. The sacred writer there mourns over the fact that, high as was the destiny of man, it was yet by no means reached. But then he turns instantly to the Lord within the veil, and sees in the "glory and honour" with which He is crowned the pledge of the "glory" to which God will immediately bring His "many sons."

—suffering here, glory hereafter. It was a single thought,—glory shining now through suffering, and gradually swallowing that suffering up in perfect victory.

The effect of all this was that the whole history of the Christian Church down to the Second Coming of the Lord in glory was embraced from one point of view and in one thought. It was a framework within which there was set the expression of one great idea. It was from its beginning to its end the final dispensation, the last time, the Lord's day, which was to close God's dealings with man in a present world, and to bring to full light the principles upon which the Church was guided to her eternal rest.

Hence, accordingly, the course of time disappears from view. The one idea to be expressed fills up the scene, and it is not surprising that it should do so. In an ideal representation intended to set forth the inherent tendencies and the ultimate issues of a course of action, events which, in their evolution, will occupy a long time, may with perfect propriety be set forth in one picture from the writer's pen, because the same principle runs through them all. The first contains the last in germ. The last only develops what was implicitly in the first. Time is therefore unthought of. It comes in simply because we cannot think of the accomplishment of an idea except in time. But time so viewed is summary, rapid, short, with the end at hand. Even if the Seer had not believed, as he may have believed, that the Judge was standing at the door, he could hardly, in the circumstances, have conceived of the matter in any other way. This alone he knew, that the long-expected King of Israel had come, and that God had begun to judge His people with righteousness and His poor with judgment.

We have no right, therefore, in interpreting the Apocalypse, to interject into it the thought either of a long or a short development of events. It is a representation in which an idea, not the time needed for the expression of the idea, plays the chief part.

II. While the Apocalypse thus embraces the whole period of the Christian Dispensation, it sets before us within this period the action of great principles and not special incidents. In this respect it follows closely the lines of our Lord's last discourse in the three earlier Gospels.   In both allusion is made to events of a general character,—to wars, pestilences, famines, false teachers, persecution, defection from the faith, preservation of the faithful, and so on; but this is not the prediction of particular events.   Of such prediction there is almost none either in the last discourse of Jesus or in the visions of His disciple.   If we except in the former a small portion which seems to refer to the destruction of Jerusalem, we learn from neither one single word of the special history of the future, of the impending revolutions of its kingdoms, of the changes of its parties, of the rise or fall of its statesmen or conquerors or monarchs.[1]   Both, too, preserve a similar

[1] Kliefoth (D. O. J. *Einl.*, p. 37, etc.) endeavours at great length to prove that, even in speaking of Jerusalem, our Lord had far greater and more remote events in view than the destruction of that city by the Romans.

silence as to individual misfortunes or triumphs of the Church. No one would even attempt to detect particular events of either kind in our Lord's discourse on the last things, and they are equally absent from the Apocalypse. When the disciples asked Jesus of the future, He uttered with His own lips all that He thought necessary for their encouragement. When He gave His revelation to the Seer in Patmos He gave no more. What distinguishes the revelation from the discourse is not the greater minuteness of its contents but the form in which its truths are clothed. The instant we lose sight of this we begin to look in the Apocalypse for what it does not contain, and we are in danger of becoming the prey of hasty and idle fancies.

In the respect now mentioned the Apocalypse resembles all true prophecy which, whether in the Old Testament or the New, contains mainly the enunciation of great principles of God's government of men, and not the prediction of special events. Even when the latter are predicted it is generally less for their own sake than for the principles they illustrate. A minute correspondence between every minor particular of the prediction and the result is not required to convince us that we are dealing with the insight or the inspiration of a true prophet. It is enough if the prophet connected together, in a way generally conformable to the facts as they occurred, a course of conduct, whether good or evil, with the consequences which followed it.

Thus, then, we are not to look in the Apocalypse for

special events, but for an exhibition of the principles which govern the history both of the world and the Church. These principles may not even be new. They may be those which had appeared more or less clearly in the words of all former prophets, or which fell from the lips of our Lord Himself. They may pervade the whole Old Testament Dispensation. Nay, we may even find yearnings after them, just as we find yearnings after a Messiah, in the poets of heathenism. No circumstances of that kind detract in the slightest degree from either their value or their force. What distinguishes them here is that we are not merely told of them as coming ; we see them come. We behold an old and sinful world going down in order that a new and better world may take its place; the hatefulness, the danger, and the punishment of sin, contrasted with the beauty, the security, and the reward of righteousness ; and the ever-present though unseen Ruler of the universe watching over His own, making the wrath of man to praise Him, and guiding all things to His own glorious ends. The book thus becomes to us not a history of either early or mediæval or last events written of before they happened, but a spring of elevating encouragement and holy joy to Christians in every age. In this sense it was strictly applicable to St John's own day : but it has been not less applicable to after times, and it will continue to be equally so to the end.

Hence also the easy possibility of the fact already dwelt on, and a clear recognition of which is of the utmost importance for the interpretation of the book,—

that the period of history covered by it extends from the beginning to the close of the Church's pilgrimage upon earth. That possibility is easy because the book deals with principles, and these are always essentially the same. The laws of the Almighty's moral government are as unchangeable and eternal as those by which He regulates the course of nature. They are not less the expression of Him who is the same yesterday, and to-day, and for ever. They may reveal themselves in new applications because the phenomena to which they apply may assume new forms. Their action may be more intense as the ages run on, but they do not really change; and even therefore in a book so short as the Apocalypse they may find, what all the important events of the Church's history could never find, a full and adequate expression.

III. A third principle of interpretation must still be noticed. We are both entitled and required to interpret in a spiritual and universal sense that language of the Apocalypse which appears at first sight to be material and local. The book is full of words and figures taken from Jewish history, and associated with the memories and the anticipations of the Jewish people. The question, therefore, naturally arises, May not the book be Jewish? May it not be occupied throughout with the fortunes of the Jews? What right have we to interpret such words as Israel, Jerusalem, Zion, the temple, the altar, the key of David, the palms of the feast of Tabernacles, the " people" (claimed by Christ as His), and other similar words, in a wider and more spiritual sense than that which they naturally bear ? May we not, in doing so, put into them a meaning unthought of by the author ? The answer to these questions depends upon a prior question, What were the views of the author of the Apocalypse in regard to the Christian system as a whole ? If we have reason to believe that they were of the widest, most comprehensive, and most spiritual kind, his local words and figures will not necessarily carry with them a local meaning. The spirituality and universality of St. Paul's views are admitted, yet he frequently employs similar language. In Gal. vi. 16 he speaks of the whole Christian community as " the Israel of God." In chap. iii. 7 of the same Epistle he is even more special in his designation of believers, " Know therefore that they which be of faith, the same are the sons of Abraham." In 2 Cor. vi. 16 he says to the Corinthian Christians, who were unquestionably for the most part Gentiles, " for we are a temple of the living God " (R. V.) In Eph. ii. 21 he describes the united Church as " a holy temple in the Lord;" and in Gal. iv. 26 he declares that " the Jerusalem that is, above is free, which is our mother." Expressions of the same kind occur in other writers of the New Testament and in the mouth of Christ Himself ; but these are chosen from St. Paul, because in that apostle's case the spirituality and universalism of the sentiments conveyed by them are never questioned. What we know of his general views sheds light upon such language, and we should no more think of charging him with judaizing, than of laying that charge at the door of a Christian minister who should speak of Christians as wanderers in a wilderness, or as pilgrims to a land of promise.

When, in like manner, we turn to the Apocalypse, it is undeniable that its leading ideas are as purely Christian as any ideas of the New Testament. Nothing can be more strikingly so than its conception of Christ. Throughout the book He is the Lamb—the Lamb sacrificed, the Lamb risen and glorified. In other words, He is the Lamb who has passed through death to glory, and who now, at the right hand of the Father, reigns in His spiritual and universal kingdom. Again, there is the same spirituality and universality in St. John's conception of the Church. No language can be a clearer proof of this than the language of chap. vii. 9, where those standing before the throne and before the Lamb are described as " a great multitude, out of every nation, and of all tribes and peoples and tongues;" or that of chap. v. 9, 10, where the four and twenty elders sing their new song, saying, " Worthy art Thou to take the book, and to open the seals thereof : for Thou wast slain, and didst purchase unto God with Thy blood men of every tribe, and tongue, and people, and nation, and madest them to be unto our God a kingdom and priests ; and they reign upon the earth." Once mroe, nothing can indicate more strongly the spirituality and universality of the writer, or his complete elevation above the limited ideas of Judaism, than the statement of chap. xxi. 22, when, speaking of the New Jerusalem, he says, " And I saw no temple therein."

Passages like these reveal a width of view on the

part of the author of the Apocalypse, whoever he be, which are wholly inconsistent with a narrow attachment to Judaism and Judaistic hope. It would in fact be far more reasonable to ask whether he recognises the Jewish, than whether he recognises the Gentile, branch of the Church. All the seven cities, the congregations of which represent the Church, belong to a Gentile land. When the Trumpet judgments, those upon the world, are nearly ended, and we are about to deal with judgments on the Church, it is intimated to the Seer that he must "prophesy again over many peoples and nations and tongues and kings;"[1] and there can be no doubt that the struggle with the three great enemies, the devil, the first beast, and the false prophet, is the struggle of the Church after she has gone out into the whole world. We have much more need therefore to ask for traces of the Jewish than the Gentile Christian Church.

But the truth is that the Church in the Apocalypse is one. She has an aspect indeed both to Israel and the Gentiles. Twenty-four elders, twelve for each branch, represent her in her heavenly triumph ; and the redeemed sing the song described at once by an Old Testament and a New Testament designation— "the song of Moses the servant of God and of the Lamb." These are only her outward aspects ; internally, essentially, she is one. In such circumstances we cannot hesitate to acknowledge both the spirituality and the universalism of the author of this book ; and,

____

[1] Chap. x. 11.

that being so, we must apply to him the same rule that we apply both to the other writers of the New Testament and to our Lord. His Jewish figures are the embodiment of Christian, not of Jewish, thought.

For the three principles now spoken of we shall have immediate need in considering the special object which the author of the Apocalypse had in view.

LECTURE V.

THE previous lectures ought to have prepared us for the next point to which our attention must be directed, the Design and Scope of the Apocalypse. But, in order to understand this better, it will be well to look for a moment at the circumstances in which the Seer was placed.

The time was one of the deepest anxiety and suspense to the Christian Church in general, and more especially, we may well suppose, to the aged apostle who for many years had been the solitary survivor of the apostolic band. Events of the most momentous character had happened, or were happening, to the Jews, among the Gentiles, and in the world. Israel, so long God's favoured people, and the literal glory of whose future seemed to be spoken of in so many passages of the Old Testament, had been extinguished as a nation. Jerusalem had fallen amidst horrors as yet unequalled in the bloody list of sacks and massacres which had stained the history of man. The Jews had been driven from their homes, and the sanctuary, so long revered and loved with all the ardour of the Jewish heart, had been levelled with the dust. The Gentiles were hardly less involved in every calamity that can fill the breasts of nations with hopelessness and despair. The mighty fabric of the Roman Empire had arisen, a new monster from the sea of the nations, and more terrible than the worst of previous tyrannies—its military despotism degraded in itself and degrading all beneath its sway; its soldiers claiming the right to sell the crown to the highest bidder; its subject nations crushed under the exactions of selfish and greedy procurators; the old freedom of the Republic gone, and a grinding tyranny substituted for it; the throne filled from time to time by profligates or villains, a Nero, a Caligula, a Domitian, men whose names have drawn down upon them the execration of every succeeding age ; no security for life or property; no justice; no mercy; but crimes heaped on crimes till, at the very mention of them, the blood runs cold, and we wonder how the earth could longer bear the burden of its misery.

Into this sweltering mass of dissoluteness and lawlessness and vice the Church of Christ had just been sent, like a lamb into the midst of wolves. It is difficult for us to realise the thought as it must have presented itself to St. John. He had been accustomed to think of the kingdom of God as protected within the Jewish fold. Where was that fold now? Its walls were broken down ; its hireling shepherds had failed to fulfil their commission and were fled; the timorous sheep were gathering into corners, or were looking round with startled gaze to see from what quarter the next blow would come. Nor was it long of coming. The followers of Christ were everywhere the objects of the world's scorn. Persecution in all its forms of cruelty raged against them. They were imprisoned, tortured, burned, thrown to the lions in the amphitheatre, treated as if they were abandoned criminals whom no eye should pity and no hand should spare. They that killed them imagined that in doing so they were offering service to God.[1]

Even nature appeared to feel for and to sympathise with the woes of man. The latter half of the first century was marked by an unusual amount of her more terrible phenomena.[2] Earthquakes were numerous and destructive. Asia Minor in particular, the seat of the seven churches, was to such an extent a centre of their action that before the end of the century several of her cities had been overthrown. Famines followed the convulsions of nature, and plagues followed famine. The darkest language of ancient prophecy was hardly too strong to express the terrors with which the earth was visited. And amidst them all St. John was himself a sufferer, an exile " for the word of God and the testimony of Jesus,"[3] torn from his flock, perhaps never to return to it.

In these circumstances what was more natural than that, with his mind penetrated, filled, saturated, with the thought of his Master's life, and with the teaching

[1] John xvi. 2.

[2] Comp. Renan, *L'Ant.*, p. 325, and article "Apokalypse" in

Schenkel's *Bibel Lexikon*, i. p. 161.

[3] Chap. i. 9.

in which our Lord had so closely identified His people with Himself, that life should rise before him with renewed vividness and power, and that he should behold it repeated in the fortunes of His Church? Now we know from the fourth Gospel how St. John thought of the life of Jesus. It was the life of One who, though " the only begotten of the Father, full of grace and truth," had been regarded as an alien by the very persons whom He came to save. "He was in the world, and the world was made by Him, and the world knew Him not : " " He came unto His own home, and they that were His own received Him not."[1] What sadness and sorrow had encompassed Him! What a struggle had that been in which love and tenderness and self-sacrifice were repaid with hatred and cruelty and death! Yet there had been glory too. Ever and again Christ had manifested His glory.[2] He had permitted it to shine through the "flesh" which for the most part veiled it.[3] It had appeared in the confounding of His enemies, in the increasing attachment of His friends, in the wonderful discourses of the upper room at Jerusalem, in the high-priestly prayer, in the rising from the grave.

All this, then, St. John felt was repeated in the history of the Church. Once again, as before, to his eyes, "the light shineth in the darkness, and the darkness overcame it not."[4] That is the thought of the Apocalypse.

It is a vision of the Church as, encompassed by trials

---

[1] John i. 10, 11.

[2] John ii. 11.

[3] John i. 14.

[4] John i. 5.

similar to those of her Redeemer, she passes on under the same protecting care of a Father in heaven to a similar reward.   To the eye of sense all may seem dark and hopeless.   But the eye of faith beholds " the Revelation of Jesus Christ," and the eternal principles of God's government working beneath apparent defeat, and coming more and more to victory.   The Seer in his Divine inspiration penetrates the darkness.   The clouds roll away ; and, as the glorious prospect spreads before him, he can only lift up his heart and proclaim, in the visions of this book, his message of encouragement and hope.

The Apocalypse is, accordingly, the revelation, in the case of the members of Christ's body, of the three great ideas which St. John had already beheld exemplified in the history of Christ Himself,—those of conflict, preservation, and triumph.   These ideas he does not describe : he *sees* them ; and he tells us what he saw.

Let us look at them a little more particularly.

1. In the first place, there is the idea of conflict.   It could not be otherwise.   From its very nature darkness must be opposed to light, error to truth, sin to holiness, Satan to Christ.   These opposites can never be at peace with one another, and the dearest bonds of earth must be broken for the sake of the issues of the struggle between them.[1]   The Apocalypse, therefore, is full of the thought of war and suffering for the children of God.   We misunderstand it if we think only of its pictures of judgment on the wicked.   It contains a

---

[1] Comp. Matt. x. 35.

thought prior, deeper, more intimately bound up with its whole structure, than even the punishment of sin ; and that thought is the cross, which every follower of Christ must bear when he listens to the words "Follow thou Me."[1] It is the idealised expression of what the Christian feels more and more powerfully in proportion as he enters more fully into the spirit of his Master,— that the world, constituted as it is, whatever it may be to others, must be to him, not a place of rest and peace, but of struggle, of suffering, of discipline, of longing for a better. This stamp is impressed upon all its visions. Those to whom it is written are partakers with the writer " in the tribulation and kingdom and patience which are in Jesus."[2] The characteristics of the glorious Person described in the first vision, which are obviously enumerated with a view to the necessities of His people, tell us of victory not yet gained, and of enemies who are yet to be overwhelmed. In each of the Epistles to the seven churches the promises are made to him that "overcometh."[3] Upon the two faithful witnesses the beast makes war, and they are killed.[4] The first great enemy of the Church is over-come by those "who loved not their lives unto the death."[5] The second "makes war with the saints," who are comforted with the assurance that " if any man leadeth into captivity, into captivity he goeth; if any man shall kill with the sword, with the sword must he be killed."[6] The third is able to secure that " as many

---

[1] John xxi. 22.
[2] Chap. i. 9.
[3] Chaps. ii. iii.
[4] Chap. xi. 7.
[5] Chap. xii. 11.
[6] Chap. xiii. 7, 10.

as should not worship the image of the beast should be killed." [1] We read of "the war of the great day of God, the Almighty," [2] of the battle of Har-Magedon, [3] and of the "armies which are in heaven" following Him who is "arrayed in a garment sprinkled with blood," the blood of His enemies, and "out of whose mouth proceedeth a sharp sword, that with it He should smite the nations." [4] Before they are finally destroyed "the beast, and the kings of the earth, and their armies, gather together to make war against Him that sat upon the horse, and against His army;" [5] while the very last vision, before the great white throne is set for judgment, tells us of the gathering together of the nations to the war, "the number of whom is as the sand of the sea." [6] Throughout the whole book in short we deal with conflict, with armies, with battles, with the bow and the sword and the war-horse and blood, with a mighty struggle between good and evil, between light and darkness, between righteousness and unrighteousness, between Christ and the devil, between the Church of God and the synagogue of Satan.

This is not all. It appears to be the idea of St. John that, in the case of every true follower of Christ, conflict leads to martyrdom. Inattention to this fact on the part of commentators has greatly marred the interpretation of the Apocalypse. That book does not speak of a select company of martyrs to be distinguished from the whole number of Christ's faithful people. It

[1] Chap. xiii. 15.
[2] Chap. xvi. 14.
[3] Chap. xvi. 16.
[4] Chap. xix. 13-16.
[5] Chap. xix. 19.
[6] Chap. xx. 8.

draws no distinction between ordinary believers and those to whom in our use of language the term " martyr " is more properly applied.[1] The Seer of course knew well that many followers of Christ had fallen asleep, that many would still fall asleep, in their own beds, tended by family and friends in their departing hour. But it is another instance of his singular idealism that all such knowledge gives way to the deeper thought, that the essence of Christian life, and the true manner of Christian death, is martyrdom.   It had been so under the Old Testament Dispensation. The souls under the altar, described at the loosing of the fifth seal as " slain,"[2] cannot be a select number of these saints ; they must be all of them ; and if, to the eye of St. John, they all were martyrs, much more may we expect the same style of language to be applied to the saints of the New Testament. This, therefore, appears to be the case. " The great tribulation " mentioned in chap. vii. 14 is no special tribulation at the close of the world's history. It is that of Matt. xxiv. 21, and it refers to the trials experienced by the saints of God throughout the whole period of their pilgrimage, at one time greater than

---

[1] Comp. Keble, *Christian Year, St. Stephen's Day.*

> " So on the King of Martyrs wait,
> Three chosen bands in royal state,
> And *all earth owns of good and great*
> Are *gathered in that choir*."

Keble quotes Wheatly on the " Common Prayer : "—" As there are three kinds of martyrdom, the first both in will and deed, which is the highest ; the second in will but not in deed ; the third in deed but not in will ; so the Church commemorates these martyrs in the same order : St. Stephen first, who suffered death both in will and deed ; St. John the evangelist next, who suffered in will but not in deed ; the Holy Innocents last, who suffered in deed but not in will."

[2] Chap. vi. 9-11.

at another, but always great. It is also universal, including both Jewish and Gentile Christians; while the peculiar expression "they that come" (not "came") leads us to think of the appellation, "He that cometh," applied elsewhere to our Lord, and of that identification of believers with Him which is so characteristic of the writings of St. John.[1] As, in one of its aspects, the fourth Gospel may be called the history of the martyrdom of Jesus, so, in one of its aspects, the Apocalypse may in like manner be called the history of the martyrdom of the members of His body. Christ Himself submitted to the inevitable law, "Except a corn of wheat fall into the earth and die, it abideth by itself alone; but if it die, it beareth much fruit." [2] How can His people escape submission to the same law? St. John knew no Christianity that does not, in one way or another, conduct the believer through tears and blood, through suffering and the cross, to the heavenly reward. It is a part of the teaching that came from his inmost soul that an easy prosperous Christian upon whom the world smiles, and who returns its smiles, is no real follower of Christ.[3]

2. In the second place, this idea of the conflict is accompanied by that of the preservation of Christ's people. Whatever may be their trials they are pro-

---

[1] Comp. *Comm. in loc.*

[2] John xii. 24.

[3] Fairbairn sees clearly to what an absurd length it would lead us were we to think only of actual martyrs in the passage above referred to. He gets over the difficulty by arguing that the description is to be understood of the martyrs "symbolically, as representative of the cause and kingdom of Christ" (*On Prophecy*, p. 461). This is virtually conceding the view contended for in the text.

tected by Him who walks in the midst of the seven golden candlesticks ; and, even if at times apparently defeated or martyred, their defeat is instantly turned to victory. While the judgments of the Seals rage around them they are "the oil and the wine" which the rider upon the black horse of famine is not permitted to hurt.[1] Before the judgments of the Trumpets rush upon the world they are stamped with the seal of the living God, so that the mystic number of 144,000 is complete—not one is lost.[2] The locusts of the fifth Trumpet are permitted to touch none that have the seal of God on their foreheads.[3] All who worship in the sanctuary are measured.[4] The 144,000 appear a second time standing with the Lamb upon Mount Zion, as complete in number as before ;[5] the "book of life" obviously contains a definite number of names ; and, when we come to the reign of the thousand years, the glory of that reign is bestowed upon all such as "worshipped not the beast, neither his image, and received not the mark upon their forehead and upon their hand."[6] The redeemed, even when their blood is shed, are never permitted to forget that, though crushed beneath the world's power, it is only for a time.

On the other hand, as if to bring out into still greater relief this preservation of the saints, there is for the enemies of the Redeemer nothing but judgment. It has indeed been often thought that this is not the

---

[1] Chap. vi. 6.

[2] Chap. vii. 2, 3.

[3] Chap. ix. 4.

[4] Chap. xi. 1.

[5] Chap. xiv. 1.

[6] Chap. xx. 4.

case, but that the Apocalypse anticipates the conversion of the world, and that its revelations of God's dealings with mankind are of a mixed character, presenting at one time His judgments upon the impenitent, at another His offers of mercy made to them, and the invitations addressed to them in the Gospel of His Grace. This view cannot be sustained. The Apocalypse says nothing of conversion. Its point of view is different from that which would lead to conversion being thought of. It contemplates men as persons whose lot has already been decided, who are already ranged either with Christ or with His enemies. Its business is to reveal the true character and to foreshadow the certain fate of the two opposing ranks. By deliberately adopting the spirit of the devil, the ungodly have confessed the devil to be their father. In the very nature of the case, therefore, they must perish. They may not be saved against their will.[1]

Special passages confirm what has been said. It is only by mistaken interpretation that the prayers of chap. viii. 4 are regarded as prayers for the conversion rather than for the destruction of the world;[2] that other passages are supposed to speak of an extended proclamation of God's grace; and that the prospect set before us for the present dispensation is considered one of advancing progress towards a joyful time when the kingdoms of the world, by acceptance of the Gospel,

---

[1] It is allowed by Godet (*Biblical Studies*, p. 312) that the Apocalypse does not recognise any conversion of the pagan world. But in chap. xi. 13 he sees the conversion of the Jews (p. 314).

[2] *Comm. in loc.*

shall become the kingdoms of our Lord and of His Christ.[1] The prayers thus alluded to are no prayers for mercy to the world. They are prayers that God will vindicate His own cause by avenging His people's blood upon their persecutors. The message proclaimed to a guilty world is everywhere one of judgment, not of salvation. Even when Christ is seen with a rainbow round His head, the meaning, so far as the ungodly are concerned, is only that the judgments inflicted upon them by the Lord shall be felt all the more terribly, because committed against One who would so fain have given them peace ; and, when the universal reign of Messiah is established, it is not by the submission of the world to His cross, but by the overthrow which, as King of kings and Lord of lords, as " a man of war," He brings upon it. Nothing, in fact, is more strikingly characteristic of the Apocalypse than the manner in which the two great divisions of mankind are from the very first viewed as separate and complete. There is no passing from the one to the other. There is only, here a rising to ever higher victory, there a sinking into ever heavier woe. In no vision of the book is either the extension or the diminution of the number of Christ's chosen people so much as hinted at. There is indeed, as we proceed through the visions, that climax which has been already noticed, because mercy has been despised and sin has grown more ripe for its merited doom. But during all the time embraced by them, a time covering the whole history of the militant

[1] Fairbairn *On Prophecy*, p. 408.

and struggling Church, the field upon which the scourges of God are inflicted neither widens nor contracts its boundaries. There is no change of darkness into light, or of light into darkness. There is brightening light; there is deepening darkness; but the two lines are always distinct, antithetical, opposed.[1] The preservation of the saints amidst all their troubles is secure.

3. The idea of preservation is followed by that of the final triumph and the perfected happiness of Christ's people. Destruction overtakes all by whom they have been persecuted. On them are visited plague after plague, each more terrible than its percursor, and all of them together bringing with them such an intolerable weight of woe that the guilty desire to die, though death flees from them. Babylon drinks of the cup of the wine of the fierceness of God's wrath. The beast is taken, and with him the false prophet that wrought signs in his sight, and both are cast into the lake of fire. The flesh of kings, and of captains, and of mighty men, and of horses, and of them that sat on them, and the flesh of all men, both free and bond, and small and great (who had been upon their side),[2] is made a supper for the devouring birds. The devil that deceived the nations is cast into the lake that burneth with fire and brimstone; and death and Hades, together with all whose names were not found in the book of life, share a similar

---

[1] This singular line of thought is not less characteristic of the fourth Gospel than of the Apocalypse (see Appendix II.). The same thing may be observed in the First Epistle of St. John, in which every one belongs either to Christ or Antichrist.

[2] It should hardly be necessary to say that this is implied in the statement.

fate.[1] Nothing is wanting to their overthrow. On the other hand the saints are rewarded with all that may compensate for their past wrongs and sufferings. They are made priests in the heavenly sanctuary. They obtain royal dignity and glory. They are set down upon the same throne with their exalted Lord. As yet, indeed, they lead the hidden life, but that life is in reality a life of glory like their Lord's. They are already essentially possessors of His glory, and they wait only for the time when no eyes shall rest upon them that regard that glory as their shame. Therefore may they be said even now to shine as the sun in the kingdom of their Father; and, amidst the splendours of the new Jerusalem, having followed the Lamb whithersoever He goeth, they hunger no more, neither thirst any more; neither does the sun strike upon them, nor any heat: for the Lamb which is in the midst of the throne is their Shepherd, and He guides them unto fountains of waters of life: and God wipes away every tear from their eyes. Wrong is for ever ideally redressed : right is established in her sole and eternal triumph.

More particularly, this triumph of the righteous is connected with that *manifestation* of the glorified Lord to which we commonly apply the term His " Second Coming." The expression indeed is hardly Biblical. What we read of in the New Testament is rather the " Coming," the " Manifestation," the " Revelation " of the Lord, His "Parousia" or "Presence," His "Epiphany," and the " Epiphany of His presence."[2] Such expres-

<hr>

[1] Chap. xx. 15.   [2] Comp. Züllig, i. 23.

sions point rather to a *revelation* of One who is come; who is with us, though unseen; who has said, " Lo, I am with you alway, even unto the consummation of the age; " and who needs only to make manifest the glory with which He is even now clothed within the veil.

However this may be, there can be no doubt that the Apocalypse, in speaking of the final triumph of the righteous, connects it with the coming of the Lord, and that in doing so its design corresponds most closely with that of the general teaching of the New Testament. There this coming is continually referred to for instruction and encouragement and warning and comfort; and there is not a single passage that justifies our substituting for the thought of it the thought of our own death. With it then the Apocalypse, from its beginning to its end, is occupied. Twenty times, it is said, does St. John speak of it throughout his book; and on many of these occasions with a force and vividness peculiarly his own. It is hardly necessary to say that there is nothing sensuous in the idea. The manifestation of Christ in glory is rather the appropriate and necessary complement of His appearance in the weakness of mortal flesh. We have no more right to resolve it into a mere progress of Christianity than modern Judaism, rejecting the Christ of history, has to resolve its yet unfulfilled hope of a Messiah into the thought of the general ad-. vancement of the race. The departure of the King, after having given to His servants their various talents, is naturally followed by His return to see how they have used them. The Christian elevation of humanity is not completed in the cross ; and, if the agency of the Spirit alone is sufficient to perfect us, it will not be easy to show that the same agency might not have been enough to start us upon the path of progress.

In the manifestation, in the Epiphany of the Presence, of Christ, accordingly, the Apocalypse sees the completion of all God's plans of mercy for His people. Their Lord will then " be manifested " in the glory that belongs to Him, and they also " shall be manifested with Him in glory." " If He goes and prepares a place for them, He comes again, and will receive them unto Himself; that where He is, there they may be also." [1]

The Apocalypse has been described in these lectures as a book which presents in a highly poetic and symbolic form the general principles that mark the Church's history in the world. But this remark has to be qualified by one most important consideration. We must distinguish in the book before us between the whole Church as an organised body and the faithful remnant within the body, the Church within the Church, the " elect " within the " called." The Church as a whole degenerates. She repeats the experience of the old Theocracy, becomes false to the trust reposed in her, yields to the influences of the world, and eventually falls beneath judgments as much greater than those which overtook Israel after the flesh as the position she had occupied was higher, and the privileges she had enjoyed more exalted.

----

[1] Col. iii. 4 ; John xiv. 3.

Let us look at the facts of the case as they are presented to us by the sacred writer.

In doing so, we turn naturally in the first place to the Epistles to the seven churches in chaps. ii. and iii. All the elements of the future history of the Church are found in one part or another of these two chapters. If the world is ever to prevail within the Church, we may be sure that we shall find traces of such a state of matters there.

Now it seems undeniable that we do so. When we consider the manner in which the Seven Epistles describe the Church in her relation to the world, there is a marked distinction between the first three and the last four. In the former the Church stands over against the world, listening to the voice of a present Lord as He speaks by His faithful apostles, meeting the severest trials without shrinking, and holding fast her Lord's name and faith at a time when persecution rages even unto death. It is true that she is not perfect. Perfection is not reached here below. There are symptoms of decay in the leaving of her first love, and in the existence in her midst of positive sin. Yet, taken as a whole, she is true to her position and to the demands of her great Head. She can remember from whence she is fallen, can repent, and do the first works (chap. ii. 5); and, if transgressors of the Divine precepts of purity are among her members, they are not many in number, they are only "some" (chap. ii. 14). When we pass to the second group of Epistles a striking difference is at once perceptible. With the exception of Philadelphia, the churches in the three other cities named have yielded to the influences of the world, and those who remain loyal to Christ are but the smaller portion of their members. Thyatira is thus addressed, " But to you I say, to (not as in the Authorised Version ' and to ') the rest that are in Thyatira, as many as have not this teaching, which know not the deep things of Satan, as they say; I cast upon you none other burden. Howbeit that which ye have, hold fast till I come " (chap. ii. 24, 25). It is simply " the rest," the remnant, that have here maintained their faith. The bulk of the Church tolerate those who seduce Christ's servants to commit fornication and to eat things sacrificed to idols; nay, even when time has been given them to repent, they will not repent of their fornication (verses 20, 21). In Sardis a similar state of things is still more marked, " Thou hast *a few names* in Sardis which did not defile their garments : and they shall walk with me in white; for they are worthy " (chap. iii. 4). Philadelphia, as we have stated, does not appear to be blamed, although even here it is not certain that there is not at least a gentle intimation that there had been failure, when it is said, " Thou hast a *little* power," and, again, " hold fast that which thou hast," *i.e.* thy little power (verses 8, 11). But there can be no doubt as to the condition of Laodicea. There the victory of the world is almost complete ; not indeed wholly so, for she is still able to receive warnings, and " any man " within her who will listen to the Judge standing at the door has addressed to him the most glorious promise made to any of the churches. Notwithstanding this the temptations of worldly wealth (verse 17) have proved in her case irresistible, and the last picture of the Church is the saddest of all.

To these considerations let us further add the fact that the churches thus yielding to the world are four in number—four being the number of the world,—and it will be impossible to resist the conclusion that the Lord of the Church sees that, in the course of her history, the Church will not be always faithful to Himself. There will come a time when, as a whole, she will be more carnal than spiritual, more worldly than heavenly. The true members of Christ's flock will be fewer in number than the false. Even within the Church the remnant only is expected to overcome. The world will penetrate into the very sanctuary of God, and will not be rooted out until the Judge of all takes to Himself His great power and reigns.

From the Epistles to the seven churches we proceed to another passage which seems to contain a similar lesson. At the beginning of chap. xi. we read, " And there was given me a reed like unto a rod : and one said, Rise, and measure the temple of God, and the altar, and them that worship therein. And the court which is without the temple cast out, and measure it not ; for it hath been given unto the nations : and the holy city shall they tread under foot forty and two months." In these words a distinction is drawn between the " temple," that is, not the whole building, but the *naos*, the innermost sanctuary, the Holy of Holies, and the outer court. Yet both of them were not only within the sacred precincts ; they were parts into which Israelites alone might enter, and which no Gentile foot might tread without profanation. They cannot, therefore, here represent Israel, the Church of Christ, upon the one hand, and the world upon the other. They can only represent two portions of the Church of Christ, the one that portion which is always true to Him, and in which the light of His presence dwells ; the other that portion which has fallen from truth and purity. The one of these is measured for preservation; the other is to be cast out. The one continues to be the object of the Redeemer's constant care and love ; the other becomes the object of His righteous indignation.

This conclusion is confirmed by the remarkable use of the word, "cast it out" (ἔκβαλε, not "leave it out," as in the Authorised Version). The use of the word is altogether novel in such circumstances as these. No one would dream of saying to another "cast out" a certain large space of ground with all the buildings on it from thy measurement, if all he meant was that these things were not to be measured. He would certainly say, as our translators of A.D. 1611, true to the instinct of the English tongue, make the Seer say, " Leave them out." But another thought is in the mind of the speaker here, He is thinking of excommunication from the synagogue (compare John ix. 34, καὶ ἐξέβαλον αὐτὸν), as when it is said of the blind man whom Jesus restored to sight, " they cast him out." This, however, distinctly implies that the persons thus cast out once belonged to the community of Israel, and that they must represent a portion, which can only be a degenerate and faithless portion, of the 'Church. Not less clearly then than in the Epistles of chaps. ii. and iii. does it appear in the vision of the measuring that the world penetrates the Church, and that within the same outward framework there is the true salt destined for everlasting preservation, and the salt which has lost its savour, and is destined to be trodden under foot of men.

A third passage, the most interesting of all, must still be noticed in its bearing upon this point. It is the history of what in the Apocalypse is called Babylon. For Babylon is no pagan city of the past, no world metropolis of the future. It is only another name for an apostate Church that has forsaken her Betrothed, and broken her covenant relation to Him.

In this picture of Babylon one supreme aim of the Revelation of St. John is reached. To the interpretation of this picture the efforts of every student of the book ought to be chiefly directed. Until we understand it all our labours in other directions will prove vain. There is no scene in the Bible of more dark and terrible sublimity; and none upon which colouring of more inimitable power has been employed. At one moment we behold the city in her brightness, her gaiety, her rich and varied life. We hear the voice of her harpers and minstrels and flute-players and trumpeters. Her crafts-men are busy at their work. Her merchants are the princes of the earth. Her lamps glitter in the darkness ; and the cheering voice of the millstone, together with the joyful voice of the bridegroom and the bride, falls upon our ear.   The next moment the proud city is cast down, " as it were a great millstone," into the sea, and the successive companies of chap. xviii. come forth with their pathetic lamentations, crying, " Woe, woe, the great city, for in one hour is she made desolate."[1]

What is the meaning of all this? What does Babylon represent ? Only one answer can be given to this question. "The great city" is the emblem of the degenerate Church. As in chap. xii. we have, under the guise of a woman, that true Church of Christ which is the embodiment of all good; as the same picture is repeated in chap. xxi. in which we meet " the bride, the wife of the Lamb," so in Babylon we have, under the guise of a harlot, that false church which has sold her Lord for the sake of the honours, the riches, and the pleasures of this earth. Babylon is a second aspect of the Church. Just as there were two aspects of Jerusalem in the days of Christ, under the one of which that city was the centre of attraction both to God and Israel, under the other the metropolis of a degenerate Judaism, so there are two aspects of the Church of Christ, under the first of which we think of those who within her are faithful to the Lord, under the second of which we think mainly of the great body of merely nominal Christians who in words confess, but in deeds deny, Him. The Church in this latter aspect is before us under the term "Babylon;" and it would appear to be the teaching of

---

[1] Burns, with his keen poetic instinct, recognised the power of this passage. It is one of the Scripture passages referred to as read at the family worship in the "Cottar's Saturday Night," "And heard great Babylon's doom pronounced by heaven's command.",

St. John, as it is certainly that of both Jewish and Christian history, that the longer the Church lasts as a great outward institution in the world, the more does she naturally tend to realise this picture. As her first love fails she abandons the spirit for the letter, makes forms of one kind or another a substitute for love, fixes her affections upon the things of time, as if her portion were to be found in them, allies herself with the world, and by adapting herself to it secures the ease and the wealth which the world will never bestow so heartily upon anything as upon a Church in which the Divine oracles are dumb.

One point of this interpretation requires to be carefully guarded. There are many who will readily accept it if it be allowed that by the degenerate Church now spoken of is meant the Church of Rome. But Babylon is not the Church of Rome in particular. Deeply no doubt that Church has sinned. Not a few of the darkest traits of "Babylon" apply to her with a closeness of application which may not unnaturally lead us to think that the picture of these chapters has been drawn from nothing so much as her. Her idolatries, her outward carnal splendour, her oppression of God's saints, her merciless cruelties with torture, the dungeon, and the stake, the tears and agonies and blood with which she has filled so many centuries,—these and a thousand circumstances of a similar kind may well be our excuse if in "Babylon" we read Christian Rome. Yet the interpretation is false. The harlot is *wholly* what she seems. Christian Rome has never been wholly what on one side of her character she was so largely. She has maintained the truth of Christ against idolatry and unchristian error, she has preferred poverty to splendour in a way that Protestantism has never done, she has nurtured the noblest types of devotion that the world has seen, and she has thrilled the waves of time as they passed over her with one constant litany of supplication and chant of praise. Above all, it has not been the chief effort of Rome to ally herself with kings. If at times she has done so, there have been other times still more characteristic of her, when she has rather trampled kings beneath her feet; and when, in the interests of the poor and the oppressed, she has taught both proud barons and imperial tyrants to quail before her. For deeds like these her record is not with the beast, but with the Lamb. Babylon cannot be Christian Rome ; and nothing has been more injurious to the Protestant churches than the impression that the two were identical, and that by withdrawing from communion with the Pope they wholly freed themselves from alliance with the spiritual harlot. Babylon embraces much more than Rome, and illustrations of what she is lie nearer our own door. Wherever professedly Christian men have thought the world's favour better than its reproach ; wherever they have esteemed its honours a more desirable possession than its shame ; wherever they have courted ease rather than welcomed suffering, have loved self-indulgence rather than self-sacrifice, and have substituted covetousness in grasping for generosity in distributing what they had,— there the spirit of Babylon has been manifested. In snort, we have in the great harlot-city neither the Christian Church as a whole, nor the Romish Church in particular, but all who anywhere within the Church profess to be Christ's "little flock" and are not,—denying in their lives the main characteristic by which they ought to be distinguished,—that they "follow" Christ.[1]

The considerations now adduced lead us to the thought of one great part of the Design of the Apocalypse which is too frequently lost sight of. That book is written not simply to describe the conflict, the preservation, and the triumph of Christ's true people, but

---

[1] In Note xi., p. 509, to his work on *The One Mediator*, Canon Medd gives a valuable contribution to the proof that "the 'great city,' the 'Babylon' of the Apocalypse, is Jerusalem." The argument is most forcible and conclusive, but is weakened, as appears to the author of this volume, by one fault. According to it Babylon is "none other than the old, the earthly, the apostate, the doomed Jerusalem of A.D. 30 to 70." The argument of this lecture is not indeed thus invalidated, for the old Jerusalem undoubtedly lies at the bottom of the description given of Babylon. But Babylon is not primarily that city itself. There are features in the picture drawn from those of the old Jerusalem, but the portrait is not her portrait. It is that of *her Gentile successor*, of the Church when she has become in the midst of the Gentiles what old Jerusalem was in the midst of the Jews. This is a common manner of the prophets, particularly in the Psalms. The Psalmist contemplates David's victories (Ps. ii.) or Solomon's marriage (Ps. xlv.) or peaceful reign (Ps. lxxii.). He has these in the foreground, though it is not them that he describes. His heart is bursting with a goodlier matter. He sings of a greater king, a holier bride, a better sovereign. So St. John took some features of his description of Babylon from Rome, some from Tyre, some from the literal Babylon, some from Jerusalem, but his picture is not of the last-named city *literally*, but of the Gentile Church become, in the mass both of her rulers and members, a Babylon, not a Zion.

to warn against the coming degeneracy of His professing Church. If in no book of Scripture do we find so
striking a view of the glory of the Church both here and
hereafter, there is also none that sets before us so
melancholy a picture of the degree to which, in the course
of her history, the world is to prevail in her. Yet, after
all, the lesson is not different from that taught us by
our Lord when, comparing Himself to the true vine, He
adds, "Every branch in Me that beareth not fruit, he
taketh it away. If a man abide not in Me, he is cast
forth as a branch, and is withered; and they gather
them, and cast them into the fire, and they are burned."[1]
There are two sets of branches in the "true vine." If
we think of it only as it bears the one, it shall be
gathered unto life eternal; if, as it bears the other, it is
destined to be burned. The two sets of branches must
be separated from one another, and the one only can
be the "Bride" prepared for marriage to the heavenly
Bridegroom.

The truth is that, in this whole delineation of Babylon,
we have a fresh illustration of what has been spoken of
as the principle lying at the foundation of the structure
of the Apocalypse. That principle is that St. John
beholds the history of the future mirrored in the events
of the life of Christ with which he had been himself
familiar. Nothing, as we see in his Gospel, had struck
him more than that a Divine theocracy intended to
prepare for the First Coming of the Lord had degenerated
into a carnal and worldly institution, *out of which* Christ

---

[1] John xv. 2, 6.

was to be the door.[1]   He turns to the Church of Christ, intended to prepare the way for the second manifestation of the Lord, and he beholds the same scenes re-enacted.   The world again enters into the Church.   Its riches and honours and ease are again welcomed instead of persecution and the cross.   The Church ceases to prepare for the future.   She lives for the present; she is satisfied with the world as it is, especially when viewed in the light of her efforts to amend it.   She consoles herself with the thought, " I sit a queen, and am no widow."[2]   The voice which says, " Yea, I come quickly," loses its attractive power, or is resolved into a shadowy amelioration of society.   The Pharisee, the Sadducee, the Herodian, the Priest, the Scribe, sweep by upon her stage, all of them citizens of the Holy City, members of the new Divine theocracy.   The hearts that sigh and cry for a pure and spiritual righteousness are few in number, and are not heard amidst the disputations of the Sanhedrin or the clash of instruments in the Temple.   What can happen but that the Lord of the poor and lowly and meek shall at length say, " Come forth, my people, out of her, that ye have no fellowship with her sins, and that ye receive not of her plagues " ?[3]

Such then are the Design and Scope of the Apocalypse.   It contains no continuous history of the Church from the beginning to the end of her historical course.   It is not a mere revelation of events that are immediately to precede the Second Coming of our Lord. It is no mere prophecy of the early doom of those

[1] See *Comm.* on John ix. 35 ; x. 3, 4.   [2] Rev. xviii. 7.   [3] Rev. xviii. 4.

enemies of Christian truth whom the Seer beheld around himself. The book is not predictive. It contains no prediction that is not found in the prophecies of Christ. It gives us no knowledge of the future that is not given first by our Lord, and then by others of His inspired Apostles. It is simply the highly idealised expression of the position and fortunes of that "little flock" which, against the world and against the Church in the ordinary sense of that word, listens to the Good Shepherd's voice and follows Him. It is the utterance of one idea, but that the greatest of all ideas, "to assert eternal providence, and justify the ways of God to men." [1]

Perhaps it may seem at first sight to many that to look at the book as we have done is in a great measure to destroy its value. They may miss its application to the special events, whether of the past, the present, or the future. They may even urge that to find in it no predictions except those which are contained in the words of Christ is to reduce it to a monotonous repetition of what we already know. Yet surely to think that the truths of the Apocalypse are monotonous, because they are not absolutely new, is to think that the waves of the sea must be monotonous because they have swelled up from the bosom of the same ocean under the force of every gale that has swept across its surface from the beginning until now. The waves of the sea are never monotonous;—nor the judgments of God. These are

---

[1] Isaac Williams well says of it, "It is an embodiment not so much of historic incidents as of divine philosophy ; descriptive of good and evil in their influences and progressive results" (*The Apocalypse*, p. 401).

always new to the generation upon which they fall; and the proclamation of them is always new, both to those who have seemed to sin without suffering, and to those who have been the martyrs of truth and goodness without any Divine intervention to avenge their cause.

But this is not all. A little reflection may show us that, viewed as we have viewed it, the Apocalypse presents itself in a far worthier and nobler aspect than if it had told us of the revolutions of earthly empires, of the fall of earthly kingdoms, of the changes of political parties, of wars and famines and pestilences, of earthquakes and cities overwhelmed by them. It will be time enough to know such things when they come. What the Church needs is to learn the true nature of her position in the world, to be directed to her true strength, and to fix her eyes more intently upon her true hope ; and these purposes the plain interpretation of the Apocalypse here contended for is best fitted to serve.

1. It teaches the Church that her true position in this world is that of her Lord, of Him who said, " Man, who made Me a judge or a divider over you ? " [1] and who lived among men only to labour, to suffer, and to die for them. The Apocalypse has been thought to foment spiritual pride. There is no book of Scripture which, rightly interpreted, is more full of the lessons of humility, self-denial, and self-sacrifice. It identifies, in a thousand ways and to the most remarkable degree, the fortunes and the work of Christ's Church on earth with

---

[1] Luke xii. 14.

those of Christ Himself. It makes that Church-life, the very name of which so many fear, a service. It makes the universal Christian priesthood a body whose commission in the world is to forget itself for the world's good. The ideas of the Church and of the priesthood are among the fundamental conceptions of the book; and it is because they are so that it teaches us, as no other book of the New Testament does, the wisdom, the power, and the glory of the Cross.

2. It directs the Church to her true source of strength. It has always done so. We should be wrong in thinking that the Church has in past times been strengthened by the Apocalypse as she has been, because she beheld in it predictions applicable to her own days. The general tone and spirit of the book, even when the details were not thoroughly comprehended, have been her strength. As it has pointed out to Christians the glory of their risen and exalted Head, shown them His constant and watchful care over His Church, exhibited to them the true nature of the conflict in which they were engaged, and described for them their final triumph, their souls have been stirred, as by the sound of a trumpet, to feel more powerfully than ever how noble was their calling, and how worthy a thing it was to hold fast "their boldness, and the glorying of their hope, firm unto the end."[1]

More especially in times of trouble, amidst surrounding darkness, when every refuge seemed to fail, and when faith threatened to sink in stormy waters, this book, apart from all predictions supposed to be contained

---

[1] Heb. iii. 6.

in it, has been often like the hand of the Saviour to the apostle Peter in his hour of need. It has lightened the Christian's gloom. It has presented to him, when perplexed by the many apparent anomalies of God's dealings with His children, a magnificent panorama of the Divine purposes. It has sent forth a cheering voice, nerving him to patient action and persevering steadfastness. It has helped to sustain him when in the prison or at the stake for Christ's cause. It has supplied texts which, age after age, as in the Greyfriars churchyard in Edinburgh, tell us from the martyrs' tomb that these victims of bloody persecution died in hope and rest in peace. If it is sometimes less than this to us, it may be because, in easier days, we have so little experience of outward trials, because we are less acquainted than we ought to be with the outward as well as the inward cross. But let troubles come again; let us realise more fully than we do what it is to follow in the footsteps of One whose whole life on earth was the bearing of a cross; let the soul, let the Church, be in her Patmos "for the word of God and the testimony of Jesus Christ," and then will the Apocalypse be once more as precious to us as it was to the beloved disciple whose lonely rock of the Ægean was lightened, as he beheld it, with the glory of the New Jerusalem.

3. It calls the Church to fix her eyes more intently upon her true hope. For what is that hope? Is it not the hope of the revelation of her Lord in the glory that belongs to Him? No hope springs so eternal in the Christian breast. It was that of the early Church, as

she believed that He whom she had loved while He was on earth would return to perfect the happiness of His redeemed.   It ought not less to be our hope now. "Watching for it, waiting for it, being patient unto it, groaning without it, looking for it, hasting unto it, loving it—these are the phrases which Scripture uses concerning the day of God."[1]   And surely it may well use them; for what in comparison with the prospect of such a day is every other anticipation of the future? Shall the fondest expectations of our hearts be then really fulfilled?   Little as the faith of Christ has yet prevailed among men, shall a bright day dawn for it, and the period of its full triumph come?   Shall sin be yet completely rooted out of our own hearts, and be yet completely banished from the world?   And shall that earth, which even now retains so many traces of its primeval beauty, put on in expectation of its Lord "as a maid her jewels and as a bride her attire"?   Above all, are we in ignorance of the time when this blessed change shall happen?   May it be in a century, in a year, while we ourselves yet live?   At all events shall the delay, whatever it be, when looked at in the light of eternity, be brief?   Then we may well ask whether the communication of such a prospect, and the stirring us up to dwell on it, do not make the Apocalypse infinitely more precious than if it contained those manifold details of the future progress of this earth which, if known, would be far more likely to overwhelm us with sadness than to elevate us with hope.

[1] *His Appearing and Kingdom*, p. 19.

LECTURE VI.

A FITTING close to these Lectures might have been found
in giving, had it been possible, a short summary of the
teaching of the Apocalypse in its successive paragraphs.
General principles and views have engaged so much of
our attention, that even those who have listened to all
that has been said may complain that the meaning of
any particular passage is still dark to them. A running
commentary upon the whole book would therefore have
been desirable.[1] But it is out of the question to attempt this now, and all that can be done in that way
is to select some one part of the visions before us for
such treatment. The portion of the book extending
from chap. xix. 11 to chap. xxii. 5 may be appropriately
chosen for this purpose ; partly, because it contains the
most interesting and difficult visions recorded by the
Seer ; but especially, because the interpretation of these
particular visions has a closer than ordinary bearing

---

[1] The author may be permitted
to refer his readers to his " Commentary on the Apocalypse " in
the last volume of the *Commentary*
on *the New Testament*, edited by
Prof. Schaff, D.D., etc., and
published by Messrs. Clark, Edinburgh.

upon the principles to be applied to the interpretation of the others. It has been urged in these lectures that the Apocalypse contains nothing that is not found elsewhere in Scripture, and more particularly in the discourses of our Lord. Here, if anywhere, objection may be taken to the statement. Have we not, it may be said, in the part of the Apocalypse referred to, the Millennium and the New Jerusalem? Is not the reign of the saints for a thousand years entirely new? Is not the descent of the New Jerusalem from heaven, in like manner, if not wholly, yet almost wholly, new? By these passages, more than by any others of the book, may we test the theory that the Apocalypse is no more than the expansion, in its own peculiar form, of ideas taught in other passages of the New Testament.

At the point, then, where we stand, chap. xix. 10, Babylon, the degenerate and apostate Church, has fallen, and at verse 11 another vision follows. Heaven is opened, and the victorious Redeemer comes forth upon a white horse, the armies of heaven following Him "upon white horses, clothed in fine linen, white and clean." It is the beginning of the picture of final triumph over every foe, when all Christ's enemies shall be made His footstool. Christ Himself is arrayed in a garment sprinkled with the blood of His enemies; many diadems, symbols of the many kingdoms now owning His authority, are upon His head; and He has on His garment and on His thigh a name written, KING OF KINGS, AND LORD OF LORDS. He is the suffering and conquering Messiah, and all His enemies are now to be destroyed for ever. In the first place, therefore, they are gathered together to meet their fate,—kings, and captains, and mighty men, and horses, and they that sit thereon, and all men (that is, obviously, all wicked men), both free and bond and small and great. In this the last moment of their career their old enmity is still unsubdued. Their opposition to the Lamb is not less fierce than formerly ; and to bring this out, it is said in the nineteenth verse of the chapter that they "gathered together to make war against Him that sat upon the horse, and against His army." The battle is not to be thought of as literal. It is but a figure to set forth the fixed, undying hatred of the world to God and His people. But no hatred is of avail against the overwhelming power of Him whom the world would oppose. The beast and the false prophet are taken and cast alive into the lake of fire that burneth with brimstone ; and the rest, consisting of the kings of the earth and their armies, and of all who set themselves up against the Lord and His anointed, are slain with the sword of Him that sat upon the horse, even the sword which came forth out of His mouth ; and all the fowls are filled with their flesh. Thus we reach the end of chap. xix.

In now approaching chap. xx., with all its yet unsolved difficulties of interpretation, it is of essential importance to observe, in the first place, the relation of the chapter to what immediately precedes. It is not an entirely new subject on which the Seer is entering ; on the contrary, he is distinctly continuing the prosecution of a theme he had before begun. In the previous portion of his book three great enemies of the saints of God had been introduced to us—the devil, the beast, and the false prophet. These were the main opponents of the Lamb, in one way or another stirring up all the efforts that had been made against Him by the kings of the earth, their armies, and their followers. For a time they had appeared to succeed. They had persecuted the saints, had compelled them to flee, had overcome them, and killed them. This, however, could not continue ; and it was to be shown that in the end complete victory shall rest with those who had suffered for the sake of righteousness. In chap. xix. we have the beginning but not the close of this victory. Of the three great enemies only two, the beast and the false prophet, perish in that chapter. The destruction of the third is reserved for chap. xx., and is effected at the tenth verse of the chapter. The following verses, from verse 11, then describe the judgment of those who had listened to these enemies, but who, though defeated or even killed [1] or devoured by fire out of heaven when in their service,[2] had not yet been consigned to their final doom. Thereafter nothing remains, in order to complete the victory of Christ and His saints, but that death and Hades shall also be removed from the scene and cast into the lake of fire.

These considerations are of themselves sufficient to show that *the overthrow of Satan*, and not the reign of a thousand years, is the main theme of the first ten verses

---

[1] Chap. xix. 21.　　　　　　　　[2] Chap. xx. 9.

of the chapter. So far is the latter topic from being the culminating point of the whole book, that it is not even introduced as the beginning of any new and important section. It starts no fresh series of visions. It comes in indirectly, in the midst of a section devoted to an entirely different matter.

But what is the meaning of this reign of the saints with Christ for a thousand years; of this binding of Satan, and casting him into the abyss, and shutting it, and sealing it over him, for the same period, so that " he should deceive the nations no more until the thousand years should be finished"? And further, what is the meaning of Satan's being loosed out of his prison at the end of the thousand years, and going out to deceive the nations until he is at last defeated and destroyed?

Before giving a direct answer to these questions two interpretations of the passage must be noticed.

The first of these is that a lengthened period of prosperity and ease for the Church of Christ on earth is to intervene between the close of the present Dispensation and the general Judgment. Almost everything indeed connected with this period is a matter of dispute among those who accept the main idea—its length, the number and class of the believers who shall be partakers of its glory, the condition in which they are to live, the work in which they are to be engaged, the relation in which the exalted Redeemer is to stand to them. These differences of detail it is impossible to discuss as if they were so many separate theories, but the more important will be noticed as we proceed.

The second explanation demanding notice is that which supposes the thousand years to be a figure for the whole Christian age, from the First to the Second Coming of the Lord.

I. Turning to the first of these explanations, it would seem as if the difficulties surrounding it were nearly, if not wholly, insurmountable.

1. In the form in which it supposes a resurrection of the saints in which they shall reign upon the earth with a body similar to that which they now possess, it is inconsistent with that *spiritual character* of the resurrection body, which is so important an element alike in the resurrection of our Lord and in that promised to His people. The Christian looks forward not merely to a resurrection similar to that of Lazarus—a return to an earthly mode of life on this earthly scene, but to a glorification of his body as well as his spirit. From this point of view Scripture represents even the appearances of the risen Lord as manifestations specially vouchsafed for a special purpose. After His resurrection His proper home was heaven. He rose not to remain here, but to ascend. Only He showed Himself for our sakes; and St. Peter says that we look, not for a reign on earth, but for " new heavens and a new earth "—

> New heaven and earth
> Meet for our new immortal birth.

From the first this was the feeling of the Christian Church. Any other view seemed to the fathers to be carnal, to be a forgetting of the glory of our hope. To entertain the idea, therefore, of a future Millennium during which believers shall, after resurrection, possess their present bodies, is to place ourselves at variance with one of the great truths of Scripture, and one upon which we have need, both in season and out of season, to insist.

But difficulties do not disappear if we abandon this thought, and adopt the idea that during a Millennium upon earth the saints shall possess a glorified body. It is not less impossible, upon this view, to form any reasonable conception of their condition during the thousand years. Multitudes of them, it is allowed, have been raised from their graves through Him who is " the first fruits of them that sleep," while those who are alive at the beginning of the thousand years, and are to share the Millennial glory, are " changed." Whether raised or changed they are thus " in glory;" and we have presented to us the absolutely inconceivable spectacle of glorified saints living in a world which has not yet received its own glorification, and is in consequence completely unfitted for their residence. Nor is this difficulty obviated by either of two suppositions which have been suggested for the purpose :—first, that only Jerusalem and the Holy Land shall be transfigured, the " nations" occupying the remainder of the earth as it now is ; or secondly, that the saints shall reign not upon the earth but from heaven over it. For, as to the first of these suppositions, nothing can be more remote from all reasonable probability than the idea of an earth, one part of which shall be transfigured without the rest ; while the part chosen for this purpose is far too small to accommodate those who are to occupy it. The second supposition, again, is not less difficult to apprehend. Were it indeed meant that a certain class of the saints shall reign in glory with their glorified Lord for a thousand years before the general resurrection; in other words, that their eternal and heavenly bliss shall simply begin a thousand years sooner than that of the other saints who shall afterwards share it with them, the idea would be intelligible. But, unless compelled by the special requirements of the passage, few surely will be prepared to adopt such a supposition. It is at once too trifling, and too much opposed to the general meaning of a vision which certainly draws a distinction, in one form or another, between millennial and eternal reward. The thought of a reign *in relation to the earth* must be accepted by all, and upon that point the second supposition now before us throws no satisfactory light. The saints are with their Lord in heaven. How do they communicate with the inhabitants of earth ? Will they be visible or invisible ? Will their work be missionary or punitive ? At this point, indeed, we are brought face to face with some of the greatest difficulties attending the view now under consideration. What are to be the relations between the saints in their millennial glory and " the nations" so much spoken of throughout these verses ? Different answers are given to the question, and it is not easy to gather them together in a few sentences. But it may be enough to say that " the nations" are generally regarded as either subject to the saints, and ruled by them in peace, or as the objects of their missionary enterprise. They are thus either harmless innocents, the absence of Satan preventing all combination and organised manifestation of evil, or they are peculiarly accessible to the grandeur of the spectacle which they behold in the glorified Saviour and His people. It is needless to reply that for all this, and much more of a similar kind, there is not the slightest foundation in the apostle's words, the total absence of any mention of relations between the saints and "the nations" until we come to verse 7 being one of the most remarkable characteristics of the vision. Evidently the Seer has no thought of any complex state of matters such as would spring out of the long dwelling together of these different classes. Or, if there is to be a fresh duration of existence, is there also to be *another proba-tion* for "the nations," a Gospel preached under circum-stances very different from what we have known, and constituting a new Dispensation; while yet there is the *same* Judgment at the end, and the conditions for en-trance into happiness or woe continue as before?

The difficulties now mentioned are increased when we endeavour to conceive of the relations between the devil and "the nations" during the thousand years. Satan is bound, is cast into the abyss, is shut into it, and has it sealed over him for a thousand years, so that during all that period, by most interpreters of this class made in-definitely longer than a thousand years, "he should de-ceive the nations no more."[1] Yet these nations are "the nations," enemies of Christ, outside His kingdom, ready

---

[1] Chap. xx. 3.

to obey the behests of the devil, and to war against the saints the moment the thousand years are finished. Whence comes the evil of this long period? How is sin maintained and kept in vigour during the thousand years? This continued state of sin marking the nations is not in the circumstances more conceivable than the state of grace and glory of the saints.

The whole conception, in short, of the chiliastic view of the thousand years' reign is compassed about with so many difficulties and improbabilities, with so many notions of which we can form no clear conception, or which, when we think that we understand them, are so incredible in themselves, that, unless it be forced upon us by fairness of interpretation, there is no alternative except to abandon it. But fair interpretation, instead of demanding it, strengthens the argument for its rejection. For

2. If we interpret the thousand years literally it will be a solitary example of a literal use of numbers in the Apocalypse, and this objection alone is fatal. If, on the other hand, we regard the thousand years as denoting a period of *indefinite* length, such interpretation is not less opposed to the genius and spirit of the book. The numbers of the Apocalypse are no doubt symbolical, but the symbolism has always a *definite* meaning. They express ideas, but the ideas are distinct. They may belong to a region of thought different from that with which arithmetical numbers are concerned, but within that region we cannot change the numerical value of the numbers used without at the same time changing the thought.

Substitute the number eight for the number seven, or, in like manner, four for three or twelve for ten, and the idea which the writer intended to express by the number actually employed by him immediately disappears. We are not to imagine that numbers, in the allegorical or spiritual use made of them by the Jews, may be tossed about at our pleasure, or shuffled like a pack of cards. They are a language ; and the bond between them and the ideas that they involve is quite as close as it is between the words of ordinary speech and the thoughts of the mind which utters them. Thus 1000 years cannot mean 2000 or 10,000 or 20,000 or 365,000 years, as the necessities of the case may afterwards demand. If they are a measure of time the measure must be fixed, and we ought to be able to explain the principle leading us to attach to the number one thousand a value different from that which it naturally possesses. To all this it is no answer that, as three and a half years are described in chap. xii. 12 as "a short season," though extending over the already almost two thousand years of the present Dispensation, so the thousand years may indicate a period of proportionally long duration, or, in other words, a long season without stating how long. The three and a half years do not primarily embrace the thought of a course of years, whether short or long. They embrace the thought of the *whole* Christian age, from its beginning to its close, as of a broken, interrupted, troubled time ; and they bring into view the character, not the length, of their "short season." In contrast with three and a half therefore, we are entitled to urge that character, not length, is the idea of the number one thousand in the passage before us. Thus only do we gain the *definiteness* which must belong to the apostle's language. No man can say how long the present Dispensation may still last, but the number three and a half takes it all in, and conveys to us a distinct impression of the light in which it is regarded by the Seer. In like manner no one can say how long or how short a time the Millennial years may last. The number one thousand has nothing to do with such a question. In contrast with three and a half it does not express length as distinguished from shortness of time, but rather the idea of what is unbroken, uninterrupted, free from trouble, and full of heavenly glory.

3. There are other particulars in the vision which forbid any such interpretation as that against which we contend. The mention of " souls," for example, in verse 4 is inconsistent with the idea that the Seer beholds risen and glorified saints, clothed with the bodies, of whatever kind they be, in which they are to pass the ages of eternity. The word occurs once before in the visions of the Seer, in a connection somewhat similar to the present. In chap. vi. 9 St. John sees underneath the altar the " souls" of them that had been slain for the Word of God, and for the testimony which they held. These "souls" are obviously the spirits of saints, the spirits of the saints of the Old Testament Church, as they wait for their brethren of the New Testament. Here too, therefore, St. John would certainly not have spoken of " souls" had he meant believers in their complete personality raised and glorified.

The ideas, too, involved in the word " reign " are not

those of a royal dignity during the continuance of which subject nations admire the splendour of saints seated on their thrones.   It has been well pointed out that the conception of Christ's βασιλεία or kingdom, instead of being that of a long reign of blessedness, is rather that of a powerful and prompt overthrow of His foes.[1] When the end comes no thousand years are needed to effect His purpose.   He destroys His enemies with a sudden destruction, like a thief in the night, or like the lightning's flash.

4. Another difficulty presented by this view of the Millennium arises from the teaching of Scripture elsewhere upon the points involved in it.   The difference is not simply negative, as if the rest of the New Testament only failed to fill in certain details of events more largely described in the Apocalypse, but upon the whole substantially the same.   It is also positive, and in some of its features irreconcilable with what we are taught by others of the sacred writers.   If we suppose that the saints who are made partakers of millennial glory are a selected company, we introduce a distinction between different classes of believers at variance with the general tenor of the word of God, in which all believers enjoy the same privileges on earth, share the same hope, and are at length rewarded with the same inheritance, though, according to their capacity of receiving, in different degrees.   Even if we reject such distinctions among believers themselves, and suppose that all of them share the millennial glory, we are not entitled, unless there be

---

[1] Kliefoth, *in loc.*

no alternative, to separate between them and unbelievers in such a way as to interpose a thousand years between their respective resurrections. It cannot be denied that the New Testament always brings the *Parousia* and the general Judgment into the closest possible connection. When Christ comes again it is to perfect the happiness of all His saints and to make all His enemies His footstool.[1] The teaching of the Apocalypse itself in other passages corresponds with this.[2] The idea of masses of the nations continuing to be Christ's enemies for years or ages after He has come again is not only entirely novel, but is inconsistent with the teaching of the other sacred writers. Again, the New Testament elsewhere knows only of one, and that a general, resurrection (John v. 28, 29); and the passages usually quoted as containing partial indications of two resurrections, such as 1 Cor. xv. 23, 24 and 1 Thess. iv. 16, 17, fail to support the conclusion drawn from them. In the meantime it is sufficient to notice the fact that, while the "first resurrection" is supposed to take place a thousand or even thousands of years before the end, it is distinctly said in our Lord's discourse in the sixth chapter of St. John that the resurrection of believers takes place "at the last day" (John vi. 40).

5. Once more, the idea that before the end the Church is to enjoy a long period of prosperity and rest on earth with her Lord reigning in her midst, is inconsistent with that teaching of Scripture, which seems

---

[1] Matt xxv. 31-46 ; John v. 16 ; 1 Thess. iv. 17 ; 2 Thess. i. 28, 29 ; Acts xvii. 31 ; Rom. ii. 5-7 ; 2 Peter iii. 8-13.

[2] Chaps. iii. 20, 21 ; xi. 17, 18.

distinctly to imply that her history down to the close of her pilgrimage shall be one of trouble. That this is the meaning of the twenty-fourth chapter of St. Matthew can hardly be disputed, and the argument from that chapter is the stronger because, as we have seen, the discourse of Christ contained in it lies at the bottom of the Apocalypse, and the writer of the latter could not contradict the very authority upon which his delineation is founded. On the other hand, if it be said that Christ is to come again in person not at the beginning but at the end of the period of millennial bliss, it is not easy to understand how that bliss should be spoken of in the terms actually applied to it. Scripture leads us to believe that only in the immediate presence of their Lord shall the saints be perfected, that only as *following* Him shall they attain the consummation of their happiness. The words also contained in verse 6 of this very passage lead to the same conclusion,—they "shall reign *with Him* a thousand years."

On these grounds alone, without mentioning others, we seem called upon to reject the view which sees in the thousand years a period of prosperity and joy, either of definite or indefinite length, appointed to come between the resurrection of the righteous and the general Judgment, and either with or without the immediate personal presence of the Lord.

II. The second interpretation, of which it is necessary to say a few words, is that which understands by the thousand years the whole Christian age from the First to the Second Coming of Christ. That there is an element of truth in this view we shall see by and by ; but, looking at it in the form in which it is usually presented, it is not possible to accept it. The number one thousand is inappropriate to the purpose to which it is applied. The period in question has already been made known to us as three and a half years. To make it a thousand years now would be to throw everything into confusion. Again, the "reign" of a thousand years is obviously granted not to the generation of believers only who are alive at the Coming of the Lord, but to all who in any age have been faithful unto death. And how can it be said of them that, in whatever era they departed, they "shall reign with Christ a thousand years," if by these years we are to understand the whole period of the Christian Dispensation and that alone ? Once more, we cannot speak of Satan as having been bound and shut up in the abyss during all those ages in which the Church of Christ has carried on her conflict with the world. That there is a sense in which he is so *as regards the righteous* must be allowed, and we shall afterwards see what that sense is. But he is still permitted to act upon them. Our Lord Himself had to contend with his temptations. Can we suppose that His people shall be exempted from them when they are "made partakers of His sufferings" ? Not only so. In His high-priestly prayer our Lord prayed on behalf of His disciples, not that His Father should take them out of the world, but that He should keep them out of the evil one ; [1] and He taught them also to pray for them-

----

[1] John xvii. 15.

selves "Deliver us from the evil one." [1]   Words like
these undoubtedly presuppose such action on the part of
Satan during the militant history of the Church as is
absolutely inconsistent with the supposition that he has
been bound and cast into the abyss, and the abyss shut
and sealed over him during all that time.   The same
point is equally clear when we think of Satan's action
upon "the nations."   That action has never ceased.
He has been their betrayer and destroyer in every age.
When he was cast out of heaven in the twelfth chapter
of this book he was "cast down into the earth," and
there he persecutes the woman which brought forth the
man child "for a time, and times, and half a time." [2]
So far from his being shut up and sealed into the
abyss, the language of St. Peter is a more correct
description of the case, when that apostle speaks of him
as "a roaring lion, walking about, seeking whom he
may devour." [3]   This view too, not less than the one
last considered, perplexes our ideas as to what is to
happen when the Christian Dispensation has run its
course.   At that point the thousand years expire ; and,
as they have been understood of time, it becomes necessary to allow some additional space of time for the
closing war.   We are thus brought into fresh conflict
with other statements of Scripture relating to the same
subject.   The second proposed solution is not more
satisfactory than the first. [4]

[1] Matt. vi. 13.
[2] Chap. xii. 9, 14.
[3] 1 Peter v. 8.
[4] It may be well to notice here a theory proposed by Canon Medd in his work on *The one Medi-ator*, which, from its simplicity, seems at first sight to have much

Having set aside these two views let us turn directly to the explanation now to be offered of this passage. Two preliminary points have to be noticed.

I. The fundamental principle to be kept clearly and resolutely in view is this, that the thousand years express no period of time. Like so many other expressions of the Apocalypse, their real is different from their apparent meaning. They are not to be taken literally. They embody an idea; and that idea, whether applied to the subjugation of Satan or to the triumph of the saints, is the idea of *completeness*. Satan is bound for a thousand years—*i.e.* he is completely bound. The saints reign for a thousand years—*i.e.*

to commend it. Canon Medd (p. 353) understands "the things which must shortly come to pass" of Rev. i. 1 as a series of things closing with the destruction of Jerusalem, upon which "was to follow the millennial period, a long, but wholly indefinite period, to be closed by the general resurrection and judgment." Such an interpretation assigns an importance to the destruction of Jerusalem inconsistent with the remarkable declaration of our Lord to the high priest in Matt. xxvi. 64, "Nevertheless I say unto you, from this time forth (not as the Authorised Version, "hereafter," or even as the Revised Version "henceforth") ye shall see the Son of man sitting at the right hand of power, and coming on the clouds of heaven."

The events to which our Lord alludes were to begin, not thirty-five years afterwards, when Jerusalem fell, but ἀπ' ἄρτι, immediately, with His crucifixion, resurrection, and glorification,—what St. John calls His being "lifted on high." Canon Medd's view is equally inconsistent with the tenor of the Apocalypse generally, the first nineteen chapters of which must then precede the destruction of the holy city. The "age to come" does not begin with the downfall of Jerusalem (p. 352), but with the completion of the work of Jesus upon earth, in His resurrection, ascension, and session at the right hand of the Father. Comp. the words of Jesus on the cross, "It is finished," and Daniel ix. 26, 27.

they are introduced into a state of perfect and glorious victory.

That years may be understood in this sense there can be no doubt. In Ezek. xxxix. 9 it is said that the inhabitants of the cities of Israel shall prevail against the enemies described, and "shall set on fire and burn the weapons, both the shields and the bucklers, the bows and the arrows, and the hand-staves and the spears, and they shall burn them with fire *seven years.*"—*i.e.* they shall utterly destroy them, not a vestige shall be left. Again, at the twelfth verse of the same chapter, when the prophet speaks of the burying of "Gog and all his multitude," he says, "and *seven months* shall the house of Israel be burying of them, that they may cleanse the land." In these passages the *seven years* or *seven months* mark only the thoroughness with which the weapons should be burned, and the land cleansed from heathenish impurity. The use of "years" in the passage before us seems to be exactly similar; and the probability that it is so rises almost to certainty when we remember that, as proved by the vision of Gog and Magog in the subsequent part of the chapter, this prophecy of Ezekiel is before the Seer's eyes, constituting the foundation upon which his whole delineation rests.

The only difficulty in connection with this view is that afforded by verses 3 and 7, where we read of the "finishing" of the thousand years and of that "loosing" of Satan which is to follow "after this." But the difficulty is more specious than real. Let us familiarise ourselves with the thought that the thousand years, regarded simply

as an expression, may denote completeness, thoroughness, either of defeat or victory.   Let us remember that
the Seer has expressed the defeat of Satan by the statement that he was bound for a thousand years. Finally, let
us notice that, as we shall immediately see more fully,
this defeat has reference only to the righteous, and that
although bound, defeated, in regard to them, Satan is to
go forth on his malign mission against the unrighteous,
and we shall immediately see that in no way could this
latter onset be more appropriately expressed than by
saying that it took place when the thousand years were
finished. The thousand years being a symbol not of time
but of completeness, it belongs to the same symbolism
to use the word "after," not in a chronological sense, but
rather with the force of subordinating the secondary
to the primary effect. To revert for a moment to the
image of Ezekiel, when he said that Israel should burn
the weapons of its enemies " with fire seven years,"[1] let
us suppose that the prophet had next wished to describe
some secondary effect of the great victory which preceded the burning, and what more suitable expression
could he have used than either "after this" or "after
the seven years were finished" ?   The one expression is
only the natural consequence of the other.

II. A second preliminary point is the meaning of the
last words of verse 3, " he (*i.e.* Satan) must be loosed for
a little time." What is this "little time" ?   Is it a little
time following the thousand years which had, in their
turn, followed the close of the present dispensation ? No.

---

[1] Chap. xxxix. 9.

It is something altogether different.   The words take us directly to that conception of the *Christian age* which is so intimately interwoven with the whole structure of the Apocalypse—that it is all a "little time."   We see this in the application of the very same words to the souls under the altar in chap. vi. 11, "and it was said unto them, that they should rest yet for a *little time*, until their fellow-servants also and their brethren, which should be killed even as they were, should be fulfilled."   The "little time" there is undeniably the whole Christian age.

But, if it be so there, we are entitled to suppose that the very same expression, when used in the passage before us, will be used in the same sense, and that when it is said Satan shall be loosed "for a little time," the meaning is that he shall be loosed for *the whole Christian age*.   Again, in chap. xii. 12, we read "the devil is gone down unto you, having great wrath, knowing that he hath but a short time."   The "short time" here referred to must include the whole period of Satan's action in this world, and the manner in which that period is designated corresponds closely with the description of the time during which he is to be loosed.   Again, in chap. x. 6, the angel swears that there shall be "time" no longer, using the same word for "time" that we meet with in the verse now under consideration, so that it would appear as if to the author of the Apocalypse the word "time" or "season" were a kind of technical term by which he was accustomed to denote the whole period of the Church's probation in this world.   Lastly, this conclusion is powerfully confirmed by the many passages of the Apocalypse in which it is clear that the Christian Dispensation from its beginning to its end is looked upon as a "little while," as *hastening* to its final issue, and as about to be closed by One who cometh quickly.[1] The "little time," therefore, of chap. xx. 3, the "little time" during which Satan is loosed, and which, when more fully expanded, is the time of the war described in verses 7-9 of the chapter, is the historical period of the Christian Dispensation during which Satan is permitted to deceive the nations and to lead them to the war against the camp of the saints and the beloved city. It is, in short, the time between the First and Second Coming of our Lord. *The period, so often sought in the thousand years of verse 2, is really to be found in the " little time" of verse 3.*

Keeping these two preliminary points distinctly before us, we may now apply to the whole passage the hypothesis which they suggest, and may ask whether we do not thus obtain for it a clear, appropriate, and Scriptural meaning.

It has been already stated that the main object of the Seer in chap. xx. is to describe, in continuation of the preceding chapter, the overthrow of Satan, and not any Millennium of the saints. But before he proceeds to this, before as in the case of the beast and the false prophet he even mentions " war," he is invited to behold in vision the complete security of those over whom Satan has no power. Whatever influence the great adversary may exert over others, *they* are safe. They

---

[1] Chaps. i. 3 ; ii. 16 ; iii. 20 ; xvii. 10 ; xxii. 20, etc.

belong to Him who is King of kings and Lord of lords, who rules in the armies of heaven, and who will not suffer one of His faithful warriors to perish. How suitable was it that such a vision should be presented to St. John's view! About to follow Satan to his final overthrow, he sees him gathering his hosts to the war in which he shall be signally defeated. But, before he describes that war, it is in harmony with his whole method of delineation that he shall find utterance for that preliminary truth which here fills his mind. Again and again throughout his book he has done the same, and before speaking of the trials of the righteous has shown us that they shall be affected by no judgment, however terrible, by no hosts of evil, however mighty. They have been purchased with the blood of Christ. They have died, yea rather, they have risen again to glorious and endless life. They share the throne of their glorified Lord. His rule is their rule, His kingdom their kingdom. Satan cannot harm them. He is already bruised beneath their feet.

From this point of view let us trace, as briefly as possible, the course and meaning of the vision that is here presented to us.

1. In the first place, let us look at the condition of Satan. That head of all evil is bound for a thousand years, and is cast into the abyss, which is shut and sealed over him, so that he shall deceive the nations no more until the thousand years should be finished. The meaning of this is simply that, by the work of Christ, Satan in his character as the deceiver of the nations has

been in principle, completely, and for ever, overcome. It was not at the end of a long series of ages that the Redeemer was to conquer the great enemy of man. He did it once for all by that redemptive work which He accomplished. Satan's power was then wholly broken. He had no longer either right or authority to act in his proper character,—that of the deceiver of the nations. He met in reality the fate which he was able, in a shadowy and temporary form, to inflict on Jesus,—he was bound and shut up in the abyss, and the abyss was sealed over him. Such is always the teaching both of St. John elsewhere and of our Lord Himself. To both the judgment of Satan is not so much a future as a present thing: "For this end Christ was manifested, that," from His incarnation onward, "He might destroy the works of the devil." [1] Jesus Himself, *when He was upon earth*, exclaimed, "*Now* is the judgment of this world; *now* shall the prince of this world be cast out." [2] He declared that "the prince of this world (not is or shall be but) *hath been* judged." [3] In conformity with these passages He elsewhere said, "I beheld Satan fallen as lightning from heaven." [4] He gave His disciples reason to hope that they should "bind the strong man." [5] He told them that they had authority from Him "to tread upon serpents and scorpions, and over all the power of the enemy;" [6] and He granted them a foretaste and experience of this authority when He enabled them to heal those that were possessed with

[1] 1 John iii. 8.

[2] John xii. 31.

[3] John xvi. 11.

[4] Luke x. 18.

[5] Matt. xii. 29.

[6] Luke x. 19.

demons.   There is a sense, therefore, in which, *for the followers of Jesus*, from the very beginning of their Christian career, the devil is not a foe to be conquered, but one already bound, shut into an abyss, and the abyss sealed over him—the very lesson of this vision. "This is the *victory* that hath overcome the world, even our faith;"[1] the victory before the war.

2. In the second place, before noticing the loosing of Satan, let us look at the condition of the righteous as it is here depicted.   In doing so, a passage in the fifth chapter of St. John's Gospel ought to be distinctly in our minds.   "Verily, verily," are there the words of Jesus, "I say unto you, the hour cometh, and now is, when the dead shall hear the voice of the Son of God; and they that have heard shall live;"[2] and again, a little later in the same discourse, "Marvel not at this: for the hour cometh, in which all that are in the tombs shall hear His voice, and shall come forth."[3] Compare these two verses with one another, and we discover the source whence the idea of the "first resurrection" comes.   It is not an actual resurrection from the grave, although that resurrection is potentially involved in it. It is a spiritual resurrection in an hour *"that now is."* This is "the first resurrection" of the Apocalypse, and the fact that it is so is brought out still more clearly by the intimation that what St. John saw was "souls," whose resurrection bodies had not yet been given them.

Nor is this all.   The other features of their condition correspond with the ideal conception of the condition of

---

[1] 1 John v. 4.   [2] Verse 25.   [3] Verse 28.

the righteous even in a present world. They sit upon thrones: but we have been already told, at chap. v. 10, that they "reign upon (or rather 'over') the earth," and the whole description is but another way of expressing what St. Paul has said when he speaks of believers as already blessed with every spiritual blessing "in the heavenly places in Christ."[1] "Judgment is given them," words which seem only capable of bearing that sense which is so peculiar to St. John—that for believers there is no judgment; all the judgment through which they have to pass is over. They "live" with Christ; but Christ Himself had said in the Gospel, "Because I live, and ye shall live."[2] They "reign" with Christ; but that is only another method of saying that they sit on thrones. Over them the "second death hath no authority"—they have passed from that death with which judgment is connected into life.[3] Nothing is said of them that does not find its parallel for the *present* life of believers either in St. John's other writings or in the later writings of St. Paul. Still further, it is to be observed that this picture of the blessedness of the saints during the thousand years is really the counterpart of that ascension of Jesus to His heavenly Father which had been described in chap. xii. before the troubles of the saints began. In that chapter it is said of the Son, the man child, who is to rule all nations with a rod of iron, that immediately after His birth "He was caught up unto God and unto His *throne*,"[4] and then the statement

---

[1] Eph. i. 3.

[2] Chap. xiv. 19, R. V., margin.

[3] John v. 24 ; 1 John iii. 14.

[4] Verse 5.

follows that "the woman fled into the wilderness." Two things have to be remembered here; first, that Christ and His people are (throughout the Apocalypse) so identified that it is impossible to separate them from one another; and secondly, that it is the manner of St. John to give more fully in one place what he touches more lightly on in another. When we remember this, we can hardly fail to see that the two visions now spoken of are the counterpart of one another. Before Christ suffers in the members of His Body He is safe within the throne of God : before the members suffer they are safe, sitting upon their thrones, and reigning in the glory of their Head and King.

Putting all these circumstances together we can have no difficulty in understanding either the binding of Satan or the reign of the saints for a thousand years. The vision here presented to us describes no period of blessedness to be enjoyed by the Church at the close of the present dispensation, between the first resurrection of the saints and the general resurrection to follow, when a thousand years expire; nor is it a picture of the Church's history from the beginning to the end of the Christian age. Alike negatively and positively, alike in the binding of Satan and in the reign of the saints for a thousand years, we have simply an ideal picture of what was effected by the Redeemer for His people, when for them He lived and suffered and died and rose again. Then He bound Satan for them; He cast him into the abyss; He shut him in; He sealed the abyss over him—so that against them he could effect nothing.

He is a bruised and conquered foe. He may war against them, afflict them, persecute them, kill them, but their true life is beyond his reach. They live already a resurrection life, an ascended life; for it is a life hid with Christ in God, a life in that "heaven" from which the devil has been finally and for ever expelled. They rest upon, they live in, a risen and glorified Redeemer; and, in whatever age or country or circumstances their lot is cast, they sit with their Lord in the heavenly places and share His victory. He has been always triumphant. At the opening of the first Seal He had gone forth "conquering and to conquer,"[1] and in every song of praise which meets us in the book, sung by the Heavenly host the Church and redeemed creation, His had been "the blessing, and the honour, and the glory, and the dominion, for ever and ever."[2] In this triumph of Christ the saints on earth not less than the saints in heaven have their share. The glory which the Father gave to the Son the Son has given them.[3] They cannot sin because they are begotten of God.[4] He that was begotten of God keepeth them, and the evil one toucheth them not.[5] This is the reign of the thousand years, and it is the portion of every believer who in any age of the Church is a sharer in the life of his risen and exalted Lord.

3. In the third place, we may now easily comprehend what is meant by the loosing of Satan when the thousand years are finished. No point in the future is

[1] Chap. vi. 2.

[2] Chaps. v. 13 ; vii. 12 ; xi. 15 ; xv. 3 ; xix. 7.

[3] John xvii. 22.

[4] 1 John iii. 9.

[5] 1 John v. 18.

there referred to. The point of time when Satan was loosed is in the past. He was loosed to exert his rage in the world immediately after he was completely conquered. He was loosed as a great adversary who, however he may persecute God's children, cannot touch their inner life, and who can only " deceive the nations," —the nations that have despised and rejected Christ. He has never been really absent from the earth. He has gone about continually, " having great wrath, knowing that his time is short." [1] But he has never been able to " hurt " those that have been kept in the hollow of the Lord's hand. No doubt he has tried it. That is the meaning of the description extending from verse 7 of this chapter to verse 9—the meaning of the war which Satan begins against the camp of the saints and the beloved city when the thousand years are finished. In other words, no sooner was Satan, as regarded *the saints,* completely bound than, as regards *the world,* he was loosed ; and from that hour, through the whole past history of Christianity, he has been stirring up the world against the Church. He has been summoning the nations that are in the four corners of the earth, Gog and Magog, to gather them together to the war. But all in vain. They war, but they do not conquer, until at last fire comes down out of heaven and devours them ; the devil that deceived them is cast into the lake of fire and brimstone, where are also the beast and the false prophet ; and they shall be tormented day and night for ever and ever.

[1] Chap. xii. 12.

The whole picture of the thousand years thus presented to us is, in all its main features, in the binding of Satan, in the security and blessedness of the saints, and in the loosing of Satan for the war, a striking parallel to the scenes in chap. xii. of this book. There Michael and his angels contend with the devil and his angels, and the latter prevailed not (comp. the very remarkable parallel in John i. 5, " and the darkness overcame it not "), but were cast out of heaven into the earth, so that the inhabitants of heaven are for ever safe from them. There the child who is to rule all the nations with a rod of iron, and from the thought of whom it is impossible to separate the thought of those who are one with Him, is caught up unto God and unto His throne. Finally there also the dragon, though unable really to hurt the saints, " the rest of the woman's seed which keep the commandments of God and hold the testimony of Jesus," makes war upon them, but without result. This picture in chap. xx. is a repetition, but at the same time a fuller development, of that in chap. xii. ; and when we call to mind the peculiarities of apocalyptic structure formerly spoken of, we seem in this fact alone to have no small evidence of the correctness of the interpretation now proposed.

Finally, it may be observed that the solution of the difficulties of chap. xx. here offered is not arbitrary, or framed to suit the exigencies of a theory. It rests upon a careful examination of the Seer's own words and a faithful application of well-known and universally recognised exegetical laws. That it is wholly free from

difficulty would be too much to say ; but it is presented
to the Church as being, first, a fair interpretation of the
passage ; secondly, as avoiding the insuperable difficulties of other interpretations ; and thirdly, as in harmony
with the general teaching of Scripture, and especially of
the Apocalypse itself, on the points with which it deals.[1]

[1] It is impossible to defend at length the interpretation of this difficult passage here proposed. One or two very brief remarks may be permitted. The writer would ask his readers to bear in mind, in considering it (1) That no interpretation hitherto proposed has succeeded in commending itself to anything like general acceptance ; (2) That the interpretation now offered, whatever may be the difficulties attending it, is in thorough harmony with all the other teaching of Scripture upon the point. This applies in even a special degree to the interpretation of the words of verse 3, "a little time." Yet the interpretation is in no degree the result of any effort to harmonise Scripture. It suggested itself gradually to the writer's mind, and as the result of the combined interpretation of many passages, each considered independently and on its own merits.

There are, however, two great difficulties connected with it that may be noticed, the one presented by a clause in verse 3, the other by a clause in verse 5.

1. In the first of these two verses we read that Satan was bound and shut up into the abyss, "that he should deceive the nations no more, until the thousand years should be finished." These words seem to mean that there must be a time during which Satan, because bound, does not "deceive the nations," while we have urged in the text that he was no sooner completely subjugated for the righteous than he was let loose to deceive the unrighteous. In reply to this difficulty we suggest that the words, "that he should deceive the nations no more," are not designed to indicate that action on Satan's part was for a time to cease, but rather to bring out and express that aspect of Satan by which he is specially distinguished in the Apocalypse. In chap. xii. 9 we have been taught to know him as "the deceiver of the whole world"— words which describe him as he *is*, and not simply in what he *does*. The clause now under consideration, therefore, may mean that Satan was bound and shut up in the abyss in that character which best describes him—the deceiver of the nations. The meaning of the passage will then be, that the

A description of judgment follows, in which it is too often supposed that both the righteous and the wicked are included. Such, however, is not the case. For the righteous there is no judgment. Judgment, as we read

main result of our Lord's redemptive work was the securing His own people in their state of exalted and glorious privilege, or, in the language of the apocalyptic writer, in their reign of a thousand years. Until this was done we can only think of Satan, the deceiver of the nations, as conquered and in the abyss. But as soon as victory over him was gained, and *we see* that it was gained, our thoughts are free to pass on to the fact that for the world, for the nations, for the ungodly, he is loosed. Thus may it be said that the abyss was sealed over Satan, that he should deceive the nations no more until the thousand years should be finished, *i.e.* that he should not be himself, or be permitted to act like himself, until the saints were ideally secured in all the privileges of their new estate.

The interpretation of verse 3 now proposed will be rendered more probable should it be allowed that it may not be necessary to understand the words τὰ ἔθνη in that verse in the strict sense of the *ungodly nations*, but in the wider sense of the nations generally, without special regard to their spiritual condition. In that case the meaning above suggested will be still more obvious, and there will be little difficulty in taking the words, "that he should deceive the nations no more until," etc., as simply meaning that Satan, *the deceiver*, was bound until, etc. But this interpretation has much to confirm it. More particularly is the special definition of verse 8 worthy of notice, "*the nations which are in the four corners of the earth, Gog and Magog.*" Why this definition here? Why this limitation of "the nations," unless it be to draw a distinction between the nations of verse 3 and those of verse 8? It may be further noticed that in chap. xxi. 3 we read of the redeemed as the Lord's "peoples" (λαοί not λαός). If under the theocratic notion "peoples" many nations may be included, so in the worldly designation "nations" peoples of God may have a place. It appears also from John xi. 50-52 that there is a sense in which the theocratic people are "a nation," and the heathen gathered into the flock of Christ a part of His "people" (comp. Comm. *in loc.*). Lastly, the distinction drawn in the fourth Gospel between "the Jews" and "the multitude" may supply an in verse 4, had long before been "given them." They may, indeed, as the Shorter Catechism puts it, be "openly acknowledged and acquitted in the day of judgment," but there "remaineth" for them even now

important Johannine parallel. These two classes in the Gospel are always to be carefully distinguished from each other, the one being self-steeled against the truth, the other presenting a field open for its reception. It may be so here. The nations which are in the four corners of the earth, Gog and Magog, may find their parallel in "the Jews," the nations generally in "the multitude." The object of the middle clause of verse 3 may then simply be to tell us that Satan, *the deceiver*, was no longer permitted to carry on his work of deception until, after having been first completely conquered, he was again let loose.

If this view of these words be admitted, no difficulty need be felt with regard to those of verse 7, "and when the thousand years are finished," or rather, "when the thousand years should be finished," for the word $\tau\epsilon\lambda\epsilon\sigma\theta\hat{\eta}$ ought certainly to be translated in the same way as in verses 3 and 5. We have here simply the second, because subordinate, half of the thought of which we have already spoken, —when the saints are secured in their position Satan is permitted to resume his work of deceiving the nations.

2. The second difficulty demanding notice is presented by the clause in verse 5 in which we are told that "the rest of the dead lived not until the thousand years should be finished." This difficulty may perhaps be met in either of two ways.

a. "The rest of the dead" may be understood to mean the ungodly; but there is a serious obstacle to this, in so far as we shall thus be compelled to lower the meaning of the word "lived" in the same clause, and to understand it simply in the sense of coming into the field of action. In other words, the meaning will be that at the moment of Christ's completing His victory there was a pause. After the victory was completed the ungodly again stirred, moved, acted, "lived." In this we should have a close parallel to John xviii. as compared with xvii. But even although at the close of verse 4 it may not be necessary to connect "lived" as well as "reigned" with the words "with Christ" (comp. verse 6, where we read only "they shall reign"), it is not easy to take its high spiritual mean-no condemnation or judgment tending to it. They are "in" Christ, who sits upon the seat of judgment. They have long since passed out of death into life.[1] The wicked alone are judged and cast into the lake of fire; while death, the last enemy, and his follower Hades, are also judged, and are cast into the same lake of fire.[2]

One vision still remains, described in chap. xxi. and in the first five verses of chap. xxii. The new heavens and the new earth are beheld wherein dwelleth

ing out of the Johannine "lived."

b. A second solution is suggested by a valued friend, who asks whether these "rest of the dead" in verse 5 may not be the Old Testament saints of chap. vi. 9. These Old Testament saints were, by the completion of the Lord's redeeming work, brought up to the level of the New Testament Church (comp. Comm. on vi. 9, etc.) May not the meaning of chap. xx. 5 therefore be, The New Testament Church had *first* bestowed upon it a complete redemption, and only *after that* were the same white robes given to the Old Testament Church, the succession being again one of thought rather than time. The advantages of this rendering appear to be— first, that it marks out *all* the members of Christ's body as having been νεκροί before they "lived," thus identifying them with their Lord in chap. i. 18 ; secondly, that

"*the rest* of the dead" then belong to the *same* class as that previously spoken of, and not to a different class ; thirdly, that it makes the position of the words at the close of verse 5, "this is the first resurrection," more natural, when they thus follow what is *wholly* a description of the blessed ; and fourthly, that we preserve by this rendering the full Johannine meaning of the word "lived." Upon the whole the second rendering is to be preferred, and it appears to offer a fair solution of the difficulty. But, whether that difficulty is solved or still awaits solution, the writer of these Lectures trusts that the explanation proposed in the text may be accepted as in the main correct, or as, at all events, helping forward the interpretation of the passage by leading to further investigation.

[1] Comp. John v. 24.

[2] This point will be further spoken of in Appendix II.

righteousness.   The holy city, New Jerusalem, the true Church of God wholly separated from the false Church, is beheld coming down from God out of heaven, prepared as a bride adorned for her husband.   Her eternal marriage with the Lamb takes place—a marriage in which there shall be no unfaithfulness on the one side and no reproaches on the other, but in which, as the bridegroom rejoices over the bride, the Lord shall for ever rejoice in His people, and they in Him.   The tabernacle of the Lord is pitched among men, and He dwells among them.   They are His people, unchangeably, eternally His, free from sin and free from sorrow.   The tears are wiped away from their eyes; and there is no more death, neither sorrow, nor crying, nor pain, for the former things are passed away, and all things are made new.

Then follows, still further to enhance the picture, a description of the true Church under the figure of the city which had just been spoken of.   The treasures of language are exhausted that the thought of her beauty and her splendour may be suitably impressed upon our minds.   In her foundations, in the courses of stones resting upon them, in her height and fair proportions, she is thought of as ideally perfect, and not according to the strict realities or possibilities of things.   All the outward helps actually needed by men to aid them in leading the life of God in their present state of imperfection are dispensed with.   There is no temple in the city, for the Lord God Almighty and the Lamb are the temple of it.   It has no need of the sun, neither of the moon to shine in it, for the glory of God lightens it, and the Lamb is the light thereof. There is no sin there, and every positive element of happiness is provided in abundance for its blest inhabitants. The river of the water of life, full and clear, flows there ; and on either side of the river is the tree of life, not bearing fruit once a year only but every month ; not yielding one only but twelve manner of fruits, so that all tastes may be gratified, having nothing about it useless or liable to decay. Its very leaves are for the healing of the nations, and it is evidently implied that they are always green. Finally, the curse is for ever removed. The servants of the Lord serve Him. They see His face. His name is in their foreheads. They are priests unto God in the service of the heavenly sanctuary, and they reign for ever and ever.

One question still remains. What aspect of the Church does the holy city Jerusalem, thus come down out of heaven from God, represent ? Is it the Church as she shall be in the supposed days of millennial bliss, the Lord Himself reigning in it among His people ? Or have we before us an ideal representation of the true Church of Christ as she exists now, and before a final separation has been made between the righteous and the wicked ? After all that has been said there ought to be little difficulty in answering the question ; and hints in the passage appear to confirm the answer that must be given. *The New Jerusalem is an ideal picture of the true Church now.* Just as we saw that the Millennium is come, as it came with the finished work of Christ, as it comes in principle to every heart that rests upon its Lord in faith, so the New Jerusalem has come, has been in the midst of us for more than eighteen hundred years, is now in the midst of us, and shall continue to be in the midst of us wherever its King has those who love and serve Him, walk in His light, and share His peace and joy. Let us look at the words of chap. xx. 9, where we read of "the beloved city." That city is none other than the New Jerusalem about to be described in the following chapter, and yet it is spoken of as *in the world*, and as the object of attack by Satan and his hosts *before the judgment.* Let us look at chap. xxi. 24, where we read, " And the nations shall walk amidst the light thereof: and the kings of the earth do bring their glory into it." Who are these "nations" and these "kings of the earth "? The constant use of the same expressions in other parts of the book, in which there can be no doubt about their meaning, compels us to understand them of nations and kings beyond the pale of the covenant, who must therefore be still existing in the world *after* the descent of the New Jerusalem. Let us look at chap. xxi. 27, where we read, "and there shall in no wise enter into it anything unclean, or he that maketh an abomination and a lie: but only they which are written in the Lamb's book of life," and these words distinctly intimate that the time had not yet come for that separation of which we read in chap. xx. 15, " And if any was not found written in the book of life, he was cast into the lake of fire." Finally, let us look at chap. xxii. 2, where we are told that " the leaves of the tree were for the healing of the nations," and we see that even after the city had descended to earth there were nations to be healed.

Nor are even those parts of the description which it appears at first sight most difficult to reconcile with the idea that we have before us the true members of Christ's Body upon earth, and not the Church in heaven, out of keeping with other statements of the New Testament. The intimation of verses 8 and 27 that sin is banished from the city is not stronger than the words of St. John in his First Epistle, "Whosoever is begotten of God doeth no sin, because his seed remaineth in him: and he cannot sin, because he is begotten of God;"[1] while the assurance of verse 4, that "the first things are passed away," has its perfect parallel in the language of St. Paul when, writing to the Corinthians and occupied with the very same thought of the risen Lord as that which is here prominent, he exclaims, "The old things are passed away; behold, they are become new."[2] In addition to this it is well to remember that the most glowing descriptions of the Old Testament, when it speaks of the coming kingdom of Messiah, apply to the age now passing over us; and these descriptions the Apocalypse adopts and seals.[3]

[1] Chap. iii. 9.

[2] 2 Cor. v. 17.

[3] It may be well to notice in a note another consideration upon this point, which will be allowed to be of weight by those who admit the existence of that principle of structure in St. John's writings upon which it rests. St. John is often marked by a tendency to return at the close of a section of his writings to what he had said at the beginning, and to shut up, as it were, between these two statements all he had to say. So here in chap. i. 3 he introduces his Apocalypse with the words, "for the time is at hand." In chap. xxii. 10 he returns to the thought, "Seal not up the words of the prophecy of this book; for the time is at hand." That is, the whole intervening Apocalypse is enclosed between these two statements; all of it precedes the "time" spoken of; the New Jerusalem comes before the end.

In the New Jerusalem, therefore, we have essentially
a picture, not of the future but of the present, of the
ideal, condition of Christ's true people, of His "little
flock" upon earth in every age. The picture may not
yet be realised in fulness, but every blessing lined in
upon its canvas is in principle the believer's now, and
will be more and more his in actual experience as he
opens his eye to see and his heart to receive. We have
been wrong in transferring, as we have done, the thousand years' reign and the New Jerusalem to the future.
They belong to the past and to the present. They are
the Church's heritage at the very time that she wars
and suffers ; and the thought of them ought to console
her amidst her trials, and to make her burdens easy to
be borne. Oh, if the Church, if believers, only felt this
more, what a *millennium* of happiness and glory would
each enjoy ! With what triumph would each lift up
his head as he paced the streets of that New Jerusalem
of which he is a citizen ! And in what a light would
he feel called upon to present himself to the eyes of
men, not mingling in the strife of human tongues, or
interested in worldly wealth and honour, but already
radiant with the glory of his heavenly home ! The
Church has mistaken her mission, and has misinterpreted
the Scriptures of the possession of which she boasts.
She has transferred all her blessedness to the future, and
has asked men to accept for the realities of the present
and the seen her dim and shadowy, too often her fantastic, pictures of the future and the unseen. That is
not the method of our Lord or of His servant John in

the Apocalypse. They do not try to convert men by hopes of heaven. They deal with realities now to be grasped, with visions of glory now to be realised. They invite us, indeed, to a glorious and eternal future ; but, as at once the evidence and the beginning of that future glory, they invite us, in the first place, to the possession here and now of "things which eye saw not, and ear heard not, and which entered not into the heart of man."[1] They tell us that the brightness of the New Jerusalem ought to be within us and around us, shining through every earthly sorrow, so that we may lighten the dark places of " the nations " with its purity and peace and joy.

It is unnecessary to dwell upon the Epilogue which begins at chap. xxii. 6. With the previous verse the special visions of the Apocalypse had come to an end, and the book which had presented so many dark traits of Paradise lost had closed with the glorious picture of Paradise regained. Only one thing more was needed— that the Lord Himself, long waited for, should come, to transmute each promise into fulfilment and each ideal into its corresponding real. Even so. " Amen : come, Lord Jesus." Meanwhile we cannot doubt that to St. John the lone isle of Patmos was lightened with the glory of what he saw ; and, be it that we too are in our Patmos, the same glory will lighten us, if only we are among them which keep the sayings of this book.

<hr>

[1] 1 Cor. ii. 9.

APPENDICES

APPENDIX I.

AUTHORSHIP OF THE APOCALYPSE.

In entering upon the discussion of this question it seems unnecessary to enumerate at length the various testimonies of the early Church to the authorship of the Apocalypse by the apostle John. These will be found gathered together in many books which are easily accessible, and of which the following may be named :—Alford's " Prolegomena," in the last volume of his *Commentary on the New Testament;* Davidson's *Introduction to the New Testament;* Westcott on the *Canon of the New Testament; Canonicity,* by Dr. Charteris ; and Archdeacon Lee's *Introduction to his Commentary on the Revelation.* Numerous works of continental scholars containing similar summaries of the facts may also for the present be omitted. It is the less necessary to do more than mention the above, because it is well known that there is no book of the New Testament the reputed authorship of which is more generally, or in stronger terms, allowed by inquirers of all schools of thought, and not least by the chief members of that school of negative criticism which is so often found opposed to the traditions of the Church. Thus it is that Dr. Baur has expressed his opinion that few writings of the New Testament can claim evidence for an apostolic authorship of a kind so ancient and undoubted (*K. U.,* p. 345). Zeller follows in his master's steps with the declaration that the Apocalypse is the real and normal writing of early Christianity, and that among all the books of the New Testament it is the only one which, with a certain measure of right, may claim to have been composed by an apostle and immediate disciple of Christ (*T. J.,* 1842, p. 654). Schwegler (*N. Z.,* ii. p. 249) and Hilgenfeld

E. in d. N. T., p. 448, etc.) bear similar testimony to the authenticity of the book; while, in our own country, Dr Davidson thus speaks, "Enough has been given to prove that the apostolic origin of the Apocalypse is as well attested as that of any other book of the New Testament. . . . With the limited stock of early ecclesiastical literature that survives the wreck of time, we should despair of proving the authenticity of any New Testament book by the help of ancient witnesses if that of the Apocalypse be rejected" (*Intr. to N. T.*, i. p. 318) Having such testimonies from scholars who cannot be suspected of the slightest desire to uphold the traditional views of the Church, we might almost dispense with further argument. Ye some parts of the evidence are in themselves so interesting that it would be improper to omit them.

This remark may be particularly applied to the evidence of Papias, who is said by Eusebius to have spoken in his book concerning the "Oracles of the Lord" of a corporeal reign of Christ upon the earth for a thousand years after the resurrection from the dead (*H. E.*, iii. 39). It is not indeed stated in this passage that the opinion referred to was taken from the Apocalypse, and Papias may have adopted it from some other source But the probability that he is speaking upon the authority of St. John is in no small degree confirmed by the fact that Andreas and Arethas, two Bishops of Cæsarea, in the second half of the fifth century, when the work of Papias, now lost was still in circulation, distinctly say—the one, that Papias regarded the Apocalypse as worthy of trust; the other, that he had the book before him (*Canonicity*, pp. 338, 339). No doubt indeed would probably have been entertained upon the point had not Eusebius, contrary to his custom, failed to tell us that Papias had the Apocalypse in his eye; and had he not raised the question whether the " Presbyter John," with whom Papias had conversed, might not be a different person from the apostle The first of these difficulties is easily removed when we remember that Eusebius, a keen antimillenarian, and one who speak with contempt of Papias for his millenarian proclivities, must have been most unwilling to connect such opinions with a sacred book, and that he was even doubtful whether the Apocalypse ought to be regarded in this light. The second difficulty again would at once disappear were it allowed, as there seems every reason to think is the case, that the apostle and the " Presbyter are identical. But, even if this cannot be spoken of as estab

shed, it is worthy of notice that in another work Eusebius
couples the names of Papias and Polycarp of Smyrna together
s acknowledged hearers of the apostle (*Chron. Bipart.*, quoted
i the Speaker's *Commentary on the New Test.*, iv. p. 408). The
onclusion is strengthened by the date of Papias's birth, not
ter than A.D. 70, and by the scene of his ministry, at no great
istance from Ephesus.

Omitting many intervening authorities we pass to another
nteresting testimony connected with these early times, that of
renæus. No one disputes the acquaintance of this father with
he Apocalypse, or that he distinctly ascribes it to St. John.
he point of importance is that, as we learn from his beautiful
tter to Florinus (Stieren's *Irenæus*, i. p. 822), he had been a
isciple of Polycarp, who in his turn had been a disciple of St.
ohn, and that he delighted in after life to call to mind the
ccounts which his teacher used to give of his intercourse with
he apostle; an intercourse so truly transmitted to his pupils
hat Irenæus, in describing it, speaks with obvious artlessness,
ot of eye-witnesses of Jesus, but of "eye-witnesses of the
fe of the Word."

Testimonies such as these are of the highest value, but the
uthers who have left them are supported by many others.
Without passing beyond the first half of the third century we
ame only Justin Martyr, Dionysius of Corinth, Melito of
ardis, Polycrates of Ephesus, Theophilus of Antioch, Clement
f Alexandria, and Origen, in the East; and in the West, Ter-
ullian, Cyprian, the letter of the Churches of Vienne and
yons, the old Latin version of the New Testament, and the
ocument known as the Muratorian Fragment. It is needless
o enlarge. External evidence of a more satisfactory and con-
incing nature could not be desired. One or two circumstances
orthy of notice add to its importance.

In the first place, there is a singularly close connection
etween the sources of no small portion of the evidence and the
istrict in which the apostle laboured. Papias was Bishop of
Hierapolis; Polycarp, so intimately associated with Irenæus,
vas Bishop of Smyrna; Irenæus belonged to Asia Minor; Melito
vas Bishop of Sardis; Polycrates was Bishop of Ephesus; and
ustin Martyr wrote at Ephesus. In the second place, some of
he men to whom we owe these testimonies gave them under
onditions peculiarly favourable to their knowledge of the facts.
ustin Martyr, the earliest and most important, was not only

possessed of singular ability and an inquiring mind, but ha〈
travelled over most of the then known world, enjoying in thi〈
way the most ample opportunities of becoming acquainted witl
the convictions of the Church.   Irenæus discusses the famou〈
reading in Rev. xiii. 18 ; and, in doing so, refers to "all th〈
good and *ancient* copies," as well as to the "attestation to th〈
received reading, of those who had themselves seen John fac〈
to face."   Origen, the extent of whose scholarship and th〈
acuteness of whose criticism would have distinguished the mos〈
enlightened ages of the Church, came to his conclusion in spit〈
of all his prejudice against that chiliasm which the Apocalyps〈
appeared to favour.   In the third place, it would seem as if w〈
had in no case cited by us to deal only with individual opinio〈
It is upon the tradition of the Church that our witnesses res〈
their conclusion, thus taking us back to a period much more r〈
mote than their own, and to those historical authentications 〈
what they say which, though since lost, existed in their time〈
and were relied on by them.

Internal evidence confirms the conclusion drawn from the e〈
ternal.   The most important parts of it, indeed, like so man〈
other points connected with our subject, will find a more appr〈
priate place in the second appendix to these lectures.   But on〈
point claims attention now.   Both in the opening and closin〈
verses of the book the writer calls himself John (chaps. i. 1, 4, 9〈
xxii. 8), telling us at the same time that he was "in the isl〈
that is called Patmos, for the word of God and the testimony 〈
Jesus" (chap. i. 9).   Who could this John be but the apostle 〈
He speaks to the churches of Asia as possessed of authorit〈
which none can question : antiquity knows of but one John t〈
whom such a position may be assigned.   He had been banishe〈
to Patmos (the only natural interpretation of his words) for th〈
cause of Christ ; antiquity speaks only of one of his name wh〈
had experienced such a fate.   An attempt has indeed been ofte〈
made to show that a conjecture of Dionysius (Eusebius, *E. H.*〈
vii. 25), the probability of which is hesitatingly allowed b〈
Eusebius (iii. 39), may be well founded, and that the "John〈
of the Apocalypse may have been the person known as "Joh〈
the Presbyter" (Düsterdieck, *Einl.* § 4 ; comp. Bleek, *Intr.* t〈
N. T., ii. p. 202).   The probability, however, is that no suc〈
person as John the Presbyter ever existed (see the author'〈
paper in *Kitto's Journal,* Oct. 1867 ; and comp. Riggenbach〈
Die Zeugnisse, f. d. E. Joh. ; Steitz, in *Herzog's R. Encycl.*〈

üller, *Die Offenbarung, Joh.*, p. 703). Even if he did exist,
e cannot have occupied the place in the estimation of the
hurch which belongs to the author of the Apocalypse, or we
ould have known more about him ; nor do we meet anywhere
ith the slightest hint of his banishment to Patmos. The
tempt, therefore, to fix upon him as the author of the Apoca-
pse is vain ; and, so far as we may judge from the general
ne of the most recent literature upon that book, it seems to
ave been abandoned. Besides him there is no other John who
m be for an instant thought of. Upon the assertion that some
ie may have written it who pretended to be the apostle (see
leek's *Intr. to N. T.*, ii. p. 201) it is unnecessary to dwell.
he supposition is as destitute of probability as of proof.

To the conclusion naturally following from the above testi-
ionies various objections have been urged. The most formidable
f these are drawn from a comparison between the Apocalypse
id the fourth Gospel, not a few of the most distinguished
ipporters of the Johannine origin of the latter being of opinion
iat its difference from the former is in many respects so great
i to render it impossible to ascribe both to a common author-
iip. To this point, which may be considered the kernel of
ie whole question, and for the discussion of which it is de-
rable to reserve as much space as possible, we shall immediately
roceed. In the meantime one or two other objections, having
o relation to this comparison, call for notice.

These objections resolve themselves into the statement that
ie voice of antiquity is not unanimous in favour of the Johan-
ine origin of the Apocalypse, and more particularly that
istinct evidence of an opposite kind is borne by Caius, usually
esignated as a Roman Presbyter, by the sect known as the
logi, and by Dionysius, Bishop of Alexandria, in the third
ntury.

1. That of Caius. In Eusebius (*H. E.*, iii. 28) we meet the
illowing words, " About the same time, we have understood,
ppeared Cerinthus, the leader of another heresy. Caius, whose
ords are quoted above, in 'The Disputation' attributed to him,
rites thus respecting him : ' But Cerinthus, by means of revela-
ons which he pretended were written by a great apostle, also
ilsely pretended to wonderful things, as if they were shown him
y angels, asserting that, after the resurrection, there would be an
irthly kingdom of Christ, and that the flesh, *i.e.* men, again
ihabiting Jerusalem, would be subject to desires and pleasures.'

Being also an enemy to the Divine Scriptures, with a view to deceive men he said 'that there would be a space of a thousand years for celebrating nuptial festivals.'" These words of Caius, it is alleged, refer to the Apocalypse, and prove that he regarded it as a forgery of Cerinthus; while Dionysius of Alexandria must have had Caius and his statement, so interpreted, in his mind when, speaking of the Revelation of St. John, he says, "*Some indeed before us* have set aside, and have attempted to refute, the whole book, criticising every chapter, and pronouncing it without sense and without reason. They say it has a false title, for it is not of John, . . . but that Cerinthus, the founder of the sect of the Cerinthians, so called from him, wishing to have reputable authority for his own fiction, prefixed the title" (Eusebius, *E. II.*, vii. 25). Both conclusions are obviously hasty. The words of Dionysius, "some before us," can hardly refer to Caius, for the description given of the efforts of these persons in the passage quoted by Eusebius has little or no resemblance to what, as we learn from the same historian, Caius must have written. Dionysius speaks of persons who attempted to refute the whole book of Revelation, criticising every chapter, a thing which Caius could not have done in a work which was simply a dialogue or disputation against a certain Proclus in connection with the heresy of Montanism (Eusebius, *E. II.*, ii. 25; iii. 31; vi. 20). It is true, no doubt, that in that "Disputation" the books of Scripture were referred to, but not in the manner described by Dionysius. The probability, therefore, is that the Bishop of Alexandria is not alluding to Caius, but to other persons who rejected the Revelation of St. John and ascribed it to Cerinthus.

Again, it is by no means clear that the "pretended revelations of a great apostle" spoken of by Caius is the Revelation of St. John. As justly noted by Lardner (*Works*, ii. p. 402), St. John, or whoever was the author of the book, does not expressly give himself the title of Apostle. He simply calls himself "John." Why, then, should Caius speak of Cerinthus as claiming to give the revelations of "a great apostle" instead of pretending to give those of John? The description, too, of the contents of Cerinthus's work does not apply to our canonical book, and has a much closer affinity to some of those apocryphal *apocalypses* of which so many were in circulation in the early Christian Church. There is more ground to think that Caius refers to a book written by Cerinthus himself, in which he

claimed to have had visions ; and this conclusion is strengthened
by the fact that Cerinthus is distinctly said by Theodoret to
have "feigned certain visions which he professed to have seen"
(Speaker's *Comm. N. T.*, iv. p. 439, *note* 3), and the contents of
which were from Jewish sources (Smith's *Dict. of Christ.
Biogr.*, i. p. 449). Still further, it is in the highest degree improbable that Caius could have had the Apocalypse of St. John
in his eye when he used the language ascribed to him by Eusebius. For when he wrote at the beginning of the third century
the Apocalypse was accepted in the Roman Church, to which
he belonged, as the work of St. John, and in that Church Caius
appears to have been held in high estimation for his learning and
prudence. He is described by Eusebius as λογιώτατος (*E. H.*,
vi. 20). To these considerations may be added the statement
of Dr. Westcott when he says, " I may express my decided belief
that Caius is not speaking of the Apocalypse of St. John, but
of books written by Cerinthus in imitation of it. The theology
of the Apocalypse is wholly inconsistent with what we know of
Cerinthus' views on the Person of Christ " (*On the Canon*, p.
307, *note* 2).

The whole controversy regarding Caius would at once be
brought to a termination could we adopt the conjecture of the
present Bishop of Durham, that the controversy against Proclus
was conducted not by Caius, but by Hippolytus, whose first
name was Caius, and that the "Disputation" containing the
account of it was written by him (*Journal of Philology*, i.
p. 98 ; Smith's *Dict. of Christ. Biogr.*, i. p. 386). In that case it
would be utterly impossible to refer the description given as that
of Caius to the work of St. John, for the views of Hippolytus
on the Apocalypse are well known. He not only admired and
constantly referred to it, but he wrote a work entitled " A
Defence of the Apocalypse and Gospel of the Apostle and Evangelist John " (Smith's *Dict. U. S.*, iii. p. 99). Apart from this,
however, and allowing the existence of Caius as a person distinct from Hippolytus, there is no reason to think that the
authority of the Apocalypse was opposed by one in the important position of the Roman Presbyter. Dionysius has probably
in view persons whose difficulties rested mainly, if not wholly,
on the strange and enigmatical character of the book. Nay,
even if we admit that the words of Dionysius, "*some before us*,"
are to be understood of Caius, they are of much less weight
than is generally attributed to them. *Caius belonged to*

Dionysius's own time.[1] He *wrote* in the beginning of the third century : Dionysius was born in the last decade of the second, and was an already ordained Presbyter in A.D. 233 (Smith's *Dict. of Christ. Biogr.*, i. pp. 384, 850). The two men must have been of very nearly the same age. Thus the words, "*some before us,*" even when understood of Caius, take us back to no remote point in the history of the Church, and indicate no broken tradition with regard to the Apocalypse at a date much anterior to the days of Dionysius himself.

2. From Caius we may pass to those known as the Alogi. Lardner indeed doubts whether such a sect ever existed, so slight and confused are the notices regarding it that have come down to us (*Works*, viii. p. 629). Our information regarding them rests mainly on the accounts of Epiphanius (*lib.* l. 1, 3), who himself, after a fashion not confined to this single instance, invented the name by which they are known, intending to describe by it both their opposition to the idea that Jesus was the Divine *Logos*, or Word of God, and the unreasonableness of their views. They belong to the last quarter of the second century, and seem to have been persons marked by strong opposition to the chiliasm of the time. The fact that they rejected not only the Apocalypse, but also the fourth Gospel, ascribing both to the heretic Cerinthus, is of itself a proof that they were incapable of conducting critical investigations. No one would dream for a moment of accepting their conclusion upon the latter point ; and their opposition to the Johannine origin of the Apocalypse is thus materially weakened. It proceeded wholly upon internal grounds, and was in no degree supported by that reference to history, or that tradition of the Church, which is alone of weight for the present stage of our inquiry. The nature of the opposition, however, offered to the Apocalypse by the Alogi throws light upon two important points connected with our subject. It implies a recognition by the Church of both the Gospel and the Apocalypse about A.D. 170, and an acknowledgment of the unity of authorship of the two books.

3. We have still to speak of Dionysius of Alexandria. Great interest has always been taken in the statements of this father, who flourished in the first half of the third century

---

[1] If the Caius referred to in the letter of Dionysius to Domitian and Didymus be the Caius of whom we speak, then Dionysius describes him as a contemporary and companion in suffering (Eusebius, *H. E.*, vii. 11). This, however, may be another Caius; the name was a common one.

(† 264), and much importance has been justly attached to them. They are given at considerable length by Eusebius (*H. E.*, vii. 25), and they indicate an ingenuousness, sobriety, and critical discernment worthy of one of the most distinguished pupils of the illustrious Origen. The general opinion of Dionysius on the Apocalypse is expressed in the following words : " Having formed a conception of the subject of the Apocalypse as exceeding my capacity, I consider it also as containing a certain concealed and wonderful intimation in each particular. For, though I do not understand, yet I suspect that some deeper sense is enveloped in the words, and these I do not measure and judge by my private reason ; but, allowing more to faith, I have regarded them as too lofty to be comprehended by me, and those things which I do not understand I do not reject, but I wonder the more that I cannot comprehend."

Regarding the Apocalypse in this light, Dionysius did not hesitate *to quote it as Scripture* (Eusebius, *H. E.*, vii. 10); nor did he "venture," he tells us, " to set it aside, as there were many brethren who valued it much " (*ibid.* vii. 25). He agrees that it was " the work of some holy and inspired man," and he did " not deny that the author saw a revelation, and received knowledge and prophecy." His doubts centre wholly on the composition of the book by the Apostle John. With this idea he could " not easily agree," and he was of opinion that it was most probably the work of a second Ephesian John (the first being the beloved disciple) whose tomb he had heard (" they say ") was shown at Ephesus. This John was the person known as " the Presbyter," the tradition regarding whose grave has been preserved by Eusebius (*H. E.*, iii. 39). Had it not been for the fact that the John Mark of the Acts of the Apostles seemed to have had no connection with Asia, Dionysius would obviously have been more inclined to associate the authorship of the Apocalypse with him. In speaking thus he distinctly rejects that part of the tradition of " some before us " (to which so much importance has been attached), which would imply that the book was the composition of Cerinthus, and that it had " a false title, for it was not of John."

What concerns us most, however, is the ground upon which Dionysius rested his conclusion. It is remarkable that he anticipates to a large extent the more recent criticism of those who, holding the Johannine origin of the Gospel, deny a similar origin to the Apocalypse. Consideration of his difficulties may therefore be postponed, and, in the meantime, it is enough to say that, so far from indicating any interrupted tradition of the Church upon the point, Dionysius is a most important witness to its continuity. He obviously feels that he is arguing, not in favour of a disputed opinion where on either side there was an almost equal balance of authority, but against the *general tradition* of his time. He is opposing himself to *the Church ;* and hence in no small degree the care, the hesitation, and the modesty with which he states his views. The point to be chiefly noticed in connection with these views is, that they were wholly the result of *internal* considerations. There is not one word of appeal to any external authority thought worthy of regard. Dionysius finds it difficult to reconcile the language, the style, and the dogmatic contents of the book with what we otherwise know of the writings of St. John ; and, because of this, he resorts to a theory which he seems to have been the first to broach, that the author must have been another John than the apostle. The opinion thus expressed had little or no influence even upon the Alexandrine Church (Westcott *On the Canon,* p. 413).

Here, therefore, we are entitled to pause. So far as the external, and much at least of the internal, evidence goes only one conclusion can be drawn, that the Apocalypse is either the work of the Evangelist and Apostle, or that we have no means whatever of identifying the author. In the latter case the book would occupy a position in the Canon similar to that of the Epistle to the Hebrews.

One other point ought to be noticed. An attempt has been made by several recent writers, most elaborately by Keim (*J. of N.*, i. p. 217, etc. ; comp. Holtzmann in Schenkel's *B. L.*, iii. p. 332 ; Schenkel, *Ch. Bild. I. Einl.* c. ii. and appendix 2 ; Wittichen, p. 101, etc. ; also, in reply, Steitz, *St. u. Kr.*, 1868, part iii. p. 487), to show that St. John cannot be the author of the Apocalypse, because he had never any connection either with Ephesus or with Asia Minor, and because in fact he, as well as all the other apostles, had died before the destruction of Jerusalem. Could the premiss be established the conclusion would almost inevitably follow. So intimately is the book associated with the churches of Asia, so directly do the fathers who ascribe it to the apostle ascribe it to him in his supposed connection with that district, that, if no such connection existed, the whole tradition of the early Christian Church respecting St. John as the writer of the Apocalypse must be set aside as unworthy of reliance. A few words, therefore, upon this latest phase of the controversy seem to be required.

The texts relied on to prove the death of St. John before the destruction of Jerusalem are Luke ix. 49, etc., 51, etc.; Mark iii. 17; ix. 38, etc.; to which are added, as showing that all the apostles were dead before the Apocalypse was written, Rev. xviii. 20; xxi. 14. We can only recommend our readers to compare these texts with the conclusions drawn from them, that they may judge for themselves how flimsy are the foundations upon which not a little of that modern criticism rests which is so confidently urged on our acceptance. The argument against any connection between St. John and Ephesus is more elaborate. It depends partly upon the statement that there is no mention of such a connection in several of those early documents in which we might naturally have looked for it, and partly on the endeavour to prove that Irenæus, our chief authority upon the point, was led " under the combined influences of misunderstanding and of the necessities of the time " to confound the " Presbyter John," of whom we have already spoken, with the far more important John the Apostle. Of the former, not the latter, had Irenæus, while yet a boy, heard many memorable things from Polycarp: the former, not the latter, had been the " Lord's disciple," had succeeded to the sphere of St. Paul's labours in Asia Minor, had lived in Ephesus, had written the Revelation and the Gospel, and had died at a very great age in the reign of the Emperor Trajan. To all this has to be added that, according to a recently-discovered passage of the lost work of Papias (Nolte, *Theologische Quartalschrift*, forty-fourth year, p. 466, in Schenkel's *B. L.*, iii. 333, Παπίας ἐν τῷ δευτέρῳ λόγῳ τῶν κυριακῶν λογίων φάσκει, ὅτι ὑπὸ Ἰουδαίων ἀνῃρέθη), the apostle John was put to death by the Jews, that is, in Palestine, not at Ephesus. From these circumstances the conclusion is drawn that the whole story with regard to the apostle's having spent the last years of his life in Ephesus is mythical. It sprang up in Asia Minor late in the second century from the desire, everywhere experienced, to possess apostles as channels of the pure tradition in opposition to Gnosticism, and it was aided in its growth by the fact that there had been a John at Ephesus whom it was easy to confound with the apostle. But in reality the apostle never was in Asia; and it is thus impossible that the Apocalypse can be his work.

The argument cannot be accepted as either conclusive or

satisfactory. The first part of it obviously proves nothing.
We have no right to fix beforehand what a writer is bound to
say; and, if we are to reject statements of antiquity as false,
because in the scanty remains of early ecclesiastical literature
that have reached us fragments are found which do not mention them, even when it would have been natural to do so, we
shall have little left us to believe. Hilgenfeld calls attention to
the fact that Papias makes no mention of St. Paul (*Einl.* p.
396). The documents referred to are also silent, not only as to
the apostle's connection with Ephesus, but as to his existence,
and to that silence surely no importance is to be attached. As
to Ignatius, again, whose silence in his Epistle to the Ephesians
is thought so particularly inexplicable, it is to be observed (1)
that in chap. xi. he speaks not of St. Paul only, but of the
apostles with whom they had companied or been in accord, and
that in the number thus referred to St. John may have been included; (2) that if in chap. xii. the name of St. John is not
coupled with that of St. Paul, it is because it was not suitable
to his purpose. "Ignatius is speaking of the relations of the
Ephesians with martyrs. John died peaceably in extreme old
age at Ephesus" (Lightfoot's *Ignatius*, vol. ii., section i., p. 64).
Besides this "the life of St. Paul had a peculiar attraction for
Ignatius, owing to the similarity of their outward circumstances"
(*ibid.*) It is to be remembered too that St. Paul, not St. John,
had founded the Church at Ephesus; and all that has come down
to us from Christian antiquity bears witness to the importance
everywhere attached to such a fact. Nor is this even all that
may be said. The force of the argument from the silence of
Ignatius depends upon the assertion that the story with regard
to the apostle's residence at Ephesus sprang up about the time
of the publication of the fourth Gospel. Those therefore who
place the publication of that Gospel in the middle, or beyond
the middle, of the second century, may say that the silence in
question is best explained by the circumstance that there was as
yet no tradition of the kind. But Keim's own conclusions as to
the date of the Gospel close this refuge against him. Before
the letter of Ignatius was written the Gospel had appeared.[1]

---

[1] If, as seems to be generally agreed on, Ignatius was martyred during the persecution by Trajan, it could hardly be before A.D. 110 or A.D. 112. The latter is the date of Pliny's letter to Trajan (Lightfoot's *Ignatius*, vol. i. p. 56). The letter of Ignatius to the Ephesians was written only a very few weeks before his martyrdom.

The fable, supposing for the moment that it was only a fable, had sprung up. Ignatius must have known it. Yet he says nothing on the point. His silence must in consequence be attributed to other causes than such ignorance of the fact as may be employed to prove that the fact had no existence.

Again, Keim's theory compels us to suppose that Irenæus, in speaking as he does in his letter to Florinus of the intercourse of Polycarp with "John," was mistaken as to the John to whom Polycarp had referred, and had, without being aware of his error, substituted the apostle for "the Presbyter." The words of the letter are themselves the best answer to such a supposition, "I saw thee," says Irenæus, "when I was yet a boy, in Lower Asia with Polycarp, faring prosperously in the royal palace and endeavouring to commend thyself to him. For I remember better the things that then took place than those that have happened in more recent years (inasmuch as the things which we learn while we are boys grow up with our minds themselves and become a part of them), so that I am able to name the very place in which the sainted Polycarp was wont to sit and hold discourse, his goings out and comings in, the manner of his life and his personal appearance, his discourses to the multitude, and the narratives he used to give of his intercourse with John and the others who had seen the Lord. At these times Polycarp would recall the words which they had spoken, and would describe what he had heard concerning the Lord and His miracles and His teaching from those who had been eye-witnesses of the life of the Word, all that he related being in agreement with the Scriptures. These things through the goodness of God I was then in the habit of listening to with eagerness ; I stored them up not on paper but in my heart ; and from that time till now I am ever, through the Grace of God, revolving them faithfully in my mind" (see the letter in Stieren's *Irenæus*, i. 822). Can any impartial person read that letter, and for a moment imagine that the writer had mistaken the John of whom Polycarp so loved to speak ? Can there be here "a delusion which Irenæus disastrously transferred from his youth to his manhood" ? and was Polycarp "not the disciple of the apostle but of the other John the disciple of the Lord" ? (Keim, i. p. 221, 222). We have but to read the letter, so simple, so definite, so loving in its recollections, so true in its statement both of the process and the explanation of the process by which the aged writer was able to revivify the days of

his boyhood, in order to be satisfied that, in the absence of
positive contradiction from other quarters, we have in that
letter one of the most trustworthy documents of the early
Christian age.   Irenæus could not be mistaken as to these
memories ; and so clear is this that Scholten, supporting Keim
in his general position, found it necessary to assail the genuine-
ness of the letter (Smith's *Dict. of Christ. Biogr.*, ii. p. 544).   In
this undertaking he has, so far as we are aware, had no support ;
nor has the mistake thus attributed to Irenæus the slightest
countenance from any writer of the Church during the first
seventeen hundred years of her existence.

Still further, the theory now before us elevates into a great
historical personage a Presbyter of whom, if he ever existed, we
know nothing but the name.   Keim's theory forbids him to rest,
as so many have done, in the supposition that there were two
Johns at Ephesus, the one the Apostle, the other the Presbyter.
He is compelled to get rid of the former altogether, and he does
so by resolving him into the second bearer of the same name.
His argument may be taken advantage of by those who, on the
other hand, doubt the existence of the Presbyter, and are inclined to resolve him into the Apostle.   But it is unnecessary to
plead that point now.   Enough that the effort to ascribe all that
is said of "John" to one man, and that one man "the Presbyter," involves in it a series of improbabilities so great that in
this part of his conclusion Keim appears to have no followers.

Lastly, the tradition with which Keim's theory is at variance
is one of the earliest, most continuous, and best authenticated
which the second century presents.   Holtzmann allows that all
the church fathers are at one upon the point (Schenkel, *B. L.*,
iii. 332).   It is true that the fact is not alluded to in the Acts
of the Apostles or in the Epistles of St. Paul, because in all
probability the Apostle's residence at Ephesus did not begin
until these books were penned, but it is authenticated by a
succession of ancient Christian writers, some of whom from their
official position in that city, others from early or later connection
with it, had the best opportunities of being accurately informed,
while all of them are our most reliable authorities for the general
history of the time.[1]   Such were Polycarp, Polycrates, Irenæus,
Apollonius Presbyter of Ephesus, Clement of Alexandria, Origen,

---

[1] A long list of authorities for
the tradition will be found in
Archdeacon Lee's *Comm.*, p. 428 ;
in Renan, *L'Ant.*, p. 207, *note;*
and in Hilgenfeld, *Einl.*, p. 394,
etc.

and the historian Eusebius. Although, too, Scripture is silent upon the point, it is to be remembered that the false teaching directly condemned in the First Epistle of St. John is the heresy of Cerinthus, who taught in Asia Minor at the close of the first century, and who is placed by tradition in immediate connection with the apostle (comp. Westcott, *Epp. of St. John, Introd.*, p. xxxii.). The relation between St. John and Ephesus is thus confirmed from another point of view. Little need be said of the recently-discovered passage of Papias, quoted on p. 245. Knowing it only as it is given in Schenkel's *B. L.*, the writer of these pages may fail to do it justice. But, taking it as quoted by Holtzmann, there is no connection between the statement that St. John was removed ὑπὸ ʼΙουδαίων and the inference that his death must have taken place in Palestine. Instead of this the words are *against* the supposition that the " Jews " spoken of are to be sought in Palestine. Had such been the author's meaning we should almost certainly have had the article before ʼΙουδαίων. But he speaks simply of " Jews, " and Jews in all their persecuting bigotry, as the martyrdom of Polycarp bears witness, were nowhere more numerous than in Asia.[1]

Upon few things not mentioned in Scripture may we rely with greater confidence than upon this, that the Apostle John occupied a position of great authority among the Churches of Asia Minor before his exile to Patmos, and that after his deliverance from exile he returned to Ephesus, where he died.[2]

From all that has been said it ought to be manifest that the arguments, drawn chiefly from internal considerations, against the authorship of the Apocalypse by the Apostle John, are not sufficient to shake the decided and clear testimony of antiquity, that the John who speaks in that book is no other than " the disciple whom Jesus loved."

---

[1] Nolte himself thinks that the passage is probably corrupt, and that the reference in it applies to James, not John.

[2] It may be well to quote the words of Renan upon the point :— " Like almost all the accounts relating to the lives of the apostles, the traditions regarding the stay of John at Ephesus are subject to doubt ; yet they have their plausible side, and we would rather accept than reject them " (*L'Ant.*, p. 207).

APPENDIX II.

RELATION OF THE APOCALYPSE TO THE
FOURTH GOSPEL.

HAVING in the previous Appendix discussed the question of
the authorship of the Apocalypse, both on external and internal
grounds, a writer on the subject would in ordinary circumstances
have no more to say. But it so happens that, in the present
instance, there is one branch of internal evidence which of
itself prevents many from adopting the conclusion that the
Apocalypse is the work of the Apostle John. That book and
the fourth Gospel cannot, it is urged, have been written by the
same hand. The writer of these pages has elsewhere declared
and defended his belief in the Johannine origin of the Gospel
(*Comm.* vol. ii., *Intr. to Gospel of St. John*). He has also now
contended for the Johannine origin of the Apocalypse. Throughout the "Lectures" of this volume unity of authorship in the
case of these two books has been taken for granted and proceeded on. An effort must be made to show that the two
beliefs are not inconsistent with each other.

The confidence with which the statement, that there is an
irreconcilable difference between the two books before us, is
made by many distinguished ornaments of the later criticism of
the New Testament is very great, but it is unnecessary to give
many quotations from their works. Two, often referred to with
approbation both on the Continent and in England, may be
enough. "In the criticism of the New Testament," says De
Wette, "there is nothing established with such certainty as
that the Apostle John cannot have written the Apocalypse if
he be the author of the Gospel and Epistles, or that, if he be

he author of the former, he cannot also be the author of the
atter" (*Einleitung*, § 189, 4). The same conclusion is other-
vise expressed by Baur when he says : "The Evangelist's point
f view is not merely different from that of the Seer, it is
horoughly opposed to it" (*Die K. Ev.*, p. 347).

I. How far, we have now to ask, is this the case ? Several
ninor particulars require, in the first place, a moment's notice.

It is urged that in the Gospel St. John does not name him-
elf, that in the Apocalypse he does ; that since his name is
;iven in the latter book it ought to have been given with a
ulness resembling that with which he makes himself known to us
n the former as "the disciple whom Jesus loved ; " that, coming
»efore us in the one case as an apostle, we might have expected
iim in the other to describe himself by a higher designation
han a "servant" of Christ (chap. i. 1)'; and that a spirit of
rue humility would have led him to avoid speaking of himself
s he does when he tells us that the wall of the New Jerusalem
iad "twelve foundations, and on them twelve names of the
welve apostles of the Lamb" (chap. xxi. 14).

These objections are to a great degree inconsistent with one
.nother ; but, without dwelling upon this, the first of them is
t once disposed of by remembering the difference of the two
»ooks ; the one historical, and intended only to bring forward
he Redeemer while keeping the writer out of view ; the other
.pocalyptic, and needing a distinct voucher, on the part of the
.uthor, for the marvellous revelations granted him. Usage too
lemanded his name in the latter book. Every one of the Old
Testament prophets names himself. In particular, how often
lo we read in the book of Daniel, so largely followed in the
Apocalypse, the words, "I, Daniel"! (chaps. vii. 15 ; viii. 27,
tc.) Why not also in the Apocalypse, "I, John"? To the
econd objection it may be replied that the introduction of the
vords, "the disciple whom Jesus loved," for the simple designa-
ion "John," would not only have been cumbrous, but would
iave led to the charge that a fabricator was endeavouring to
»ass for the apostle. The humility alluded to in the third
»bjection has its parallel in the case of the other apostles who
requently speak of themselves in a similar way (Rom. i. 1 ;
? Cor. iv. 5 ; Gal. i. 10 ; Titus i. 1 ; James i. 1 ; Jude verse 1),
»esides which St. John, in the Apocalypse, writes less as an
.postle whose authority no one might despise than as a
'brother" of all persecuted saints, a "partaker with them in

the tribulation and kingdom and patience which are in Jesus "
(chap. i. 9). They were suffering members of Christ's body ; so
was he. Such was the deepest aspect of the Christian position,
that in which Christians were most like their Master. Why
assert apostolic dignity and honour when in the furnace of
affliction all had been welded into one? Finally, the fourth
objection disappears if we consider that the words complained
of are an exact echo of those of St. Paul when he tells us
that Christians are "built upon the foundation of the apostles
and prophets" (Eph. ii. 20), and that they express a fact borne
witness to by the selection of the twelve. Nor can any one who
recalls the light in which the "Lamb" is always set before us
in the Apocalypse doubt that the glory of the apostles of whom
the writer speaks lay in nothing in themselves, but in their
having been summoned to be "Apostles of the Lamb."

The above objections are trifling. We turn to one or two of
a more important character drawn from the style and language,
from the tone and spirit, from the method of delineation, and
from the teaching, of the book.

1. *The style and language.*—A negative argument first meets
us here which it may be well to notice. The Apocalypse, it is
said, fails to exhibit characteristic expressions of the Gospel,
such as ἡ ἀλήθεια, ποιεῖν τὴν ἀλήθειαν, εἶναι ἐκ τῆς ἀλήθ., ζωὴ
αἰώνιος, ὁ κόσμος, ὁ πονηρός, ὁ ἄρχων τοῦ κόσμου τούτου, τὰ
τέκνα τοῦ θεοῦ, ἐκ τοῦ θεοῦ εἶναι and γεννηθῆναι, τὰ τέκνα τοῦ
διαβόλου, σκοτία and φῶς, παρρησία and others (Düsterdieck,
p. 78; Schenkel, *B. L.*, iii. 339). But many characteristic expres
sions of St. Paul in his Epistle to the Romans are not found in
his equally undisputed First Epistle to the Corinthians ; and
an author's language is determined by the subject on which he
writes. No argument of weight can be built on such negations.
A similar remark applies to the complaint that the Apocalypse
has in many respects a terminology not found in the Gospel
Neither the one book nor the other, nor both together, exhaust
the terminology of the language which the writer employs.

It is at once to be allowed, however, that the style and
language of the Apocalypse are very different from those of the
other Johannine writings contained in the New Testament
The fact has constituted a difficulty from very early times. It
was dwelt on by Dionysius of Alexandria in the middle of the
third century with an acuteness not surpassed by any later
critic ; and the following words of Holtzmann may be taken as

d expression of the opinion of many modern
ing of De Wette's canon, already quoted, Holtz-
iis canon rests above all on the fact of thorough
uage and style, on the striking contrast between
iess, the multitude of linguistic roughnesses and
ipecifically Jewish Apocalypse on the one hand,
reek of the Gospel with its Alexandrian colour-
" (Schenkel's *B. L.*, iii. p. 339). Objections of
: summed up in the statement, that the differ-
language between the Gospel and the Apoca-
:d and penetrating as of itself to render the
of authorship untenable; that the barbarisms
the Apocalyptist cannot have proceeded from
and that even when the two writers use the
connect with them different thoughts.
: to the points thus indicated we may at once
hly unsatisfactory explanation of the diversity
;, the assertion that, at the date of the com-
iospel, the long residence of St. John in Asia
n him a better acquaintance with the Greek
had possessed when he wrote the Apocalypse.[1]
ioment that the interval between the writing
, was as great as supposed, it may yet be main-
ifidence that the grammatical and stylistic
the Apocalypse are not the result of ignorance.
the book displays more than ordinary freedom
: Greek tongue. It is written in a far more
in that of the calm and simple narratives of the
gurative, poetic, impassioned. In various passe-
e description of the fall of Babylon in chap.
if the New Jerusalem in chap. xxi., it rises to a
ce unsurpassed by anything that has come down
: antiquity. No tyro acquiring a knowledge of
ild have penned such passages. The writer is

xplanation even   gery between the Apocalypse and
  In his Essay on   the later writings of St. John, due
the Three," ap-   allowance being made for the dif-
imentary on the   ference of subject;" and, in a
he thus speaks: note, he adds that "the difficul-
re than thirty   ties are greatly increased if a late
he midst of a   date be assigned to the Apoca-
n will explain   lypse."
nguage and ima-

at home not only in his thoughts but with his words. Had he not been so his poetic inspiration would have been quenched. Still more decidedly must we dismiss the idea, supported by no mean names, that the Apocalyptist wrote Greek which he wished to be recognised as bad ; that he avoided customary expressions in order to bring his language into closer correspondence with his extraordinary revelations ; and that he set the ordinary rules of grammar at defiance, because he had already defied the ordinary forms of thought. Such a course is too trifling to be ascribed to him. It would be out of keeping with his seriousness and intensity of feeling. Whatever we do we must start with the conviction that, in writing a *revelation*, the Seer desired to be understood ; and that, if different forms of expression occurred to him, he would choose the most common and intelligible as the best fitted to his end. Once more, the idea of some that the linguistic peculiarities of the Apocalypse are due to a certain harshness and roughness in the mode of speech that belongs to age compared with youth, is to be set aside as not sufficiently supported by the experience of literary men. Our explanation of the phenomenon before us, if explanation can be given, must be sought in some other than any of these ways now mentioned.

Again, little need be said of results to be expected from an amended text. It is true that there are passages in the book in which objection taken to the language has been removed by later readings. It is so, *e.g.*, in chap. vii. 10, where κράζουσι is now read for κράζοντες ; in chap. viii. 11, where ἐγένετο is now read for γίνεται ; in chap. xi. 9, 10, where all the futures are now read as presents ; and in chap. xi. 11, where the simple αὐτοῖς ought to be read instead of either ἐπ᾽ αὐτούς or ἐι αὐτοῖς. Other examples might no doubt be added ; but the effect produced would be so slight that it is unnecessary to dwell upon it.

For the same reason we may omit all reference to passages where apparent anomalies of grammar are abundantly confirmed both by classical and New Testament usage ; as, *e.g.*, the frequent use of the nominative for the vocative, and of the plural for the dual, or the occasional use of the accusative to denote a point, as well as continuance, of time. Too many parallels to such constructions can be adduced to make it needful to say more of them than that they ought never to have been spoken of in this connection (comp. Moulton's *Winer, passim*).

We turn to real anomalies.

A very large part of the question connected with them belongs to the consideration of *intention*. If there be proof that the author was not only acquainted with ordinary usage but that he commonly employed it; and if, at the same time, it can be shown that, when he departs from it, he does it in such a manner, and on such occasions, as to make it clear that his departure was *designed*, the difficulty now dealt with is in a great degree removed. These peculiarities of construction are then no longer to be spoken of as barbarisms, or as indications of an imperfect knowledge of Greek. The contrary inference must be drawn. To violate the grammar or the genius of a language, either without knowing what we are about, or loosely, irregularly, and without evident intention, is unquestionably a token of ignorance; but to do so with design, however it may indicate folly, or vanity, or bad taste, is not. Departure from ordinary idiom then presupposes an acquaintance with it; and if, instead of being foolish or vain, the writer was obviously possessed of the opposite qualities, it is no unfair inference that he must have had a full hold of the speech that he employs. The departures of such a writer as Thomas Carlyle from the ordinary idiom of his contemporaries presuppose a more than ordinarily perfect, rather than an imperfect, acquaintance with the English tongue. Nor does it matter although, in judging of such a phenomenon, we may not always be able to discover exactly what the *intention* is. In a book of such peculiar structure as the Apocalypse, many of the figures of which baffle the skill of the interpreter, nothing else is to be expected. We must be prepared for inability to penetrate into those innermost feelings of the author which reveal themselves in a manner so remote and delicate. Let us turn to some of the anomalies complained of. In doing so we shall keep chiefly in view the objections of Lücke, who has treated the point with all his usual care and fairness (*Versuch*, p. 448, etc.).

The very first that meets us is one not only of the most remarkable, but of the most convincing, that the point of view under which we are now regarding these anomalies is correct. It is the construction of ἀπό in chap. i. 4, ἀπὸ ὁ ὤν καὶ ὁ ἦν καὶ ὁ ἐρχόμενος. The preposition is used thirty-nine times in the Apocalypse; and, in every instance, one of them occurring in the verse before us, and in the words immediately following those quoted, it is construed, in regular usage, with the genitive. Can there be a moment's doubt that Winer is right when he says that "the nominative is here designedly treated as an indeclinable noun" (Moulton's *Winer*, p. 227). Again, feminine nouns are followed by an adjective or a participle in the masculine, τὰς ψυχὰς . . . λέγοντες; φωνὴν λέγοντα; φωνὴ λέγων (chaps. vi. 9; ix. 13; iv. 1). Yet the construction not only of feminine adjectives in general, but of these *particular feminines*, with the feminine nouns that properly belong to them, is perfectly familiar to the writer. In the verse immediately following the first of the above examples we meet with φωνῇ μεγάλῃ; and, again and again, as in chaps. xiv. 18; xvi. 1, 17; xviii. 2, 4, etc., the same thing occurs; while in chap. xvi. 3 a similar observation holds with regard to ψυχή.

Again, neuter nouns are followed by plural verbs in many passages (chaps. iii. 4; v. 6; xi. 13, 18; xv. 4, etc.), but they are often also construed with the singular (chaps. ii. 27; viii. 3; xiii. 14; xiv. 13; xvi. 14; xix. 14, etc.) In chap. i. 19 we have even both constructions in the same verse.

Again, the nominative is met where we should have expected an oblique case corresponding to the case of the word with which the former is evidently in apposition. Many illustrations of this, given by objectors, are hardly indeed to be accepted as such. In chaps. xix. 6; xx. 2 the reading is too doubtful to be relied on, and chaps. ii. 20; v. 12; viii. 9; ix. 14; xiv. 7, 14; xxi. 12, are susceptible of other and simple explanations. Still a sufficient number of instances remains to arrest attention, such as chap. i. 5, where we have μάρτυς in apparent apposition with χριστοῦ; chap. iii. 12, ἡ καταβαίνουσα with Ἰερουσαλήμ in the genitive; chap. xiv. 12, οἱ τηροῦντες with τῶν ἁγίων, and perhaps others. But this construction is by no means a prevailing one throughout the book; and passages like chaps. iv. 9; vi. 1; vii. 1; viii. 13, establish in a perfectly incontestable manner that the writer was familiar with ordinary rules, and able to apply them when it suited him to do so.

Again, the present is said to pass into the future in chaps. i. 7; ii. 5, 16, 22, 23; iii. 9, and the aorist to be used for the future in chap. x. 7. But the use of these tenses is so regular in innumerable passages as to force us to the conclusion that, when there is a departure from it, which however there is not in several of the instances referred to, that departure is intentional.

Once more, there is a class of constructions with the verb δίδωμι presenting a singular contrast to what we should expect in a classical writer (comp. chaps. iii. 8, 9 ; viii. 3 ; xiii. 7, 16 ; xvii. 17), but the explanation is obvious. The verb referred to is one of the key-words both of the Apocalypse and the fourth Gospel. In the former it is used no fewer than fifty-eight times, and the object is to guide us, even at the expense of correctness of idiom, directly to Him who is the source of all blessing, and the Giver of all good. Translators, even the recent Revisers of the New Testament, in order to preserve the idiom of their own tongue, have often neglected such peculiar constructions (Rev. iii. 8 ; viii. 3). It may be doubted whether they have been right in doing so.

Enough has been said to establish the only point at present under consideration, that the constructions of the Apocalypse objected to as anomalous are the result of deliberate intention on the writer's part.

· The argument now adduced gains force from the consideration that we can to a large extent discover what the intention is. It is the writer's aim, though not so much his *deliberate* aim as one arising out of the conditions amidst which he writes, to conform to the spirit of that prophetical and rhetorical method of address to which he and his readers had been accustomed in the language of the Old Testament. Nor is it strange that it should be so. Every one will admit that the Apocalypse is steeped in the essence of that style of thought by which the Old Testament prophets are marked. Shall not its language also be largely coloured in a similar way ? The imagery of the Old Testament certainly lived in the mind of the Seer with not less vivacity than in the minds of its original authors. He uses it far too freely to admit of any other supposition. There is no laboured effort to mould it to his purpose. There is no sitting down with the passage of an ancient prophet before him, and directly adapting it to his end. The prophets and their words are in his heart. He breathes their atmosphere, sees with their eyes, hears with their ears, and is in every respect one with them. In these circumstances it is only most natural that their modes of expression should also influence him. Even in our own day one who lives much in the thoughts and language of the Bible will often use language, when speaking on sacred subjects, that at other times would appear ungrammatical. He will use " which " for who, and " let " for hinder ; and his hearers, so far from considering this a fault, will own that it lends to his words a weight of sacred association which they

would not otherwise possess.   The very same thing could hardly
fail to mark the writer of the Apocalypse ; and it is only necessary to remember further that, in his case, this influence would
flow from a double source—the Hebrew Bible and the Septuagint, for both can be proved to have been equally familiar to
him.[1]   When, accordingly, it is objected by Holtzmann, in the
article above referred to, that the strong Hebraising of the
Apocalypse is a proof, among others, that it cannot have proceeded from the author of the Gospel, we at once reply that
this very Hebraising, so far from being itself the difficulty to be
contended with, is a large part of the explanation of the real
difficulty, the anomalous constructions.   If indeed the Hebraistic
thoughts and figures could not have been used by one who wrote
the Gospel, an argument that would also prove that the author
of the *Pilgrim's Progress* could not have written *The Jerusalem
Sinner Saved*, we should be compelled to allow the force of the
objection.   But once admit that the Hebrew *figures* of the
Apocalypse are not inconsistent with the position of the fourth
Evangelist, and the Hebraising of the *style* follows as a natural
consequence.

The writer does, then, intentionally Hebraise.   Upon a
point like this no authority can be quoted equal to that of
Ewald, and that all the more because he rejects the identity of
authorship for which we contend.   Yet nothing can be more decided than his statement that the imitation of Hebrew idiom
in the Apocalypse goes so far as to lead to many a change in
Greek construction with the view of imitating the constructions
of the Hebrew tongue ; a statement which he immediately proceeds to illustrate by reference to a number of those cases most
eagerly urged against the book.   Such are ἵνα with a καί
following, chaps. iii. 9 ; xiii. 16 ; xxii. 14 : the change from the
genitive to the accusative in chap. xvii. 4 : the interchange of
the accusative and nominative in chaps. iv. 4 ; vii. 9 ; x. 8 ;
xi. 3 ; xiii. 3 ; xiv. 14 ; xx. 4 : the giving a double gender to
ληνός : the use of the masculine for other genders in chaps.
xiii. 14 ; xvii. 3 ; xi. 4 : and of the neuter for the masculine in
chap. xii. 5 (*Die Joh. Schr.*, ii. p. 53).   The statement must be
accepted as conclusive.

[1] Proof of his acquaintance with
the Hebrew Bible will not be
asked for.   Referring to his acquaintance with the LXX., and
illustrating his statement by
examples in a note, Ewald says,
"It cannot be doubted that our
author knew the LXX., and had
read it much" (*Die Joh. Schr.*, ii.
p. 52).

Still further, however, the influence of the Septuagint has to be noted ; and, when it is so, many other difficulties connected with the language before us disappear. The use of ἰδού, *e.g.*, instead of ἴδε, is at once explained, the former being not only the more sonorous and impressive word, but being that also invariably employed in those Old Testament prophecies between which and those of the Apocalypse the resemblance is so close. The same remark explains the use of παντοκράτωρ and σκηνὴ τοῦ μαρτυρίου; while it at once disposes of the objection that in the Apocalypse we always meet with Ἰερουσαλήμ, though in the Gospel we invariably read Ἰεροσόλυμα, for the first of these two forms is that usually met with in the LXX.

The explanation applicable to these usages prepares us for its application to others ; and the inference is confirmed by facts. Thus, the neuter plural noun is followed by the plural, not the singular, verb in such passages as Zechariah ii. 11; x. 7; xii. 3 : Ezekiel xxxviii. 10 ; xxxix. 7 ; Nahum ii. 5 ; iii. 10, and that too although, as we see in Ezekiel xxxviii. 10, the ordinary usage was known to the writers. Thus the repetition of the preposition before a series of nouns, objected to in such a text as Rev. xvi. 13, continually meets us in the language of the prophets (Zechariah i. 4, 6 ; vi. 10, 14 ; viii. 7). Nay, the tendency to repeat other words of a character still more marked is equally to be observed, as in Zechariah viii. 12, 19 ; and the desire to give a measured and solemn march to the language at once supplies the explanation. Thus, too, the use of a present and a future verb in the same clause occurs quite as frequently in the Old Testament as it does in the Apocalypse (Zechariah ii. 9, 10 ; xi. 6, where the future is not used for the present any more than in chap. iii. 9 the present is used for the future).[1]

The conclusion from what has been said is obvious. The grammatical constructions of the Apocalypse arise not from ignorance, but from design, and from the fact that, in an apocalyptic book, the writer naturally employs a style of language which he had come to regard as not merely an appropriate, but as the only appropriate, vehicle of visions such as his.

We are not wholly without analogy in this matter. Short as is our Lord's prophetic discourse in Matt. xxiv., and although so recorded that we cannot be sure that every word used is the exact equivalent of that originally spoken, it yet exhibits extremely similar phenomena. There is the same tendency to

[1] Comp. also such a use of δίδωμι as is found in Zech. iii. 9.

employ peculiar words, ἐκολοβώθησαν, διχοτομήσει (verses 22,
51); the same ἰδού, not ἰδε (verses 23, 25, 26); the same use
of the present for the future (verses 40, 41, 44). Had the discourse been as long as the Apocalypse; still more, had it been
marked by the disposition of that book to drive the prophetic
style to the utmost limit of intelligibility, we can scarcely doubt
that a much larger number of the anomalies which startle us in
the one case would also have met us in the other.

In connection with the point now before us, it is still further
urged that not only are there anomalies of construction in the
Apocalypse which forbid our ascribing its authorship to the
writer of the fourth Gospel, but that the style of the books
differs materially in at least two important particulars, in the
connecting particles employed in each, and in the different senses
in which the same words are used.

The first of these particulars can hardly be spoken of as important. An author is not bound to use the same connecting
particles in different books, and he cannot even be expected to
do so if his whole subject, aim, and sphere of thought are
different. Prophetic enthusiasm is so unlike calm narrative as
almost to forbid that the binding particles of sentences, or the
descriptive tenses used, shall be the same in both. The contrary
is rather to be looked for. The sameness thus desiderated
would really be an indication that the state of mind professed
by the writer was, in one or other of his works, not genuine;
that he had not really passed into the mood of which his book
claimed to be an utterance; and that he had not yielded himself to that flow of living thought which, as it lives, weaves a
garment for itself. Thus, to take one or two illustrations from
the books we are examining. Why complain that οὖν is so
much used as a particle of transition in the Gospel, and καί in
the Apocalypse? It will be found in almost every case quoted
from the former that οὖν is much more than a mere copula. It
introduces a reason why the second statement follows on the
first. But καί in the latter is not intended to do so. It merely
accumulates, one after another, successive parts of the visions of
the Seer. Let the inquirer take the fourth chapter of the
Gospel, or any other where οὖν frequently occurs, and let him
substitute for it the simple copula, he will immediately discover
that the meaning intended by the Evangelist is not brought
out; or let him select any chapter of the Apocalypse where
the καί is as frequently to be met with, and let him substitute

οὖν, he will see at once that the simply successive character of the visions is destroyed. The different particles are used with perfect propriety; and, however attached a writer might be to one of them, he could not have given it a place where the other was demanded by the progress of his thoughts. In the correct reading of the First Epistle of St. John, too, the particle οὖν does not occur at all, and yet the close connection of that Epistle with the Gospel is, so far as concerns our present purpose, undisputed. Again, why complain that the historic present, although not unfrequent in the Gospel, is not used in the Apocalypse ? Let us allow that the use of one of the commonest turns of Greek grammar may constitute a peculiarity upon which an argument may be built, is it not enough to observe that it is the intention of the Seer to introduce his visions as something belonging to the past, and not to lend them additional liveliness of delineation by speaking as if they swept before his eye at the moment when he wrote ? Again, why complain tha the sentences of the Gospel, though not of the Apocalypse, frequently begin without any copula at all ? The argument, if good for anything, will tell equally against the Johannine authorship of the First Epistle of St. John, in which the same peculiarity constantly occurs (chaps. ii. 22, 24 ; iv. 4, 6, 7-10, 11-13 ; so also ii. 5, 6, 9, 10 ; iii. 2, 4, 5, 9, 10 ; comp. Westcott, *The Epp. of St. John*, p. xl.). Once more, why urge that, because in the Gospel (chap. i. 38) the Hebrew term 'Ραββί is followed by the words ὃ λεγεται ἑρμηνευόμενον, Διδάσκαλε, a different writer appears in Rev. ix. 11, because we there read ὄνομα αὐτῷ ἑβραϊστὶ 'Αβαδδών, καὶ ἐν τῇ ἑλληνικῇ ὄνομα ἔχει 'Απολλύων ? The Greek term in the latter case is not, as in the former, the strict interpretation of the Hebrew ; and the writer does not intend to present it to us as if it were. The Greek for אֲבַדּוֹן is ἀπώλεια (comp. LXX. Ps. lxxxviii. 12 ; Job xxviii. 22), and only when we turn to the root of the Greek name Apollyon do we discover that it expresses the same meaning as the Hebrew. In all these cases, and many others might be taken did space permit, it is difference of thought that produces difference of words.

The second statement above mentioned, that even when the same characteristic words are used in our two writings, they are used in a different sense, is much more important than the one now considered. A writer of thoroughly marked individuality of character and views, however different at different times may be the purpose of his books and the style of their composition, will hardly use the same words with much diversity of meaning.   His ideas we may expect to be the same, and his words are the expression of his ideas.   Any well-grounded charge, therefore, that peculiar words of the Gospel, meeting us again in the Apocalypse, or *vice versâ*, bear a different sense in the two books would certainly constitute an argument of weight against identity of authorship.   Many illustrations of the alleged difference are given by Lücke (*Versuch*, p. 675, etc.)   It will be proper to examine them, and that in the order in which they are adduced.   We take first one mentioned by Lücke in a different connection, but properly belonging to the point before us (p. 673).

Ἔργα,—not found in the Seven Epistles in its genuine Johannine sense of Christian works of God (*Christliche Gottes-werke*) ;—but why limit us to the Seven Epistles, and not quote chap. xiv. 13, where this very idea is met with in its clearest form ?   Or why omit the many passages in which the " works " of the wicked are spoken of in a strictly contrasted sense, thus showing us, on the principle of contrasts already explained, p. 110, the precise idea which the Seer attached to the word when he applied it to the righteous ? (chaps. ix. 20 ; xvi. 11 ; xviii. 6 ; xx. 12, 13).   Even in the Seven Epistles ἔργα meets us in this sense (chaps. ii. 2, 19 ; iii. 1, 2).   The real truth, however, is that both in the Gospel and in the Apocalypse the word ἔργα is used in its purely Johannine force,— to indicate, not so much isolated deeds, whether good or evil, as the whole character of the life making itself manifest to men.

We turn to the examples upon which Lücke seems especially to depend—Ἀληθινός in the sense of the real, the only existing, or the true, in the Gospel ; synonymous with πιστός, δίκαιος, ἅγιος in the Apocalypse (chaps. iii. 7, 14 ; xix. 11), and there associated with the λόγοι, κρίσεις, ὁδοί of God rather than with God, or such symbols of Christ as " light " and " bread."   The facts are that in the Gospel ἀληθινός is used twice of God (chaps. vii. 28 ; xvii. 3), three times of Christ, in His character as the Light, the Bread from heaven, and the Vine (chaps. i. 9 ; vi. 32 ; xv. 1), once of worshippers (chap. iv. 23), once of a λόγος (chap. iv. 37), once of Christ's κρίσις (chap. viii. 16), and once of a μαρτυρία (chap. xix. 35) ; that in the Apocalypse it is used once of God (chap. vi. 10), three times of Christ (chaps. iii. 7, 14 ; xix. 11), once of the ὁδοί of Him who is κύριος (chap. xv. 3),

twice of the κρίσεις of the Lord (chaps. xvi. 7 ; xix. 2), and
thrice of His λόγοι (chaps. xix. 9 ; xxi. 5 ; xxii. 6).   No more
need be said to show how closely the usage corresponds ; while
the passages above referred to, in which it occurs along with
other appellations, need only to be looked at in order to see
that it is *not* synonymous with these, but that it has its own
proper and distinctive meaning.   Were similarity not only in
the use of a particular word but in the *special meaning* of that
word desired, a better example could hardly be found than in
ἀληθίνος.   Ἀγάπη and ἀγαπᾶν are said to have neither the
same emphasis (*accent*) nor the same idea in the Apocalypse as
in the Gospel.   The two words occur six times in the Apocalypse.   Three of these are abandoned by Lücke (chaps. i. 5 ; ii.
4, 19) ; and, as one of the three is "to Him that loved us," a
fourth (chap. iii. 9), "I have loved thee," must be added to
the list.   Only two remain, "they loved not their lives unto
the death," and "the beloved city" (chaps. xii. 11 ; xx. 9),
with which it seems enough to compare John xii. 43, "they
loved the praise of men," words showing that the Evangelist
also could apply the expression to other objects than God, or
Christ, or our Christian brethren.   Σκηνοῦν is said to be used
by the Evangelist in the technical sense of the dwelling of the
Shechinah of the θεὸς λόγος, and with the preposition ἐν, while
it is used in the Apocalypse of God with a distinct reference to
the σκηνὴ τ. θεοῦ, and with the prepositions ἐπὶ or μετὰ, or, as
in chaps. x. 4 ; xx. 3, in the sense of "dwelling" in general.
These last references must be intended for chaps. xii. 12 ; xiii.
6, and they supply an exact parallel to John i. 14, where the
reference is not to the Shechinah of the θεὸς λόγος but to the
"Word made flesh" whose glory the Evangelist had "beheld."
Besides this, the meaning of the word in the Apocalypse has
been misapprehended by Lücke.   It denotes much more than
the mere general notion of dwelling.   There lies in it one of the
particulars of that identification of Christ and His people which
is fundamental to the Seer.   Jesus "tabernacled" (John i. 14) ;
they also "tabernacle."   The reference in chaps. xii. 12 ; xiii.
6, it will be observed, is not to angels or spirits in heaven, but
to the ransomed family of God in their condition of heavenly
privilege upon earth.   They "rejoice," while "woe" falls
upon the "earth" and the "sea," or, in other words, upon
the ungodly.   It may be further noticed that the verb is found
in the New Testament only in the two books of which we speak.

Lücke's observations on μαρτύρια and μάρτυς might almost be passed by as belonging rather to a different department of the subject. It may however be observed that in the Gospel the time was hardly come to speak of "witnesses" of Jesus, that in the Apocalypse it was; and further that in John iii. 11, 32, 33; v. 31, the use of μαρτύρια is precisely analogous to its use in such passages as Rev. i. 2, 9; xii. 17. Ἔχειν μέρος is said to be construed in Rev. xx. 6 with ἐν, in John xiii. 8 with μετά. Construction in the former case with μετά would be impossible, and the use of the preposition is determined by the idea to be expressed. With far more reason might it be urged that Romans and 1st Corinthians cannot have the same author, because in chap. xi. 25 of the former we have ἀπὸ μέρους, and in chap. xi. 18 of the latter μέρος τι, to express not a different but the same idea. Σφραγίζειν, it is alleged, is frequently used in the Apocalypse in the sense of closing fast (chaps. x. 4; xx. 3), or of putting a mark on one (chaps. vii. 3, etc.), while it is met with only twice in the Gospel (iii. 33; vi. 27), and then with the meaning of confirming or legitimising. The interpretation thus given to the word in the Gospel is incorrect. The fundamental idea in John vi. 27 has nothing to do with confirmation or proof. It denotes the act by which God has marked out the Son as what He is, in the office He is to fill, and in the blessings He is to bestow; precisely the same idea as belongs to it in Rev. vii. 3, etc., where the servants of God are marked out as His. Again in Rev. xx. 3 the word includes no thought of "holding fast," which had already been expressed in the previous ἔκλεισεν. It calls attention only to the mark or seal impressed upon the abyss (comp. Daniel vi. 17), by which the Almighty signifies that the enemy within is kept there for His own purposes, with which none can interfere. The same idea appears also in chap. x. 4, although obscured in the authorised translation by the words having been rendered "seal up" instead of "seal." The use of ἰδού has already been considered, and nothing further need be said of it. The use of ὁ νικῶν in the Apocalypse is allowed to present an important resemblance to its use in the fourth Gospel and in the Epistles of St. John; yet even here, it is urged, there is a difference, the verb being in the former absolute, in the latter having an object such as κόσμον or πονηρόν. Let our readers turn to Rev. xi. 7; xii. 11; xiii. 7; xvii. 14, passages not referred to by Lücke, and they will not only find an object associated with the verb, but the very same object as that in 1 John iv. 4. The resemblance in the use of $\tau\eta\rho\epsilon\hat{\iota}\nu$, not less striking than that in the use of $\nu\iota\kappa\hat{\alpha}\nu$, is allowed, but it is objected that in Rev. xiv. 12 we have $\tau\grave{\eta}\nu$ $\pi\acute{\iota}\sigma\tau\iota\nu$ $'I\eta\sigma o\hat{\upsilon}$ as an object to the verb, an object never found in the Evangelist, who uses the word $\pi\acute{\iota}\sigma\tau\iota\varsigma$, except in the Apocalypse, only in 1 John v. 4. But it is Christ Himself who uses the different expressions in which this verb occurs in the Gospel, and it was much more natural for Him to speak of "keeping His sayings, His word, His commandments," than of "keeping His faith." The further objection, that the words of Rev. ii. 26, "he that keepeth My works unto the end," is a formula which would hardly have entered into the thoughts of the Evangelist, is difficult to answer, because the Evangelist has given no indication that it might not. This much, however, cannot be forgotten, that the word $\check{\epsilon}\rho\gamma\alpha$ in the fourth Gospel denotes in a very peculiar manner the whole working of the Redeemer, all in which He naturally expressed himself, and that $\tau\eta\rho\epsilon\hat{\iota}\nu$ might therefore be as easily connected with it as with $\lambda\acute{o}\gamma o\iota$ or $\acute{\rho}\hat{\eta}\mu\alpha$ or $\acute{\epsilon}\nu\tau o\lambda\alpha\acute{\iota}$. Any objection founded on the use of $\Sigma\alpha\tau\alpha\nu\hat{\alpha}\varsigma$ is abandoned by Lücke himself, who compensates, however, for its abandonment by attaching all the more importance to the fact that the appellation "Lamb," so often applied in the Apocalypse to the exalted Redeemer, is there expressed by the term $\grave{\alpha}\rho\nu\acute{\iota}o\nu$, while in the Gospel we read only of $\grave{\alpha}\mu\nu\acute{o}\varsigma$. Yet the use of the former instead of the latter in the Apocalypse admits of a simple and natural explanation, which again binds our two writers together instead of separating them from each other. For the word $\grave{\alpha}\mu\nu\acute{o}\varsigma$ is not once used by the writer of the fourth Gospel in any description of his own. It occurs only twice in that work (chaps. i. 29, 36), and both times in the mouth of John the Baptist. The word $\grave{\alpha}\rho\nu\acute{\iota}o\nu$ again is found only once in the Gospel (chap. xxi. 15), and then in the lips of Jesus. Can we suppose that this was the only time during a three years' ministry that our Lord, who seems often to have used of Himself the figure of a shepherd, spoke of his $\grave{\alpha}\rho\nu\acute{\iota}\alpha$? Hardly will any one for a moment think so. If we may not say that it is certain, we may at least look upon it as in the highest degree probable, that the tender expression must have been often in the Good Shepherd's mouth, and in that circumstance alone we have an ample explanation of the fact that St. John should have preferred it to $\grave{\alpha}\mu\nu\acute{o}\varsigma$, a word associated with no such endearing recollections. The memory of the Evangelist guides the Seer.[1] That the Apocalyptist should speak in chap. xxi. 6 of the fountain τ. ὕδατος τῆς ζωῆς, while the writer of the fourth Gospel speaks of ὕδωρ ζῶν, cannot be deemed of consequence, as Lücke himself allows the phrase ὁ ἄρτος τῆς ζωῆς to be equivalent to ὁ ἄρτος ὁ ζῶν ; and that in Rev. ii. 17 we should meet, instead of the latter expression, with the phrase τὸ μάννα, is at once explained when we remember that every one of the figures of the latter book is taken from the Old Testament. Finally, it is urged that in Rev. xix. 13 the expression ὁ λόγος τοῦ θεοῦ, while bearing an unmistakable resemblance to the conception of the Prologue of St. John's Gospel, is distinguished from it by the fact that in the former the term is applied to the historical, in the latter to the prehistorical, Christ. The objection is again unfounded. The "name" of the *historical* Christ is that referred to in the 12th, not the 13th, verse of chap. xix.   It is the "name which no one knoweth but He Himself," which expresses the character of His whole redeeming work, and which can only be "known" (*i.e.* in the Johannine sense, *known with inward and experimental knowledge*) by the Father who plans the work (comp. Matt. xi. 27), the Son who executes it, and the members of Christ's Body when their union with their Lord is perfected (chap. ii. 17).   The name of verse 13, "The Word of God," is the name which belongs *originally* and *essentially* (κέκληται) to the rider upon the white horse, and which is again fittingly applied to Him in the moment of His final victory, when the historical conflict is ending, and when He who says "I glorified Thee on the earth, having accomplished the work which Thou hast given me to do," immediately adds, "And now, O Father, glorify Thou Me with Thine own Self with the glory which I had with Thee before the world was" (John xvii. 4, 5).   One consideration again is sufficient to remove any apparent force belonging to the statement that in the Gospel we read only of the ὁ λόγος, without the genitive θεοῦ which accompanies it in the Apocalypse. No one will deny that the Apocalypse, if not the work of the author of the fourth Gospel, must have supplied to that work its special view of the Redeemer. The author of the Gospel, therefore, can have seen no difference of meaning between the words he found before him

---

[1] Füller, in his *Comm. on the Apoc.*, suggests that St. John's love of the word ἀρνίον may have been determined by the direct contrast which it affords to θηρίον, the wild beast, the enemy of the Lamb.

and the shorter term employed by himself, or he would certainly
have made the resemblance more complete.

We have thus examined all those cases of a different use of
the same words in our two documents which are adduced by
Lücke to prove diversity of authorship. In every one of them
we have either found the alleged difference disappear, or resolve
itself, when the words were properly interpreted, into identity
of meaning. A few additional illustrations of the same kind
might be found in other writers, such as De Wette or Davidson, but those who have followed us thus far will not ask a
further prosecution of the argument. Instead of proving a
difference of authorship it seems rather, so far as it has gone, to
favour the conclusion that, notwithstanding many apparent indications to the contrary, the authorship of the two books is one.

2. A second objection to that unity of authorship for which
we are contending is drawn from *the tone and spirit* of the
books. The heat and fire which appear in the Apocalypse are
said to be entirely out of keeping with the quietness and gentleness of the fourth Gospel and the First Epistle of St. John.
But to ascribe such a tone to these writings is either to misunderstand them or to view them superficially. There is,
indeed, one section of the Gospel, chap. xiii. to chap. xvii., when
the great conflict is over and Jesus is alone with His disciples,
which breathes nothing but an atmosphere of the most perfect
love and peace. The other chapters leave a wholly different
impression upon the mind. The " Son of thunder " is there
beheld in every incident and in every discourse of Jesus which
he records. In none of the earlier Gospels is the idea of struggle,
of conflict, of tumultuous and excited passion, so constantly or
powerfully impressed upon the mind. Even the denunciations
of the Scribes and Pharisees in Matt. xxiii. are not for a moment
to be compared in intensity of rebuke with the language of chap.
ix. of the Gospel of St. John. The single term " the Jews,"
used by the writer to describe the opponents of Jesus, carries in
it, when properly appreciated, a depth of indignation and scorn
to which the rest of the New Testament affords no parallel;
while the manner in which the persons so designated are presented to us in chaps. xviii. and xix., when they accuse Jesus
before Pilate, reveals to every one who reads in the style of a
narration the narrator's feelings, a depth of emotion on the
writer's part in which all the most eager passions of the soul
were stirred. Similar remarks may be made upon the First

Epistle of St. John. Where else do we find such expressions as
"If we say that we have fellowship with Him, and walk in the
darkness, we lie;" "He that saith, I know Him, and keepeth
not His commandments, is a liar;" "Who is the liar but he
that denieth that Jesus is the Christ?" "Whosoever hateth his
brother is a murderer;" "The whole world lieth in the evil
one"? (chaps. i. 6 ; ii. 4, 22 ; iii. 15 ; v. 19). These expressions
prove that, whatever may be the tone of calmness and love
which in some respects characterises this Epistle, there is a
slumbering fire beneath ready to break out when occasion calls
for it. No well-founded contrast can be drawn between the
spirit disclosed by the Gospel and Epistle upon the one hand,
and the Apocalypse upon the other. Nor can any criticism
betray more imperfect appreciation of the tone of these several
writings than that of Düsterdieck when, comparing the Apocalypse with the other writings of St. John, he declares that
"another spirit thinks, another heart beats, and another mouth
speaks in it" (*U. S.*, p. 71). The peaceful pictures of the former
are not more touching than those of the latter. The severity,
the indignation, and the storm of the latter are not more intense
than those of the former.

3. A third objection to the unity of authorship we are now
considering relates to *the method of delineation* marking our two
books. The one, it is urged, is sensuous, the other spiritual
the one is full of concrete and plastic representations, and denotes its objects by fixed measures and numbers, the other
moves in the region of pure thought, making itself manifest in
all the freedom of truth, in speculative depth, and in a rich
power of grace for the life (Baur, p. 346, etc. ; Düsterdieck, p.
69, etc.) To the contrast thus drawn it is not sufficient (with
Füller) to reply that, in the Apocalypse, the Seer is little more
than a passive instrument relating what is presented to him in
vision. However true the Divine source of what he sees, he
must have entered fully into its spirit ; and, in his descriptions,
he must be understood to reveal not merely the impressions
made upon him by an external Divine agency, but habits and
modes of thought which he had made his own. It is more,
therefore, to the purpose to say that the two methods of delineation are not inconsistent with each other, that the prominence of one at any particular moment is determined by the
circumstances of the case or the object which the author has in
view, and that the inward appreciation of Christ's Kingdom in

s utmost spiritual power may consist with the liveliest percep-
ion of its outward fortunes in the world. The parable of the
eaven has a different meaning from that of the mustard seed ;
et the same lips of Jesus uttered both.

Even this is not all that may be said, for the decided way in
which the two books are opposed to each other rests, partly upon
n imperfect appreciation of the form of the Gospel, and partly
pon a false interpretation of the Apocalypse. Nothing, for
xample, is more characteristic of the Gospel than the extra-
rdinary degree to which it brings spiritual truths before us in
material forms. Each miracle recorded in it is an illustration
f this fact, while the details of the narratives are often so
rouped as to show that each detail, to the ordinary beholder a
matter of insignificance, was to the writer full of spiritual mean-
ig (comp. paper by the writer in *Br. and For. Ev. Rev.*, Oct.
871, and *Intr. to Gospel of St. John in Comm.*, p. xxv.). The
ame similarity will afterwards be pointed out with regard to
umbers (p. 274). On the other hand, the importance attached
y Düsterdieck (*U. S.*, p. 70) to the Nero-fable, as showing that
he Apocalypse cannot be the work of the Apostle, disappears
when we consider that there is no such fable in the book
comp. Lect. vi. and Appendix iii.). No doubt the two books
re very different, but we have too many examples (witness
Goethe) of a high poetic genius delighting in the plastic figures
f the imagination, combined with speculative depth and the
ower of uttering pure thought in its purest forms, to make it
mpossible to suppose that the two gifts could be united in one
man.

Of the fact that the Apocalypse is pervaded by pure Christian
hought, however much it may be presented in the forms of the
Old Testament, we have already spoken.

4. A fourth objection to the unity of authorship now claimed
or the fourth Gospel and the Apocalypse is taken from *the
teaching* of each book. The points especially selected by
Düsterdieck to establish diversity of authorship are the follow-
ig:—the first and second resurrections of chap. xx. ; the thou-
and years' reign of the same chapter ; the doctrine of antichrist
nd his opposition to the Redeemer ; and the manner in which
he λόγος is described. Of the last of these four points we
ave already said enough (p. 266). The first two have also been
iscussed (Lect. vi.), and an effort has been made to show that,
nstead of a difference in the teaching of our two books, their

unity in this respect is of the most striking kind, any supposition to the contrary arising from imperfect interpretation. A few words have still to be spoken on the third point, the doctrine of antichrist. The objection rests on the idea that, in the Apocalypse, antichrist is a person who appears in chap. xvii. 11, instead of a spirit of hostility to Christ. But there is a want of evidence that this representation is correct. The beast of the passage referred to is in reality identical with the beast of verse 8 of the same chapter. It is an eighth, though not numerically so in the same line with the seven. Then it would be an eighth *head;* but the Seer is dealing with *the beast itself*, not with its heads, and it is spoken of as an eighth, simply because it follows the seven, and because in its final condition the malice and evil of its previous conditions are concentrated. It is also "of the seven." The meaning cannot be that it is one of the seven, when it had just been described as distinct from them. The preposition "of," too, in the usage of St. John, denotes origin and, with origin, identity of nature. The beast is thus the essence, the concentrated expression, of the seven, and the embodiment of their spirit. In all this we have nothing of a personal antichrist; we have simply the last and worst manifestation of the ungodly power of the world. Not only so. When we attend less to any particular text than to the general strain and bearing of the Apocalypse, the resemblance between the teaching of that book and other writings of St. John on the subject of antichrist comes still more strikingly into view. In 2 John, verse 7, we have a definition of antichrist, "They that confess not that Jesus Christ cometh in the flesh. This is the deceiver and the antichrist,"—words upon which Dr. Westcott thus comments, "The thought centres upon the present perfection of the Lord's Manhood, which *is* still, and is to be manifested, and not upon the past fact of His coming" (*in loc.*). And what is this but the keynote of the Apocalypse, distinctly struck in chap. i. 17, 18, and sounding throughout the book? The Seer has constantly before him the risen and glorified Redeemer, who, for the present unseen, is about to manifest Himself in the brightness of His glory. Opposition to Him in that aspect is the antichristian spirit; and the opposition, when it reaches the extreme point of its development, is antichrist. If the Apocalypse does not *define* in the same terms as the Epistle, it utters the very same thought from its beginning to its close. It centres in the same "perfection of

he Lord's Manhood." Its enemy of Christ, its antichrist, is
o other than St. John's in his Epistle.

II. We have considered the most important objections urged
gainst the unity of authorship of the Gospel of St. John and
he Apocalypse; but it is not enough to answer objections.
'hose who defend the traditional view of the Church are entitled
o approach the subject from the positive as well as the negative
ide, and the importance of the question at issue calls on them
o do so. Our plea is that the two books so closely resemble
ach other in many essential particulars as to lend powerful
onfirmation to the idea that they spring from the same source.
)f these particulars we notice the Language, the Structure, and
he Teaching of both books.

1. Their *Language.*—We have already found Düsterdieck
nd others objecting to the identity of authorship for which we
lead on the ground that many characteristic expressions of
ach book are not found in the other, and we have allowed that
o a certain extent the statement is correct. But a wider con-
ideration of the language of both discloses an amount of simi-
arity which it is impossible to disregard. We take first some
ndividual and characteristic words.

'Αληθινός, a word so characteristic of St. John that, while
ound only once in the Synoptic Gospels, once in a Pauline
Epistle, and four times in the Epistle to the Hebrews, it occurs
ine times in the fourth Gospel, four times in the First Epistle of
t. John, and ten times in the Apocalypse, and in every instance
n these three latter books in *its own distinctive signification.*
'he word is allowed to be characteristic of the fourth Gospel.
t is equally characteristic of the Apocalypse. Not less marked
 the use of the verb δίδωμι. The word is in itself simple, and
 often met with in the different books of the New Testament;
ut the following passages in the Gospel show a characteristic
mployment of it—chaps. iii. 35; v. 22, 27, 36; vi. 65; vii.
2; xiii. 3; xvii. 6. A similar remark applies to the following
exts in the Apocalypse—chaps. ii. 23; iii. 8, 9; vi. 4; vii. 2;
iii. 3; xi. 3; xiii. 7, 16; xvi. 8; xvii. 17; xx. 4. These
assages have only to be looked at in order to satisfy us that
 both books the word is used in circumstances in which we
ould certainly have expected some other form of expression.
'he word νικᾷν is not less characteristic. Found only four
ther times in the New Testament, it occurs six times in the
irst Epistle of St. John and sixteen times in the Apocalypse,

while its special force appears to rest upon the words of our Lord in John xvi. 33. However this may be, it is undoubtedly characteristic of that idea of the Christian life as a victory in the midst of conflict which marks so strongly the views of the beloved disciple. Μαρτυρεῖν and μαρτυρία, it is on all hands allowed, express a characteristic idea of the fourth Gospel and the First Epistle of St. John. The words and the idea are also characteristic of the Apocalypse. The same thing may be said of the word τηρεῖν, which, from its use in the Gospel and Epistle, we are entitled to call a peculiarly Johannine word. But it is not less characteristic of the Apocalypse, and that too in its own peculiar sense (as distinguished from φυλάσσειν) of "keeping," in the exercise of active and strenuous care, rather than of watching over to preserve. In not one of the passages in which the former verb is used in the Apocalypse could we substitute the latter without changing the idea which we learn from the Gospel (especially from chap. xvii. 12, where it is used in conjunction with φυλάσσειν) to attach to it. Of the use of the word σκηνοῦν we have already spoken. To these instances may well be added the singular use of the preposition ἐκ in the Apocalypse. This preposition seems to be used in that book one hundred and twenty-seven times, and its proper signification in almost every case is "out of;" yet so strange, and apparently so unidiomatic, would be the result of such a rendering (comp. especially such passages as chaps. ii. 7, 21, 22; vi. 4, 10; viii. 11; ix. 18; xiv. 13; xv. 2; xvi. 21) that the New Testament Revisers have only felt themselves able to adopt it forty-one times out of all that number. On other occasions they resort to such renderings as "of," "from," "by," "with," "on," "at," "for," "because of," "by reason of," "from among." Compare this with the use of the same preposition in the fourth Gospel, where we meet it in a similarly strange and apparently unidiomatic way, so that the Revisers have again thought it necessary to depart from their original, and to substitute "of" or "from" for "out of," though at the cost of sacrificing the peculiar meaning of St. John (comp. chaps. iii. 31; iv. 13; vi. 13, 39, 51; viii. 23, 44; ix. 6; xi. 1; xii. 3, 27, 32; xvii. 15). In cases such as these, and others might be added, the preposition springs out of a mode of thought characteristic of the writer, is far from being equivalent to ἀπό, and is without a parallel in the other New Testament books.

In addition to what has now been said, two or three special

passages deserve a moment's notice—Rev. i. 7 compared with John xix. 37, in both of which Zech. xii. 10 is quoted, and the Hebrew is rendered not, as in the LXX., by the Greek $\kappa\alpha\tau o\rho\chi\epsilon\hat{\iota}\sigma\theta\alpha\iota$, but by a word of wholly different signification, $\dot{\epsilon}\kappa\kappa\epsilon\nu\tau\epsilon\hat{\iota}\nu$. The efforts made to escape the force of the conclusion to be drawn from this are allowed by Dr. Davidson to be futile (*Intr.*, i. p. 334)—Rev. xxii. 2 compared with John xix. 18, the position of the tree of life relative to the two sides of the river of life being described by the phrase $\tau o\hat{\upsilon}\ \pi o\tau\alpha\mu o\hat{\upsilon}\ \dot{\epsilon}\nu\tau\epsilon\hat{\upsilon}\theta\epsilon\nu\ \kappa\alpha\iota$ $\dot{\epsilon}\kappa\epsilon\hat{\iota}\theta\epsilon\nu$, the position of Jesus on the cross relative to the two thieves who were crucified with Him by $\kappa\alpha\grave{\iota}\ \mu\epsilon\tau'\ \alpha\dot{\upsilon}\tauo\hat{\upsilon}\ \ddot{\alpha}\lambda\lambdao\upsilon\varsigma$ $\delta\acute{\upsilon}o\ \dot{\epsilon}\nu\tau\epsilon\hat{\upsilon}\theta\epsilon\nu\ \kappa\alpha\grave{\iota}\ \dot{\epsilon}\nu\tau\epsilon\hat{\upsilon}\theta\epsilon\nu$. The similarity is rendered more striking by the fact that the other Evangelists employ an entirely different phrase in relation to the crucifixion, $\epsilon\hat{\iota}\varsigma\ \dot{\epsilon}\kappa\ \delta\epsilon\xi\iota\hat{\omega}\nu\ \kappa\alpha\grave{\iota}$ $\epsilon\hat{\iota}\varsigma\ \dot{\epsilon}\xi\ \epsilon\dot{\upsilon}\omega\nu\acute{\upsilon}\mu\omega\nu$ (Matt. xxvii. 38; Mark xv. 27; Luke xxiii. 33)—Rev. xi. 8 compared with John xix. 20, the true reading of the latter passage supplying the rendering, which even the Revisers have ventured to place only in the margin, "For the place of the city where Jesus was crucified was nigh at hand." This reading has indeed been ridiculed on the ground that it makes St. John say that Jesus was crucified within the city, when the fact was well known to every one that he had suffered "without the gate" (M'Clellan *in loc.*). So far from doing so, it affords one of the most striking coincidences of thought to be found in the writings we are examining; the language in both cases, however different, being used for the purpose of bringing the guilty city of Jerusalem into closer connection with the crime of the crucifixion of its Lord.[1]

[1] In addition to the illustrations spoken of in the text many others may be briefly referred to in a note. Attention ought to be paid not to particular words alone, but to the general idea or the turn of thought. For the sake of the English reader we shall give the English translation rather than the Greek. Rev. i. 1, "God gave," comp. John vii. 16, xii. 49; i. 2, "signified," c. J. xii. 33, xviii. 2; i. 16, "had," in sense of possession, c. J. xiv. 21, 30; i. 6, "hand," as hand of power, c. x. 28; i. 18, "the living one," c. J. i. 4, v. 26; ii. 7, "eat," c. J. vi. 51; ii. 13, "my name," c. J. *passim;* ii. 17, "knoweth," in sense of the knowledge of experience, c. J. iv. 32; ii. 21, "*willeth* not to repent," c. J. v. 6, vi. 21; ii. 22, "except they repent of *her* works," a remarkable expression, c. J. ix. 4; iii. 10, "earth," as opposed to heaven, c. J. iii. 12; iv. 2, "set," c. J. ii. 6; v. 8, idea of fulness, c. J. ii. 7, xix. 29, xxi. 11; v. 10, unexpected use of third instead of first person, c. J. xvii. 3; vii. 9, "a great multitude," c. J. xii. 12; ix. 1, "well of the abyss," c. J. iv. 11, 12; x. 4, trial before knowledge, c. J. ii. 22, xii. 16; xi.

2. *The Structure* of the two books.—Of the structure of the Apocalypse we have already spoken at considerable length. It remains only to ask whether, or to what extent, the same structural characteristics are to be traced in the fourth Gospel.

(1.) The similarity appears in the dominating power of certain numbers. Of the number seven it is unnecessary to say more than has been said already (p. 61). But the number three still claims attention. The part played by it in the Gospel is hardly less worthy of notice than its part in the Apocalypse. Upon this point Keim will probably be allowed to be an unexceptionable witness. In his *Life of Jesus* he speaks of the trichotomy of the Gospel as lying at the foundation of its plan, connecting this, whether rightly or wrongly it is unnecessary to ask, partly with Jewish methods of conception, partly with the Divine mystery of the Trinity. " Jesus," he says, " is three times in Galilee, three times in Judæa, twice three feasts fall within the period of His working, especially three passovers, at its beginning, its middle, its end. He performs three miracles in Galilee, and three in Jerusalem. Twice three days He is occupied in the neighbourhood of John. Three days mark the history of Lazarus, six the Passion week. Three words are spoken on the cross. Three times did he appear as the risen Saviour " (*Life of Jesus*, i. p. 157). Even better examples might have been found, such as the threefold division of chap. ix., verses 1-12, 13-34, 35-41 ; or the three figures in the earlier part of chap. x., the shepherd, the door, the good shepherd ; or the three questioners in chap. xiv. ; or the three parts of the highly-priestly prayer in chap. xvii., verses 1-5, 6-19, 20-26 ; or the three confessions of

2, " cast without," c. J. ix. 34 ; xi. 13, " names " used to express persons, c. use of " name " in the Gospel ; xii. 5, " of man's sex," c. commentary *in loc.* and J. xvi. 21 ; xii. 1-6, c. J. i. 1-5 ; xiii. 14, " make an image," c. commentary *in loc.* and J. viii. 44 ; xiv. 5, " lie," c. J. viii. 44 ; xv. 4, " fear," c. commentary *in loc.* and J. v. 20 ; xvii. 8, " ascend," " go," c. commentary *in loc.*; xix. 3, " a second time," c. J. iv. 54 ; xx. 15, c. commentary *in loc.*; xxi. 2, " prepared," c. J. xiv. 3 ; xxi. 3, " tabernacle," c. J. i. 14 ; xxi. 6, c. commentary *in loc.* ; xxi. 8,

" liars," c. J. viii. 44 ; xxi. 25, " night," c. J. xiii. 30 ; xxii. 5, c. commentary *in loc.* ; xxii. 7, " keepeth," c. J. xiv. 15 ; xxii. 11, c. commentary *in loc.* Other illustrations of the same point may be found in the *Intr. to the N. T.*, by Dr. Davidson, who shows great fairness in the matter, and whose conclusion is that, " after every reasonable deduction, enough remains to prove that the correspondences are not accidental, and either betray the same author or show that the writer of the book was influenced by the ideas and language of the other" (i. p. 332).

the glory of Jesus made by Peter, Philip, and Nathanael in chap. i. ; or the tripartite division of that chapter, verses 1-18, 19-34, 35-51 ; or a similar division of the first of these three sections, verses 1-5, 6-13, 14-18 ; or a similar division of verse 1. Many other illustrations of the same point might be given, but those mentioned are enough to show that the same tendency to group his materials under the influence of the number three, which so strongly marks the writer of the Apocalypse, marks also the author of the Gospel.

(2.) The principle of *contrasts* appearing in so marked a manner in the Apocalypse appears also in the Gospel. Upon this point it may be enough to quote the language of Dr. Davidson when he says : "The contrasts in the Gospel are striking. Light and darkness, God and the world, heaven and earth, spirit and flesh, life and death, truth and error, love and hatred, the eternal and transitory, Christ and the world, Christ and the devil, the Church and the world, the children of the world and the children of the devil, present Christianity attaining to victory through contest" (*Intr.*, ii. p. 348). No reader of the Gospel indeed can hesitate to acknowledge that, although its contrasts may not be exhibited in such minute detail as those of the Apocalypse, the tendency to see the kingdom of heaven standing over against the kingdom of this world is as strong and deep in the one book as in the other. Nor is the ironical or mocking contrast which we so often meet with in the Apocalypse wanting in the Gospel. A striking illustration of this appears in its description of Jesus on the Cross (chap. xix. 28-37). The particulars of the scene here presented are in perfect harmony with those of the other Evangelists, but a careful study of them is sufficient to show that they are grouped under the dominating influence of the idea of the Passover. Few will deny that on the cross Jesus is the Paschal Lamb. This being the case, He is there that Lamb, not in the moment of death, but at the later stage when it was prepared for, and eaten at, the paschal meal, and the Evangelist sees the Jews around the Cross celebrating an inverted and contorted passover. [1] The view thus indicated throws a fresh and striking light upon the whole conduct and fate of those who at the time were crucifying their Messiah and King. At chap. xviii. 28 they had not entered

---

[1] The writer has endeavoured to bring this fully out in two papers in the *Expositor*, July and August 1877, on "St. John's view of Jesus on the Cross."

into the judgment hall of Pilate "lest they should be defiled, but that they might eat the passover." They had not eaten it then. Amidst the tumult and stormy passions of that dreadful morning when had they an opportunity of eating it? St. John does not tell us that they found one. Rather is the whole narrative so constructed, so full of close, rapid, passionate action, that it is impossible to fix upon any point at which we can insert their eating, until it was too late in the day to make it legal. *May it not be that they found no opportunity?* They lost their passover. Lost it? Nay, the Evangelist seems to say, they found a passover. Follow them with me to the Cross, and, in their cruel mockeries of the true Paschal Lamb, let us see the righteous dealings of God, as He makes these mockeries take the shape of a passover of judgment, of added sin, and deepened shame.

(3.) The principle of *prolepsis or anticipation* appearing in the Apocalypse (see p. 114) appears also in the Gospel. Thus we have repeated anticipatory allusions to the desire of the Jews to "kill Jesus" (chaps. vii. 1, 19, 20, 25; viii. 37, 40), allusions which, made long before the time when the deed was to be executed, the Jews themselves disown. So also in chap. xi. 2 the mention of Mary's act as that by which she is especially distinguished anticipates the narrative of the act itself at chap. xii. 3; while in chap. xii. 7 the anointing of Christ and the allusion to His burial anticipate what actually takes place in chap. xix. 39-42.

(4.) *Double representations of the same thing* meet us in the Gospel, the second representation standing in a climactic relation to the first. We have already alluded to this characteristic of the Apocalypse (p. 116), and have only to show that it also marks the Gospel. Let us take an incident related in the first chapter, verses 29, 35, 36.

In the first of these verses we are told that "on the morrow he (the Baptist) seeth Jesus coming unto him, and saith, Behold, the Lamb of God, which taketh away the sin of the world!" In the last two we read, "Again on the morrow John was standing, and two of his disciples; and he looked upon Jesus as He walked, and saith, Behold, the Lamb of God!" Why mention a circumstance of this kind twice? and that, too, when the Evangelist feels that he has so much to relate, that were he to tell it all, "even the world itself would not contain the books that should be written" (chap. xxi. 25). If there is no difference between the two statements, there seems to be a waste of space ; if there is a difference, wherein does the difference lie ? We have before us one of the double pictures of St. John. It is of peculiar importance to him to bring out that aspect of Jesus in which He appears as the Lamb of God. At the close of His earthly career Jesus will be seen to be so (chap. xix. 36, 37). But what He was at the close He was also at the beginning, beneath all the lowliness of His lot,—the Divine Lord who changes not. The Baptist had, in all probability, often spoken of Him as the Lamb of God. The Evangelist fixes upon two occasions when he did so, and the repetition lends force to the declaration. More, however, is necessary in order that the incident may fall within the range of that principle of structure which we are considering. In the mention of the second when compared with the first there must be climax. Climax is at once traceable here. At verse 29 the Baptist appears to have been alone, and his words have the form of a soliloquy. At verse 35 two of his disciples stand beside him, and his words are intended for them ; they " heard him speak." Again, no effect is connected with the first utterance ; at the second " the two disciples followed Jesus " (verse 37). Once more let us look at the exclamation in itself. At first sight it may seem as if climax failed, as if the Baptist's words were richer and fuller the first time than the second. In reality the reverse is the case. Let us remember that the paschal lamb lies at the bottom of the figure. The words in verse 29 therefore, " which taketh away the sin of the world," limit us to one aspect of the benefits conferred by that great sacrifice, which contained in it all the ideas of Israel's sacrificial system as a whole. They bring out the pardon and removal of sin, but nothing further. Let us drop the addition, and dwell only on the shorter form, " Behold, the Lamb of God," and everything included in the thought of the paschal lamb comes into view. Above all, we have now room for the highest, the culminating, idea of the paschal sacrifice—that of nourishment, of food for the life, of the feast as a communion and fellowship with God. The second of the two statements, brief as it is, is far wider and more comprehensive than the first. We take another passage, chap. xii. 1-19. In this passage a double picture of the reception given to Jesus, in the remarkable circumstances in which He was at the moment placed, arrests our attention. It is of importance to observe that, when introduced to us at the beginning of the chapter, Jesus had not only been condemned to death by the highest religious authorities of the land (chap. xi. 50, 53), but that "they had given a commandment that, if any man knew where He was, he should show it, that they might take Him" (chap. xi. 57). The virulence of His persecutors has thus been indicated with more than ordinary force; and the object of the first nineteen verses of chap. xii. is to illustrate the fact that, although thus outwardly defeated, He is still the Conqueror; that in the lowest stage of His humiliation He draws to Himself the affection and admiration of men. This object is attained by means of the two pictures, the anointing in Bethany and the triumphal entry into Jerusalem. That these two scenes really form a double picture designed to illustrate the same thought is clear from different considerations. On the one hand, both are obviously an act of homage to Jesus. On the other, Jesus is brought before us in both with the doom of death resting upon Him. More than this, it is to be noticed that with the thought of the death of Jesus is distinctly combined in both the thought of His power over the grave. In both Lazarus is associated with Him. In the first he is actually present, and that as one raised from the dead; "Jesus," it is said, "came to Bethany, where Lazarus was, whom Jesus raised from the dead;" "Lazarus was one of them that sat at meat with Him" (verses 1, 2). In the second, Lazarus raised is present to the minds of the people; "The multitude therefore that was with Him when He called Lazarus out of the tomb, and raised him from the dead, bare witness;" "For this cause also the multitude went and met Him, for that they heard that He had done this sign" (verses 17, 18). The sentence of death, in short, is in each of the two pictures upon Jesus; and in each He is the Resurrection and the Life. The striking combination of these ideas in both, not less than the homage expressed in both, proves the unity of the two scenes. While, however, the principles marking the two tributes of adoration are thus essentially one, and while the two may be regarded as parts of the same tableau, the idea to be expressed comes before us in the second at a higher stage than in the first. At the opening of the first Jesus is indeed the selected victim upon which sentence of death has been passed. But before the second opens He has been anointed for His burial (verse 7). In the first He is only at Bethany, in the quiet village, perhaps in the quiet house, where He had so often rested, and in which friendship and love ministered to Him consolation under His many trials. In the second He has bidden farewell to rest, hospitality, and comfort; and has entered upon His last short journey to Jerusalem, where He is to die. Death is nearer now. In the first He is borne witness to by a number of Jews from Jerusalem who had "seen Lazarus" (verse 9); in the second the witness is borne by a multitude, brought together from all quarters, who had only "heard" (verse 18) and yet had believed; and we have but to look at chap. xx. 29 to see how much more valuable is the latter than the former faith. In the first the tribute paid is a silent act of reverence and love; in the second it is a loud acclaim of praise (verse 13), while Jesus Himself appears not as a longed-for guest, but as Israel's eagerly expected King (verse 15). In the first the hope of the chief priests and Pharisees, that they will be able to accomplish their end, has been high (chap. xi. 57); in the second they begin to despair, and their plot seems in danger of being baffled (verse 19). In the first many Jews are led to faith (verse 11); in the second "Lo, the world is gone after Him" (verse 19). Finally, we are not told that the disciples had any difficulty in comprehending the first; but the second belongs to that higher order of things which can only be understood when light has been thrown upon it by time and the wonderful events of Providence (verse 16). The climactic relation of the two pictures cannot be mistaken.[1]

(5.) A fifth point demanding a few moments' consideration is the use of *Episode*. Enough was formerly said of the Episodes of the Apocalypse (p. 125). Their existence is denied by none. But we have an unquestionable Episode in the Gospel (chap. iii. 22-36), introduced, exactly as the apocalyptic episodes are introduced, in the middle of a section, and with the view of preparing us for a greater manifestation of mercy (in the Apocalypse of judgment) immediately to follow. Another such Episode is probably to be found in chap. x. 22-42, the middle point of it being verse 28, and the Episode as a whole being intended to prepare us for the wonderful event to be recorded in the next chapter.

Characteristics of the kind now illustrated are of great importance in helping us to come to a conclusion upon the identity or difference of authorship of two different books. They are not of an outward kind. They lead us into the depths of the

---

[1] For other illustrations of the point we refer to three papers in the *Expositor*, second series, vol. iv. pp. 264, 368, 430.

author's nature, into the inmost frame and habit of his soul. The mere language of a writer, indeed, his mere *delectus verborum*, may frequently in no small degree guide us to a determination upon the point at issue. Yet the argument seems to possess far greater strength when it is founded less upon the words themselves than upon the *form* into which they are cast, or the *manner* which they display. A man may change his thought and, with this, the words in which he utters it. He is not so likely to change the mould or framework within which all his thinking is conducted. This becomes like his walk or the tones of his voice. He may walk faster or slower ; he may speak more loudly or more softly ; there is in each case something beneath that we recognise, even at a distance. However great his transition from one set of ideas to another, the fashion in which he presents them will most probably be the same. More particularly if, as we are often told, we are not to think of deliberate and skilful imitation in the early Christian age ; if there was a simplicity in writers and a credulity in readers which then made the task of fictitious authorship easier than it is now, the value of these inner marks of identity is greatly raised. Two different men, writing with a long interval of time between them, and in entirely different circumstances, could hardly have resembled one another so closely in the whole tone and habit of their minds.

III. *The Teaching* of the Apocalypse and of the fourth Gospel.—In considering this, it is impossible to pass in review the whole teaching of the two books. We confine ourselves to a very few leading and characteristic points.[1]

1. The teaching of each regarding *the Saviour and His kingdom.*—Of Christ Himself little need be said. It is allowed that the most marked coincidence is apparently in the Christology (Davidson, *Intr.*, i. p. 333) ; and the admission, though hardly in every respect correct, is enough to justify us in passing rapidly over this part of the subject. In addition, therefore, to what has been already said of the distinctive appellations, " The Word," or " The Word of God," and " The Lamb," applied to Jesus in these two books of the New Testament alone, it is

---

[1] A minute comparison of the teaching of the two books on special points will be found in Gebhardt's *Doctrine of the Apocalypse*, translated in Clark's *Foreign Theol. Libr.* We take, for the most part at least, a different course from the one followed in that book.

enough to recall the Divine attributes everywhere ascribed to Him in both; the prominence given to the conception of Him as a shepherd, a conception only distantly alluded to in the earlier Gospels, but brought out fully in the fourth; the importance attached to the idea of His being the faithful and true Witness; His bestowing "the hidden manna," that is Himself (*Comm.* on Rev. ii. 17), equivalent to the "true bread out of heaven," which He is (John vi. 32, 35); His dwelling among His saints; His supplying them with the water of life; and His being the Bridegroom of His Church. The existence of these conceptions in the Apocalypse, and that too in a marked degree, is not denied; and they incontestably lead us to the thoughts of the fourth rather than any of the other Gospels.

No doubt it is still urged that there is a difference in the mode by which the "glory" belonging to Christ in our two books is made manifest in each. As revealed in the Apocalypse it is said to be outward might and dominion; while in the Gospel it is revealed only to the inward eye, or to the faith which beholds in the Redeemer the sum of Divine grace and truth (Frommann, *Der Johann.*, *Lehrb.*, p. 545; comp. Davidson's *Intr.*, i. p. 335). To the same effect Lücke: "The apocalyptist brings especially forward the external development and completion of the Divine kingdom and judgment in the great convulsions of the world and nature, while the quiet internal development and completion springing from the power of the Divine word and spirit of Christ in humanity passes into the background. The eschatological process which, according to him, begins with the first manifestation of Christ, chap. xii. 1, etc., is viewed by him more according to its external historical appearance than the inward ground of the oppositions which it unfolds; more in its external epochs, progresses, and resting points than in the internal continuity of its development in the spiritual life of humanity; more in the external destruction of the world's powers of evil than in their conquest and condemnation from within" (*Versuch*, p. 719). Baur adopts these representations, and sums up the whole argument in the following words: "The difference, therefore, lies mainly in this, that the mode of thinking and the whole representation is so internal in the Gospel, and so external in the Apocalypse" (*D. K. E.*, p. 347).

The contrasts thus alluded to undoubtedly exist to a large

extent, but the statement of them in these extracts is exaggerated ; while Lücke, in referring Rev. xii. 1, etc., to the historical
Christ, has failed to catch the real meaning of the passage
(*Comm. in loc.*).   Nothing indeed is more strikingly characteristic of the visions of the Apocalypse than the manner in which,
up to the very last, the Saviour Himself is withheld from view.
In the visions constituting by far the larger portion of the
whole, He is not once introduced to us in His outward glory ;
and it is not until we reach chap. xix. that He comes forth in
the sight of the nations.   Up to that time the world has not
beheld Him.   Even if we adopt Lücke's interpretation of chap.
xii., He was in the instant of His birth caught up unto God
and unto His throne (verse 5).   From His unseen place in
heaven He has directed the contest and exercised His rule.   No
hostile eye has witnessed the glory which belongs to Him.
Even His people do not behold it until the final stage of the
conflict is reached.   St. John himself has seen it in the first
chapter, yet only in the spirit (verse 10) ; they have not.   It
is not as those upon whom outward glory has shone that they
are spoken of, but as those who " have washed their robes and
made them white in the blood of the Lamb " (chap. vii. 14)
The glory of the slain Lamb is all that they have seen ; and is
not that the very glory which meets us in the beginning of the
Gospel, " The Word was made flesh and dwelt among us, and
we beheld His glory, the glory as of the only begotten of the
Father, full of grace and truth " ? (John i. 14).

Let us turn to Christ's kingdom.   So far as the idea o
" development " enters into the Apocalypse, it is fundamentally
the opposite of what it is represented to be in the passages
above quoted.   Instead of having only an " external " character
it is really, in the strictest sense of the word, in the first place
internal, both as regards the piety to be blessed and the impiety
to be doomed.   In the visions of the book there is no *externa*
development whatever of the Divine kingdom, as if that king
dom were making an outward progress in the world, and
gradually bringing one part of mankind after another under it
sway.   There are no successive chronological epochs and period
within which the people of God gain a more prominent position
in the world and inflict more striking defeats upon their enemies
Only one great epoch is taken note of, and that the whole
period extending from the First to the Second Coming of the
Lord.   This is the three and a half years, the forty-two months

e one thousand two hundred and sixty days, so frequently
ferred to. The period of the Seals covers it all; so does the
riod of the Trumpets; so does the period of the Bowls. All
ese periods extend from the beginning to the end of the
hurch's militant history. Within that space of time the
embers of Christ's flock are from the first ideally complete.
he names of all of them are written in the Lamb's book of
e. God has known all that are His, and has kept them all
the hollow of His hand. There is indeed a progress of things
ithin this period, implied in the climactic character of the
ree great series of visions. But the *development* alike on the
rt of the Church and of her enemies is internal, not external.
is a development of the one to ever higher stages of meetness
r the accomplishment of Christian hope, of the other to ever-
creasing ripeness for eternal woe. Development of any other
nd—external development—we not only have not, but cannot
ve. The plan of the book will not permit it; for that plan
not to trace the Church's growth as she rises from her
ustard-seed beginning into a mighty tree: it is to take her
om the first as ideally complete, and to show us by a series of
ctures rising one above another how, as the world hastens to
s end, her trials increase, grace to sustain her increases, and
dgment on her foes increases also.

In so far again as there does exist a contrast between calmly
orking grace and external manifestation of might, such a con-
ast lies necessarily in the object of the two books. The
ntrary impression has arisen from the idea that the aim of
e Apocalypse is to set forth a history in continuation of that
resented in the Gospel. Its real object is rather to set forth
e manifestation of an idea to be realised in history after the
ork of grace delineated in the Gospel is supposed to have
tained its purpose. It deals with the Redeemer not so much
an earlier stage of a continuous development as in a stage
together different. In the Gospel we have the Christ in His
umiliation, in the Apocalypse in His exaltation; in the former
He was a sufferer on earth, in the latter as He is glorified in
eaven; in the one as He carries on the educative process by
hich light is raised to brighter light and darkness deepened
to thicker darkness, in the other as He brings to view the
nal issues of the education He has given. But this leads
cessarily to external manifestations, and anything of that kind,
erefore, appearing in the Apocalypse, proceeds not from a

difference of authorship, but from a difference of object in t
one author of both books.

2. The teaching of both regarding *the field of the Saviou.
work, and the precise nature of the work He has to do in it.*-
Nothing is more strikingly characteristic of the Apocalypse th
the light in which it presents this point to us.   From the fir
vision to the last there is the most marked antithesis betwe
the Church and the world, between the followers and t.
opponents of the Lamb.   There is no neutral ground.   All m
are divided into the two great sections, light or darkness, tru.
or falschood.   What we see of them is not a passing from dar
ness into light, or from light into darkness, but a brightenix
of the already existent light and a deepening of the already e
istent darkness.   It may at first sight strike us with extrem
surprise that a book, intended to be the stay and comfort of tl
Church amidst her trials, and written when as yet she he
made no great progress in the world, should in all its visio:
not possess one to tell her of that increase in number of h
adherents, of that missionary success, which should reward h
labours.   Yet such is undoubtedly the fact.   The visions
the Seals, the Trumpets, and the Bowls relate to the same fiel
No extension of the Church's borders is even incidentally allud
to under any of them till the very end is reached ; and even the
" the kingdoms of the world become the kingdoms of our Lo
and of His Christ," not by the conversion, but by the destru
tion, of the Church's foes.   There is no change in the sphe
in which the action of these three great series of visions
played out.   The same thing may be said of the visions
comfort interposed at various points of the delineation, of tl
sealing and harping visions coming before the seventh Seal, tl
measuring and witnessing visions coming before the seven
Trumpet, and the vision of the Lamb upon Mount Zion su
rounded by His saints coming before the seven Bowls.   Th
field of blessing is not enlarged ; the Church is ideally as stror
at the beginning as at the end.   There is no passing of darl
ness into light ; there is no sinking of light into darknes
There is ever-brightening light ; there is ever-deepening darl
ness.   The two lines are from first to last distinct, antithetica
opposed.

The very same method of representation marks the Gosp
and the Epistles of St. John.   In the field of the Saviou
working there presented to us mankind are again divided in

o great classes, one of which has already a receptivity for the
.th, while the other resolutely opposes it ; and the work of
sus consists in a separation of the two classes, and in *making
.nifest the tendencies of each*, rather than in bringing the one
.ss over to the other.   The general impression conveyed to us
· the earlier Gospels of the state of those not yet interested in
.rist, is that they are miserable in their sinfulness, and are to
led by a gracious Redeemer to the happiness which they
ed, and for which they long.   Not that their sinfulness is un-
ought of, but it is not so prominent as their misery.   They
labour and are heavy laden ;" they "faint and are scattered
road as sheep having no shepherd ;" they suffer from "in-
mities" and "sicknesses" which Jesus bore ; they stand in
ed of the "rest" and healing which the Good Physician alone
n give (Matt. xi. 28, 29 ; ix. 36 ; Mark ii. 17 ; Luke v. 31).
) all of them, therefore, Jesus addresses Himself as if they
cupied substantially the same ground.   On all He has equally
 bestow the blessings of His salvation, if they will not now,
ter they have listened to Him, cast away His offered gift.
St. John's point of view in the fourth Gospel is entirely
fferent.   Not, indeed, that the salvation to be found in Jesus
 not designed to be universal, that there is even one who may
)t be saved if he will only turn to the light that shines around
m, and let that light shine within him.   "God so loved the
orld that He gave His only begotten Son, that whosoever
·lieveth in Him should not perish, but have eternal life ;" "I
.me not to judge the world, but to save the world" (chaps. iii.
5 ; xii. 47).   Nor, again, that men are considered as so
.sentially identified with the two classes into which they are
.vided as to deprive them of responsibility for the reception or
.jection of the truth.   It is conclusive against any such idea
.at, as regards the one class, St. John says in the very opening
: his Gospel, "As many as received Him, to them gave He
.wer to become the Sons of God" (chap. i. 12) ; as regards
.e other, "This is the condemnation, that light is come into
.e world, and men *loved* darkness rather than light, because
.eir deeds were evil" (chap. iii. 19).   In both cases moral
.sponsibility is implied.   Still the fact remains that there are
.wo classes, and these not simply formed *after* the work of
.hrist has tried and proved the world but *before* it, and while
.he Logos is not yet incarnate.   Almost the very first words of
.he Gospel introduce us to this conception.   We do not see

only a world of sinners, all equally alienated from God, all
that earliest stage of natural sinfulness to which no moral di
cipline has been as yet applied.   There has been such a disci
line, although its history is not unfolded to us, and we nc
witness the result.[1]   From the first two classes appear; on tl
one side there is alienation, deep, deliberate, confirmed, "t'
light shineth in darkness, and the darkness overcame it no
(verse 5); on the other side there are those who "receive
the Word incarnate, and who because they received Him h
that faith implanted in them by which they became the childr
of God (verse 12).   And this antithesis of light and darkne
of truth and falsehood, of life and death, runs throughout tl
whole Gospel.   It knows only of two classes of men repi
sented by these terms; and, from the moment these classes a
introduced to us, they are completely separated from o
another.   There is the class of those who receive the Saviou
and of those who do not receive Him; of those who recogni
His glory as the glory of the only begotten of the Father, ai
of those who do not recognise it—mark the emphatic "we"
chap. i. 14; of those who know Him, and of those who kno
Him not; of those who see, and of those who are blind;
those who are the children of God, and of those who are
their father the devil.   Nor is this antithesis conceived of
an antithesis of states into which men gradually rise or sin
but as all along fully formed, as *chosen* by such as respective
belong to either side, as developed and mature.   In short, tl
contrast between the followers and the enemies of Christ, b
tween the Church and the world, is from the first and alwa
presented to us in the sharpest and most distinctive lines.   Tl
separation is decided.   The two have no point of connectic
with each other.   Various circumstances connected with S
John's mode of speaking illustrate what has now been sai
Let us advert to one or two of them.

---

[1] In considering the difficult
topic here before us it may be well
for our readers to take along with
them the following words of Dean
Alford.   He is commenting on
John iii. 17, and showing that
that text is not in contradiction
to ix. 39, "for judgment I am
come into this world," and he
says, "The κρίμα there, as here,
results from the separation
mankind into two classes—tho
who will not come to the ligh
and that result itself is not tl
purpose why the Son of God can
into the world, but is evolved
the accomplishment of the high
purpose, viz. love, and the salv
tion of men."

It is thus, *e.g.*, that, in his writings, even false brethren are not those who have fallen away from the Church. They never belonged to it. They were the world in the Church. "They went out from us, but they were not of us; for if they had been of us, they would no doubt have continued with us; but they went out, that they might be made manifest how that they all are not of us" (1 John ii. 19). It is thus that he recalls the words of Jesus regarding Judas, "Did not I choose you the twelve, and one of you is a devil? Now He spake of Judas the son of Simon Iscariot, for he it was that should betray Him, being one of the twelve" (John vi. 70, 71). Judas is to outward appearance one of the twelve, but he really belongs to an altogether different class—he is a devil. It is thus that the present condition of man is viewed without heed being given to the fact that the righteous may fall away, that the wicked may be converted and saved—"He that believeth on Him is not judged: he that believeth not hath been judged already, because he hath not believed on the name of the only begotten Son of God;" "He that believeth on the Son hath eternal life; but he that believeth not the Son shall not see life, but the wrath of God abideth on him" (chap. iii. 18, 36). Above all, it is thus that St. John seems often to look wholly away, or to bring Jesus Himself before us as looking away, from some of the most important steps in what we should call the conversion of the sinner, and that not a few of his texts present in this light serious difficulties to the interpreter. "He that is *of God* heareth the words of God: for this cause ye hear them not, because ye are not of God;" "But ye believe not, *because ye are not of my sheep;*" "Every one that is *of the truth* heareth my voice;" "They are *of the world:* therefore speak they as of the world, and the world heareth them. We are *of God:* he that knoweth God heareth us; he who is *not of God* heareth not us" (John viii. 47; x. 26; xviii. 37; 1 John iv. 5, 6),—all, words in which the expressions "of the truth," "of God," "of the world," must be referred, not to a stage of the spiritual history when Christ's words have been either received or rejected, but to a stage anterior to that, when the bias to the one course or the other is thought of as already existing in the soul. The spiritual history of man is, in such passages, taken up at a point earlier than that in which the eye only rests on the natural disinclination of all to godliness. Man is viewed as if he were marked by a predisposition to either good or evil; as

if some were from the first inclined to receive, and others to re
ject, the full communication of the light that shines in Christ
as if the germ of the ultimate result were previously existing in
the soul ; and as if the true point of departure for our considera
tion of what we are were that where the divinely-implanted
love of the truth is the foundation for higher blessings, where
the devil-implanted love of a lie, and the free clinging to it
is the foundation for final doom. We need hardly say that, in
all this, there is not the slightest essential divergence from the
doctrine of the universal corruption of human nature, and of our
entire dependence upon the grace and spirit of God for the very
earliest dawnings of the Divine life within us. That doctrine is
set before us by St. John as distinctly as by the other writers of
the New Testament. It is simply a mode of viewing the matter
peculiar to him. It marks him out at once from the rest of the
apostles ; and it is so essentially embedded in his nature that it
colours his whole language, and is interwoven with his whole
style of thought.

The antithesis now noted leads to a corresponding modifica-
tion in the aspect of Christ's work in the Gospel. That work
consists not so much in converting all classes as in separating
the two of which we have spoken, and in cultivating in the one
the germ which is to issue in the possession of life, in visiting
judicially in the other the germ which is to end in death in its
deepest and fullest sense. It becomes a work of sifting. The
unbelieving Jews grow more and more confirmed in their obstinacy ; the believing disciples are united to their Master in bonds
constantly closer and more endearing. To the one He can only
speak in terms of severe reproach, "How can ye believe ?"; "Ye
are from beneath;" "Ye are of your father the devil" (chaps.
v. 44 ; viii. 23, 44) ; the other are in ever-increasing degree
His friends ; He washes their feet ; He addresses to them His
most consolatory discourses ; at the Supper one of them leans
upon His bosom ; till at length, in His last intercessory prayer,
the separation is indicated in the most solemn and awe-inspiring
manner, "I manifested Thy name unto the men whom Thou
gavest me out of the world : I pray for them, I pray not for the
world" (chap. xvii. 6, 9).

3. *The appropriation of Christ's redemption and the relation of believers to their Lord.*—Upon this point St. John has
undoubtedly much that is common to the other writers of the
New Testament, but there is also much that is peculiar to

himself. In the fourth Gospel and in the First Epistle of St.
John salvation is such an appropriation of life in Christ that
believers are identified with Him. They and He are in one
another, as the branches of the vine are in the stem or the stem
in the branches. They are placed in His relation towards God ;
and, now that He has gone to the Father, they have to take up
and carry on His work in the world. What He was, nay, what
He is, they are ; one with Him in privilege, in duty, in suffering, in essential, though as yet unmanifested, glory.

To quote passages from the fourth Gospel in proof of what
has been said would be an almost endless task. The whole
Gospel is penetrated by, and filled with, the idea. Nowhere
is it more strikingly brought out than in the Prologue, its
place there, in verses which contain a summary of the book,
lending it peculiar importance,—"But as many as received
Him, to them gave He the right to become children of God "
(chap. i. 12). "Received" is more than "accepted," for it indicates not simply the accepting will but the possession gained ;
"children" is more than "sons," for sonship may be that of a
mere adoption, while the expression used leads to the thought
of actual (though spiritual) paternity ; and for the words "gave "
and "right" ($\dot{\epsilon}\xi o\upsilon\sigma\iota\alpha$) we may fitly compare chap. v. 26, 27,
"For as the Father hath life in Himself, even so *gave* He to
the Son to have life in Himself : and He *gave* Him authority
($\dot{\epsilon}\xi o\upsilon\sigma\iota\alpha\nu$) to execute judgment, because He is a Son of man "
(marginal and correct reading of Revised Version).

The keynote thus struck in the Prologue is continued
throughout the body of the Gospel. In particular we see it in
the remarkable use of the words $\dot{\epsilon}\nu$ $\dot{\epsilon}\alpha\upsilon\tauo\hat{\iota}\varsigma$ applied to believers,
to which the Authorised Version does so much injustice (chaps.
v. 42 ; vi. 53 ; comp. v. 26), and which are obviously intended
to bring out that independence of standing, rising out of dependence, which is granted to the believer when he is identified
with his Lord. We see it in the foot-washing, where the words,
"Know ye not what I have done to you? Ye call Me Master,
and Lord : and ye say well ; for so I am. If I then, the Lord
and the Master, have washed your feet, ye ought also to wash one
another's feet. For I have given you an example ($\dot{\upsilon}\pi\delta\delta\epsilon\iota\gamma\mu\alpha$),
that ye also should do as I have done to you " (chap. xiii.
12-15), when viewed in the spirit of the whole passage, express
much more than the power of example. Above all we see it in
the language of the last discourses of chaps. xiv.-xvi., and in the

high-priestly prayer of chap. xvii.　These are full of words of
Jesus which can only be understood on the principle for which
we now contend (comp. chaps. xiv. 19, 20 ; xv. 3, 4, 5 ; xvi.
26 ; xvii. 8, 18, 22, 23, 26).　The late Dr. Candlish has spoken
of the "wonderfully gracious identification" thus established
by our Lord between His disciples and Himself (*Fatherhood of
God*, p. 111), and the authority of that eminent theologian will
be of weight with many who might otherwise shrink from the
word in the connection in which we have used it.

One thing is clear, that this identity or identification of the
members of Christ's Body with their Head, extending as it does
not only to their relation to the Father, but to their work in
the world, and to sufferings there endured even unto death
(comp. 1 John iii. 16), is one of the most characteristic parts of
the teaching of the fourth Gospel.

When we turn to the Apocalypse the same teaching meets
us.　It is true that at the time when that book was written
Christ had gone to the Father.　St. John had not forgotten
that in his First Epistle (chap. iv. 17), and he cannot forget it
now, because it is with the glorified Redeemer that his visions
deal.　But with that Redeemer as He had been on earth,
and ideally with Him as He is now in heaven, believers are
everywhere identified.　We meet the thought in the Prologue,
where we are taught that, through Him that loveth us and
loosed us from our sins in His blood, we have been made "a
kingdom, to be priests unto His God and Father" (chap. i. 6),
He Himself being everywhere throughout the book Priest and
King ; and where too the writer describes himself as "partaker"
with the churches "in the tribulation and kingdom and patience
which are in Jesus" (chap. i. 9).　In every later description of
believers the same tone of thought is observable.　We know
that the "garment down to the feet" with which the glorious
Personage who appeared to the Seer in chap. i. was, as a priestly
garment, white, and it is unnecessary to quote texts telling us
of the white garments of the redeemed.　The people of God
everywhere "*have* the word of God and the testimony of
Jesus" (chaps. i. 2 ; vi. 9 ; xii. 17 ; xix. 10).　Jesus is the
"faithful witness," and they are the "witnesses of Jesus"
(chap. i. 5 ; ii. 13 ; xvii. 6).　Jesus says of Himself, "I overcame," and they also "overcome" (chaps. iii. 21 ; ii. 7, 11,
etc.).　Jesus has "works" and they have "works" (chaps. ii.
2, 19, 26, etc.).　Jesus "walks" in the midst of the seven

golden candlesticks, and they shall "walk" with Him (chaps. ii. 1; iii. 4). "As a shepherd shall Jesus tend all the nations with a sceptre of iron," and the believer, having had authority given him over the nations, shall "tend them with a sceptre of iron" (chaps. xii. 5; ii. 27). Jesus has His "new name" written upon Him, and that new name shall be written upon His people (chaps. xix. 12; iii. 12). Jesus having completed His work received the reward of victory, and He Himself says to Laodicea, "He that overcometh, I will give to him to sit down with Me in My throne, as I also overcame, and sat down with My Father in His throne" (chap. iii. 21). Even now in the midst of all their trials the saints "reign upon the earth" (chap. v. 10), and in the power of the resurrection life which they enjoy in a risen and glorified Redeemer they "live and reign with Christ a thousand years" (chap. xx. 6).

It is, however, in struggle, suffering, and death that the identification of Christ and His people comes out most strongly in the Apocalypse. The degree of this is indeed dependent upon the special interpretation of several important passages of the book, and it is possible that all may not accept the interpretation given of these in a previous Lecture (Lect. v. p. 167). But the more carefully that interpretation is considered, the more, we persuade ourselves, will it prove itself to be correct. Struggle, suffering, a martyr-death, are, in the view of the Seer, the portion of all believers. "Follow thou Me" means not merely, Be obedient to My commandments, imitate My character, but follow Me to shame and reproach and persecution and the cross. He who would be Christ's disciple must drink His cup and be baptized with His baptism. Then, the Lord's in death, He will also be His in glorious, everlasting, life.

There is no need to deny that various points of connection may be traced between such teaching as this and the teaching of other books of the New Testament than the writings of St. John. Our contention simply is that this style of thought has a precision, a clearness, and a fulness in the fourth Gospel and in the Apocalypse which it has nowhere else. Whether or not the person was the same, the mind that dictated these two books was one.

4. *The termination of the saints' earthly course and their entrance upon their eternal reward.*—What has to be said upon this point will be to a considerable degree dependent for its force upon an admission that the manner in which we have pro-

posed to interpret the reign of the thousand years is just (comp.
Lect. vi. p. 210, etc.).   Yet not wholly so ; and it will be well for
the reader to mark carefully how much hangs upon that interpretation, and how much not.   The first point that meets us,
for example, is only partially connected with it.   The life given
by the Lord to the members of His Body is of such a kind that
it rises superior to both death and judgment ; or rather the
believer does not die in the sense in which we know death, and
he does not enter into judgment.   In the Gospel of St. John
the first of these points is indicated with great distinctness by
the words of our Lord to Martha at her brother's grave : "I am
the Resurrection and the Life : he that believeth in Me, though
he die, yet shall he live: and whosoever liveth and believeth in
Me shall never die" (chap. xi. 25).   To a similar effect are
such words as those of Jesus in John iv. 14, which ought to be
translated, neither as in the Authorised nor in the Revised
Version, but " The water that I shall give him shall become in
him a fountain of springing water, unto eternal life ; " and the
meaning is that the life referred to, not simply attained in the
remote future, begins and is actually present now in every one
who receives the living water (comp. also chap. vi. 47, etc.).
The conception, in short, of the Gospel of St. John is that when
we believe we pass wholly out of one sphere into another, out
of the evil one into God, out of death into life (chap. v. 24 ; 1
John v. 11).   This life is in its own nature eternal.   It is the
life of God, the life of Christ.   The believer "has" it.   It is
"in himself."   The result is necessary.   He in whom such a
life is formed cannot die in the ordinary sense.   Even the sword
or the flame cannot touch his true life.   Like his Lord he may
" bow his head and deliver up his spirit " (John xix. 30), but
he does not die.   Such is the teaching of the Gospel, and on its
characteristic nature it is needless to enlarge.

The teaching of the Apocalypse is precisely similar. "Death"
is never spoken of in connection with Christ's faithful ones.
They may be "slaughtered," as were the true sons of the old
Dispensation (chap. vi. 9), but that death, a sacrificial one
($\sigma\phi\acute{a}\zeta\epsilon\iota\nu$), only sets the true life free.   They may be "be-
headed " (or slain with the axe), like those who are afterwards
enthroned in the millennial bliss, but though thus cruelly put
to death they "live and reign with Christ a thousand years "
(chap. xx. 6).   True, we read in chap. xiv. 13, " And I heard a
voice from heaven saying, Write, Blessed are the dead which die

in the Lord from henceforth ; " but the context leads us to the thought of troubles and persecutions in the midst of which they die, and the words "in the Lord," when interpreted in the spirit of the book, seem to imply that the death referred to is such a death as His. The expression, therefore, "die in the Lord," does not bear that sense of quiet falling asleep in Jesus which we generally attribute to it. It brings out the fact that in Him His people meet persecution and death, and that, though not all in the strictest sense martyrs, they have all the martyr spirit. Even when they perish then they do not die ; "they rest (in contrast with verse 11) from their labours, and their works (an entirely different word from 'labours') follow with them ; " their Christian character and life, giving them a meetness for the "rest," follow *with* them. They enter the state beyond the grave fitted for its joys. Once more, in the New Jerusalem, which we have seen cause to interpret as the ideal of the Christian Church on earth, "death shall be no more" (chap. xxi. 4). On the other hand, "death," in the Apocalypse, is always associated (just as it is in 1 John iii. 14) with the evil, the hateful, the unloving, and the wrath of God (chaps. ii. 23 ; vi. 8 ; ix. 6 ; xiii. 3, 12 ; xviii. 8 ; xx. 13, 14), until it culminates in the "second death," which is "the lake of fire" (chap. xx. 14). In no part either of the Gospel, the First Epistle, or the Apocalypse, do we read of the second life.

Not only, however, does the life given in Christ, according to both the fourth Gospel and the Apocalypse, rise superior to death, it rises also superior to judgment. Nothing can be more emphatic in this respect than the teaching of the Gospel. " He that heareth My word," says our Lord, "and believeth Him that sent Me, hath eternal life, and cometh not into judgment, but hath passed out of death into life" (chap. v. 24). The preceding verses stated the work of the Son *as it has been given Him by the Father;* this verse states the same work *in its effect upon believers.* All judgment is given unto the Son (verse 22) ; into this judgment he that believeth does not come (verse 24). The believer has passed into a state to which judgment does not apply. He has received into himself that word which (chap. xii. 48) will at the last day judge all who reject it. In like manner we read of Christ, " He that believeth in Him is not judged " (chap. iii. 18). No teaching could be either more definite or more characteristic.

But the very same view meets us in the Apocalypse, and, of

all the books of the New Testament, in the Apocalypse alone. Thus in chap. xi. 18 the action of that great day when the Lord takes unto Him His great power and reigns is clearly distinguished into two parts, one, "And the nations were wroth, and Thy wrath came, and the time of the dead to be judged;" the other, "And the time to give reward to Thy servants the prophets, and to the saints, and to them that fear Thy name, the small and the great." In the great day spoken of none of the latter classes here mentioned are "judged." The most important proof of the same point is to be found in chap. xx. 11-15, in the description given of what is so often supposed to be the general judgment. A more careful examination of the passage leads to the conclusion that it describes, not the general judgment, but a judgment of the wicked alone. In the first place, the word $\dot{\epsilon}\kappa\rho\dot{\iota}\theta\eta\sigma\alpha\nu$, "were judged," of verse 12 can properly apply only to them. It is used seven times in the Apocalypse in addition to the two times it occurs in the verses before us. One of the nouns derived from it ($\kappa\rho\dot{\iota}\sigma\iota\varsigma$) is used four, and another ($\kappa\rho\dot{\iota}\mu\alpha$) three times. In every case these words denote, not a mere process of trial where a sentence of acquittal *may* be pronounced, but a judgment tending to condemnation. The use of "were judged" in the passage now under consideration would be a solitary exception to this rule did it here refer to the judgment of the good as well as the wicked. The improbability is therefore great that it has such a reference. In the second place, the books opened in verse 12 are books containing the record of none but evil deeds. In direct contrast to them the "book of life" is spoken of with the names written in it of the saved. It harmonises with this, that the book of life is not expressly mentioned as used to prove of any that they were to escape the lake of fire, but only (verse 15) that the condemned were condemned justly, because their names were not found written in it. In the third place, the mention of the quarters from which "the dead" appear leads to the same conclusion. They are three, "the sea," "death," and "Hades." That "the sea" is not the ocean can hardly admit of a moment's doubt. In that sense it would form no proper parallel to death and Hades; few comparatively could come from it; and in chap. xxi. 1, where we read, "And there was no more sea," it cannot be literally understood. The "sea," therefore, is the emblem of all disorder and confusion; from it the wicked alone can rise. "Death," again, cannot be the neutral grave, for it is cast into the lake of fire ; and a similar remark applies to Hades (comp. chap. vi. 8). The sea, death, Hades, all are symbolical, and symbolical only of what is bad. Not one of them has in it any righteous to give up. The whole passage is applicable to the judgment of the ungodly, and to that alone. For the godly there is no judgment, or it is already past.

This view is sufficiently remarkable, but it is not more so than the statement of the Apocalypse regarding (apparently) two resurrections in chap. xx. We have already considered the question connected with the two resurrections, and have seen that the "first resurrection" is purely spiritual,—a resurrection of "souls" out of death into life (Lect. vi. p. 217). Upon this point it is needless to say more.

Let us turn to the fourth Gospel, and is there any part of its teaching more characteristic than that contained in the words of Jesus to the Jews at the pool of Bethesda? "Verily, verily, I say unto you, An hour cometh, and now is, when the dead shall hear the voice of the Son of God; and they that have heard shall live. . . . Marvel not at this : because an hour cometh, in the which all that are in the graves shall hear His voice, and they that have done good shall go forth unto a resurrection of life, but they that have committed evil unto a resurrection of judgment" (chap. v. 25, 28, 29). In these words we have the same two resurrections, if the "first resurrection" necessarily imply a second, that we find in chap. xx. of the Apocalypse. The "dead" of verse 25 are the spiritually dead. In regard to them alone could it be said that the "hour" spoken of has already begun ("an hour cometh, *and now is*"), or would the limitation of the last words of the verse, "*they that have heard,*" be in place. They that have so heard, though they were dead, live,—the first resurrection. That in verses 28, 29 the future alone is spoken of is clear from the omission of the words, "and now is," found in verse 25. This resurrection is wholly different from the last, for the words, "all that are in the graves" (not "all that have heard") shall "go forth" (not shall "live"), together with the mention of two great classes, "they that have done good unto a resurrection of life," "they that have committed evil unto a resurrection of judgment," show that a general, or second, resurrection is before us.

One point still remains to be noticed, not because, like those now considered, it is in any special sense characteristic of the two books of which we speak, for it pervades the whole New

Testament, but because its presence in the fourth Gospel has been often and emphatically denied. We refer to the Second Coming of the Lord. Of that topic the Apocalypse is full; but it is urged that the Gospel understands by Christ's Second Coming something purely spiritual, the establishing of His dominion in the hearts of men. Such a view can only be taken where the Gospel is misunderstood. The words of chap. xx. 22, "If I will that he tarry till I come, what is that to thee?" admit of no interpretation but that of a personal, local, coming of the Lord. The same thing may be said of the frequent allusions to the subject in chaps. xiv.- xvi. There the "coming" is always in direct contrast to the "going away;" and, if we are to understand the former of an inward manifestation by Jesus of Himself to the believer, we shall be compelled to understand the latter of His leaving the believer to spiritual separation from Him. The impossibility of doing this will be felt by any one who substitutes, in such passages as John xiv. 3, 18, 19, 23, 28; xvi. 5, 7, 16, 17, 22, the latter for the former thought. The words are instantly deprived of all meaning; and that personal, local departure must be understood which shall be followed by a personal and local return. In its expectation of such a "coming" of Christ, the fourth Gospel, while no doubt laying greater emphasis upon the believer's present possession of eternal life, does not differ from the other books of the New Testament or from the Apocalypse among them. The eschatological teaching, therefore, previously adverted to, may be left to make its full impression on the mind.

The various points of comparison between the Apocalypse and the fourth Gospel which have now been adduced are sufficient to show that the two books so greatly resemble one another as to lend a high degree of probability to the belief that both proceeded from the same pen.

It may indeed be urged that in what has been said we have dealt largely in details, and that details afford no proper basis of argument in a matter of the kind. To a certain extent this is true, and the following remarks of Reuss may be unhesitatingly accepted—"Details can furnish no conclusive proof, either by the analogies or the variations they may offer, because, after all, it is unquestionably apostolic and Christian teaching that we have before us (he means in both books), and it is inevitable that certain evangelical facts and fundamental convictions should be occasionally reproduced, and that the particular design of each book, and other external circumstances, should modify the choice and the expression of them. It will not be, then, by the comparison of individual texts or formulas that any decisive result will be reached in a critical inquiry of this kind" (*Christ. Theol. of the Apost. Age*, ii. p. 507). This remark of the veteran critic is true; but the following observations may be made.

(1.) Details in which a certain correspondence might be expected have not alone been dealt with. Those selected have been for the most part *characteristic of the writer* among the different writers of the New Testament. They have pointed to a strongly marked individuality both of thought and of expression. They have been such as to enable us to say with perfect confidence that the writer of the fourth Gospel was neither one of the first three Evangelists nor St. Paul, St. Peter, or St. Jude, and that from these persons the writer of the Apocalypse is equally distinct. Is it possible, then, that the author of the former book may also have been the author of the latter? We have seen in a multitude of particulars that the same characteristics appear in both, that the individuality of each is the same, and that the correspondence between them leads to the conviction that in the one we recognise the other. Details of such a nature form the legitimate basis of an argument.

(2.) To details even of this kind we have not confined ourselves. Let the reader recall the particulars adverted to; more especially let him recall what has been said in the lectures of this volume, and he will not deny that the "general tone and tendency" of the two books have been as much before us as details. The main stress of the argument has indeed been rested on this fact. There is in each book a mode of conceiving the whole purpose and plan of God in His dealings with mankind, the whole manifestation of Christ, and the whole nature of the Christian Dispensation which, while it distinguishes the writer of each from the other sacred writers, brings them into the nearest possible relation to one another. While studying visions of the Apocalypse, such as those of the "glories" of chaps v. and vi., of the death and resurrection and ascension of the two witnesses in chap. xi. (comp. John xii. 20), of the woman with the man child in chap. xii. (comp. John xvi. 21), and of the assault of the ten horns and of the beast upon the harlot in chap. xvii., the student is often startled to find how powerfully he is reminded of passages of the fourth Gospel conveying the very same truths

in a didactic form. So far from meeting, as Reuss alleges,
"two types of Christian teaching which could not dwell simul-
taneously in the same mind" (*U. S.* p. 507), he meets *precisely
the same type*, differing only in this, that in the one case the
light is revealed in Christ, in the other in the members of His
body; that what is taught historically of the former is taught
in symbol of the latter; and that the period of Christian
development treated of in the Gospel belongs to Christ's conflict
with the world as it revealed itself in "the Jews;" while in
that treated of in the Apocalypse the Church is in conflict with
the world as revealed in the tumultuous surging of the Gentile
nations. No book of the New Testament goes farther beyond
the scope of Judaism than the Apocalypse; none is more ideal
in its conception of the universality, the completeness, or the
spirituality of the Christian Church. Reuss's mistake is that
of the ordinary interpreters of the book, who look on it as
historical instead of ideal, and who fail to see that it is simply
the completion of that compound thought connected with
Christ's coming which the Gospel had but partially disclosed.
The Gospel sets this thought before us so far as to show the
manner in which at His coming Christ entered into the hearts
of men. The Apocalypse starts with the fact that in this
respect He has come, and has only further to guide those who
have received Him through the same trials as His own to that
glory which He enjoys now, and which shall also be made
theirs when He comes again without sin unto salvation. It is
absurd therefore to dwell upon a tone of love in the Gospel and
of vengeance in the Apocalypse, as if the two were inconsistent
with each other. Even were there not, what we have seen
there is, as much severity in the former as in the latter, as
much love in the latter as in the former, the vengeance spoken
of is determined by the object. Nor is it really vengeance. It
is the vindication of righteousness. It is the echo of the words
of Jesus, "Hear what the unrighteous Judge saith. And shall
not God avenge His elect which cry to Him day and night?"
(Luke xviii. 6, 7), or of the words of the Old Testament adopted
by St. Paul, "Vengeance belongeth unto me : I will recompense,
saith the Lord" (Rom. xii. 19). There is no more inconsistency
between Christ's being at once the Lion of the tribe of Judah
and the Good Shepherd than between the two aspects of His
manifestation of Himself in the tender Gospel of St. Luke, in
which He is at once the Physician of souls and the corner stone

ry one that falleth shall be broken to pieces;
ver it shall fall, it will scatter him as dust"
Even Reuss allows that this type of teaching
ible with the idea of the Gospel" (*U. S.* p.
irther and say that the two types not only may
ne mind, but that they must do so in exact
e approach the mind of Christ. In whom
refore have been more united than in "the
sus loved"?
se object of the argument ought to be kept dis-
The defender of that unity of authorship for
s not in the position of a person who has one
into his hand as the production of the Apostle,
show by internal evidence that the other pro-
same source. The two books come to him
unanimous tradition of the Church in favour
n. From the beginning both were believed to
ven to the world as, St. John's. That some
sprang up upon the point is true. But the
ed, and even gained strength, in the midst of
hus proved its vitality more effectually than it
had no such doubts existed. It was the firm
ost all for seventeen centuries; and this "almost
iolars, writers, commentators, historians, men
well as of sluggish minds, and heretics as well
What is required of us therefore, is not to
own author, but to inquire into the probabilities
accepted authorship, and to ask whether the
to it are so powerful as to constrain us to yield
just weight of authority in favour of the
ve advocated, though clearly open to question
ow its ability to defend itself, ought never to
when we review the grounds of a definite con-
point.
mbent on the opponents of the Church's belief
it a hypothesis having some claims to take its
have been made to do so. The most specious
hich ascribes the Apocalypse not to the apostle
ter John—we have already considered and dis-
never found its way to anything approaching
e even among those who advocate the double
two books. A similar remark may be made

on the hypothesis of Baur. That distinguished man was so much struck with the points of resemblance between the Gospel and the Apocalypse that the former became to him a "spiritualised Apocalypse" (*K. E.*, p. 380), in which the writer, who only professes to be the Evangelist, elevates and transfigures to their purest spiritual height the conceptions he had learned from the Jewish Revelation. This hypothesis implies that the Apocalypse was written about A.D. 70, and that long afterwards, not necessarily so long as Baur imagines, some one undertook to spiritualise its picture of the Christ, and produced the Gospel. The theory is inconceivable. Even with the help of the Synoptic Gospels it is impossible that any one should have framed out of the Apocalypse such a life of Jesus as that of the fourth Gospel. Surely in thought at least (not necessarily in date) the Gospel preceded the Apocalypse, not the Apocalypse the Gospel. We can understand that a writer, different from the writer of the Gospel but with the Gospel in his hand, might depict the struggle of the Church in a manner corresponding to that of her Lord ; but that one should think of drawing up from the Apocalypse a corresponding life of Christ, and should embody his ideas in the life given us by the supposed St. John, is utterly incredible. The individual might suggest the general. The general could never have suggested the individual. It was a fitting thing that the servant should be as his Master, but there was no need that the Master should have been as the servant. Besides this He is not. In Baur's view, while the servant has outward suffering, although rising superior to it, the history of the Master is an inward and spiritual process. The very key-note of the theory is that the elements which the Apocalyptist had appropriated out of the realities of the Church's life and had thrown into a transcendental future, the Evangelist transforms into the immanent presence of a clear and peaceful self-consciousness in Jesus. The distant heaven of the persecuted saint, for example, is transformed into the present heaven of the Redeemer's breast. But this is completely to reverse the order of things. The writer of the Gospel, as a student alike of the Old Testament and of history, must have learned the lesson of St. Paul, "Howbeit that is not first which is spiritual, but that which is natural" (1 Cor. xv. 46). From the outward carnal picture of the Church, which had long been familiar to him, he could hardly have travelled backward to a conception of her Head so inward and

piritual as that of the Johannine Jesus. We may accept
Baur's strong language as to the close resemblance of our two
books, but not his solution of the problem; and nearly all later
inquirers have declined to do so.

No hypothesis, indeed, has as yet been offered with regard
to the composition of the Apocalypse which, while rejecting the
idea of its Johannine origin, has been able to command more
than the adhesion of a few; and, till this is done, the defender
of unity of authorship in the case of the two books before us is
entitled to the benefit of the traditional view upon the point.
Nor is this all. Let us proceed upon that view. Let us try
the hypothesis of ascribing both books to the same author, and
that author the apostle John; and, though it cannot even then
be said that every difficulty will disappear, it will be found that
we are in a far better position than we should otherwise occupy
for explaining the origin and meaning of both. Their harmony
of plan will be made manifest; and rules of interpretation will
be suggested which will cast such a flood of light upon passages
otherwise almost unintelligible as to afford no small test that
our hypothesis is true.

APPENDIX III.

THE DATE OF THE APOCALYPSE.

In the Lectures on the Apocalypse contained in this volume it has been taken for granted that the composition of that book is to be assigned to a date subsequent, and not prior, to the destruction of Jerusalem, in A.D. 70. So far, however, is this from being generally conceded, that the very reverse is the case. Recent scholarship has, with little exception, decided in favour of the earlier and not the later date. It is impossible, therefore, to dispense with an attempt to defend the position which has been here assumed. Apart from this, too, the inquiry possesses so much interest and importance that no layman even, desirous to understand the book with which we are concerned, should pass it by. We shall endeavour, while not omitting any important argument, to make the matter intelligible to every reader.

For all practical purposes the inquiry really is, Whether the Apocalypse was written about A.D. 68, before the fall of Jerusalem, or about A.D. 95 or 96, towards the close of the reign of the Emperor Domitian? Züllig has indeed placed it so early as A.D. 44 to A.D. 47, under Claudius, who reigned from A.D. 41 to A.D. 54; and others, among whom may be named Grotius and Hammond, have assigned it to the same reign, though not necessarily to so early a part of it. On the other hand, the writer of a tract on "The life and death of the apostles and disciples of our Lord," supposed, but falsely, to have been Dorotheus, Bishop of Tyre, at the close of the third century, speaks of the reign of Trajan, A.D. 98 to A.D. 117, as the time when the Apocalypse was produced. The first of these dates is so universally allowed to be too early, the second too late, that

it is unnecessary to discuss them. At the one end of the scale
we are limited to a date immediately preceding A.D. 70. At
the other the evidence affords no resting-place till we reach the
late date (A.D. 95 or 96) in the first century already mentioned.
Between these two the question lies. The evidence is both
external and internal, and it will be well to take its two branches
in their usual order.

*I. External evidence.—The first witness who claims our
attention is undoubtedly Irenæus, appointed Bishop of Lyons,
A.D. 177, in succession to Pothinus, whose age, ninety years,
takes us back to the generation that saw the last of the apostles,
and with whom Irenæus, as one of his Presbyters, can scarcely
have failed to have had familiar intercourse. The words of
Irenæus have been preserved by Eusebius (*H. E.*, v. 8), "for
no long time ago was *it* (the Revelation) seen (οὐδὲ γὰρ πρὸ
πολλοῦ χρόνου ἑωράθη), but almost in our generation, at the
end of the reign of Domitian." An effort has no doubt been
made to evade the force of the conclusion to which these words
lead, by suggesting that the subject of the verb ἑωράθη in the
sentence quoted is not "the Revelation" but St. John himself
—not "it" was seen but "he" was seen. Argument against
such a supposition may be dispensed with. Although supported
by an able writer (generally supposed to be Dr. Goodwin) on the
Apocalypse in the *Biblical Review* (vol. i. p. 175), and by Dr.
Macdonald in his *Life and Writings of St. John* (p. 169), no
Greek scholar would for a moment endeavour to defend it. The
testimony of Irenæus is therefore clear. The meaning of his
statement is indisputable; and we must either accept it or
allow (what may certainly have happened) that he was mistaken.
But Irenæus was not likely to be mistaken, and several considerations add weight to the witness that he bears with so
much precision.

. The following may be mentioned: (1) His nearness to the
apostolic age; for he cannot have been born later than A.D.
130 (*Dict. of Christian Antiquity*, IRENÆUS), while many have
contended that his birth should be placed at least twenty or
twenty-five years earlier in the century. (2) The well-known
fact that he had been a disciple and friend of Polycarp, Bishop
of Smyrna, who had been a contemporary of the apostle John
himself, who had held intercourse with him and who was wont to
relate in the circle of his friends incidents out of that deeply
interesting past. In this respect Irenæus's own letter to

Florinus (see p. 247), in which he details the nature of his intercourse with Polycarp, will always remain one of the most precious monuments of Christian antiquity, showing as it does in the clearest manner the spirit of inquiry, the intelligence, the vivacity, and the effort to form distinct conceptions of times anterior to their own, by which these old fathers of the Church were marked. (3) The object which Irenæus had in view in making the statement now commented on. He had been discussing the number of the beast as given in Rev. xiii. 18, and he goes on to explain that it was only at some risk that any one could endeavour to interpret it; for, had the apostle desired "the present time" to know the interpretation, he would himself have given it, inasmuch as the vision had been granted him on the very borders of the generation to which Irenæus spoke. The date of the book was thus no trifling matter in the eyes of this father, for it powerfully affected the relation in which he stood to one of the most difficult mysteries of the Apocalypse. (4) The confidence of Eusebius in the statement made by him. This confidence, it will not be denied, appears in all that Eusebius has said upon the point; and no one could have known better than he any counter-opinions which are supposed to have existed long before his day, and to have formed another and wholly different current of tradition.

It is unnecessary to say more. There need be no hesitation in asserting that in regard to few facts of early Christian antiquity have we a statement more positively or clearly given than that of Irenæus, that the Seer beheld the visions of his book at the end of Domitian's reign, that is, about A.D. 96.

We turn next to the testimony of Clement of Alexandria, who flourished towards the close of the second and in the early part of the third century (A.D. 165 to A.D. 220). For this we are again indebted to Eusebius, who quotes from Clement the beautiful story of the young robber, in order to prove that, after the death of Domitian (μετὰ τὴν Δομετιανοῦ τελευτὴν), the apostle John returned from his exile in Patmos to Ephesus, and presided over the churches there (*H. E.*, iii. 23). It is true that, in his account of the story, Clement does not name Domitian, saying merely that John had returned "after the death of the tyrant" (τοῦ τυράννου τελευτήσαντος). But no one can read Eusebius without seeing that he at least distinctly understood Clement to mean that John had been banished to Patmos by that Emperor, and that, at a period subsequent to

Domitian's death, he had presided over the Church in the neighbourhood of Ephesus. Nor is there any force in the objection that, if so, the apostle must have lived into the second century, because the incidents of the story, beginning only about A.D. 95, would require some years for their complete development. Nothing is told that might not have happened in the course of a single year; while, if we suppose, and it is the only other possible supposition, that St. John's return took place after the death of Nero, when he was in all probability not more than sixty years of age, many expressions of the narrative of Clement, such as "forgetful of his age," and "thy aged father," lose their force, and *the whole object of its quotation by Eusebius is destroyed.* At the close of the second century, therefore, the impression certainly prevailed in Alexandria that St. John's return from his banishment to Patmos had taken place under Domitian, and that before that date the book of Revelation could not have been penned.

The evidence of Tertullian, but little later than that of Clement († A.D. 240), may appropriately follow. His own words indeed will hardly justify any positive conclusion upon the point, for, after having spoken of Nero as the first persecutor of the Christians, he merely adds, "Domitian, too, a man of Nero's type (*portio Neronis*) in cruelty, tried his hand at persecution; but, as he had something of the human in him, he soon put an end to what he had begun, even restoring again those whom he had banished" (*Tertullian*, in Clark's *Library*, i. p. 64). But Eusebius notices the passage in such a manner as to show that he believed St. John to be included among those to whom Tertullian refers (*H. E.*, iii. 20).

Passing to another region of the Church, we are met by the testimony of Victorinus, Bishop of Pettau in Pannonia, who was martyred under Diocletian, A.D. 303. So far as is known he is the earliest commentator on the Apocalypse; and it is natural to think that, as a commentator, he would take a greater than ordinary interest in such a question as is now before us. His testimony is of the most specific kind, for, commenting on chap. x. 11, he says that "when John said these things he was in the island of Patmos, condemned to the labour of the mines by Cæsar Domitian. There, therefore, he saw the Apocalypse" (*Tertullian*, in Clark's *Library*, iii. p. 417).

In still another quarter we meet Eusebius, Bishop of Cæsarea (A.D. 260 to A.D. 339) a man whose inquiring spirit led him to

search out, and to preserve in his writings, many ancient documents of incalculable value to the student of early Christian
antiquity. Of his opinion there can be no doubt. We have
already found him citing Irenæus and Clement as authorities in
favour of everything in connection with this matter for which
we need to contend ; and, in his own historical account of the
fourteenth year of Domitian's reign, he says of the Apostle John
that " he was banished " at that time " to Patmos, where he saw
the Apocalypse, as Irenæus shows " (*Chron.* cap. xiv.). Nor is
there any ground for the assertion that Eusebius simply repeated what Irenæus had said more than a century before.
That he relied greatly upon Irenæus is unquestionable. His
very object was to collect and preserve the testimonies which
seemed to him to warrant a definite conclusion. But he did
not depend upon Irenæus alone. Referring to the point before
us, he in one place names also Clement of Alexandria as his
authority (*H. E.*, iii. 23), and in another the " tradition of the
ancients " (ὁ τῶν παρ᾽ ἡμῖν ἀρχαίων παραδίδωσι λόγος, *H. E.*,
iii. 20).

This list of witnesses may be fitly closed with Jerome
(† A.D. 420), the most learned of all the fathers except Origen,
and one who, as is well known, devoted himself to the study of
Scripture with a zeal not even surpassed by that of his illustri-
ous predecessor in the same field. Speaking of St. John in his
Treatise on Illustrious Men, he says of him that, " having been
banished in the fourteenth year of Domitian to the island of
Patmos, he wrote the Apocalypse " (cap. 9).

Testimonies subsequent to these, however clear, hardly
possess so much authority as to entitle them to quotation.

Looking back upon what has been said we have the following result. From the first witness who speaks upon the point
in the latter half of the second century down to the first half of
the fifth we have a succession of fathers bearing testimony with
one accord, and in language which admits of no misunderstanding, to the fact that St. John was banished to Patmos under
the reign of Domitian, and that there he beheld those visions
of the Apocalypse which he afterwards committed to writing.
These fathers, too, are men who in their interest in the subject
immediately in hand (to say nothing of other subjects), in
ability, learning, and critical insight into the history of bygone
times, surpass all the fathers, except one to be afterwards mentioned, of their respective eras. In their spheres of labour, i

.ey belong to the most different and widespread
Church, to Gaul, Alexandria, the proconsular
rth Africa, Pannonia, Syria, and Rome. They
eat degree independent of each other, and they
e incontestable impression that, for at least the
ries of the Christian era and over the whole
hristian Church, it was firmly believed that St.
l the visions of the Apocalypse in the days of
ot of Nero.[1]
er, has to be said, for various considerations of
ier than an internal kind are favourable to this
us the persecution under Domitian appears to
h more widespread than that under Nero, by
 must have been banished if the earlier date of
 be correct. The almost unanimous voice of
favours the supposition that the Neronic per-
i it may have provoked echoes in some of the
iot extend beyond the city of Rome (Gieseler,
mpletely adopts the conclusions of Dodwell in
gainst Orosius ; Keim, *Rom und das Christen-*
Aubé, *Histoire*, p. 109 ; Overbeck, *Studien*, p.
therwise with Domitian, for, even although the
hat emperor can hardly be spoken of as general,
uded inquiries made with regard to descendants
 the house of David (Eusebius, *H. E.*, iii. 20),
ll have touched places intermediate between
ome. Again, there is the clearest evidence even
f Tacitus (*Annal.* xv. 44), confirmed by all the
 which has come down to us, that the persecu-
ro had no relation whatever to the religious
victims, or to the interests of the State. It was
; of the tyrant's rage, and of his effort to avert
e indignation of the people at the horrible crime
as the reputed author (comp. Keim, *U. S.*, p.
in, as we have already seen, had much more of
ious considerations, and Christians in his time

<table>
<tr><td>

ioned by Lücke
is also not with-
ere. That writer
martyrologies and
Andreas place the
tipas (Rev. ii. 13)
nitian, "because

</td><td>

the Apocalypse appeared to them
to have been written at that time."
The belief illustrates the continu-
ous nature of the current tradi-
tion.

[2] Lücke (*Versuch*, p. 437) ad-
mits the limitation.

</td></tr>
</table>

were much more numerous.[1] The words of Rev. i. 9 have no
relation to the former, and are at least much more suitable to
the latter state of things. Again, if importance is to be attached
to the fact that the Apocalypse bears the marks of *immediately*
surrounding persecution, these will be found more readily at the
later than at the earlier date. It was in the last year of his
reign that Domitian became a persecutor, and in the same year
the apocalyptic visions were seen. On the other hand, several
years of rest to the Christians elapsed between the date of the
Neronic persecution and the reign of either Galba or Vespasian ;
for the city of Rome was fired in July 64 ; the persecution broke
out in the following September ; and the idea entertained by
some that Nero's persecutions continued at intervals till his
death in A.D. 68 is not only destitute of proof, but has been
pronounced by Keim to be "fully unhistorical" (*U. S.*, p. 196).
Once more, there appears to be no mention, in any ancient
writer, of exile as a means of punishment resorted to by Nero.
We read of imprisonment, confiscation, hunting to death with
dogs, crucifixion, beheading, drenching with oil and then setting
fire to the miserable victim : banishment is never named. In
the case of Domitian we have not only Eusebius reporting from
"the historians of the day," and expressly from Tertullian, a
decree of the Roman Senate recalling those whom Domitian had
unjustly expelled (*II. E.*, iii. 20), but we have the detailed story of
Domitilla (whether there were not two of that name who experienced a similar fate it is needless to inquire), the wife of Flavius
Clemens, Domitian's own cousin, whom that Emperor banished
to Pandateria near Naples (*Suet. Dom.*, c. 18 ; *Dio Cassius*,
lxvii. 14). In this instance also the charge against the accused
was of a religious kind, that of atheism or Judaizing, and such
continued to be the character of Domitian's persecutions to the
end of his reign (Keim, *U. S.*, p. 213).

These considerations powerfully confirm the probability that
the tradition of the early Church, connecting the composition of
the Apocalypse with the reign of Domitian rather than of Galba
or Vespasian, is correct.

It has indeed been urged that the voice of antiquity is
not so distinctly in favour of an early date as might be supposed from the above remarks ; and different testimonies have
been appealed to which are thought to lead to an opposite con-

---

[1] Comp. Keim, *U. S.*, p. 210, whose words are *Die verfolgten sind
also Christen.*

clusion. Of these the earliest is from the Muratorian fragment, ascribed by Bunsen to Hegesippus, A.D. 170. The words of the fragment are, "The blessed Paul himself, following the order of his predecessor (*prodecessoris sui*) John, writes to seven churches only by name;" and the argument is, that the Apocalypse is here stated "to have preceded the death of St. Paul, who suffered martyrdom in the reign of Nero" (*Bibl. Rev.*, i. 172). If this, however, be the meaning, the Apocalypse must have preceded not only the death of St. Paul, but the writing of at least the last of his Seven Epistles to the churches; that is, it must have preceded the year A.D. 62, a conclusion fatal to the idea of St. John's banishment by Nero, the persecution of that Emperor having begun in A.D. 64. But it is not necessary to say this. The obvious meaning of the word "*prodecessor*" is that St. John had been called to the apostleship earlier than St. Paul (comp. Gal. i. 17, "them which were apostles before me"). Nor does the word "following" necessarily involve the idea that St. Paul had St. John's "order" before him when he wrote. It may mean no more than that the writer of the fragments, passing in his statement from the Gospels to the Epistles, and thus *from* St. John *to* St. Paul, was struck with the fact that the latter had written only seven Epistles; and that, as the earlier apostle had done the same, he spoke of the one as following the example of the other.[1]

Origen, too (A.D. 186 to A.D. 253), has been cited as in favour of the early date of the Apocalypse, but his words contain no definite information of the kind. In his commentary on St. Matthew he tells us that John was condemned to Patmos by "the King of the Romans," adding that the apostle had not mentioned in Rev. i. 9 by whom he was condemned ($\mu\grave{\eta}$ λέγων τίς αὐτὸν κατεδίκασε). He may, therefore, not have known whether the "king" in question was Nero or Domitian; or, even if he knew, he may have said nothing upon the point, because he thought it proper to follow the example of St. John himself, whose silence, as we may infer from his use of $\mu\grave{\eta}$, he regarded as intentional.

Thus far the evidence adduced on behalf of the composition

---

[1] Tregelles (*Can. Mur.*, p. 44) says, "It cannot be that the author thought that St. John saw and wrote the Apocalypse before St. Paul had written his Epistles;" and he adds his own explanation, "John had been previously spoken of by the writer as the author of the Gospel and his First Epistle." Lücke (*Versuch*, p. 809) has no hesitation in adopting the explanation given above.

of the Apocalypse before the fall of Jerusalem may without impropriety be spoken of as unworthy of regard. It is somewhat different when we come to Epiphanius, appointed Bishop of Salamis A.D. 367, and one of the most voluminous writers of his age. Lücke, anxious as he is to find proof of the earlier date, speaks of him as the first to interrupt the Irenæan tradition (*Versuch*, p. 806). What does the interruption amount to? Epiphanius has spoken upon the point in two passages. In the first (li. c. 12) he says that John, though he shrank from the task, was constrained by the Holy Spirit to write a Gospel " in his old age, when he had spent ninety years of life, after his return from Patmos, which took place in the reign of the Emperor Claudius " (see in Lee's *Prolegomena*, p. 419). In the second (c. 33) he speaks of the apostle as having prophesied in the time of the Emperor Claudius, when he went to the island of Patmos. The impossibility of receiving these statements must be at once apparent. The Emperor Claudius died A.D. 54, so that we have the incredible assertions that St. John was even then ninety years old, and that he wrote his Gospel at that time. Besides this, it is to be observed that Claudius did not persecute the Christians generally, though they may be included among " the Jews " whom (Acts xviii. 2) he banished from Rome. The universal voice of early Christian antiquity is that Nero was the *first* persecutor, Domitian the second (comp. among many others *Tertullian*, *Apol.*, p. 5 ; comp. also the strong statement of Stuart upon this point, *Comm.*, p. 226). How Epiphanius was led into his mistake, whether by that general inaccuracy and want of critical acumen for which he is noted (comp. *Dict. of Christian Biogr.*, EPIPHANIUS), or by some misapprehension connected with the words of Acts xviii. 2, it is impossible to say ; but that there is error either on his part or on the part of those who copied him there can hardly be a moment's doubt. This is rendered the more probable by the singular fact that the story of Epiphanius appears never to have made the slightest impression upon those who came after him. No tradition in that form exists ; the statement seems to have been forgotten until revived by Grotius and Hammond ; and it now stands in the pages of its author, a striking instance of the perplexity which one single inaccuracy may introduce into our efforts to reconstruct the past.

In addition to Epiphanius one or two other authorities from the first Christian centuries are quoted on behalf of an early date for the Apocalypse. Thus a statement to that effect is contained in the superscription of a Syriac version of the Revelation, first published A.D. 1627, and belonging, as seems to be generally allowed, to the sixth century. The superscription bears that the Revelation was "given by God to the Evangelist John on the island of Patmos, to which he had been sent by the Emperor Nero." Even allowing to this statement the full weight which it is supposed to possess, and giving no heed to the conjecture that by Nero is meant Domitian, who was known as a second Nero (comp. Elliott, *H. A.*, i. p. 43), the singular point to be noticed is that here, *for the first time*, we have the banishment of St. John assigned to Nero. An allegation of this kind so late as the sixth century is of little moment. Andreas, Archbishop of Cæsarea in Cappadocia, about the beginning of the sixth century, in his commentary upon Rev. vi. 12, tells us that "there are not wanting some" who apply the mention made of the "great earthquake" there to the destruction of Jerusalem by Titus, from which the inference is drawn that those who did so must have believed that the Apocalypse was written before that event. Even if they did, it by no means follows that they rested upon any tradition to that effect. Their idea of the date of composition may have sprung from their interpretation of the text, and not their interpretation from any historical information at their command. Andreas himself decidedly rejects the interpretation, but says nothing of the question of date. Andreas was succeeded, how long afterwards is disputed, in the same See by Arethas, but the commentary of the latter on the Apocalypse, in which he simply followed Andreas, and which is also referred to in this controversy, leads to the same conclusion.[1] Finally, Theophylact is mentioned,

---

[1] The writer may be permitted to express his own conviction, although he ventures to do it only in a note, that the words of Andreas have been misunderstood. Referring to those who are spoken of as applying the words of the Seer to the destruction of Jerusalem under Vespasian, Lücke (*Versuch*, p. 810) says, "These persons therefore took for granted a banishment of St. John to Patmos before that date." When we look at Andreas's own commentary this inference of Lücke's seems to be by no means justified. The words of Andreas (chap. vii. 1) are, *Etsi isthæc ad illa incommoda a quibusdam referantur quæ Judæi quondam a Romanis perpessi sunt; arbitrantur enim per quatuor mystica animalia*, etc.; *multo tamen rectius ad antichristi adventum locus hic refertur.* What Andreas contrasts in these words is not an opinion of some that, in Rev. vi. 12, etc., we have a prophecy of the fall of Jerusalem, and an opinion of others

who says in his preface to his commentary on the Gospel of St.
John that that apostle was "an exile in the island of Patmos
thirty-two years after the ascension of Christ." But the curious
thing is that Theophylact makes this statement in connection
with the writing not of the Apocalypse but of the fourth Gospel,
and in that respect at least no one doubts that he is wrong.
Apart from this the late period, the eleventh century, in which
he flourished, deprives his evidence of weight as to that earlier
tradition of the Church of which we are in quest.

Glancing for a moment over the external evidence as a whole,
it is clear that Lücke, notwithstanding his own conclusion in
favour of the earlier date, only states the matter with his usual
fairness when he says (*Versuch*, p. 811) that "the oldest and
most wide tradition is certainly (*allerdings*) that which proceeds
from Irenæus, according to which the apostle John beheld and
wrote the Apocalypse towards the end of the reign of Domitian."
It is unfair to say with Stuart (*Comm.*, p. 221) that "ancient
testimony is divided mainly between the time of Domitian and
that of Nero," or with Davidson (*Intr.*, i. p. 348) that there is
an "absence of external evidence," or with the writer in the
Biblical Review (i. p. 178) that the "evidence is rather in
favour of the early date than against it." So far as it goes the
external evidence is, on the contrary, both clear and definite. It
begins no doubt with Irenæus, and with some one it must begin. But Irenæus makes his statement in such a way as to show
that he gives in it the opinion of the Church, and for more than
three centuries there is no disturbing voice except that of Epiphanius, of whose story of the relation of St. John to the
Emperor Claudius no one will venture to say more than is said
by Stuart at the moment when he quotes him to show "that
the voice of antiquity is not unanimous on the subject,"—"This
opinion of Epiphanius stands alone among the ancients. . . .

that the words relate to the coming
of Antichrist. He rather contrasts
the latter with the idea entertained
by some, that St. John in the
verses spoken of must have *drawn
his description from what he knew
of the fate of the holy city.* The reference to others, in this respect
corresponding to every passage of
his own commentary bearing upon
the point, thus implies on the part
of the *quidam* the belief that
Jerusalem had fallen when the
Apocalypse was written. These
persons are thus witnesses for the
later not the *earlier* date. Arethas
(on Rev. i. 9) is still more precise
than Andreas, for he tells his
readers, on the authority of Eusebius, but in such a way as to show
his own belief in the statement,
that John had been banished to
Patmos by Domitian.

We must dismiss this matter, therefore, merely with the remark that no good grounds of it are given, nor can any be well imagined " (*Comm.*, p. 218).

If any other conclusion than that which asserts the late date of the Apocalypse is to be adopted, it must rest upon overpowering evidence supplied by its own contents.

II. *Internal Evidence.*—Such evidence is supposed to exist, many modern scholars, not more distinguished by their ability than by their sobriety and reverence of spirit, even accepting it as decisive. The evidence relied on may be said to divide itself into two branches : first, the interpretation of particular texts ; secondly, the general character of the contents and style of the book.

1. *The interpretation of particular texts.*—It is urged by Hilgenfeld that passages such as chaps. vi. 9-11 ; xvi. 6 ; xvii. 6 ; xviii. 24 ; xix. 2, refer to the persecution of the Christians by Nero (*Einl.*, p. 447) ; while Bleek (*Lectures*, p. 118) depends mainly upon the first of these passages for the same conclusion as at least the " most probable." But, properly interpreted, Rev. vi. 9-11 has no reference to any persecution of Christians. These souls under the altar are the souls not of Christian martyrs but of *Old Testament saints*, who had been waiting for that perfection which was to be brought to them by the coming of Christ (*see this point fully discussed in Comm. in loc.*). A moment's attention, again, to the other texts quoted is sufficient to show that they are equally applicable to any persecution of Christians whatever, and that there is absolutely nothing to connect them with Nero rather than Domitian. On the contrary, if we believe, as there seems every reason to do, that persecution under the latter Emperor was more severe and widespread than under the former, we shall, by referring these texts to persecutions under him rather than Nero, be better able to explain the strong expressions which direct our thoughts not only to Babylon (supposing for the moment Babylon to be Rome), but to the whole " earth " (chaps. xviii. 24 ; xix. 2).

Chap. xi. 1, 2 is referred to with great confidence in this connection (Lücke, *Versuch*, p. 825 ; Bleek, *Lectures*, p. 248 ; Stuart, *Comm.*, p. 226 ; Düsterdieck, p. 52 ; *Parousia*, p. 373, etc.) The passage relates to the measuring of the temple (ναός) and the treading of the holy city under foot by the nations ; and it is supposed to prove partly that the temple must still have been in existence when the words were written ;

partly that the Jewish war, which began A.D. 66, must then have been in progress, inasmuch as the writer expects that Jerusalem and the outer court of the temple will be destroyed by the heathen. The following considerations may be noted in reply. (1) As the act of "measuring" relates, and is admitted by almost all interpreters to relate, to the *preservation*, not to the *destruction*, of the "temple," that is, of the inner sanctuary, it will follow that, on the application of his words now spoken of, the expectations of the Seer were falsified by the event. That inner sanctuary was the very part of the temple buildings into which the Roman soldiers pressed with peculiar zeal, and which they utterly consumed with fire (Josephus, *Jewish War*, vi. 4, 5). A similar remark applies to the treading of the holy city under foot of the nations for three and a half years. If, as is sometimes done, this period is fixed between February of A.D. 67, when Vespasian received his commission from Nero, and August of A.D. 70, when the city fell, it is sufficient to point to the obvious meaning of the text, that the treading should only begin after and not before Jerusalem was taken. Or if, to escape this difficulty, the three and a half years are placed after the city's fall, there is no historical event corresponding to the cessation of the treading at their close. Besides this, the events detailed from verse 3 to verse 13, which obviously belong to the three and a half years, cannot, if we interpret literally, have occurred at a time when the foot of foreign oppression was trampling the city in the dust ; while, at the same time, it will be impossible to explain various indications given in these verses that the events referred to took place, not within the limited area of Jerusalem, but on the wide area of the World. (2) As it is obvious that, on the above supposition, the writer, deceived in his expectations, was not inspired, we are entitled to ask as to the grounds upon which, at the very outbreak of the Jewish war, he could either anticipate the destruction of the greater part of the sacred building, or could distinguish, as upon a correct interpretation he so clearly does, between the preservation of the inner sanctuary and altar upon the one hand, and the casting out of the outer court upon the other. In no case could he have done either. Was he, as so often supposed, a fanatical Jewish Christian, who was giving utterance only to his own expectations, he could have entertained but one idea, that the Almighty would yet, as He had often done before, interfere on behalf of His ancient people, and guard the Zion

which He loved. Or if, as is rendered probable by a comparison of Rev. xi. 2 with Luke xxi. 24, he proceeded upon the
prophecy of Christ, how could he shut his eyes to the fact that,
at a moment when all the buildings of the temple were before
Him (Matt. xxiv. 2), and when from the Mount of Olives His
eye would peculiarly rest upon the loftiest part,—the inner
shrine,—our Lord had said, "The days will come in which
here shall not be left here one stone upon another that shall
not be thrown down" (Luke xxi. 6). The words of chap. xi.
1, 2 cannot be understood literally without raising both psycho-
logical and historical difficulties which it is impossible to overcome.
3) Not less formidable are the exegetical difficulties of this
interpretation; for even those who understand the temple, the
altar, the outer court, and the city, literally, are compelled to
acknowledge that other parts of the same passage, the measuring reed and the measuring, the two olive trees, the two candlesticks, and the beast, must be understood symbolically. A
line of distinction thus arbitrarily drawn between what is literal
and what is symbolical leaves it in the power of an interpreter
to make anything that he pleases of the words before him.
4) The whole style of the book requires us to interpret
the passage symbolically. In the vision of Ezekiel (chap. xl.
3, etc.) upon which the delineation rests, the "measuring" of the
prophet is undeniably symbolical. How natural was it that,
with such a prophecy in his eye, St. John should adopt symbolism of the same kind! His own words, too, bear testimony to
the fact. The witnesses are described by him as "the two
candlesticks" (verse 4), and he had himself explained his use of
that term in chap. i. 20, "the seven candlesticks are seven
churches." Nowhere indeed throughout the book do we find
descriptions drawn from the institutions or rites of Israel employed in a literal sense. Even the mention in verse 8 of this
chapter of "the great city where also their Lord was crucified,"
so confidently appealed to by Lücke (*Versuch*, p. 828), is not
strictly literal. It may be more so than is allowed by Hengsten-
berg, against whose argument Lücke's may have force; but it
is not, properly speaking, the mere historical Jerusalem that is
mentioned. It is Jerusalem *under one of its aspects*, the guilty
degenerate city of "the Jews" (comp. *Lect.* v. p. 182).
5) Lastly, the 19th verse of the chapter distinctly shows us
that the Seer has in his eye not the Herodian temple at all, but
the tabernacle in the wilderness; for he there tells us that when

the "temple" of God that is in heaven was opened, "there was seen in the temple the ark of His covenant." In the Herodian temple the ark could not have been seen, for it had disappeared at the destruction of the first temple, long before the days of St. John.   No doubt the temple spoken of in chap. xi. 19 was in heaven, but to the Seer things in heaven were the type and pattern of things on earth ; and throughout the Apocalypse the saints dwell not on earth but in heaven.   The imagery of verse 19, where we have the heavenly sanctuary (ναός), being thus drawn from the tabernacle, the sanctuary (ναός) of verse 1 must be suggested from the same source.   It is true that the Seer immediately passes to the "holy city" (verse 2), not the "camp," of Israel.   He could not do otherwise.   The antitype of the "camp" was not the "holy city," but the " beloved city " (chap. xx. 9),—was Jerusalem under an aspect altogether different from that under which it is here contemplated.   It may be asserted with the utmost confidence that chap. xi. 1, 2 does not prove that the temple in Jerusalem was standing when the Apocalyptist wrote.

Still greater importance is attached by those who argue for the early date of the Apocalypse from individual texts to chap. xiii. 1 compared with chap. xvii. 11 ; and in connection with the same view to chap. xiii. 18.   It is not necessary to refer to authorities different from those mentioned in connection with chap. xi. 1, 2.   The argument is, that the "beast" of these passages, or the head of the beast slaughtered unto death and healed, is the emperor Nero ; that this head is at the same time to be identified with the last of the five kings who in chap. xvii. 9 are " fallen," and that the sixth head is either Galba, who immediately followed Nero, or Vespasian, who succeeded to the throne after what is then regarded as the *interregnum* of Galba, Otho, and Vitellius.   Either Galba or Vespasian becomes thus the king who in chap. xvii. 10 "is" at the moment when the author writes and, in that short expression, discloses the date of his composition.[1]   That date must then be either between the autumn of A.D. 68, the date of Nero's, and the spring of A.D. 69, that of Galba's, death ; or it must be in the early part of Vespasian's reign, that is, early in A.D. 70.   Düster-

---

[1] Renan is probably the most eminent of those who assign the date of the Apocalypse to the reign of Galba, and this on the ground of chap. xvii. 10.   At the same time Prof. Bruston has called attention to the fact that, in numbering the seven emperors,

lieck even goes so far as to fix upon Easter day of A.D. 70 as
pre-eminently the "Lord's day" of the year as that when the
apocalyptic visions were beheld (p. 53).

Some remarks have been already made upon this point (Lect.
v. p. 142); but its importance renders it desirable to consider it more fully.

The theory starts with the supposition that the seven heads
of the beast are seven emperors of Rome. We leave this
point untouched (comp. *Comm.* on chap. xvii. 10), remarking only
that there ought to be more agreement among the advocates
of a theory upon which so much is based as to who the seven
are.[1] The essential point is that by the head, the stroke of
whose death was healed, we are to understand Nero, who,
in popular expectation, had either returned or was about to
return from the grave.[2]

To say that, if the author of the Apocalypse adopted such
an idea, his book is degraded into a paltry puzzle is true, but
not an argument of which we can here avail ourselves. We
make our appeal simply to the general and special exegesis of
chaps. xiii. and xvii.

(1.) The supposition that the beast is Nero fails to draw

Renan begins with Julius Cæsar,
in which case the sixth, under
whom chap. xvii. 10 shows that
the book was written, is Nero
(Julius, Augustus, Tiberius, Caligula, Claudius, Nero)! Is not
Bruston right in denouncing the
"scientific frivolity" which can
lead to such a "strange absurdity"?
Le Chiffre 666, p. 17, *note* 3).

[1] Some begin the enumeration
with Julius Cæsar, when Nero
becomes the sixth king, and the
Apocalypse is written under him.
But, this being wholly unsuitable
to the idea that Nero is the subject of chap. xvii. 8, the favourite
computation is that beginning
with Augustus, in which case we
obtain Nero for the fifth king who
is to return after he has fallen.
Others again, when they have
reached Nero, omit Galba, Otho,
and Vitellius, and pass on to Vespasian. "Thus, by changing the
usual starting-point, or leaving
out of the usual list of the Cæsars
any number found convenient, any
view we please may be substanti-
ated by this kind of interpretation" (Alford, *Prol. to Rev.*, p.
235). It may be observed that,
though there is a difference of
opinion among scholars as to the
first of the imperial line of Rome,
the Jewish, Christian, and apocryphal Christian chronology of early
times begins with Julius. So it is
in Josephus, the Chronicon Pas-
chale, and at least one of the
Sibylline books. The different
authorities are summarised by
Lücke (*Versuch*, p. 839, *note* 2).

[2] Düsterdieck substitutes for Nero
personally the thought of the
Roman power in the abstract,
which was so severely shaken by
the death of Nero, but restored
under Vespasian.

that distinction between the beast and its heads which is demanded by the whole passage. It rather identifies the two. It starts with the supposition that Nero is the *head*, "as though it had been slaughtered unto death," in chap. xiii. 3, and it finds the same emperor distinctly indicated in the "*beast*" of verse 18 of the same chapter. Yet nothing can be clearer than that in chap. xiii. 3 a distinction is drawn between the beast itself and the heads there spoken of. One head is killed, and the beast dies, but the head does not live again. As shown by the second αὐτοῦ of the verse, it is the beast that lives again. The τοῦ θηρίου and the τῷ θηρίῳ of verse 4 confirm this conclusion, while all that is related in verses 5-8 belongs equally to the beast, not the head. Further, the crowned horns of the beast (chap. xiii. 1) do not *historically* appear till we reach chap. xvii. 12 (they are "ten kings *which have received no kingdom as yet*"), and, as this is later than the time of the first six heads, no one of these can be the beast. Still further, the beast is not only represented as differing from any single head; it is the concentrated expression of them all. Whatever of evil there is in each of them flows from it, and must be restored to it when we would form a true conception of what it is. Then only do we know it fully when, gathering into itself every previous element of its demoniacal power, it is about to exert its last and fiercest paroxysm of rage before it goes "into perdition" (chap. xvii. 8). By the confession even of those against whom we contend (comp. Düsterdieck, p. 55) it is "the eighth" mentioned in chap. xvii. 11 ; it is "of the seven," and yet it is to be distinguished from them. Finally, that this is the correct view of "the beast" in chap. xiii. is further established by the fact that in verses 14-17 of that chapter we have the *whole* work of the second beast in its service, as well as its own work, set before us as *fully and finally accomplished*. "The beast," therefore, to which our attention is here called, cannot be the same as any one of its heads, and cannot, therefore, be Nero.

(2.) The theory entirely fails to do justice to the language of the Seer with regard both to the wounding and the healing of the head spoken of. First, in reference to the wounding ; for, as already noticed, the rendering alike of the Authorised and Revised Versions,—in the one, "as it were wounded unto death ;" in the other, "as though it had been smitten unto death,"—is an imperfect representation of the original. The Greek words are ὡς ἐσφαγμένην εἰς θάνατον (chap. xiii. 3).

The verb σφάζειν occurs eight times in the Apocalypse (chaps. v. 6, 9, 12 ; vi. 4, 9 ; xiii. 3, 8 ; xviii. 24). In every one of these cases, omitting that before us, it must be translated "slaughtered" or "slain," the former being preferable, as there can be no doubt that the word is used in its sacrificial sense, most commonly directly (chaps. v. 6, 9, 12 ; vi. 9 ; xiii. 8 ; xviii. 24), once at least in mocking caricature (chap. vi. 4). How can it be otherwise translated here ? Besides which, the statement of the verse now under consideration is the counterpart of that in chap. v. 6, where we read of "the Lamb as though it had been slaughtered." In both cases death had actually taken place, and that too at the hands of another. The "head" spoken of, therefore, cannot be Nero, who fell by his own hand. But the main point is that we have *death* before us. It will not do to say with Bleek that "the head of the beast is apparently killed by a sword wound, from which he again recovers" (*Lectures*, p. 97). The killing is real, and to regard it in any other light is to do exegetical injustice to the text. Yet the popular belief was not that Nero had died, but that he was hidden somewhere in the East. Secondly, the slaughtered head is healed. The beast lives on after the fatal stroke, the stroke of its death (ἡ πληγὴ τοῦ θανάτου αὐτοῦ). Not a return from flight, but a resurrection from death, is spoken of. The beast thus dies and lives again, a travesty of Him who "became dead, and behold, He is alive" (chap. i. 18).

Not only so. It is in this character that homage is paid to the beast. The "marvelling" after him alluded to in chap. xiii. 3 is distinctly connected with that fact, and Bleek admits it. "Recovery," he says, "contributed to procure him a large following on earth" (*in loc.*). The words, "a large following," indeed, express very inadequately the extent of the marvelling alluded to. "*The whole earth*," it is said, "marvelled after the beast" (verse 3). With the same characteristics are connected the subsequent statements of the chapter (verses 7-9, comp. also chap. xvii. 8).

Now the question is whether by any latitude of interpretation all this can be applied to Nero, or whether it can be explained by the rumour which is said to have prevailed, that after his death he would return to life, and revive the horrors of his former reign. We urge that it is totally inapplicable. It is almost certain, indeed, that no such rumour was in circulation at the time when the apostle wrote. The thought would seem, rather, to have arisen long afterwards, when the misinterpretation of this passage gave it birth. Even Renan allows that "the general opinion was that the monster (Nero), healed by a Satanic power, kept himself concealed somewhere and would return" (*L'Ant.*, p. 350). Again, the words, "the whole earth," or the other words, "every tribe, and people, and tongue, and nation," are far too comprehensive to be applied only to the Roman Empire, to say nothing of the fact that when, in chap. xvi. 13, we read of the three unclean spirits one of which comes out of the mouth of *the beast*, we are told in verse 14 that they go forth "unto the kings of *the whole inhabited earth*, to gather them together unto the war of the great day of God, the Almighty." Nothing so comprehensive could be said of Nero. Once more, the song of praise in honour of the beast in chap. xiii. 4 is equally inconsistent with the supposition we are now combating. If it applies to Nero at all, it must apply to him as *Nero redux* (comp. chap. xvii. 8). But there is not a tittle of evidence to show that homage of this kind was paid to the thought of the returned or resuscitated tyrant. The acclamations with which he had been received by the citizens of Rome, when he returned from Campania, his hands red with the blood of his murdered mother, belong to a period before his death, and afford no indication of the feelings with which he was regarded after that event. It is true that some even then cherished his memory and decked his tomb with flowers. But, as invariably happens when a tyrant dies, the sentiment of the masses underwent an immediate and profound revulsion. Suetonius tells us that "the public joy was so great upon the occasion that the people ran up and down with caps upon their heads" (*Nero*, cap. 57). Horror, rather than admiration, filled their breasts. Is it possible that St. John, who, on the theory now before us, was so much a student of contemporary history, could have deluded himself with a series of fantastic imaginations in which he stood alone?[1]

[1] It may perhaps be said that St. John is not so much describing the present as anticipating the future. But, if so, we are introduced into such a medley of correct prophecy on the one hand and unauthorised and unfulfilled expectation on the other, that it becomes impossible to form any clear conception of his mental state. Düsterdieck, who makes the "seventh king" of chap. xvii. 10 to be Titus, and the "eighth" of the following verse to be Domitian, is much exercised on this point, and can only give as his explanation that the "singular error" mingled with the truth shows "a certain incompleteness of prophetic insight without by any means wholly destroying it" (*in loc.*)!

(3.) Other statements of chapters xiii. and xvii. are hardly less decisive against the idea that the beast is Nero. Thus chap. xiii. 5 becomes in that case unintelligible. How can it be said of Nero that, after his return (for the beast's return is here supposed to have taken place), he had given him a mouth speaking blasphemies, or authority to continue forty and two months? Or what war did he then make with the saints such as that spoken of in verse 7? Again, if the beast is Nero there can be no doubt that Babylon is Rome. We shall then have in chap. xvii. 3-7 Nero bearing Rome, while Rome, his directress and guide, holds the reins and with skilful hand secures by his means the accomplishment of her plans. Does this correspond to the reality? Once more, if the beast is Nero, those who defend that interpretation ought to explain the meaning of chap. xix. 20, where we are told that the beast was "*cast alive* into the lake of fire that burneth with brimstone."

The considerations now adduced are sufficient to show that the beast of chaps. xiii. and xvii. is not Nero, and that these chapters afford no support to the argument founded upon them for the early date of the Apocalypse. Chap. xiii. 17, 18, however, has still to be examined; and there, we are told, the Seer himself settles the matter in such a way as to put an end to all dubiety. The words of these verses are, "And that no man should be able to buy or to sell, save he that hath the mark, *even* the name of the beast or the number of his name. Here is wisdom. He that hath understanding, let him count the number of the beast; for it is the number of a man: and his number is six hundred and sixty and six."

In considering these words we start with the idea that, according to the system known among the Jews as *Gematria*, the number 666 is obtained by adding together the numerical values of the letters of a name. It is not, indeed, certain that this is the case. For the imprinting of the beast's name or number or mark upon his followers is an undoubted travesty of that writing upon the forehead of the high priest which is said to be written upon every one that "overcometh" (chaps. ii. 17; iii. 12; xiv. 1), and that writing was less a name than a clause— "Holiness to the Lord." The probability is, however, that a *name* is mysteriously hinted at.

Accepting this idea, it is marvellous to think of the number of names suggested by different scholars, and in different ages of the Church, as the explanation of the apostle's words. The following list, probably the latest compiled, is taken from the second edition of Schaff's *History of the Christian Church* (ii. p. 843),—"Latinus, Cæsar Augustus, Nero, and other Roman emperors down to Diocletian ; Julian the Apostate, Genseric, Mohammed (*Maometia*), Luther (*Martinus Lutherus*), Joannes Calvinus, Beza Antitheos, Louis XIV., Napoleon Bonaparte, the Duke of Reichstadt (called " King of Rome"), Napoleon III., the initial letters of the first ten Roman emperors from Octavianus (Augustus) to Titus, including the three usurpers, Galba, Otho, and Vitellius."   To this list we may add the name recently suggested by Bruston, Professor of Theology at Montauban, Nimrod Ben Cush.

The above list is sufficient to show what a fine field is still open to the ingenious mind in this department of inquiry.   The possibilities of suggestion are by no means exhausted.   Let the inquirer go over the notable names of any important era in the history either of the Church or the world, and he will certainly discover many persons with the qualification of the beast that we are now considering.   " Is not the gleaning of the grapes of Ephraim better than the vintage of Abiezer ? "

We turn again to the list, and, with a single exception demanding more particular attention, the names on it may be disposed of by the simple consideration that not one of them has found any general measure of acceptance, and that we have no argument to produce why any one should be lifted out of the state of discredit into which all have fallen.   That exception is Neron Cæsar, the letters of which, when the name is spelled in Hebrew, נרון קסר, yield the required number,—$\textrm{נ} = 50$, $\textrm{ר} = 200$, $\textrm{ו} = 6$, $\textrm{ן} = 50$, $\textrm{ק} = 100$, $\textrm{ס} = 60$, $\textrm{ר} = 200$, in all 666.

To this suggestion an amount of value has been attached which it is hardly possible to exaggerate.   The honour of the discovery has been contended for as the seven cities of old contended for being the birthplace of Homer ; Fritzsche, Benary, Hitzig, Reuss, and Ewald have severally claimed it as their own, and it certainly seems to have occurred to each in the course of his own independent studies.   Once made, it soon attained an almost unexampled acceptance.   " It has been adopted by Baur, Zeller, Hilgenfeld, Volkmar, Hausrath, Krenkel, Gebhardt, Renan, Aubé, Réville, Sabatier, Dr. Davidson, Stuart, and Cowles.   It is just now the most popular interpretation " (Schaff, *U. S.*, p. 846).   We may add Bleck, Beyschlag, and Farrar.

Not only so. Some of these critics, whose high claim to be heard on a point of the kind no one will dispute, have adopted it with enthusiasm, as if a burden which had pressed upon the scholarship of centuries had been at length removed. In these circumstances the suggestion demands respectful and careful consideration, and in that spirit we desire to speak of it.

(1.) Much importance has been attached to the fact that, adopting the Nero-hypothesis, we may easily assign a probable reason for the mysterious manner in which St. John thus indicates the name of Nero. It would have been dangerous to state his name more plainly. St. Paul exhibits a similar caution when, in 2 Thess. ii. 6, 7, referring as it would seem to the Roman power, he describes it in the ambiguous terms, "that which restraineth," "one that restraineth now." His brother apostle had still greater reason to be guarded in his language. He lived in more critical times. The monster upon the throne had given vent to all the unbridled licentiousness of his rage, and to have pointed to him in plain language would have been to court destruction not only for a Christian writer, but for the whole Christian community. This reasoning is entitled to little weight. There is indeed no appearance of concealment upon the part either of St. Paul or of St. John. The former, when in Thessalonica, had not only " told " his converts what he was now again saying, but was satisfied that they " knew " it (chap. ii. 5, 6), and we cannot suppose that it would have been more dangerous to give a full statement of his meaning in a letter intended only for a few than to preach it at a time when he could use his living voice, and stir the whole city by his presence (Acts xvii. 1-9). St. John is not less free from alarm. The tone of the passage shows us that at the proper time, whether now or afterwards, he wishes the number and, if the number the name, of the beast to be known. If too he thought of persons beyond the pale of the Christian community, he could not fail to be aware that his veiled allusion to Nero would rather stimulate than repress curiosity, and rather increase than diminish the rage of adversaries. The words also, " Here is wisdom. He that hath understanding, let him count the number of the beast," with which he introduces his statement, do not convey the impression that we have before us a human puzzle which only mental skill can resolve. They lead us to the thought of a Divine mystery in which God has hidden solemn truth from all who will not approach it with submission to His guidance.

Or, if he wished to conceal the name of Nero, why is he not equally careful in the case of the city of Rome?   One of the arguments most relied upon by those who see Nero in the number of the beast is that it is impossible to mistake the allusion to Rome in the mention of the woman with whom the beast is so intimately associated :—"The seven heads are seven mountains on which the woman sitteth;" "The woman whom thou sawest is the great city which reigneth over the kings of the earth" (chap. xvii. 9, 18).   Be it so.   But if Rome be thus clearly indicated, who can the beast be but the emperor, and that emperor Nero?   The curtain closed by the one hand is opened by the other.

(2.) It is not the *name* but the *number* of the beast upon which St. John mainly dwells.   No doubt we are proceeding on the supposition that the number is obtained by adding together the numerical values of the letters that compose the name.   But there is a difference between an argument from a name to a number, and from a number to a name.   In the former case the name is of chief importance; in the latter the number.   In the former we must know the name before we can estimate its import; in the latter the import has all its meaning, even although the name is as yet unknown.   This seems to suggest the true meaning of the difficult clause, "it is the number of a man."   Züllig argues from these words, and upon the common interpretation, with no small force, that the beast must be a man.   But, when we compare chap. xxi. 17, such a conclusion seems to be hardly warranted.   St. John rather means, "Here is a number from which, while we gather what it expresses, we may judge, *as we judge in the case of men*, of the character of the being to which it belongs.   The argument does not require that the name of the beast should have been at that moment known.

(3.) The last-mentioned consideration suggests as a not improbable conclusion that the Seer does not give the name of the beast because he does not know it.   In the form in which it is spoken of in chap. xiii. 17 the beast had not yet appeared.   It was to appear in that form after the seventh head had been manifested, and that head was "not yet come" (chap. xvii. 10). The beast, therefore, had not yet received its personal and historical name.   But the Seer knows its number to be 666. In that number its character was expressed, and the name would in due time correspond both to character and number.

With that St. John was satisfied. It ought not to be necessary to remind the student of the Johannine writings that in them the word "name" expresses character in a far deeper and more comprehensive sense than in any other writings of the New Testament.

The observations now made are in a certain sense preliminary. We proceed to others showing more directly that the beast of chap. xiii. 18 cannot be Nero.

(4.) That interpretation makes it necessary to have recourse to the letters of the Hebrew instead of the Greek alphabet. The Hebrew character of the Apocalypse as a whole may indeed suggest to us (as it did to Züllig, ii. p. 241) that the name in St. John's mind was most probably a Hebrew one. But there is much to lead us to a different conclusion. St. John is certainly writing not with the Jewish but with the *great Gentile Church* in his eye, and this would lead him to Greek rather than Hebrew letters. Then the beast springs from a Gentile, not a Jewish, source. It ascends out of the "sea" (chap. xiii. 1); and there can be no doubt (especially when we compare with this the origin of the second beast, which is of the "earth," chap. xiii. 11) that by the "sea" we are to understand the mass of the Gentile nations. This would again lead St. John to a Greek rather than a Hebrew name. He writes his book too in Greek. On other occasions he employs the letters of the Greek alphabet in order to give, by means of letters, utterance to his thoughts (chaps. i. 8; xxi. 6; xxii. 13). When he uses the Hebrew he notifies that he does so, as if aware that his readers needed the intimation (chaps. ix. 11; xvi. 16; comp. John v. 2; xix. 13, 17; xx. 16). Few things are more certain than that the Christians of Asia Minor had little or no acquaintance with Hebrew. Even if St. John connected the name of the beast with his own day he would probably associate both its blasphemies and the homage paid to it with a language more universal than Hebrew, and that language could only be Greek. We are called to think of Greek rather than Hebrew letters, and no Greek rendering of the name of Nero gives the required number.

(5.) Even if the letters be Hebrew it is only by force that they can be made to accomplish the end for which they are appealed to. The names of Ewald and Renan stand at the very head of Semitic scholarship in Europe, and neither scholar can be suspected for a moment of leaning towards the traditions

of the Church, yet both of them have pronounced it almost, if
not altogether, impossible to believe that the words Nero Cæsar
could in the first century have been spelled in the way demanded
by the proposed solution.   The former, accordingly, first inserts
an additional letter in KSR, then substitutes Rome for Nero,
and lastly obtains the number 616 (of which we have still to
speak) instead of 666 (*D. J. S.*, ii. p. 262).   The latter, agree-
ing with Ewald as to the spelling but not as to the number
represented, gives it as his explanation that the author of the
Apocalypse has probably of design suppressed the additional
letter in order that he may have a symmetrical cypher.   With
that letter (the Hebrew *Iod* as the second letter of the word)
he would have had 676 (*L'Ant.*, p. 416).   Surely it is too
much to expect that men shall readily receive an explanation
so heavily encumbered.

(6.) The argument drawn from the various reading 616 instead of 666 possesses no substantial force.   The former number represents Nero Kesar, not Neron Kesar ; and the argument
is that a Jewish Christian, knowing that Nero not Neron was,
to Gentiles generally, the imperial name, would be led to substitute the one for the other by dropping the final letter *n*, and
would thus obtain (ו being = 50) 616 instead of 666.   At
first sight the argument is plausible, but it breaks down on the
fact that the ancient Father to whom we owe our earliest information as to the reading 616 instead of 666 knew nothing of
the proposed explanation.   Although himself offering conjectures
at the time as to the meaning of the mysterious symbols, he
makes no allusion to either Neron Cæsar or Nero Cæsar ; and,
after mentioning one or two solutions, he concludes that St. John
would have given the name had he thought it right that it
should be uttered.   It is a curious fact, illustrating the little
importance to be attached to the argument under consideration,
that the Father to whom we refer preferred another rendering,
Teitan (T = 300 ; E = 5 ; I = 10 ; T = 300 ; A = 1 ; N = 50 ;
in all 666), from which, if we drop the final n, we get Teita,
numbering 616, and a better representation than Teitan of the
Emperor Titus by whom Jerusalem was overthrown.   When
we find, therefore, that notwithstanding the desire to penetrate
into the meaning of the enigma which marked the early Church
this solution was not discovered, we have a proof that the discovery has been made by a false process, and is worthless.

(7.) We venture to ask whether in the conduct of this dis-

cussion sufficient attention has been paid to St. John's use of
the word "name," and to the precise manner in which he makes
the statement of the verse under consideration. In all the
writings of the apostle the "name" of any one is much more
than a designation by which the person receiving it is identified.
It marks the person in himself. It tells us not only who he is
but what he is. It has a deep internal signification; and importance belongs to it not because the name is first attached to
a person and then interpreted, but because it has its meaning
first, and has then been affixed, under the guidance of God, to
the person whose character or work it afterwards expresses.
*There must then be a bond of connection between the number
and the name, deeper and stronger than the fact that the letters
of a particular name yield a particular number.* Familiar as
the writer shows himself to be with the method of transposing
letters and numbers then in vogue, he must have been well
aware that *many* names would yield the number 666, probably
quite as many as the long list which swells the history of the
interpretation of this text. Of what use would it have been
merely to call attention to this? The questions would instantly
arise, Which is the true solution? Wherein is one name so
given better than another? There must be some additional
element in St. John's thought. Let us endeavour to discover
it by making the supposition that he had been dealing with the
human name of the Redeemer, "Jesus." He cannot fail to
have known that the letters of that name in Greek give the
number 888 ($\iota = 10$; $\eta = 8$; $\sigma = 200$; $o = 70$; $v = 400$; $s =
200$), but many other names must also have done so. What
would lend peculiar importance to the fact that the correspondence existed in the name of Jesus? The combination of
two things does it; first, the meaning of the figures; secondly,
the meaning of the name given by the appointment of God.
The two correspond: behold the expression of the Divine will!
The figure 8 had a Divine meaning to the Jew. It was upon
the eighth day that circumcision, the initiatory act of a new
life, was performed. The eighth day was the great day of the
feast of Tabernacles (John vii. 37). What in Matt. v. 10 is
apparently an eighth Beatitude is really the beginning of a new
cycle in which that character of the Christian which had been
described in the seven previous Beatitudes is thought of as
coming out in such a manner before the world that the world
persecutes. Upon the eighth day, on the first day of a new

week, our Lord rose from the grave, bringing His Church with Him to her true resurrection life. But the name " Jesus " has *also* a Divine meaning (Matt. i. 21). In the very spirit therefore of this passage St. John might have spoken of the number of the " name " of Jesus as 888. As it is he is occupied with one who, in his death, resurrection, and second coming, is the very counterpart of our Lord. He has a " name," a character and work, which are the opposite of Christ's. That name, known now, or to be known, will be capable of translation into numbers yielding 666. Ominous numbers falling short of the sacred seven to the same extent as the eights went beyond it; associated too with so much that had been most godless and impious in Old Testament history. The nations of Canaan had been six in number (Deut. xx. 17). The image set up by Nebuchadnezzar, and for refusing to worship which Daniel and his companions were committed to the fiery furnace, had been sixty cubits high by six cubits broad (Dan. iii. 1). The weight of gold that came to Solomon every year, in token of the subjection of the heathen nations around him, had been 666 talents (1 Kings x. 14 ; 2 Chron. ix. 13). On the sixth day of the week at the sixth hour, when Jesus hung upon the cross, the power of darkness culminated (Matt. xxvii. 45). What dread thoughts were connected with such sixes ! The argument then is,—these numbers correspond to the name of the beast when its meaning is taken into account. Both tell the same tale ; behold how God expresses Himself regarding it ! Now for all this the words Nero Cæsar were utterly useless. The second of the two words might have a meaning, but the first was meaningless. It was simply the name of an individual. Merely to count up the numerical value of the figures obtained from Nero Cæsar would not have answered the apostle's purpose, and could never have filled his mind with the awe that is upon him in this verse.

These considerations seem to show that the mere equivalence in value (even supposing the equivalence to be established) between the letters of Nero's name and the number 666 is no proof that the Roman tyrant is thus mysteriously indicated. An examination of the Seer's own words is sufficient to show that he must have had something else before him than any thought of Nero ; and we are justified in concluding that the whole Nero-theory will most probably supply only an illustration of the manner in which exegetical, not less than other, fancies may flourish for a moment and then decay.

2. From considerations in favour of the early date of the Apocalypse suggested by particular texts, we pass to those arising out of the general character of the contents and style of the book.

(1.) It is urged that, had Jerusalem been destroyed before the Apocalypse was written, the author could not have failed to notice that event. To what end, it may be replied, should he have specially noticed it? He is not writing history, either past or future. He is gathering together in one brief summary, in one *coup d'œil*, the whole general character of that "short time" which is to elapse between the coming of Christ in His humiliation and His *manifestation* of Himself in glory. What in such circumstances we should expect of an apocalyptist is, that he will have before him the character of all God's dealings with His Church and her foes, both in previous ages and in his own time, and that he will so use these as to gain from them a clear conception of the principles upon which the unchangeable Jehovah who has guided His people hitherto will continue to extend to them His protecting care. Now this is precisely what we find in the Apocalypse. The fall of Egypt or Nineveh or Babylon would have suited the writer's purpose in some respects at least not less than the fall of Jerusalem. Yet he makes no mention of any one of these catastrophes. He shows that he remembers them. He often takes advantage of particulars connected with them; but he does not notice the events themselves. A similar remark may be made with regard to the overthrow of Judaism and the destruction of Jerusalem. Neither of these is mentioned in such a way as to remind us of the historian or the prophet. But both are presupposed. So much is this the case with the former that it was the leading idea of one of the most distinguished interpreters of the book that the first half of it—to the end of chap. xi.—was designed to set forth the coming overthrow of Judaism. The idea was a mistaken one; yet the book does describe a state of things in which the overthrow of Judaism is included. The whole book is pervaded by the conception that a degenerate Judaism is the emblem of all opposition to the truth, and that as such it is especially doomed. Again, as to the latter of the two facts mentioned, the destruction of Jerusalem, is there not reason to think that, just as in the case of Egypt and of Babylon, the writer makes use of facts connected with that event, only catching their deep general significance and extending and spiritualizing them ?   If the idea of the holy city's being trodden under foot of the nations (chap. xi. 2) may be taken from our Lord's words in Luke xxi. 24 as much as from its sack by the Roman armies, the same thing cannot be said of the "*burning*" of Babylon, the false Jerusalem (chap. xviii. 9).   Our Lord had said nothing of that kind.   His words had been, "There shall not be left here one stone upon another that shall not be thrown down" (Matt. xxiv. 2 and parallels); but He had not spoken of "burning."   How came St. John to think of it ?   No answer can be given except that the actual destruction of Jerusalem was present to his mind.   That awful scene of desolation rose up before him.   He appears to "stand afar off" and to see "the smoke of the city's burning."   The thought of it supplies him with some of his most impressive imagery; and in the judgment executed upon the degenerate metropolis of God's ancient people he beholds the type of that still wider and more terrible judgment which shall be accomplished upon all who "crucify the Lord afresh and put Him to an open shame."[1]

It would indeed have been much more unnatural to find the book wanting in any specific reference to the fall of Jerusalem on the supposition that it was written before, rather than after, that event.   All writers who adopt this view explain the Apocalypse as a real or professed prophecy.   But what had been the most startling prophecy of Christ before He died ?   Had it not been that of the destruction of Jerusalem ?   And now, in A.D. 68, the prophet, unlikely as it seemed ever to be so, hears the tread of the Roman soldiers and sees their desolating march. How must the prophecy, supposing that he wrote at that time, have sprung up with renewed vividness before him ! and how difficult is it to think that he should have been silent as to what he knew, upon the authority of his Lord, was to be the final issue !

(2.) It is urged that the tone and spirit of the Apocalypse

---

[1] It has indeed been sometimes thought that the idea of the "burning" referred to is taken from the burning of Rome under Nero.   Chap. xvii. 16, 17 shows this to be incorrect.   Rome could not be considered as a "harlot," and in Nero's atrocious deed there is nothing to correspond to the ten horns, or to God's putting it into their mind to do His will.   The epithet Sodom applied to the apocalyptic city is especially apt if we suppose it used *after* the fall of Jerusalem.   In her destruction coming, and that by fire, *after* the Christians had removed to Pella, St. John saw the antitype of the burning of Sodom on its judgment day, after Lot and his household had gone out of it.

', not a late, date ; and this particularly in two
opiousness of its imagery and the passionate
le. Both of these are thought to correspond
age of the apostle in A.D. 68 than in A.D. 95 or
not the greater age contended for by many, the
ve been thought equally inconsistent with the
The fire of youth does not generally burn after
t to dwell, however, upon this, let us look more
gument.

iousness of the imagery is a difficulty.—But the
sh, and the basis of every figure is to be found
ument. We have no flights of fancy that may
e writer's own, and no figures drawn from the
originally poetic or imaginative mind. Were
ere might be more ground to allege that St.
iculty ought to have become weakened and his
med by age. Even this may not always happen.
cal blessing of Jacob (Gen. xlix.) and the song
Moses (Deut. xxxii. xxxiii.) were both written
age. Psalms lxxi. and lxxii. are the closing
id, whose last days (Ps. lxxi. 18) were at least
ose of St. John after his return to Ephesus.
ime and Swedenborg may be appealed to as
eligious thoughts and visions may retain all
their colouring at a late period of life. It may
ly so when the mind has been nurtured amidst
ployed by it, and has felt more powerfully with
ear that the thoughts enfolded in that imagery
or it, with increasing clearness, the problems of
been said is confirmed by the next part of the
us.

rgy and passionate ardour of the style.—There
think that the heat and fire appearing in the
ocalypse belonged only to the apostle's youth.
to that period of his life, but they did not dis-
On the contrary, the stories connected with
v that to the very end there burned in him the
passion which would have called down fire upon
village (Luke ix. 54), or which led our Lord to
im the title "Son of thunder" (Mark iii. 17).
Epistles of St. John belong, by general acknow-
e last decade of the first century ; and we have

already said enough to show that it is impossible to draw a contrast between the fire of youth as it appears in the John of the first three Evangelists and the mellowed gentleness of age said to appear in his Gospel and Epistles. His vehement, keen, impetuous temperament is not less observable in the latter than in the former. We seem to trace at every step, alike while the conflict of Jesus with His enemies is described and when he denounces the opponents of a true faith in Him, the burning zeal of one who would call down fire from heaven upon the guilty "Jews."

3. Again, however, it is objected that the Apocalypse indicates in its whole tone of thought an earlier development than that of the Gospel, and that it is therefore more naturally assigned to an early period of the writer's life. The following are the words of Dr. Westcott: "It is before the destruction of Jerusalem. It offers the characteristic thoughts of the fourth Gospel in that form of development which belongs to the earliest apostolic age. It belongs to different historical circumstances, to a different phase of intellectual progress, to a different theological stage from that of St. John's Gospel; and yet it is not only harmonious with it in teaching, but, in the order of thought, it is the necessary germ out of which the Gospel proceeded by a process of life" (Speaker's *Comm.*, *Intr. to St. John*, lxxxiv. lxxxvii.). Dr. Westcott's authority is high, and it may be more readily deferred to by many because he accepts the Apocalypse as not less the work of St. John than the Gospel. But the above language is too general to carry with it conviction. Dr. Westcott allows that the Apocalypse contains the "characteristic thoughts" of the fourth Gospel, and we are entitled to ask that the earlier form of development of these thoughts shall be set over against the later. To what thoughts does the remark apply? The fundamental truth of the Divinity of our Lord is certainly not less developed by the Apocalyptist than by the Evangelist. Some even of the most striking testimonies to that truth are supplied by the former. A similar remark applies to the resurrection and glorification of Christ. This was one of those truths which, when first announced by Jesus, the disciples did not understand. They were only to comprehend it fully through the experience of later years. It is the fundamental truth of the Apocalypse. Throughout that book Jesus is the risen Lord, alive for evermore (chap. i. 18). Or, once more, let us take the thought of the universality of the

redemption given us in Christ, and nothing can be more universal than the conception of the Apocalypse upon this point. The Church of that book is the great Gentile Church in which there is neither Jew nor Greek, the Church spiritual, universal, and complete.

It is true, no doubt, that the *form* in which the characteristic thoughts of St. John are presented to us in the Apocalypse is often that of the earlier dispensation or of the early Christian age. But this sprang out of the nature of the book and of the class of literature to which it belongs. Because an early age delights in allegory and figure it does not follow that these things may not also be employed in later times. The question relates not to *form* but to *substance;* and, unless it can be shown that the substance of the Apocalypse is only St. John's thoughts in germ, the argument is of no avail. We contend that, looking at the substance, not the form, they are as highly developed in the one book as in the other, and that here again, therefore, we have no conclusive proof offered us of the earlier date.

4. It is urged that the historical notices of the condition of the seven churches of Asia, as depicted in chaps. ii. and iii., reveal a state of matters pointing to the earlier, and inconsistent with the later, date (Lücke, *Versuch*, p. 821 ; Stuart, *Commentary*, p. 224 ; *Biblical Review*, i. p. 179 ; Macdonald, p. 154). Two particulars of this condition are said to deserve special attention,—the extreme rigour as well as the source of the persecutions spoken of, and the degeneracy that had taken place alike in doctrine and practice.

(1.) The fact of persecution may be allowed, but it by no means follows that it was persecution in the days of Nero. We have already noticed various circumstances connected with it which are much less suitable to the days of that Emperor than to those of Domitian ; and Stuart, whose argument upon the point is at best a *petitio principii*, is compelled in summing it up to say, " All this may be true of the churches, and of John's relation to them in the time of Domitian some quarter of a century later, and so the argument is not conclusive " (p. 225). There is also every reason to believe that the troubles under Nero experienced by Christians in the provinces were not so much the result of systematic and severe persecution as of the dislike with which Christians were regarded (L'Enfant and Beausobre in *Lardner*, vi. p. 326 ; Neander, *History of the Church*, i. p. 130 ; Gieseler, *do.*, i. p. 82).

As to the allegation, again, that the persecutions spoken of in the seven Epistles emanated from Judaism rather than heathenism, and that after the catastrophe which befell their nation the Jews were too much crushed to exhibit so great activity and keenness, it is enough to say that the contrary was the case. The fall of Jerusalem produced upon them its natural effect in intensifying both their bitterness and fanaticism against the Christians ; and they were frequently the ringleaders rather than the led in the bitterest persecutions of the time (comp. Lightfoot, *Ignatius*, vol. ii. sect. 2, p. 966).

(2.) That indications are given in the seven Epistles of degeneracy in Christian faith and practice is not to be denied. The question is, whether it was a degeneracy along the lines noted in the Asiatic churches by St. Paul when he writes to the Ephesians and Colossians, and whether between the date of these Epistles and A.D. 68 there was time for it. Bishop Lightfoot has answered the first part of this question in the affirmative, " The same temper prevails, the same errors are rife, the same correction must be supplied " (*Coloss., Intr.*, p. 41). To a certain extent this is true. A community does not move so fast that even an interval of thirty years, much less one of five or six, shall obliterate all points of resemblance between its condition at the beginning and at the close of that period. But, along with some points of similarity, there seem to be important differences. More particularly, the Nicolaitans or Balaamites and the followers of Jezebel spoken of cannot be the same as the adherents of that Essene Judaism which had penetrated Asia Minor in the time of St. Paul. They are a different class, starting not so much from a desire to magnify Jewish ceremonial as to introduce heathen licentiousness. When we come in contact with Judaizers opposed to St. Paul, we find ourselves in the midst of churches in which the Jewish element is strong, and in which it is peculiarly necessary to uphold the freedom of the Gospel. When we read the seven, especially the last four, Epistles in the Apocalypse, we are in a different atmosphere. Not the narrowness of Judaism, but the wild immorality and worldliness of heathenism, is now striving to gain the upper hand ; and the Christian has to overcome, not Judaism, but the world in its widest sense.

It is admitted that the conditions reveal a date subsequent at least to St. Paul's connection with the Asiatic churches (Lücke, *Versuch*, p. 821, speaks strongly upon this point), and corresponding rather to the conditions of the time the coming of which the apostle had so distinctly assigned to a point "after his departure," and _to] " the last days " (Acts xx. 29 and 2 Tim. iii. 1).[1] But, if this be so, the space of time at our disposal is extremely brief, not more than A.D. 65 to A.D. 68,—long enough to degenerate if the degeneracy be along lines which previously existed ; but hardly long enough if a condition of things largely new must be presupposed in order to account for the special nature of the degeneracy.

5. Finally, to revert to the often-urged plea that the language of the Apocalypse bespeaks an early and not a late date, we have already said so much upon this point that it is unnecessary to say more (comp. p. 252, etc.) In whatever way we endeavour to account for its peculiarities, these supply no argument in favour of the early date of the book in which they occur.

The objections drawn from internal evidence to the late date of the Apocalypse thus appear, when carefully examined, to possess little or no force. If so, the external evidence is entitled to all the weight which naturally belongs to it, and only one conclusion is admissible. The book was written at the close of the reign of Domitian, A.D. 95 or 96.

It would be a mistake, however, to suppose that the general tendency of the internal evidence is in favour of the early date, and that the inquirer, while dealing with it, must be content to wage a defensive warfare. Positive grounds for a late date are also supplied by this branch of the evidence, and with these we may fittingly conclude the argument.

(1.) The fact that the book is addressed to the churches of Asia Minor is more in harmony with the idea of a late than of an early date in the apostle's life. We have no proof, but rather the reverse, that St. John was connected with that region of the Church much before the fall of Jerusalem. The general impression is rather that it was only shortly previous to that event that St. John, warned by the signs of the times, left the holy city and the holy land, and went to Asia Minor. Now it will not be denied that, in its first three chapters, the Apocalypse presupposes an intimate connection between the writer and

---

[1] It is not without importance to observe that in Acts xx. 29, 30 two sources of the coming evil are alluded to, the one (verse 29) from without, the other (verse 30) from within. Until the family idea of the Church was broken up by the destruction of Jerusalem, the former hardly existed. It was when she had passed into the wide sea of the nations that it became powerful for evil.

the Asiatic churches, a connection which it is hardly possible
to think of in any other light than as marked by affectionate
authority on the side of the former, and of willing submission
on the side of the latter. When, then, was this connection
established? Certainly not before A.D. 62, for the Epistle to
the Ephesians was written about that date; and, in conformity
with his settled rule of action, St. Paul would neither have
laboured among nor written to the Christians of that neighbourhood had St. John already established himself in their midst
(Rom. xv. 20). Nor between A.D. 62 and A.D. 68 could the
connection have grown to what it became. The time is too
short for the results. The force of this consideration ought
surely to be more acknowledged than it has been by those (such
as the present Bishop of Durham) who suppose that the apostle
did not leave the holy city till the eve of its destruction
(*Coloss.* p. 41).

(2.) St John not only addresses the seven churches of Asia in
a tone of authority, he addresses them as *representative of the
whole Christian Church.* That is, seven Gentile churches are
fixed upon as a suitable embodiment of the idea of the Church
of Christ in her most general or universal aspect. Could this
have been the case before the fall of Jerusalem? However the
views of apostles and apostolic men had widened so as to receive the Gentiles upon equal terms with the Jews into the one
Body of Christ, can we believe that, before the great catastrophe of A.D. 70, the thought of the Judæo-Christian Church
could have been entirely dropped, and that seven churches
amongst the heathen, and certainly made up for the most part
of converts from heathenism, could have been selected as the
exclusive type of the one Church of Christ? In exact proportion too as, after the manner of the defenders of the early date,
we imagine that St. John was animated, for more at least than
the first sixty years of his life, by a narrow Judaic instead of a
wide Christian spirit, must we allow that before A.D. 70 he
could hardly have extended his interests and his sphere of action
so widely as the first three chapters of this book show him to
have done. If he was about A.D. 60 what he is supposed to
have been, it is simply impossible that during the quiet closing
years of Nero and the uneventful period following down to
Galba or Vespasian he could have undergone a change so great
as that indicated by the selection of seven Gentile churches to
represent the one Catholic Church of the Redeemer.

(3.) The whole character of the Apocalypse seems to point to the conclusion that it is occupied with wider issues than those which the early date presupposes. That date is intimately bound up with the idea that the book deals only with one matter of interest and importance, the reign of Nero, the persecution instigated by that tyrant, and the prospect of his final overthrow. Without discussing individual texts, it is enough to ask whether such an idea harmonises with the general character of the book. We at once and fully allow that local circumstances lie at the bottom of the delineation. Both in his Gospel and in the Apocalypse it is the method of St. John to behold the general in the particular and the ideal in the actual. But are we really to believe that the circumstances connected with the Neronic persecution exhaust the meaning of all the passionate pictures, whether of denunciation or of promise, that fill the pages of the latter work? The importance of that persecution has been greatly exaggerated.[1] In the proper sense of the word it was not a persecution but a simple outburst of selfish craft and demoniacal cruelty. It had no reference to Christians as such, but only to Christians as despised and hated by the mob for reasons which the mob would have been wholly unable to explain. It was short-lived in the extreme; and no sooner was it over than things returned to their former state. Few things are more improbable than that local circumstances of a duration and a range so limited were all that occupied the mind of the Seer of Patmos when he wrote his Apocalypse. The general strain of his language seems rather to show that he was thinking of persecution on a wider scale, and that his mind was excited by far more momentous events. Unity and harmony, too, which are wanting on any other supposition, are thus introduced into the book.

(4.) The relation of the Apocalypse to the fourth Gospel tends to establish the same conclusion. That Gospel cannot be placed earlier than towards the close of St. John's life, and we have already seen (Lect. ii.) how dependent the two books are upon one another in their structure. The problem to be solved then

---

[1] The works of Aubé, Keim, and Overbeck referred to in this Appendix show clearly how mistaken Lücke is when he speaks of the persecution under Nero as the beginning of a long series of tyrannical oppressions, becoming continually more merciless and more general, on the part of the Roman government towards Christians (*Versuch*, p. 437).

is, which came first?   When we look at them in their order of
thought there can be no hesitation as to the answer. The Gospel
came first.   But the order of thought may not be the same as
that of writing or publication.   A man may have a subject long
in his mind—perhaps, as it would be necessary to think in the
case before us, thirty years—before he summons courage to present it to the world in a book.   In the meantime he may write
what, though founded upon that subject, seems to be more
urgently demanded by the position which he occupies or by the
force of surrounding circumstances; and the last years of life
may come upon him before he returns to his first love.   In such
a case the inquirer of a distant age would obviously be wrong in
saying that, because the subject or thought of the last book preceded that of the first, the last must also have been the first to
appear.   Thus in the present instance the thought of the Apocalypse may have been founded on that of the Gospel, while the
Gospel may have been last written or published.   Yet the probabilities are surely all the other way.   Let it once be granted
that the key to the Apocalypse lies, where we have endeavoured
to find it, in the Gospel of St. John, and it will not be easy to
suppose that the former appeared more than thirty years before
the latter.

We have discussed this subject at what will no doubt seem
to many unnecessary length.   But the length will not be complained of if we have to any extent succeeded in establishing
the point in view.   The indirect issue of the discussion may
then even be more valuable than the direct, if the young student
is taught not to yield too readily to great names and bold assertions, but to examine and judge in all such matters for himself.

APPENDIX IV.

UNITY OF THE APOCALYPSE.

IF a consensus of opinion, marking all different schools of
thought in the Church, seemed to justify our omitting many
details of the argument for the authorship of the Apocalypse by
the apostle John, much more may it do so when we turn for a
moment to the unity of the book. It may be asserted with
the utmost confidence that there is no other book of the New
Testament to which unity of authorship has been ascribed with
less hesitation, or even with more unhesitating conviction, in
all ages of the Church and by all inquirers. The Apocalypse
has been assigned to different dates ; some portions of it
even have been thought to belong to one period in the
writer's life, and others to another. But that it proceeded
from one mind has seldom been seriously disputed ; or, if
disputed, the theory of a various authorship has never found
a firm or lasting footing. To so great an extent has this
been the case that commentators often feel no call to discuss
the question. The latter course might have been followed
here had not long-exploded doubts recently experienced a
temporary revival. Dr. D. Völter, Repetent in the University
of Tübingen, published in 1882 a pamphlet upon the point
which attracted some notice in Germany. He was indeed immediately answered both in his own country and in Holland
and America. In particular Prof. Warfield of Allegheny, Pa.,
in the United States, reviewed the pamphlet in the *Presbyterian
Review* for April 1884, in a manner so well-informed, careful,
and exhaustive, as to produce a widespread feeling of satisfaction
that the attack had been made. The real danger came to be
that the higher criticism, in itself so valuable, might have
suffered through one of its latest manifestations. In these

circumstances it will not be necessary to enter into many particulars. A very brief sketch of Völter's argument and of the manifest objections to it may suffice.

According to this critic the Apocalypse may be divided into five different parts, belonging to eras of the Church more or less remote from each other, and written by at least four different persons. These parts are not indeed loosely attached to one another. Those first written interested the Church at particular points of her later history to such an extent that authors were induced not only to add to, but to revise, them. The new was fitted into the old with care and skill. Interpolations of longer or shorter passages were made in order to bring the additions into harmony with the original building, and thus the book passed through several recensions, assuming its final form between A.D. 160 and A.D. 170. The arguments leading to this conclusion are four,—the want of sufficient connection between different parts of the book; its repetitions not demanded by the course of thought; its representations resting upon historical persons and events long subsequent to the date from which much of it cannot be separated; and finally its dogmatical more particularly its christological ideas, in different parts too widely divergent from each other to permit their being reduced to the single type which must have proceeded from a single mind.

Our space is too limited to permit our taking up in detail each of these four points with the view of illustrating the author's method of treatment. One illustration belonging to the chronological argument must suffice. In Rev. xiii. 11 we meet with the second beast, and Dr. Völter is so satisfied with the identification he discovers of this beast that upon it, as "a thoroughly ascertained result," he feels he can take his stand, in order to determine the exclusion of a series of other passages of the present from the original Apocalypse (p. 29). With great interest, therefore, we naturally ask after the grounds of this conclusion. They are as follows: The beast from the "land" of chap. xiii. 11 evidently occupies a position of close proximity to, and contrast with, the beast from the "sea" of chap. xiii. 1. The latter beast, however, is the Emperor Antoninus Pius, for in the Sibylline books we read of an emperor who "bears the name of the neighbouring *sea*" (which must be Hadria), and we are thus led to think first of Hadrian, but immediately afterwards of his adopted son and successor, who incorporated his predecessor's name with his own,—Titus

Actius Hadrianus Antoninus Pius. It is true, no doubt, that the person to be identified as the false prophet or second beast did not exactly come from the "land" *in contrast with* the "sea," for he was born at Ionopolis or Abonoteichos, a small town on the coast of the Euxine; but the contrast between "sea" and "land" is only to be thought of in a general way (this had hardly been the case with "sea"), and as intended to bring out that there is something very definite in the distinction between the first and the second beast. Pursuing our inquiry we now learn from Lucian that in the days of Antoninus, the first beast, there flourished a very famous impostor of the name of Alexander of Abonoteichos; and the characteristics of this presumptuous deceiver so closely resemble those of our second beast that, taken in conjunction with the proof already given that Antoninus is the first, we can have no hesitation in assuming that we have found the second. For (1) Alexander styled himself a prophet, and Lucian styles him a "false prophet," the very description of the second beast in Rev. xvi. 13; xix. 20; xx. 10. (2) The second beast "spake as a dragon" (chap. xiii. 11), and Alexander, in order to delude the people, had fastened the representation of a dragon's head to a serpent, and then had so connected these by strings with a tube and an attendant that he could make the dragon's mouth open and shut, its tongue dart out, and a voice issue from it proclaiming the oracles of God. The second beast of the Apocalypse has indeed two horns "like unto a *lamb*" (verse 11), and it is only its *voice* or its *utterances*, not its head, that is like a dragon's, but the word "dragon" occurs in both cases, and how can the reader fail to be convinced? (3) The second beast caused "that as many as should not worship the image of the (first) beast should be killed." Alexander on one occasion commanded the bystanders to stone an Epicurean who had ridiculed his rites; and the murder would have been effected had not the scoffer been rescued. In addition to this Alexander always displayed peculiar enmity to the Christians. (4) The second beast caused all to receive a mark on their right hand or upon their forehead. Alexander caused small images of his dragon-god to be circulated in great numbers, and the people "perhaps" regarded them as a charm. (5) The second beast made fire to come down of heaven upon the earth in the sight of men (verse 13). Alexander, it is true, did nothing of the kind, but the Apocalyptist lived so far away from the scene of that deceiver's working that the report of what he did might easily have taken an exaggerated form by the time it reached him. (6) In the Apocalypse we read of worship of the first beast only (verse 15), not of worship of the second, while in Lucian's account of Alexander we read of worship of the second beast only, not of worship of the first; but the Apocalyptist allowed the two cults to flow together into one, while the close relation between them is established by the fact that the Emperor (the first beast) caused coins to be struck bearing upon them the image of Alexander (the second beast). (7) This mingling of the two cults also explains the circumstance that, while the inhabitants of the earth make an image to the first beast, Alexander fashions only *his own dragon-god*, without thought of thereby increasing the worship of the Emperor. The author of the Apocalypse had been led to confound the worship of the second beast with that of the first. (8) Lastly, the same circumstance explains the transference to the first beast of that *coercion* to worship which, in Lucian's story, has reference only to the worship of the second beast.

The illustration of the higher criticism thus given may be left to make its own impression on the reader, and from it the nature of the arguments adduced by Dr. Völter to prove his point may be sufficiently judged of.

As every attempt made in the past to shake the unity of the Apocalypse has been unsuccessful, it is probable that the same fate will attend every similar attempt in future. So peculiar are the characteristics of the book that greater difficulties could not fail to be experienced in intercalating forged passages into it than into any other book of the New Testament. Its method, its style, its figures and its language are all so remote from those of an ordinary writer that it would be almost impossible to find in different ages men who, without betraying themselves, could insert in it portions of their own composition. Apart from this too the book is in itself a perfect unity. Take away any part of it and that harmony of its proportions to which the writer evidently attached so much importance is at once destroyed. We have seen that its earlier parts anticipate its later; and that its later look back upon its earlier. We have found many expressions occurring in it which require for their explanation the thought of others far remote from them. We have seen that even long passages, such as that extending from chap. xvii. 1 to chap. xxii. 5, are so articulated by being framed

upon the number seven as to make it utterly out of the question
to imagine that one of their sections flowed from one pen and
another from another.   In short, our attention has been directed
in the lectures of this volume to such an amount of *plan* in the
construction, not only of the work as a whole, but of its several
parts, that either these particulars must be shown to be incorrect, or unity of authorship be admitted as a necessary inference.
Throughout the whole book, too, there is the same style, the
same tendency to depart from the ordinary forms of speech, the
same method of referring to the Old Testament, and of dealing
with its figures in a spirit at once of love and freedom.   From
first to last all its parts are fitly joined together, and not one of
them can be taken away without leaving an unexplained and
inexplicable blank.

To what has been said of the internal characteristics of the
book we have to add the evidence supplied by the testimony of
the Church.   Sixteen centuries of Christian history had passed
before a doubt as to its unity was raised.   Amidst all the
suspicions entertained of it in earlier times, the thought of its
having proceeded from different sources never entered into the
mind of a single doubter ; and every allusion to it implies that
the work spoken of by one father after another was the same.
" We are asked," says Prof. Warfield, " to believe that edition
after edition of the Apocalypse was put before the Church in
quick succession,—no less than three between A.D. 145 and 170,
—each differing essentially from its predecessors, and that the
docile people received each and all not only as genuine, and
John's own writing, but as divinely given for their guidance, and
never asked one uncomfortable question.   The second century
was, on this view of it, a very heaven for forgers, if we may not
even say of it a paradise of fools " (*U. S.*, p. 257).   It is
unnecessary to prolong the argument.   There is probably no
point connected with the origin of the New Testament books
upon which we may more cordially adopt the language of
Lücke, when he says that not only is even every apparent
ground for accepting the theory of a various authorship of the
Apocalypse wanting, but that its original completeness and
unity may be regarded as thoroughly and positively established
(*Versuch*, p. 887).

Printed by R. & R. CLARK, *Edinburgh*.

BY THE VENERABLE ARCHDEACON F. W. FARRAR, D.D., F.R.S.,
ARCHDEACON AND CANON OF WESTMINSTER.

The Fall of Man, and other Sermons. Fourth Edition.
Crown 8vo. 6s.

The Witness of History to Christ. Being the Hulsean
Lectures for 1870. Sixth Edition. Crown 8vo. 5s.

Seekers after God. The Lives of Seneca, Epictetus, and
Marcus Aurelius. New Edition. Illustrated. Crown 8vo. 6s.

The Silence and Voices of God. University and other
Sermons. Sixth Edition. Crown 8vo. 6s.

In the Days of Thy Youth. Sermons on Practical Subjects,
preached at Marlborough College from 1871 to 1876. Seventh Edition. Crown
8vo. 9s.

Eternal Hope. Five Sermons, preached in Westminster Abbey,
November and December 1877. Crown 8vo. 6s. Twenty-second Thousand.

Saintly Workers. Five Lenten Lectures, delivered at St.
Andrews, Holborn, March and April 1878. Third Edition. Crown 8vo. 6s.

Mercy and Judgment. A few Last Words on Christian
Eschatology, with reference to Dr. Pusey's "What is of Faith?" Second
Edition. Crown 8vo. 10s. 6d.

Sermons and Addresses delivered in America. With
an Introduction by Phillips Brooks, D.D. Crown 8vo. 7s. 6d.

The History of Interpretation. Being the Bampton
Lectures, 1885. Demy 8vo. _______ ____ _ [*Just Ready.*

BY THE REV. JOHN SERVICE, D.D.

Sermons. With Prefatory Notice and Portrait. Crown 8vo. 6s.

Salvation Here and Hereafter. Sermons and Essays.
Fourth Edition. Crown 8vo. 6s.

Prayers for Public Worship. Crown 8vo. 4s. 6d.

Scotch Sermons. 1880. By Principal CAIRD and others.
Third Edition. 8vo. 10s. 6d.

Frederick Denison Maurice, the Life of. Chiefly told
in his own Letters. Edited by his Son, FREDERICK MAURICE. Fourth and
Popular Edition. (Fourth Thousand.) 2 vols. Crown 8vo. 16s.
The *Spectator* says:—"The book is quite a unique piece of biography. You are
made to realise from beginning to end Maurice's constant recognition that human
faith can never measure God; that divine revelation is a condescension of the infinite Love to us, not an intuition of ours into the secrets of Infinitude."

BY THE REV. HUGH MACMILLAN, LL.D., F.R.S.E.
In Globe 8vo. 6s. each.

Bible Teachings in Nature. Fourteenth Edition.

First Forms of Vegetation. Second Edition, corrected
and enlarged; with numerous Illustrations.

The True Vine; or, The Analogies of our Lord's Allegory.
Fifth Edition.

The Ministry of Nature. Sixth Edition.

The Sabbath of the Fields. Being a Sequel to "Bible
Teachings in Nature."

The Marriage in Cana.

Two Worlds are Ours. Second Edition.

MACMILLAN AND CO., LONDON.